Song in My Heart

Also by this author:

Rena's Silver Lining

Song in My Heart

Sandy Knauer Morgan

ISBN-13: 978-0692441831

ISBN-10: 0692441832

Cover art by Sandy Knauer Morgan

In memory of Jess

for Briana

Thank you, Briana Morgan for inspiration and for reading aloud,

~~~

Thank you, Teresa Fancher for encouraging me, and for the many hours you spent nit picking. I appreciate everything you've done, more than I can say.

Chapter 1

In one of her worst departures from sanity, Momma threw her keys at me and laughed. "Go ahead since you think you're so big. Driving ain't as easy as you think."

I left the keys where a crack in the linoleum had interrupted their skid an inch from my bare foot, refusing to even look at them. Momma couldn't have been serious, and I wasn't falling for another of her tricks. I twisted my fingers and waited for her next cue.

She hooked her thumbs in her armpits and flapped her arms. "Chicken," she mocked, and followed that with cackling sounds. "You're too big a chicken to even try."

When the music stopped, she spun around to start her songs over on the hi-fi, goading me with more chicken imitations as she lifted the arm and raised the records. I held my breath. A record dropped, the needle skipped over to connect in a groove, and music blared through the scratchy speaker before I dared believe she might be serious.

Maybe it was the one time that I could be grateful she hadn't listened carefully to what I said. She was wrong; I didn't say I thought I was so big, or that I wanted to drive the car that very day. What I *did* say was that I thought my cousin Wanda was lucky because Uncle Bobby gave her a key to his farm truck and let her drive through the field between their house and Nana and Pappy's house, in celebration of her turning ten and having legs long enough to reach the pedals. I wasn't ten yet and my legs weren't that long.

Momma's nature didn't encourage the notion to be nice or fun very often so I took advantage of the opportunity while I had it. I used my foot to pull the keys over the bump in the linoleum and kept my eyes on her while I squatted to scoop them up, prepared to innocently hand them over if she turned around.

She forgot about the keys and sang along with Connie Francis. I backed out of the house, careful not to let go of the screen door until it closed without a slam. Pappy called that door the disgrace of Crayfield, Kentucky since the screen part had been missing for as long as I could remember. The only purpose the door served was to slam and let everybody know someone had come or gone, sort of like the bell hanging on the door at the bakery. I didn't want a slamming door to announce my departure to my mother, or to my grandmother in her house across the field.

I waited on the porch--crouched beside the door--for the next record change, to make sure Momma wasn't coming after me. Music claimed most of her attention, playing from the minute Daddy left for work until he came back at suppertime and turned it off, sometimes asking if she aimed to bust my eardrums and sometimes saying it gave him a headache. Either way, he wasted his breath. I had heard those songs so many times they stayed in my head long after he shut off the power, and she'd always find another way to antagonize his headaches.

When I finally decided the coast was clear, I tore out as fast as I could run. My feet hardly touched the ground as I ran to the end of the rutted dirt drive, across the grass to the edge of our property, and up to where Momma parked her old Chevy.

I grabbed the door handle and heard Nana's voice screeching from across the field. "Stop right where you are, Penny Sue Martox!" Nana meant business when she tacked Martox onto the end of my name. I sucked in a quick breath and my heart thumped like a trapped jackrabbit inside my sun suit, but I didn't turn toward her. With my thumb glued to the button on the chrome door handle, I carefully reviewed the situation and its potential consequences.

She was too far off to have seen or heard my reactions, and too fair to hold me responsible for a command that I hadn't heard. However, she might insist that I should have known better than to get in Momma's car, even without her warning, and spit out a few of her favorite threats. I let them echo in my head while I considered what to do next.

"I ought to tan your hide, Penny Sue." No, she wouldn't.

"I have a notion to box your ears for not listening, little girl." No, she wouldn't.

"I swear, child, I should haul you up to the funny farm and have your fool head examined." Never.

I deserved all of them if I proceeded, but knew a threat was the worst Nana would actually deliver, or maybe a lecture. Consistency was the main thing that set my grandmother apart from my parents, and one of the things I loved the most about her.

Some of her consistencies were good, like her big heart and the way she protected me. Some weren't so good, like her big mouth and the way she protected me. I was much older before I understood how the same thing could be both good and bad, but even back then I was smart enough to appreciate knowing exactly where she stood with everything and everybody, and what to expect from her.

Nana fried chicken on Sunday and breaded pork chops on Wednesday. She scrubbed the porches with bleach water and a brush on Saturday, and painted them in May, right after she planted tomatoes. She ironed everything in the house on Tuesday. Her right eyelid fluttered like a hummingbird's wing when she had problems on her mind. If she was wearing anything except pastel pedal pushers, she was going in town or to church. She loved Daddy and me every minute of her life, and didn't like Momma for one second of any day.

I didn't let on but I knew that she watched me like a hawk from behind her ruffled kitchen curtains every time I played outdoors. She worried I would break my neck when I climbed the Dogwood tree, or get killed if I walked too close to the road, the pond, or the quarry.

"She spies on her like a communist, just looking for reasons to criticize me," Momma complained to Daddy.

Occasionally, Daddy promised to talk it over with Nana. Other times, he defended his mother, explaining that she was concerned about me, or that she got a kick out of watching me play and there was no harm in that. Momma usually said she'd like to give Nana a good kick or show Daddy a little harm, but sometimes she just slammed a door and said nothing.

Nana would deal with me herself, or wait on Daddy to come home from work. By then he'd be tired or have a headache and wouldn't want to get Momma started in a tantrum.

With a heavy heart, I ignored Nana and climbed inside the car, where I immediately shoved the key in the ignition and started the engine.

Keeping in mind Nana's repeated prediction that I'd end up at the bottom of the quarry one day, I paused with my hand on the gearshift. It couldn't be that hard to shift into reverse, otherwise, Momma wouldn't pull the car up to the very edge when she was mad at Daddy or Nana, which was almost every day.

Nana yanked the car door opened and pulled me out. I felt another jackrabbit in her heaving chest as she hugged me close and choked out a brand new threat. "Penny Sue, you're going to miss me after you cause me to have a heart attack."

The words were harsh but her tone wasn't. I was sure I could calm her nerves before we passed the Oak tree, and make her forget that I had done anything wrong by the time we reached her house.

"Momma said I could," I cried. "She gave me the keys."

I would regret those words for years, and blame them for destroying the lives of everyone around me, especially my own.

Chapter 2

Nana clutched me to her chest and packed me across the field like a baby or a hurt animal. Her hair worked loose from the bun she wore on top of her head, leaving long gray strands over her eyes, and stuck to the sweat that she had worked up huffing and panting my way to safety.

I wanted to brush her hair back. Instead, I kept my fingers crossed to wish away the heart attack.

Neither of us spoke, even after she took me inside her house and deposited me on the couch, forgetting her own rules about not allowing children or men in work clothes on it. Everything was wrong. I waited for her to open the bobby pins with her teeth and reset her hair, but her hands deceived me by doing something unexpected. She put one hand on her hip and pointed at me with the other.

"You stay put. Don't think I won't tan your hide if I catch you off that couch," she ordered, restoring some hope that she was the same person I had always known. Only, I believed she might be serious about the tanning for once. I nodded my understanding and didn't move when she went to the kitchen, where I heard her blow her nose, wash her hands, and open the refrigerator.

What remained of my world shattered when she returned with a pitcher of water and only one glass. Nana was mad enough to drink in front of me without offering me a glass? I closed my eyes to hide the tears I felt collecting.

She poured a glass of water and placed it in my hand. Still silent, she dropped back into the rocking chair and finished off the rest of the water, drinking straight from the pitcher like a man. I held back the urge to ask what she expected Pappy to drink with his lunch.

After a sip, I put my glass on the end table and closed my eyes again, hoping she would think I needed a nap and leave me alone until she looked and acted normal again. We sat that way, she holding the empty pitcher and rocking, and me sitting straight up with my eyes closed, until Pappy came in for lunch.

While Pappy parked the truck and stopped on the back porch to remove his work boots, Nana confused me more. Instead of waking me, she pulled my dirty feet up on the couch and placed her good pillow under my head. Then, she moved the oscillating fan from the floor to the coffee table where it would blow directly on me and covered me with a sheet to protect me from the air she directed on me.

Pappy ordered a ham sandwich and potato salad for lunch. It was plain to see Nana was still in a state she kept on talking fast without stopping to tell him he needed to watch what he ate or he would be wear it under his belt. My cousins had recently explained the humor in that comment to me.

"First of all, Nana fixes the food and sticks it in front of him," Wanda said.

"What's even funnier," Gwen added, "is that Nana is packing a lot more under her blouse than he has under his belt. Think about it."

I laughed, to be polite, but I wasn't sure I liked my cousins making fun of Nana. This time, I wanted to laugh to myself but Nana skipped her warning and started right in talking about trouble.

"I'm telling you, that fool is the child of Satan," she said. Even though Nana was upset with me, I knew she was talking about my mother. She never called her by her name. She had several for her—the child of Satan, my son's mistake, and the blonde bimbo—but her favorite was just the fool, on account of Momma being born on April fool's Day.

That disappointed Momma because she was proud of the name Kitty Marilyn Treeton Martox. She claimed that Granny named her after Kitty Wells and Marilyn Monroe, although Granny Treeton said that was an out-and-out lie and she didn't even think either of them was famous yet when Momma was born. I think Granny Treeton came real close to agreeing with Nana Martox about Momma being Satan's daughter, only she didn't say it right out since Momma was her own flesh and blood.

Momma also took pride in her blonde hair, that everybody knew wasn't really supposed to be blonde. Most people remembered her when she had brown hair, like in the picture she screamed at Granny Treeton for keeping on the mantle in her dining room. The people who never went to Granny's and didn't know Momma when she was young could still tell by the dark roots.

"I curse the day Jerold met that witch," Nana continued. "Well, he can stay with her if he wants, but they aren't getting that baby back. Not as long as I have a breath of life left in me."

"What'd she do this time?" Pappy didn't sound nearly as worked up over the situation as Nana was, which should cause her to use a falsetto voice. Pappy never seemed to understand that Nana expected a certain amount of anger over some things, Momma being one of them. If nobody else contributed, she raised her voice and her blood pressure and delivered all the mad on her own.

Sure enough, she was louder and an octave higher when she came back at him. "She pulled her damned car right up to the edge of the quarry again, and then gave that baby the key and told her she could drive. I pulled Penny Sue out at the last minute."

"Did the car go over?" Pappy's volume didn't equal Nana's, but he didn't sound calm any more.

"No, but it's probably out of gas now. I didn't turn the engine off after the baby turned it on and I pulled her out of the car, and I doubt the fool went out to check on things. She's probably on her sixth beer of the day, and got that hi-fi up so loud she'd never hear her baby scream or her car smash against the rocks anyway. Penny Sue ain't going back this time, Claude. You'd best go find Jerold and tell him."

I hated when she called me a baby, but at least I knew by the conversation that she was madder at Momma than she was at me.

Pappy waited a spell before he answered, and then he said the wrong thing anyway. "Gladys, you can't rightfully take the child away from her parents and keep her."

"The hell I can't. I'll take her and leave town. I'll leave you and Jerold and none of you'll see either one of us again if that's what I have to do."

Nana sounded serious. I didn't know whether to feel flattered that she cared enough to leave them and run off with me, or afraid of being dragged off to who knew where with Nana in a tizzy.

Because I picked up that key and went out to the car, the whole family was going to fight. I couldn't let that happen again. I slid off the couch as quietly as I could, and snuck out the front door. Home was out of the question because that was exactly where Nana would go to look for me, and then she and Momma would get into a huge fight.

I ran as fast as my legs would carry me, across the field and past our house, where I heard Brenda Lee blasting a speaker, and hid in the overgrowth outside the fence on the far side of the house. Lying down, the grass was taller than I was.

I curled up on my side and cried myself to sleep, and didn't wake until later when I heard Daddy's voice calling for me. He used a tone that I hadn't heard from him before. He sounded scared. There were other voices too – Nana and Pappy, and Uncle Bobby and Wanda – all calling out for me, "Penny Sue, where are you?" "Penny Sue, come on in now." Uncle Bobby just yelled, "Pennnnyyyy," and I knew his hands were around his mouth to make like it was a megaphone.

Daddy's sad voice is what that finally made me stand up and walk toward the house. "Penny, baby, please come out where we can find you. Please, baby."

Granny Treeton and Momma stood arm-in-arm on the front porch looking like they forgot to hate each other for once. "Here she comes." Granny shrieked and jumped off the porch to run after me.

Granny Treeton wasn't much like Nana. She didn't have to worry about her hair falling out of a bun because she kept her hair cut nearly as short as a man's. She was as straight and skinny as a poker. And nobody ever knew what she might do next, especially me.

Momma stayed put on the porch while Granny fetched me. Daddy and the rest of the search party came running to get a closer look and make sure it was really me standing there. Daddy moved in and snatched me away from Granny, like it was her fault I hid out so now he didn't want her to touch me.

"Where have you been? You gave us all a good scare." Momma yelled at me, but didn't try to take me away from Daddy, or hug me, or offer up any words about how glad she was to see me again.

Nana butted in. "Lay off her, you crazy fool. She's already upset enough without you running your mouth. You're lucky she isn't at the bottom of the quarry because of your poor judgment."

Momma fluttered her eye lids, heavy with several layers of Cover Girl eye colors and a bunch of layers of Maybelline mascara before she went in the house, letting the door slam behind her. She didn't invite anyone in or thank them for helping find me. Brenda Lee was silent for the moment, but I suspected I would hear her again as soon as Momma passed the hi-fi and flipped the switch.

"I'm not aiming to leave Penny Sue here tonight," Nana told Daddy. "That mistake you married is going to kill her before her eighth birthday if you keep leaving her alone with that baby."

Daddy held on to me and reminded Nana that he would be there during the night, so there was no need for her to worry. I would be safe with him. She opened her mouth to speak but he got brave and cut her off.

"Penny Sue needs to sleep in her own bed after all this excitement," he said. "I'll think on what to do about tomorrow and let you know something before I head out for work in the morning."

Nana turned to Pappy for support but he was already turned and starting back toward their house. She followed behind him for a few steps and then stopped and yelled back over her shoulder. "You better not leave her alone with that crazy woman, Jerold, or I'll disown you."

Just before we went inside, Nana turned back again with a message for me. "I love you, Penny Sue. Get some sleep and I'll see you in the morning."

I waved to her, relieved she switched her anger over from me to my mother.

Momma went to the kitchen and turned on the tap to fill the sink with water, like she finally planned on washing the dishes that had been collecting for days. Daddy took me straight to my room.

I was itchy from sleeping in the grass, hungry from missing lunch and supper, and not at all sleepy. But I didn't remind Daddy that I was supposed to take my bath before I went to bed, and I wasn't about to suggest going to the kitchen where Momma was. Itchy and hungry were fit punishments for the trouble I caused.

Daddy sat on the side of my bed and stared at me while I squirmed and tried to get comfortable in my dirty clothes. For the second time in one day, I closed my eyes and pretended I was sleeping. He stayed to watch me longer than Nana had earlier. After a while, I turned over on my side, facing away from him, so he wouldn't notice that my eyes still blinked under their lids.

And, then, he went to the kitchen to light into Momma. "What possessed you to give the car keys to a seven-year-old child? Mom was right. Penny Sue could have ended up at the bottom of the quarry."

She must not have felt like saying anything about it.

"Dammit, Kitty, you knew that car was at the edge. Why would you do that?"

I put the pillow over my head and held it tight to my ears, but I still heard them fussing up a storm. I tried singing inside my head. The first song that came to me was Brenda Lee's "Dum Dum", not because of the loving people words but because dumb was how my life felt. It played over and over in my head, sometimes in Brenda's voice and sometimes in mine, but Momma and Daddy's words still came through.

"I don't need to hear about anything your mother said." Momma's voice was shrill and slurred as she slammed dishes and fussed. "That woman ought to mind her own business and stay the hell off my property."

"Kitty, you have to straighten up and look after Penny Sue better. And don't forget that it *is* my mother's business what happens to her granddaughter, and this is still her property."

I squeezed the pillow tighter around my ears, practically poking my own eardrums out with it, and turned up the volume on my mental song. I didn't want to hear that same old argument again. Nana and Pappy marked off an acre and turned an empty barn into a home for Momma and Daddy when they got married. Daddy was supposed to pay them some out of each check and Pappy would deed the property over after he paid what Momma claimed was an amount equal to highway robbery.

Momma said the whole idea was for Nana to keep Daddy up her butt and Pappy to make a killing off his own son, but Daddy disagreed. He thought Pappy wanted to help and Nana aimed to spoil me after I was born. My parents hadn't paid a cent on the debt and fought over it nearly every day.

"Don't start in on me about that," Momma said. "All I have to say about it is if you want to fork over anything to them you'd better get another job. In fact, you'd best stay off my ass about all of this and leave your mother's name outside the door when you come home, because I've had about all I'm going to take."

Daddy kept quiet, probably because he knew when it was a waste of breath to talk to Momma. But she carried on without him.

"I'm tired of living out here in the middle of nowhere, with nobody to talk to except a kid and your crazy mother. I've got a notion to take Penny Sue and leave."

"You don't care about Penny, and you wouldn't take care of her." Daddy sounded like Nana on that part but then he turned serious for once. "I won't let you leave here with her."

"I don't see as you'd have much choice. I'm her Momma and the law is behind me. I'm putting you on notice now, Jerold. Either we move to the city, away from this hellhole, or I'll take Penny Sue and move there without you."

The screen door slammed. I couldn't tell which of them left. Silence in the house told me nothing. Momma never did any housework if Daddy wasn't there so the dishwashing would have stopped either way. And Daddy didn't holler when she wasn't in the house.

I aimed to figure it out by listening to see who went for a drink. Momma kept a bottle of gin hidden in the crisper behind the vegetables. Daddy's Jack Daniels was in his toolbox in the bottom of the hall closet. I fell asleep before either door opened.

Chapter 3

Nana banged on our front door the next morning and woke everybody up. Momma and Daddy ran to the living room but I stayed in bed to listen from a safe distance.

I didn't worry about keeping my eyelids closed since they were too busy yelling at each other to look in on me. I didn't pull a song up in my head either because I wanted to listen carefully to see if anyone suggested that I should be in trouble for taking the keys and going to the car.

"You were due in at work ten minutes ago," Nana said to Daddy. "When I didn't hear from you, I thought I'd better come over and check on things."

Momma laughed, and it wasn't a happy laugh. "You mean you want to stick your nose into my business, don't you, Gladys? You want to see if your baby boy disobeyed you and left his daughter with her unfit mother?"

Daddy told Momma to go back to bed and let him deal with Nana. Even I knew that wouldn't set right with either of them.

"Excuse me for being something you have to deal with," Nana said. "I won't take much of your time because I have enough sense to know that you can't hold down a job if you keep going in late. I won't leave without Penny, so just hand her over and I'll scoot on out of here."

Momma must have left the room, but she didn't go back to bed. The next thing I heard was her screaming from the back door. "Where's my car? Which one of you took it?"

Daddy and Nana ran out the back door. I ran to join them. Sure enough, the clearing where the red Chevy had been the day before was empty.

"What did you do with it?" Momma yelled and punched Daddy in the chest with her fist.

Nana picked me up and headed across the field again. I watched my parents over her shoulder. Daddy grabbed Momma's wrists to stop her from beating the tar out of him, but he didn't hit her back. He never did, no matter how many times she punched him or how long she screamed.

I waited until we were halfway to her house to break the silence. Nana put me down once she knew Momma and Daddy weren't chasing after her to get me back, so she wasn't out of breath this time and I didn't think she was mad at me. "Where's Momma's car?"

"Your guess is as good as mine, Penny Sue. I don't much care where it went. Your Momma doesn't need a car after what she pulled yesterday."

"How will she get to Cut-N-Curl and the supermarket?" I wanted Nana to assure me that Momma wouldn't have to miss her weekly appointment at the beauty shop because she didn't know how to fix her own hair like Marilyn Monroe's.

Nana gave me another lecture about how I was the little girl, and it wasn't my place to worry about my mother. "It should be the other way around. Your Momma is supposed to do the worrying and you are supposed to have the fun. Somebody needs to teach you *and* your Momma that."

Nana didn't understand. I didn't deserve her feeling sorry for me because I was worried about me more than about Momma. When things didn't go according to Momma's plan she was so evil that nobody else could have fun. If not for that, I wouldn't care if she never got to go back to Cut-N-Curl.

Nana looked down at me and wrinkled up her face. "Don't you have pajamas? Why are you still in that sun suit, and why are the straps tied in knots instead of bows?"

Nana must have been blind not to notice that the straps were too short to make bows. If there had been any elastic left in the dingy fabric, it would have been an inch above my waist.

"This way I don't have to re-tie them every time I use the bathroom," I said, to keep her from feeling sorry for me and hating Momma more. "I just slide the straps down my arm."

She shook her head. The bun stayed in place.

"I was too sleepy to get my bath last night." I had to protect Daddy because he tried to take good care of me.

"One of them could have washed you up and changed you into your bed clothes," she said. "I'm beginning to think neither of them is fit to raise you."

I loved Nana because she always stuck up for me. But I still wasn't sure I wanted her to take me away.

"I think Momma's about to straighten up," I said, hoping that would delay her decision. "She washed the dishes last night before she went to bed so she was too busy to mess with me."

The look on Nana's face told me that wasn't enough to change her mind.

"I think she went outside and swept off the porch, too, after I went to bed," I added.

"Don't try to make up excuses for her. If you do, those thoughts will stick in your head and one day you'll wind up thinking just like her. We don't need that. The dishes and the porch should have been done already so she could see to your bath." Nana pulled a blade of dried grass from my hair. I didn't say anything else.

Pappy waited at the back door for us. He said good morning to me and then went on talking to Nana like I wasn't there.

"Kitty's car is at the bottom of the quarry, smashed to pieces," Nana said when it was her turn to talk. "Serves her right. Think Jerold pushed it over?"

Pappy picked up his coffee thermos and hardhat and said, "I doubt she did it herself."

"I wouldn't put it past her. She'd do it just so she could put the blame off on me. Jerold won't believe her, though."

Pappy had said all he was going to say on the matter. He kissed Nana on the cheek, patted me on the top of the head, and left for work.

Nana looked down at me like I was a rotten potato. "The first thing we're going to do is get you cleaned up. Go get your clothes out of my bottom drawer and I'll run your bath water."

That swept the problems clean out of my head. Nana kept one good outfit on hand for me in case she wanted to take me somewhere, or company dropped in while I was at her house. She had a brand new short set waiting for me, still in the Sears bag. I had pulled that red outfit out of her drawer to look at it so often the bag was ragged.

"Penny, you'll have that rickrack dingy before you ever wear it," she warned when I traced the white trim with my finger. "Leave it be. If you don't have reason to wear it before you grow into the next size we'll have to exchange it. And they won't take it back if it's dirty or ratty."

I went to the bathroom, with my outfit tucked under my arm, and sniffed like a hound. Nana's bathroom smelled like Ivory soap and Lilies of the Valley talcum powder. Sometimes I went in there just to sit on the rug and sniff the air. Just about everything in the room was yellow and soft; the tank and seat cover, the rugs, the walls, the hand towels that were for decoration only, and the crocheted dress and hat on the plastic doll that held a spare roll of toilet paper on her legs.

Nana put out a clean washcloth on the side of the tub, and a thick towel on the toilet seat cover. Everything fresh, just for me. Then, she smiled and pulled back the window curtain.

I clapped and squealed. "Bubbles!"

Nana poured a capful of liquid under the running water while I pulled my dirty sun suit off. I couldn't believe she was going to let me take a bubble bath and finally wear the new outfit both on the same day. Momma didn't allow bubbles at home but Nana kept a bottle hidden for me to use on special occasions, like when Momma let me sleep over, and when Nana took me in town to see Dr. Fine to get my vaccination before school started.

"I figure you need extra help to get clean after sitting in the weeds all day and sleeping in your dirty clothes," she said. "You climb in there and get yourself clean. I'll come back in a bit to wash your hair."

Nana left the room and closed the door, leaving me alone in my yellow haven. I collected bubbles on my hand and blew them off, singing "Twinkle, Twinkle Little Star" the whole time. I loaded up my cloth with Ivory and scrubbed until my skin was red, making sure to get the back of my neck and behind my ears – the first places Nana would check.

Finally, when the bubbles were gone and the water cold, I called for Nana. "I'm ready for you to do my hair."

Nana looked pleased when she came in. "You look a sight better than the last time I saw you." She checked my neck and ears and whistled. "Good job. You got everything."

I giggled and leaned back to let her massage my scalp. She lathered me up twice and then used crème rinse. I was sure my hair would be more beautiful than the girls in the pictures on the wall at Cut-

N-Curl. "This will make your hair soft so we won't have any trouble getting the rats out," Nana said.

I enjoyed having my grandmother pamper me. I had begged her to sneak me to Cut-N-Curl for a pixie cut the last time I spent the day with her because Momma had no patience for tangles. She usually wound up smacking my leg with the comb and made me cry before it was over. Nana said we would both be in trouble if she got me a pixie.

"I heard you singing in here," Nana said, while she held the towel for me to step into. "You have a beautiful voice, Penny Sue, and you carry a good tune."

I thanked her, hoping one day I'd be as good as Brenda Lee or Connie Francis so Momma would listen to me on the hi-fi. She didn't like to hear me sing in real life.

Nana had Pappy's sock drawer on the kitchen table when I came out of the bathroom. I sat in a chair and handed her one sock at a time, like the women at Cut-N-Curl did with permanent papers, and she curled my hair around the socks.

"You'll have Shirley Temple ringlets when this dries," she said. "Maybe you can sing "Good Ship Lollipop" for Pappy later."

Nana liked kid songs, that's why I picked "Twinkle" in the tub. The last time I stayed, I made the mistake of singing "It Wasn't God Who Made Honky Tonk Angels" and she didn't say one word about my pretty voice.

I sat in front of the oscillating fan so my hair would dry faster and we spent the afternoon playing Go Fish and War with a deck of sticky cards. For a while, I forgot that I was the cause of the whole family being crazy. Something seemed wrong about my causing trouble being the reason for all this good treatment, but I pushed that idea to the back of my mind.

Chapter 4

Pappy didn't come home for lunch so I asked Nana to leave the socks in my hair until he got there for supper. "Maybe he will get the Polaroid out of his closet and snap my picture, before and after, like in the magazines."

Rocking from one foot to the other, I watched for him from the front door, shouting minute-by-minute updates and fears to Nana. "He's late. What if Daddy gets here first and takes me home? Pappy won't get to see me and Momma will tear my hair out pulling the socks off my head. Still not here. No sight of him up the road."

"There's no need in you getting all worked up," she called back from the kitchen. "Your daddy went in late this morning so Pappy will get home first."

"Then what if Momma comes after me?"

"She won't. Calm down!"

I danced, paced, and fretted until I saw Pappy's truck coming down the hill. "He's on the way," I screamed, running to plant myself in the kitchen chair that faced the back door.

Nana dished up vegetables and pulled pork chops from the oven. By the time he put the truck in the garage and made his way to the back porch she had everything ready and was in her seat at the head of the table.

The door opened. I sucked my lips between my teeth to hold back giggles and rolled my eyes over to look at Nana. She winked.

Pappy said hello and went on to the bathroom to wash his hands like I had socks in my hair every day so it was no big deal. I dropped my head so Nana wouldn't see my disappointment. She patted my hand and sighed.

Pappy took his time coming back and settling into his seat across from Nana. While he prayed over the food, I scratched my head and flipped the socks with my hands, wanting him to notice before my heart broke.

He finished the prayer and looked up at Nana. "Gladys, I reckon you ought to take Penny Sue on over to that funny farm to have her head examined now. The poor child forgot where her socks belong."

I couldn't control the hysterics. I laughed until Nana called me down. "You'll get hiccups if you keep on like that," she said. "Then you won't be able to swallow your food."

"Pappy, these are your socks, not mine," I said. "Nana used them to make curls in my hair."

He shook his head and said it was the darndest thing he had ever seen. I felt special again. Nana looked at my plate so I stopped giggling and bit into an ear of corn.

"Penny Sue will look like Shirley Temple when those socks come out," Nana said to Pappy. "Soon as we finish the supper dishes, I'm going to take her hair down and she's going to sing for you. Pappy, she sounds as sweet as a song bird. You'll be so proud when you hear her."

Pappy raised his eyebrows and looked at me while he chewed his meat and took a drink of lemonade. If he didn't stop eating and say something, I figured I'd have to remind him that his food would show up under his belt.

Finally, he swallowed and wiped his mouth. "Is that so? What are you aiming to sing, little girl?"

"I know a lot of songs, Pappy. Besides all the regular kid stuff like the alphabet and "Twinkle, Twinkle Little Star", I can sing "Your Cheatin' Heart", "Where the Boys Are", "God Bless America", and just about every song Brenda Lee ever sang."

I left off "Honky-Tonk Angel" and "Don't Come Home a Drinkin" so I wouldn't set Nana off about my mother being a fool.

His eyebrows shot up again. "You expect me to believe a little girl like you has memorized the words to all those songs?"

"I did. I'll show you, I know every one of them. I left one off, I added, remembering how much he liked Hank Williams. "I know "Jambalaya", too".

"We'll see," he said, like he had trouble believing me. "I expect you to prove yourself for me later." He picked up his fork and went back to eating. I smiled at Nana, knowing we had a big surprise in store for Pappy.

"While I clean up the kitchen and Pappy reads the newspaper, you need to go out front and set up your stage," Nana said. "Move the lawn chairs out under the maple tree for us to sit in, and use the porch for your stage. That blue blanket we use for picnics should make a nice backdrop. We can put it up over the picture window."

"When are you going to fix my hair? I can't sing with socks on my head."

"We'll do that after all the work is done," Nana said. "Maybe you can put on a touch of lipstick, just for the stage."

I was almost too excited to finish dinner, but Nana had a rule that I couldn't leave the table until my plate was empty. That was the only thing she was meaner than Momma on.

Pappy had argued on my side about that once, saying it wasn't nice to force a person to eat if they were full. Nana said I ate garbage at home so she intended to fill me up on vegetables when she had me. To save them from having to say it in front of me again, I forced the last of my food down, leaving only one small slice of tomato that I knew Nana would eat.

I walked around the yard, looking for a small stick to use as a microphone. Pappy was almost as crazy about Brenda Lee as Momma was. I decided to sing "I'm Sorry" first, to make up for all the trouble I'd caused the family.

I gave up on a stick when I couldn't find one the right size, and went to move the chairs like Nana suggested. While sweeping the porch, I thought up a better idea for a microphone. Cattails grew by the pond and would work better than a skinny stick anyway.

I took off running up the hill, needing to make it there and back before Nana or Pappy noticed I was gone. I would only start a whole mess of new trouble if they caught me by the pond and the road.

The ground was muddy where the cattails grew. I'd give myself away if I went back with dirty feet so I scampered back down the hill to get the long stick that I had ruled out as a microphone and brought it back to help me reach the cattails.

I was in the grass, leaning forward as far as I could stretch to whack the perfect microphone when Granny Treeton's station wagon pulled up on the road beside me. I backed away without my cattail and tried to hide in the greenery, but Momma yelled for me to stay put.

With my eyes closed, I waited for Momma or Granny to jump out and scream at me for being so close to the pond. Instead, Daddy grabbed me around the waist and threw me in the backseat of the station wagon. Granny wasn't in the car, only Momma and a backend jam-packed with boxes.

"What the hell is in your hair?" Momma asked.

"Pappy's socks. Nana is making Shirley Temple curls with them." Suddenly I felt foolish with socks in my hair. Momma would only poke fun at me.

"Shirley Temple doesn't have black hair, and she isn't a bone rack," Momma said. "You don't look like any movie star I know of. Get those things out of your hair."

I started pulling socks out as fast as I could, which wasn't very fast. My arms weren't long enough to unroll them straight out to the end, so my hair got tangled and slowed things up. I bit my lip to keep from hollering out and making Momma madder.

Instead of driving me back to Nana's house, Daddy drove out to the main road. I got worried when he drove past our house. "Are we going to take Granny's car back?" I asked. "Nana's going to worry about me because she thinks I'm on her porch."

"It serves her right," Momma said. "She should have been watching you closer. Isn't that what she says about me?" She stuck her neck out to put her face over closer to Daddy's. "She ought to practice what she preaches."

It seemed I couldn't open my mouth without starting one adult up being mad at another. "It's my fault I ran off," I said, knowing it didn't matter to Momma whose fault it was as long as she got to be mad at somebody, or everybody.

"I'll call Nana from the payphone in front of Jake's," Daddy said. "Then she'll know you're safe with us."

I was relieved to hear we were going to get gas. Everyone in town knew that Jake closed up the only service station at dinnertime. They had to either fill up before then, or drive clear across to Leonard County if they needed gas at night.

"Are we going back to Nana's after we fill up? I'm supposed to sing for Pappy." I missed my chance on the cattail, but I could use a clothespin from the sack on Nana's back porch.

"You're never going back there as far as I'm concerned," Momma said in her most hateful tone. "Gladys Martox messed up big time when she threatened to take you away from me."

I couldn't believe what I was hearing. "But Pappy needs his socks. We have to take them back to him. It's not his fault Nana made you mad."

Momma laughed. "He can buy new socks. Better yet, let Nana worry about that, since she likes to be in everybody's business and she was stupid enough to put them in your hair."

She turned around to look at me and laughed even harder. "Well, Shirley Temple you ain't. You look ridiculous with your hair that way."

I wanted to be back at Nana's house where I could run into the bathroom, close the door, and look at myself in the full-length mirror on the back of the closet door. I wanted to see with my own eyes how I looked with curls, in my red and white outfit that nobody bothered to notice.

Daddy twisted the rearview mirror and looked at me without saying a word. I might never know if Momma was telling the truth about me looking ridiculous.

When we stopped at Jake's, Daddy told Jake's son to fill it up and check under the hood, and got out to call Nana. I leaned over in the seat and pretended I was sleeping. Just in case I did look ridiculous with my hair in curls, I didn't want the whole world to see me that way.

Daddy pulled out on the highway and headed father away from our house. I went to sleep for real then, so I wouldn't be tempted to ask questions or think about where we were going. We were parked in a motel lot with the engine shut off when Daddy woke me. He pulled me out of the car and held me close to him for a second.

"Put her down, Jerold. She can walk but my suitcase can't," Momma said.

He stood me on the blacktop where I watched a neon light flash red and blue and wondered how people could sleep with that outside the windows. I was about to find out.

"Are we on vacation?" I finally got the nerve to ask, thinking a happy question couldn't start them fighting.

"We're running away, Penny Sue." Momma sounded pleased with her announcement. "We're going to the city, where I won't have to put up with Nana's nose in my business every time I turn around.

"We're going to a big city, Penny Sue," Daddy said. You'll see lots of new things there."

"I'm happy with our old things." I guessed I was the only one concerned about Pappy's socks, and Granny's station wagon, or how I was going to second grade if we weren't near my school.

The motel room wasn't any bigger than my small room at home and the furniture was almost as shabby. There was one double bed covered with an orange and yellow spread that clashed with the red and black rug on the floor, a short dresser with only one long drawer, and a nightstand.

Daddy put the suitcase on the dresser and I pretended to help so I could sneak a look at my hair in the mirror. Momma shoved me aside and opened the bag in front of the mirror. Daddy pulled out my pajamas and handed them to me.

"Put these on. You'll have to sleep in the bed with us tonight," he said, making the mistake of not consulting Momma first.

Momma huffed. "Then she's sleeping on your side. She kicks like a mule and I won't get any sleep with her next to me."

"I can sleep on the floor," I said, so they wouldn't fight over me.

Daddy shook his head. "No, I'll sleep in the middle, so we'll be fine. There might be bugs or mice on this floor, Kitty. Use your head."

I went to the bathroom to change out of my new outfit that they still hadn't noticed and into my pajamas. I folded my red and white outfit carefully; sad to think it might be my last connection to Nana. Surely, Momma wasn't serious about never seeing her again and she'd get over being mad one day.

Daddy knocked on the bathroom door and said he had my toothbrush and the Crest. When I opened the door, he pushed his way through instead of handing my things in to me.

"Penny Sue, I think your curls look pretty," he whispered, lifting me up to see in the mirror.

I smiled when I saw my reflection. The side that was still curly didn't look ridiculous.

"I don't want to you to worry," he said. "We'll find a nice place to live in the city, and you'll have lots of new friends to play with. Momma's nerves will settle down, you'll see, and everything will be fine." He handed me the toothbrush and smiled, and I had to smile back even if tears wanted to come out.

"Daddy, Pappy needs his socks." I blinked hard. "And he wanted to hear me sing. We have to go back."

He shook his head. "He'll get over it. Nana will probably run in town and buy him some new socks first thing tomorrow."

I didn't sleep much that night for worrying about kicking like a mule. The thought of meeting new friends didn't fix anything. I just wanted to see my grandparents. And I wanted Pappy to hear me sing.

I made up my mind to get famous, so he'd hear me on the radio if I never got back to sing for him in real life.

Chapter 5

I started second grade at Midcity Elementary School in the only dress Momma had shoved into my paper bag to bring to our new life. Like most of my things, both Wanda and Gwen had already outgrown it before I got it. Their stains were so old that they had nearly faded out again but there was still a problem with this dress; I had outgrown it.

"Short skirts are in style here in the city," Momma said, like I should thank her for the fashion tip. I hoped flip-flops were also the rage since she had forgotten to reach under my bed and pull out my patent leather shoes, or the fuzzy slippers Nana had given me for Christmas. Maybe she didn't forget. Maybe she knew ahead of time that I wouldn't have a bed or a closet at the new house to keep my dresses and shoes in.

I didn't know much about city life but figured out we lived on what Nana called the wrong side of the tracks, and that was where bad people lived. I hoped Momma had earned us that position, but feared my adventure with the car may have contributed to our wrong-side status.

We rented two rooms in the back of Irene's Beauty Shop, which sat in the middle of a long block of shotgun houses. Shingles covered the houses from top to bottom, and the houses sat bunched up on top of each other with more concrete than grass between them. Most housed multiple families, or doubled as businesses with signs on the front doors or in the side yards.

Besides Irene's Beauty Shop, we had a bakery, a small appliance repair shop, and a mechanic on our side of the street. On the other side,

Mrs. Cotton took in ironing and alterations and Mr. Green sharpened blades on knives, scissors and lawn mowers.

Nobody sat on front porches, partly because the porches were too small for swings or gliders, but mostly because everyone seemed to hate each other. The only people who came outside were the ones who wanted to yell for someone else to turn down the television, or radio or to hush up their kids. Then more people came out to yell at the ones who were already yelling and the whole neighborhood turned into a screaming match.

We stayed inside and stuck to yelling at each other. Momma and Daddy had a bedroom off to one side, furnished with a saggy double bed and a dresser, but no chest of drawers or nightstand. Someone before us had flipped over a bushel basket and put it next to the bed to hold a small lamp. Daddy put his alarm clock, the only personal item he brought from home, next to the lamp.

The rest of our space was one big room with a bathroom stuck in one corner and a stove and refrigerator across on the other side. I slept on the couch in the living room side. Daddy said they should at least put a foldout couch or rollaway bed in there but Momma reminded him that kids weren't welcome there so don't push his luck asking.

Three wooden chairs and a stool that served as both a seat and a stepladder accompanied the metal table in the kitchen. Metal bookshelves and a wooden rack for drying clothes joined the couch to complete the dismal, mismatched décor.

Daddy still hadn't found a job when it was time for school to start back so he walked me the four blocks from home to school. Halfway there, he bent down to look at my face and asked, "Are you dawdling because you're nervous about starting a new school?"

"I can't skip in flip-flops," I said. "You walk too fast for me to keep up."

He barely slowed down while he reminded me again that things were going to be so much better when I met my new friends. Since he kept telling me that friends would stop me from being sad that they snatched me from Nana's yard and whisked me down the highway in Granny's station wagon, I tried to believe it was going to happen. So far, Irene was the only friend I had met and she was old. It didn't feel like things were working out. Still, I aimed to meet somebody right off and put all thoughts of Crayfield away.

No sooner than that idea settled in my head, I realized no friend could replace Nana. I didn't think Daddy cared how sad Nana and I were about losing each other, but maybe he still cared about Granny.

"Daddy, don't you think Granny misses her car?"

"She said we can keep the car as long as we need," he said. Granny wasn't generous about anything so I had trouble believing that. "She has my truck if she needs to haul something, and Grandpa's Pontiac, for church and all her other running."

"How long do you think we'll need to stay here?" I asked, afraid to hear the answer.

"Penny, we plan to make our home here. I'll find work soon, and we'll buy another car and return Granny's. We might buy a house too. Try to keep your thoughts on school and friends, and let me worry about the big stuff."

I didn't say anything else, hoping he'd think I'd switched my thoughts over to school.

After a while he asked, "Aren't you happy here?"

I couldn't figure out how to answer. He saw my sad face every day, so he must have wanted me to say yes even if it wasn't true.

I tried to pass the buck. "Momma doesn't seem any happier here than she was in Crayfield," I said. "Because of Irene's shop being open most of the day, Momma can't play her music all day." The hi-fi and her record collection were among the few things she had packed in the back of Granny's station wagon, and here they were, going to waste.

"When Momma fusses at you over not finding work and ruining her life, she has to do it in a loud whisper so Irene's customers can't hear. There isn't even much use in her getting out of bed. That's probably why she sleeps all day now."

I got up early with Daddy, even before school started, and we tried to do quiet things, like read the paper, or play cards, or color. Momma usually found a reason to be upset with us any way. We clattered our breakfast dishes, or the toilet flushed, or Daddy sneezed too loud. Everything got on her nerves.

The day Daddy dropped his coffee mug in the kitchen sink and shattered it was the worst day of all. Momma forgot all about Irene's customers and screamed until Irene had to knock on the door that separated our rooms from the shop and ask her to keep it down.

"If you can't control yourself, I'll have to ask you to move," Irene warned. She switched her eyes from Momma over to Daddy, to make sure he understood. I understood and hoped Momma would never be able to control herself.

"I was leery about letting you move in here since I don't usually allow children. But it turns out she isn't the problem. If all of you could behave as well as she does it would be a lot better."

Irene winked at me after she said the last part. Momma caught that and she said she'd better not catch me talking to Irene any more since I turned her against my own mother. I wanted to argue. I had just worked up the nerve to ask if she would fix Momma's hair like Marilyn Monroe's if I'd sweep up the hair off the shop floor in return. Now, I couldn't offer and Momma would never be in a good mood again. That might be good.

Since everything felt so wrong anyway, I decided to answer the question I had ignored. "Daddy, I liked Crayfield a lot better." I peeked up at his face and he looked as sad as I felt.

"Things will pick up here before long." He didn't sound so sure. "Give it time, Penny Sue. You'll see."

I hoped he was right, but couldn't imagine my family finding peace in the back of Irene's beauty shop. Momma didn't have a crisper in the old refrigerator that came with the apartment. Daddy didn't have a hall closet, and I didn't have Nana or a big tree to cry under. We lived with raw emotions and no escapes.

Midcity Elementary looked even bigger on a real school day than it had day Daddy walked me over to register. I thought back over that day, and how much time he had spent trying to make me comfortable.

After he filled out papers, he held on to my hand and asked the lady in the office to show us where to find room 2C. "I don't want Penny Sue to worry about getting lost when she comes back for the first day of school," he said. "Can we walk her through this?"

The lady took us to the room and back to her office. Daddy took me back to the main entrance but we didn't leave.

"We'll practice a few times, until you feel comfortable," he said, leading me from the door, around the corner and to the classroom at the end of the hall. My school in Crayfield didn't have any turns inside. The six classrooms sat three on each side of one hall, with the cafeteria at the end. Simple.

On the third trip, I led him and found the room on my own. He grinned. "You have the instincts of a bird dog, Penny Sue. You're going to do just fine."

Now, here we were again, hand-in-hand in front of Midcity, only this time there were hundreds of kids around us. Most of them were bigger than me and I didn't feel like a bird dog.

I tried to pick one person I wanted to make friends with but gave up when they kept moving and I couldn't keep my eye on anyone. A lump caught in my throat. I was afraid I would cry like a first-grader, so I squeezed Daddy's hand.

"Things might be a little confusing with all the other kids here," Daddy said. "Do you want me to walk you to your room today?"

I nodded, positive my voice would crack if I tried to force out a word. I couldn't let one tear escape. Not only did I not want to look like a baby; I was afraid of how many tears I had backed up inside of me. I had tears for Nana, and tears for the songs I didn't sing to Pappy, and tears for my cousins, and tears because I missed talking to Irene. That day, I even had some tears for the patent leather shoes sitting under the bed in Crayfield.

I pulled on Daddy's hand so he would lean over and let me whisper in his ear. "I think I need to go back home. It looks like they don't allow flip-flops at this school."

Daddy checked out the feet around us and his face pinched up. He squatted down and spoke softly. "Just for today, Penny. Tonight, we'll buy new shoes. Even if they don't allow them every day, I think they'll let you go today and just tell you not to wear them again."

The flip-flops were only for one day but the humiliation they caused lasted forever.

By the time we fought with Momma over spending money and drove to Sears, just about everyone in the whole school had already laughed at my shoes and short dress. I was sure I'd never have a friend at Midcity Elementary.

Daddy over-ruled Momma, right in the middle of Sears Department Store. I got new penny loafer shoes and three new dresses. He promised socks and two more dresses as soon as he found work. "Then you'll have a different dress for each day of the week, and you can put Wanda's green dress in the rag basket where it belongs."

Momma rolled her eyes and called me a spoiled brat.

My knack for keeping the adults in my life upset with each other had followed me all the way from Crayfield to the city. That night, with Irene's shop shut up and the rest of the neighborhood screaming back and forth at each other, Momma tore loose on Daddy like nothing I'd ever seen before. I stayed in the bathroom through most of it. I flushed the toilet every time the tank filled up, hoping to drown out the ruckus. It didn't work.

"I'm not going to bed at eight o'clock just because the brat has school," Momma said. "I'm an adult and I can stay up as late as I damned well please."

"If you'd get up at a decent hour you wouldn't need to stay up all night," he said, not even trying to keep his voice down. "It's about time you started acting like an adult, and a mother."

"Either you let Penny Sue sleep in the bed, or we go to bed so she can have quiet out here," Daddy said. "Choose one way or the other, Kitty, because she needs to get sleep for school."

Momma threw something and it hit the bathroom door. I jumped half out of my skin and climbed into the bathtub. Then the idea came to me. I could sleep there. Daddy could bring my pillow and blanket off the couch and I could sleep in the bathtub, out of everybody's way.

I got out of the tub, waited a few seconds to make sure she wasn't going to keep throwing things, and opened the door a crack.

"Daddy," I whispered loudly. "I have an idea."

"What is it, Penny? You can come out and talk to me."

I opened the door wider and walked across the room to where he stood. That set Momma off again.

"Sure, you can be nice to her. You talk to me like I'm a dog, but you're sweet to her." Momma glared at me like I had killed somebody.

"Cut it out, Kitty," Daddy said. I knew he was only going to make it worse. I shook my head. If he noticed, he wasn't in the mood for calm. "You're upsetting her."

"Well, we sure can't have your precious Penny Sue upset can we?" She kneeled down on the floor beside me and yelled so loud that her spit flew on my face. "What would you like little, Princess? Want our room? How about a few more new dresses, or maybe a goddamned chauffer to drive you to school?"

Daddy pulled Momma up by her arm and said for her to stop acting ridiculous. She smacked him across the face.

I didn't ask permission, or wait for their decision about where I was going to sleep. I grabbed my pillow and blanket off the couch and ran through the door into Irene's storage room. The bottom shelf of the rack where she stored rollers and shampoo bottles was empty. I fit perfectly in there when I curled my legs up under me.

My parents were still arguing when I fell asleep. They went back and forth, saying the same things over and over, until I got tired of listening and blocked them out by singing "Itsy Bitsy Teeny Weenie Yellow Polka Dot Bikini" in my head about a million times. It was a boy song but I didn't even care because it was happy.

Some time before morning, Daddy came into Irene's storeroom and picked me up. I pretended I was still asleep but held onto my pillow to make sure I had something to put between my face and the scratchy fabric that covered the couch. Daddy brought my blanket, tucked me in, and kissed me on the cheek before he went to the bedroom. Momma yelled at him again, only not as loud or for as long as before. I went back to sleep, thinking about which dress I wanted to wear to school first.

All the thinking the night before was wasted because when morning came I still couldn't decide which dress to wear. I made Daddy choose while I ate Corn Flakes.

He flipped through the dresses hanging on a nail on the back of the pantry door, and teased me by reciting eenie meanie miney moe.

"No, Daddy." I giggled. "Pick the one you like best. Really pick."

He closed his eyes and made a huge production out of pretending he didn't know which dress his hand was touching. "This one!" he shouted.

Momma came charging out of the bedroom. "I'll pick the damned dress if it will shut you up," she yelled. "What does a person have to do to get a little sleep around here?"

She snatched the yellow dress off the nail and tossed it on the table. "Put that on and keep your mouth shut."

I left my Corn Flakes half-eaten and took the dress into the bathroom to change, feeling bad about getting Daddy in trouble again.

"Kitty, you ought to get up with her. You're her mother. You should fix her breakfast and brush her hair before she goes to school." Daddy didn't yell. He just sounded sad.

"You're the one who couldn't keep his pants on at the right time," Momma told him. "You wanted the kid so you take care of her."

"No problem. I'll take care of her. But one day you'll regret not having a closer relationship with her."

"I'll let you know when that time rolls around. Don't hold your breath waiting," Momma said, and went back to bed.

I flushed the toilet so he'd think I was too busy to have heard the whole argument, and waited for him to tap on the door and tell me it was time to leave. When I finally came out, Daddy whistled. "You look like Miss America in that yellow dress." Momma had already ruined me ever liking that dress again.

Chapter 6

Someone poked me on the shoulder in the lunch line on the third day of school. I had memorized the seating order while Miss Keyes took roll, so I knew the ear-to-ear grin I turned around to belonged to Lori Sawyer.

"I have that same dress at home," she said. "Got mine at Sears, brand new." She sounded proud. "None of my sisters ever wore it first."

I smiled back, a little self-conscious and still afraid she only wanted to mention the flip-flops. "I got mine at Sears, too," I said. "Brand new." I probably should have added that none of my cousins had ever worn it, but I wasn't used to talking nonstop to people I had just met. I wasn't used to meeting new people at all because in Crayfield I already knew everyone.

"We can both wear them on the same day and pretend we're twins," she said. "I think it would be fun to have a twin sister and dress alike, don't you?"

That wasn't something I had ever considered. We didn't have twins in Crayfield. And, I didn't think wearing the same dress would fool anyone since twins were supposed to look alike. Lori had short, almost white hair, and she was bigger than I was. But, I didn't guess it would hurt to pretend and I wasn't about to argue with the one person who might want to be my friend.

"When do you want to wear yours?" I asked, hoping it wasn't until after I had worn all of my new dresses at least once. I had the pink one left with the tags still on it.

Lori shrugged her shoulders and said she didn't care.

"Did you get the pink dress with the pearl buttons on the front, too? It was on the same rack at Sears."

Lori shook her head slowly and rolled her eyes upward, but she kept smiling. "Nope. I only got one new dress. The rest of my dresses are hand-me-downs because I have three big sisters."

"I don't have any sisters or brothers," I told her. "My cousins, Wanda and Gwen, used to give me their clothes before we ran away from Crayfield. They don't know where to find me now so Daddy had to buy me three new dresses and these shoes to start school in." In case she would feel bad that I got three dresses and she only got one, I added, "I don't usually get spoiled this bad."

Lori looked at my shoes. I held my breath and waited but she didn't mention flip-flops. "How come you don't have pennies in them, Penny?" She giggled.

I didn't want to explain about my piggy bank being back in Crayfield, or Daddy not having a job so I wouldn't ask for any money. I mimicked her earlier body language and shrugged my shoulders. "Do you think you could call me Penny Sue so my Momma can like you? She gets mad when people leave off Sue."

She giggled again and I figured she probably did that a lot. "Sure. Do you want pennies in them, Penny Sue?"

"It doesn't matter." I really hadn't thought about that any more than I had thought about pretending to be a twin.

Lori bent over and tried to stick a penny in my right shoe. "You'll have to take it off," she said, pulling the shoe off my foot. She separated the flaps with her fingers and forced the penny in place. "Dimes go in easier, but if we put dimes in them we'd have to call them dime loafers." This time I laughed with her. "Maybe I can bring another penny tomorrow, she said, inspecting her work. "For the other one.

I said thank you but dreaded having to explain to my parents where I got the pennies, and why I accepted money from someone outside the family.

Lori sat next to me while we ate lunch. She talked so much that she didn't have time to finish her hotdog or applesauce. I was glad she did all the talking because I couldn't think of much to say.

When Miss Keyes came around to tell us it was time to clean up, I took Lori's tray and put it on top of mine. "I'll take your tray," I said. She looked at me like I was crazy. "To earn the penny you gave me."

Lori let me carry her tray but she walked right along beside me, talking and smiling the whole way over to the tray return window. In that short walk, I grew envious of the space where her two front teeth had once been.

"Did it hurt when your teeth came out?" I asked while using my dirty napkin to push the scraps off our trays into the trashcan. "I don't even have a loose tooth yet."

"The nickel from the tooth fairy makes up for hurting," she said.

After I deposited our dirty trays in the dish-washer's window, Lori took my hand.

"Want to walk to the playground with me?" Without waiting for my answer, she pulled me toward the door, gabbing all the way. "We can play jump rope or four square. Or, if you want, we can do something else, I don't care."

Lori was easier to get along with than Gwen, who had been my only playmate before then. I liked her, and wondered if this was all that was involved in making friends. Just smiling a lot and wanting to be the same didn't seem so hard.

Beth Lincoln pushed past us and turned around to walk backwards. She made an ugly face – one that Nana would have said would stick if she kept doing it – at Lori. "Ooooh, you're walking with flip-flop-head."

Tears stung my eyes. Already, I thought, I'll lose my new friend. Lori surprised me. She didn't let go of my hand. She said, "Shut up, Beth. You aren't very nice." I thought it was a good time to say shut up, even if it isn't nice.

Beth called out to two other girls, "Come here," like she was the boss. The three of them stood in a line, facing us with their hands clasped together. They chanted. "Flip-flop-head. Flip-flop-head."

I pulled up "Dum Dum Diddly Dum" in my head right away but Lori charged forward, dragging me behind her, and broke their line like we were playing red rover. "Don't listen to them, Penny Sue," she said. "They're stupid.

I wanted to laugh and cry at the same time. I was proud that Lori wanted to be my friend enough to defend me, but was sad because other voices had joined in Beth's group and Lori didn't deserve all that trouble. I already caused her so much trouble she should just go ahead and call me Penny Sue Martox.

At the end of the day, Lori and I walked out of the school building hand-in-hand. I spotted Daddy standing by the bicycle rack where he had promised to wait for me. This time, I led and pulled her along right up to Daddy.

"This is my friend, Lori," I said, positive he was going to be happy.

Daddy smiled and said, "I'm pleased to make your acquaintance," same as he would say to an adult. I was proud of him. "Is someone here to walk you home?" he asked her.

"I walk with my sisters. We live on Ash Street," Lori answered.

Ash was two blocks on the other side of Elm, where we lived. "If you want to walk with us," he said, "we'll wait here for you to go find your sisters."

Lori started to dash off and then stopped. "Thank you, Mr. Martox. I'll hurry."

"Isn't she nice?" I asked. "She has a dress just like this one and we're going to wear them on Friday and act like twins. I wish I could lose two teeth before then."

Daddy made his eyes big. "Don't rush things. The longer you keep your baby teeth, the healthier your permanent ones will be." Being reminded that I had *baby* teeth wasn't flattering or encouraging.

"Daddy, can you just call me Penny? Lori said it without saying Sue, and it made me sound bigger. You'll have to make Momma not hate it."

He closed his eyes like he had to think on it. "I'll try to remember, Penny. But, your daughter's name is a hard habit to break."

***

Daddy continued to walk me to school until he found a job, two months later, and had to leave earlier than I did. We met up with Lori and her sisters at the corner in the mornings, and at the bicycle rack in the afternoons. Daddy seemed to like Lori as much as I did. Sometimes, in the evenings or on weekends, he walked me over to the playground by her house so I could have someone to play with.

After he started his job, Momma let me walk to and from school with no adult, and she didn't care how much time I spent at Lori's house after school. Lori and I played the radio, learning the words to every new song that came out, even the ones that men sang.

"Someday when you're famous, I'll be your back-up singer, or maybe your piano player," Lori planned. "Mom said if we ever get a big house, I can have a piano and take lessons."

"In case you never get a piano, you should keep singing," I said. "I think you are good enough to be famous, too, even if you barely know who Brenda Lee is." I was sure she would learn everything there was to know about Brenda Lee if she planned on us being best friends forever.

Momma and Daddy fell into a comfortable routine of hating each other as much in the city as they had in Crayfield, and forgot all about returning Granny's car or buying a house. They mostly hated each other quietly for a long time, with dirty looks instead of hollering and punching. I guessed that meant things were a little better.

I didn't make lots of new friends like Daddy expected, but it didn't matter. Lori was the best friend anyone could want and she shared her family with me.

Midway through sixth grade, Lori's mother took a real bad attitude toward Momma on account of her deciding she couldn't stand living at Irene's any longer. Momma wasn't going to wait any longer for Daddy to make enough money to get her out so she took a job waiting tables at Harvey's Tavern.

Her original aim was to save her tips in the bank, where she'd draw interest and eventually have enough to buy a house. But she usually ended up spending her tips before she ever left Harvey's, so not much of it got to the bank.

Mrs. Sawyer said Momma wasn't respectful, and Daddy wasn't much of a man for putting up with her. I knew she said those things out of feeling sorry for me more than gossiping. She reminded me of Nana with her attitude toward Momma, only she didn't call her Satan's daughter or a fool.

I wanted to defend Daddy by telling Mrs. Sawyer there was nothing he could do to control Momma, but I kept my mouth shut since she didn't hold any of it against me. I looked forward to spending weekends at Lori's house so I knew better than to tell Momma anything Mrs. Sawyer said about her.

Often, Mrs. Sawyer had invited me to sleep over on the weekends even before Lori asked. Momma and Daddy always let me go as long as I had done my chores, which included dishes, dusting, scouring the bathroom, and sweeping and mopping the floors, which I resented more all the time. After Momma went to work at Harvey's,

Mrs. Sawyer invited me over so often it was practically like asking me to move in. I was glad she did but it wasn't as necessary as before.

Fights over sleeping arrangements ended when Momma went to work. I continued to sleep on the couch, but Daddy went to bed early and she came home late and too tired to want to be where I was.

That wasn't the only thing that worked out. We never got a new refrigerator, but Momma didn't need a crisper to hide her bottle in since she could drink all night at work. Daddy didn't need to hide anything from Momma either, because she acted like he wasn't alive. She never noticed if he was drunk or not. The only time they spoke was to fight about money, or how late she came in from work.

Lori's mother was very strict about grades and she included me in her lectures, which made me feel good. She also helped me with my book reports and special projects. With her encouragement, I made the honor roll in fourth, fifth, and sixth grades.

I kept my certificates in the World Book on the Sawyers' mantle, even after Mrs. Sawyer offered to hang them in her dining room next to the ones her own daughters got. One day, when Momma was in a good mood or she liked me more, I planned to show them to her since she never came to the Awards Day ceremonies. When I asked Daddy why Momma never came to my school for any reason, he said it put her in a sad mood because she didn't finish school.

I stopped asking about Nana after a couple of years. I figured we were never going back to Crayfield, and my parents weren't going to invite Nana and Pappy to visit. And I gave up believing they would come rescue me.

Lori said she was sad for me, but happy for her, because she'd miss me if I ever went back.

Chapter 7

The summer before I started junior high was a mixed up time. I had more fun that summer than at any other time in my life. On the other side, huge disappointments waited to erase the glow of the excitement before it had even thawed my heart. Consequently, I decided numb was the safest way to live.

Lori's dad took on a second job as lifeguard and custodian at a private swim club. Midcity Swim wasn't in the same league as the elite country clubs on the other side of town because it didn't have a golf course or tennis courts, or a fancy clubhouse for dances and weddings, but it was a step above the public pools in our neighborhood and it had a jukebox.

Lori and her sisters thought they might die of embarrassment when their dad announcement his new job. It was the first time I could remember seeing Lori upset about anything.

"Dad," she cried. "Lifeguards are supposed to be young and handsome, not my *father*."

They all changed their tune when he told them one of the benefits was that his family received free membership to the club. Lori forgave him completely when he included my name on his list of children and said I'd have to remember to call them Mom and Dad instead of Mr. and Mrs. Sawyer when we were at the pool.

The first time we went to Midcity Swim with *Dad*, we wore our regular clothes and looked around while he finished his orientation and picked up keys. There were three separate pools, lined up in a straight row. At the end where the locker rooms and concession stand were located, there was a wading pool where small children splashed in the water and their mothers sat around the edges to tan and gossip. The largest pool was next in line. It started at three and graduated to six feet deep. That was where I planned to spend most of my time, right on the grown-up side of the rope that marked off the five-foot line.

A wide, concrete patio separated the deep end of that middle pool from the diving pool, which was ten feet deep and off-limits to anyone who hadn't passed a swimming test for the lifeguards. Lori planned on passing the high dive test before the end of summer but I didn't care if I never got to go in the deep water, and certainly wasn't interested in breaking my neck learning to dive.

Webbed lounge chairs lined the concrete deck around the pool area. One of Mr. Sawyer's responsibilities was to blow his whistle and warn people when they moved their chairs past the white line that had been painted on the concrete, because that meant they were too close to the water. Beyond the lounge chairs were picnic tables, covered with yellow plastic tablecloths.

We learned several important things on that first day. If you wanted a picnic table, you had to be in line when the doors opened at ten. Leaving your towel on a lounge chair wasn't enough to hold it. Rude people threw the towels on the ground and took chairs even when they knew its occupant was only in the water or the locker room, aiming to come right back. For once, I thought Momma could come in handy. She would have put those people in their places.

More important than how to secure tables and chairs, though, we learned what it took to be cool at Midcity Swim Club. Girls needed bikinis and baby oil. The really cool ones put iodine in their baby oil to make their tans look darker. Boys could wear whatever they wanted as long as they brought quarters for the jukebox.

The area between the middle pool and the diving pool was unofficially called Teen Alley, and reserved for flirting. Boys pushed girls in the water, and girls squealed and giggled, and wiggled, from what I saw that day. Old people and little kids stayed away.

Since Lori and I had both passed our twelfth birthdays, we decided we were in our thirteenth year and could buy bikinis and baby oil and hang out on Teen Alley. I wasn't thrilled about the giggling or wiggling, and definitely didn't like the idea of someone pushing me into water that was over my head, but I did want to be cool.

I waited until Momma was at work and Daddy was half asleep, and begged until he gave me twenty dollars. He caved before it was necessary to bring up real tears. Daddy had gradually become neutral, not siding with Momma or me anymore. He didn't say much to anyone, stayed completely out of our arguments, and gave as little as possible to either of us.

Sometimes, I thought Daddy simply existed, and had given up on living altogether. When he opened his wallet to hand over the money without looking at me, I tried to talk him into taking me shopping just so we could do something together. He shook his head and walked into his bedroom to end the discussion.

Mrs. Sawyer took her daughters, Lori, Georgia, Rachel, Sue, and me, to Kresge's to buy our new bathing suits. Lori was first to find the perfect one and dart into the single dressing room.

I found a red two-piece, cut a little higher than a real bikini but still in style, and that cost less than fifteen dollars. That left enough to buy baby oil. Lori's sisters also found suits they liked. We stood in the aisle impatiently holding our finds when Lori finally opened the dressing room door and stepped out to get our opinion on hers.

Mrs. Sawyer gasped when she saw Lori in the yellow bikini, and spoke to Georgia and me from behind her hand. "It looks like Lori has lost her baby fat."

"She sure has," Georgia agreed. "She's also getting taller. I don't think she'll fit into my hand-me-downs much longer." Rachel and Sue looked agitated and made their comments so low that I couldn't hear them.

Before she put the bikini on, I hadn't noticed the changes in Lori any more than her family had. In the bathing suit, the changes that had occurred gradually over the winter and stayed hidden under her ill-fitting clothes were very obvious.

"I don't think she lost the baby fat," I said. "It looks like she just moved it all to her chest."

Georgia elbowed me in the side and laughed. "Good one, Penny."

Mrs. Sawyer didn't think it was funny. "Lori, everyone in the store is staring at you. Get back in there and change into your clothes."

Lori looked around, enjoying the attention. Mrs. Sawyer shoved her in the little room and pulled the accordion door closed.

"Thanks a lot," Lori said to me later. "Because of your big mouth, I got a long, boring lecture about how my body is changing and the boys will be all over me soon. Mom is really flipping out over this. She hates my bikini because it shows off my figure."

"Then why'd she let you get it? My mother would never let me get something she like." I couldn't imagine my mother shopping with me in the first place, but knew that if she did she would never let me buy a bikini. The two-piece was risky enough. I planned to keep it at Lori's house where Momma wouldn't see it.

"Mom lets us make our own decisions," Lori said. "Only, when we make one she doesn't like, we get the lectures to go with it." She laughed. "It's not so bad. I'll take the lecture if it means I get to keep the bikini."

To complement the figure and the yellow bikini, Lori adopted a new walk. She threw her shoulders back and her chest and pelvis out, and swung her hips to the sides. I never tried to mimic the walk, but assumed it was difficult since she moved at a snail's pace. I picked up the habit of giving her a head start when we walked from one end of Teen Alley to the other because I couldn't walk that slow.

Lori's sisters ignored her. Georgia said she was through with Lori because she turned into a stuck-up snob when boys started paying attention to her. I thought Georgia was unfair, and probably said that partly out of jealousy. Rachel and Sue had their own high school friends and didn't pay much attention to us anyway.

As far as I was concerned, Lori was still as nice as ever. When the boys gathered around her, she pulled me close to include me in their conversations. And she still said hi to everyone who was nice to her. Also, she didn't make fun of me for walking barefoot on the concrete and in the locker room because I hated flip-flops.

I knew she remembered Beth Lincoln's teasing as clearly as I did. But Lori kept quiet about things like that.

Mr. Sawyer had to go in at eight on Saturdays to clean the locker room floors with chemicals. Lori and I went with him and helped line up the lounge chairs so everything looked orderly, at least until the doors opened and rude people poured in.

We collected quarters during the week so we could play the jukebox and sing along while we worked. I stole most of my quarters out of the tip money that Momma left in the car seat or on the kitchen table. It wasn't fair that Lori's dad got my membership to the pool, and Lori's mom brought my food and drinks in her picnic basket, and that Lori had to play my music with her quarters, on top of all that, so I did what little I could to pay my share.

Lori usually played "Downtown" more than once, because she said I sounded exactly like Petula Clark when I sang it.

"I know you'll end up on Ed Sullivan one day," she told me often. "And I'll be screaming so loud I won't even be able to hear you sing."

Without Lori's expectations, I might have given up my dream of becoming a singer. I had outgrown the desire to return to Crayfield and sing for my grandparents on their front porch, and I doubted that my mother would like me even if I turned into Brenda Lee the second. There wasn't much reason to care about singing anymore, except that I couldn't disappoint Lori.

One Saturday morning I was so busy aligning the lounge chairs on my side of the pool that I didn't notice when the lifeguards and concession stand workers gathered at the foot of Teen Alley for a pre-shift meeting. Petula Clark came on the jukebox. Since Lori had spent her money to play it, I sang as loud as I could so she would hear me at her post, down near Teen Alley.

When the song ended and I turned around, the workers clapped their hands and cheered for me. "Dang Girl, you can really sing." Gary Osburn, the cutest lifeguard of them all, said those words to me. My heart raced until I thought I might faint, overriding my humiliation for a few seconds.

I thanked Gary and ran down to confront Lori. "I'm going to kill you," I whispered when I reached her. "Why didn't you tell me they were here?"

"Why would you want to kill me? They thought you were good. Penny, you can't be famous if you don't sing in front of people."

I turned to look. The pool employees had returned to their meeting like nothing happened. They weren't pointing and laughing at me. Still, I wasn't sure I could ever face them again.

Before the doors opened for members, I spread my towel on a lounge chair near Mrs. Sawyer's favorite picnic table and far from Teen Alley. I didn't want to move from that end of the pool until I was sure the employees weren't going to tell everyone what happened earlier.

Mrs. Sawyer arrived with her usual picnic basket, a thermos of lemonade, and a stack of towels for her family. She looked like a TV mom, fresh and organized, and always smiling.

The smile faded when she stopped beside my chair. "Aren't you feeling well?" she asked, adjusting her load.

I took the thermos to relieve her. "I'm fine. I thought I'd just sit over here for a while and get some sun."

She sat on the chair next to mine. Georgia came to get the picnic basket and thermos and take them to the picnic table so Mrs. Sawyer could quiz me. "I'm not sure I believe there's nothing wrong, Penny. There's just as much sun over there where your friends are as there is here. Did you and Lori have a spat or something?"

I shook my head and looked away so she wouldn't see what I was thinking. She was the exact opposite of my mother; when she read minds she got it right.

"I won't pry and make you uncomfortable, but I'm here for you if you decide you want to talk about whatever is on your mind." Mrs. Sawyer reached over and patted my arm before she went to the picnic table.

While the rest of my body ached with dread of what the day might bring, that one small spot on my arm felt wonderful. It brought back memories of Nana holding me, and Daddy hugging me. I missed my grandparents, and being touched once in a while. Daddy had even stopped kissing me goodnight, probably because he didn't want me to smell the alcohol on his breath, though, not because he didn't like me.

Tears found their way to the surface. Good thing I was at the pool where I could jump in the water and wet the rest of my face and nobody would know the difference between tears and pool water. I went under the water and swam as far as I could without coming up. It wasn't as far as usual. My lungs were so full of sorrow that there wasn't much room left for air.

I swam until kids packed the pool and it was too much trouble to swim around them, and then returned to my seat. Georgia was in my chair.

"I was saving your place," she said, getting up to let me have my chair back. "That woman over there in the black one-piece threw your towel off and was ready to take it away when I caught her."

"Thanks, Georgia," I said. "You can sit here if you want. I'll sit on my towel."

She said no and got up. When I settled in she sat on the foot of the lounge. "We can share for a few minutes. I want to talk to you."

I felt trapped, but didn't ask her to move, since it was her dad that got the membership and she had gone to the trouble to rescue my seat.

"Mom said you seemed sad when she talked to you. Is Lori ignoring you?" she asked.

I shook my head. "No, Lori hasn't done anything wrong. I just don't feel like running around today."

"Oh boy. I think I know what's wrong. Did you get your period? Are you using a tampon?"

"No!" I was horrified that she would say that out loud, and too humiliated to look around and see if anyone else had heard.

"Sorry, I didn't mean to embarrass you. I feel rotten when I get mine so I thought that might be the problem."

Tears popped up again. Lori had breasts and periods, and I didn't have either. I still had a couple of baby teeth in the back. It was just as well, because I had wondered what I would do when the time came that I needed a bra or a box of Kotex. I couldn't imagine discussing either with my mother, whose reaction would most likely be to resent the added expense.

Georgia noticed the tears. I couldn't very well jump up and run for the pool this time, since she was sitting on the end of my chair. I grabbed the baby oil and doused my face, wiping the tears away as I rubbed the oil in.

"You'll burn your face that way, and I can still see your tears," Georgia said. "What's wrong? You can tell me."

"Everything." I only got the one word out before my throat closed up.

Georgia looked over the back of my chair, then grabbed me by the hand and pulled me up. "Come on, Penny. We're going to talk to Mom."

Lori came over as soon as she saw Georgia drag me to the picnic table and sit me down opposite her mother.

"Are you still mad at me over the song?" she asked. "I didn't mean to embarrass you. Honest, I didn't."

"I'm not mad at you, Lori. I'm mad at me for being such a big baby and for messing things up all the time."

"I knew it." Georgia shot Lori a dirty look. "I knew Lori did something to upset you."

"She hasn't ever done anything to upset me." I defended Lori the way she had defended me against Beth Lincoln the first day we met, and the way she had defended me a million times since then. I told Georgia and Mrs. Sawyer about what happened that morning. "Lori didn't do anything wrong. It's my fault I didn't look around and notice other people were there."

"Penny, Gary keeps telling everybody how good you sing," Lori said. "He said he thinks you'll be on TV one day too, and Marsha agreed with him. You shouldn't be embarrassed."

Mrs. Sawyer smiled at me. "I've heard you girls sing many times, and I agree. I called George in from the yard one night to listen to how beautiful your voice was. He said the choir at church needs you. Desperately."

That made me laugh, and I felt a little better about the singing disaster. But I still felt lonely for Nana to hold me, and sad about nobody loving me enough to hug or kiss me good night.

I figured I couldn't be humiliated any worse than I already had been that day, with Gary and the others hearing me, the tears in public, Georgia's question about my period, and Lori thinking I was mad at her, so I opened up and dumped all my problems on them.

I talked about Nana and Pappy, and told them how Momma and Daddy had snatched me away before my front porch concert. I told them how disappointed I was that my grandparents had never come looking for me. I talked about the problems I had getting along with my mother, and how Daddy got so tired of it that he quit talking to both of us, and that I caused everyone in my family to not like each other. I even admitted that I was ashamed to live in the back of Irene's beauty shop, and I hoped people didn't know that my mother was waiting tables and tending bar at Harvey's.

When I stopped talking, they all stared at me. "There's one more thing," I added. "When I need a bra or a box of Kotex, will you help me?"

Mrs. Sawyer crawled out of her side of the picnic table and came around to hug me. "Honey, you can come to me for anything you need. Anytime. I already feel like you are my own daughter."

"That's true," Lori said. "She told us that before, didn't she Georgia?"

Georgia nodded.

I thanked them, wondering if I would feel like part of the family later, or if I would regret spilling my guts and be embarrassed to face them. Fortunately, or maybe unfortunately, as things turned out, I felt like part of the family after that day.

Chapter 8

My popularity skyrocketed at the pool after the day the lifeguards overheard me sing. My voice didn't measure up to Lori's breasts or outgoing personality, but it placed me ahead of the girls who had neither big breasts nor good singing voices. Even some high school guys started talking to me because Gary noticed me first.

The story spread. People said things to me like *aren't you that girl Gary Osburn said could sing so good*. Someone's mother stopped me as I walked out of the bathroom and invited me to join her church choir.

One girl bragged that she had been lucky enough to overhear me singing in the locker room once when I didn't know anyone was listening. Others seemed envious, and gathered around to ask her questions. "What was she singing?" "Is she really as good as Gary says she is?"

I didn't deny the girl's story or call her a liar, but I didn't remember singing in the locker room. I felt like a celebrity because strangers talked about me, but undeserving since I wasn't famous for real.

One bad thing came out of the experience. Some of the girls that liked Gary decided they didn't like me. "He's too old for you," one of them warned. "He's only trying to boost your ego, little girl," another added.

Gary made a habit of playing Petula Clark on the jukebox and begging me to sing for everyone. I declined his requests, partly because of what those girls had said, partly because I was still a little bit shy, but mostly because of Momma's voice ringing in my head.

The early days in the barn house stuck with me. Momma always wanted me to sit quietly on the couch while she sang with her records. I was allowed to clap and talk between songs, while we waited for the record to change. I tried to keep the music inside but far too often my singing filled up my lungs and jumped out before I could stop it.

"Hush up, Penny Sue," Momma consistently yelled. "You sound like fingernails on a chalkboard and you don't know the words."

Her criticism came back every time someone other than Lori heard me sing. On the other hand, part of me remembered when the pool workers had cheered for me, and those glorious short-lived few seconds when the elation was greater than the humiliation. If I had known for sure that the applause and the feeling of peace it brought with it would follow again, I would have worked up the courage to sing in front of everybody on Teen Alley, every day.

But fear conquered faith. What if my friends laughed instead of clapping? I'd be too disappointed to ever sing again.

Lori didn't mention my singing in public after that day but she encouraged me more than ever in private. She talked about costumes, and hair, and stage make-up—the things that she believed were important to my image as a singing star.

"You're beautiful, Penny, but I don't think you know that." She stopped talking to study me for a minute. Her scrutiny made me self-conscious. "Don't you have mirrors at your house where you can see how pretty you look?" she asked.

"I never thought about it." I lied. Truthfully, I had thought quite a bit about whether or not I was pretty when I was younger. Nana and Daddy, and even Pappy a time or two, had all told me I was beautiful.

But Momma took it back. "Don't let that go to your head, idiot. They only say that to make you feel good." Or, "You look like a wet rat because your hair is flat and you don't eat enough."

While Lori stared at my face, I thought about the many times I had studied myself in the mirror on the back of Nana's bathroom door, trying to decide who was lying, Momma, or everyone else.

As the memories rolled out, I inhaled deeply.

"Are you okay?" Lori asked. "Why are you breathing like that?"

"I'm fine. Let's talk about something else." She'd really think I was nuts if I told her I was trying to smell Nana's yellow bathroom way off in Crayfield.

"I heard Gary and Bobby talking about you over by the concession stand once," she told me. "Bobby said you are going to be a knock-out one day. Gary said you already are, for your age."

"Don't tell me that." I closed my ears.

She raised her right hand. "I swear. Gary said he would ask you out on a date if you were older, because he thinks you're pretty."

Lori thought she was helping, but I wasn't ready to think about that yet. My self-image as a wet rat who had destroyed an entire family still haunted me. Also, it was hard to see myself as attractive when my chest was still flat and I hadn't had my period, or even a first zit yet. Who could feel pretty with so much ugliness and worry inside?

"I think I'll change my name when I get famous," I said to avoid discussing my appearance. "I'm glad you stopped calling me Penny Sue, but I don't think I really like plain Penny either. Penny Martox doesn't sound like a famous name, does it?"

"Something like Raven or Ebony would be good with your black hair," she said. "If you want to be really different, you could use Coal."

At first it sounded crazy, but the idea grew on me after I thought it over a few times. "How about Raven Coal?" I asked.

"That's perfect." She said it like it was the final decision and she had done me a favor by making it for me. "Are you always going to keep your hair long? If you do, you can wear a ring of hippy flowers around your head."

"I know one thing I'm *not* going to do. I won't draw on thick eyeliner even if Petula Clark, and Dusty Springfield, and Cher use it. Not even if Brenda Lee herself does."

Lori looked confused. "My mother wears black eyeliner, thick across the bottom and top of her eyes, and curled up into a semi-circle at the corners. I don't want anything about me to resemble her. I'm just thankful she bleaches her hair blonde so I won't have to change the color of mine."

That's how our summer went. When we weren't at the pool reveling in all the attention we received from our new friends, we were either in Lori's bedroom or her backyard, planning every detail of my imaginary stardom. Lori called dibs on being the president of my fan club if she never got to take piano lessons.

One night I practiced signing autographs, using both Penny Martox and Raven Coal, and Lori practiced copying them so she could help sign the pictures we would mail to fans. Georgia caught us doing that and made fun of us, but later she came back to say the name Raven Coal really was catching, and it looked good on paper. She taught me how to make a curly C for Coal.

When August rolled around, we switched our focus to school. Nobody at the pool lived in our neighborhood, so our new friends would all go to different schools.

"I wish we could give fake addresses and go to Southwood," I confessed as I lay across Lori's bed one Friday night. "I know some of the guys from Teen Alley would talk to me in the halls. And I wouldn't have to worry about people like Beth Lincoln."

"Penny, when we get to junior high school nobody will remember that childish stuff. I'll bet the rumors about your singing will carry over to Edgeview and you'll be as popular there as you are at the pool."

I said thanks, knowing that if things didn't turn out that way she would still defend me. Lori was the best friend on earth and I was lucky to have her. Because of her, the rest of my life didn't seem so bad. I secretly hoped we would have all of the same classes because I couldn't imagine facing a room full of my peers without her.

"Are you getting new school clothes?" she asked. "Mom got a charge card at J.C. Penney and she said she'd take me there to get a couple of things since Georgia's old clothes are too short on me."

I had mentioned school clothes the weekend before but neither of my parents responded. Irene found me pouting on the side porch and offered to pay me if I'd help out in the shop. That way I could buy my own clothes. As a last resort I would accept her offer and just let Momma pitch her fit. Irene said she'd never seen anyone hold a grudge like my mother and she would have thrown her out years before if I hadn't been there.

"I'll probably get a few things," I said. "I think I'll wait until after school starts, to see what everyone else wears. Remember how we cased out the pool before we bought bathing suits?"

Her eyes lit up. "That's a great idea. I want to see if culottes really catch on before I buy them. Besides, things might be on sale if we wait, and we'll get more for our money."

I didn't have anything else to say about school clothes. I still depended on Lori to do most of the talking.

"Forget school clothes," she said, pulling a tablet and box of colored pencils from her dresser drawer. She flopped on the bed beside me. "Let's design your stage clothes."

I rolled my eyes. "Don't you ever get tired of working?"

She flipped over the cover on her tablet and started drawing, refusing to let my negativity discourage her. She drew red pants and a red top, with wide bellbottoms on the pants and sleeves, and then added yellow stars to the bells.

"These pants will look great on your skinny legs. I know red is your favorite color," she told me, holding the drawing out at arm's length to admire it.

I was just about to compliment her work when Georgia ran past the room wailing at the top of her lungs.

"Either Jimmy broke up with her again, or she gained another pound," Lori said. She put down her pencil and pad and got up to check things out.

I followed Lori to Georgia's room. Mr. and Mrs. Sawyer arrived right behind us.

"We'll deal with Georgia," Mr. Sawyer said. "You girls go back to whatever you were doing."

"Don't leave," Georgia said. "They just don't want you to know what's going on. They plan to ruin our lives and weren't even going to tell us about it until it's too late."

I wanted to disappear. The Sawyers weren't supposed to scream like my family. If they wanted to act that way, I didn't want to see or hear it. I walked past the parents, into the hall. I aimed to escape and hoped Lori would come with me.

"Daddy took a job in Chicago and I guess they weren't going to tell us until the day we move," Georgia blared out before I got away.

That's all I heard. I don't think they stopped talking, and I know I didn't leave without stopping in Lori's room to get my shoes, but I managed to shut off my ears and stop listening.

"Georgia's lying. Georgia's lying." The words repeated with each footfall as I ran the two blocks from the Sawyer house to mine, and around the side of the building to our door.

I saw Daddy through the glass in the door, his head thrown back on the couch and the television still on. He thought I was sleeping over at Lori's, so he hadn't gone to bed to leave my place on the couch. I doubted he would have anything to say to me if I went in, but I didn't want to be near anyone.

I stepped off the porch and walked to the back of the house, where a glider sat on the small grassy area between the back of the house and the alley. Lying on the glider, I tried to stop my world from spinning. Georgia had to be lying. My life was over if Lori moved to Chicago. I couldn't go to Edgeview without her. I couldn't bear my life without her. I reached under the cushion and pulled Daddy's bottle out.

***

Irene found me the next morning when she passed through on her way from the parking space in the alley to the shop. I heard her calling my name. I even felt her try to sit me up, but my body wouldn't cooperate.

"Leave me alone, please." Every piece of me hurt.

"Just come inside with me and lie down in the supply room," she said. "I can't leave you out here like this."

I didn't move. I couldn't move.

"I can't," I whispered. "I'll puke if I get up."

Irene stepped back to give me room. "Go ahead and get it over with. You'll feel better once it's out."

I said no. She said she wasn't leaving without me.

I pulled myself up, and the retching started before I made it to a sitting position. Irene walked behind the glider and held my hair back while I puked my guts up. When nothing was left but heaves, she handed me a tissue from her purse.

"Wipe your mouth and come inside with me," she said. I knew she wasn't going to take no for an answer.

Irene let me stagger on my own, all the way to the front door without offering a hand. She unlocked the door and told me to sit in the dryer chair while she got a glass of water.

I closed my eyes when she was gone and wished I were dead. I didn't want Irene's sympathy or her help. She should have left me alone.

"So you want to be like your mother?" she asked. "Or is it your dad that impresses you more?" She handed me the water and waited for me to drink it before she raised her eyebrows to demand a response to her question.

"Please, leave me alone," I begged. "I don't want to be like either one of them. I don't want to be me either."

"You don't have any choice about being you, but you do have the power to decide if you want to turn yourself into a copy of one of them or not."

I leaned my head back into the dryer and closed my eyes, hoping to stop the pounding in my head, and the tears that were ready to fall.

51

"You don't understand, Irene. I made them this way. I deserve to be just like them. I deserve the misery more than they do."

"Just a second, I'll be right back," Irene said and darted out the door. She returned in a few seconds with Mrs. Sawyer. "I saw her headed back to your door and thought I'd better stop her," Irene said.

I thanked her and closed my eyes again, too embarrassed and sad to face Mrs. Sawyer.

Irene explained that she had found me in the glider on her way in. I was drunk and sick, and she assumed that I had been there all night. She also repeated every word we had spoken to each other, including what I had said about being responsible for my parents and deserving the pain.

By the time Irene finished, she and Mrs. Sawyer were both crying. I was convinced that I was destined to ruin the life of every adult I came into contact with. These nice ladies were miserable because of me.

"Please, let me go," I asked. "Go home, Mrs. Sawyer. Go to work, Irene. Forget you ever met me and go back to your lives. I'll only hurt you."

Mrs. Sawyer cried harder and I felt my heart rip. How could I do this to her? She said I was like her own daughter, but I knew none of her own daughters would ever hurt her this way. She knelt down in front of the chair and tried to hug me.

"Don't touch me!" I yelled and pushed her away. "Don't touch me, don't talk to me, and don't ever think about me again. Take your perfect family and move to Chicago where you'll never be bothered with me again. Go!"

She backed away, but didn't leave. "Penny, I do love you."

I closed my eyes, put my hands over my ears, and sang. I couldn't let her waste those words on a loser like me.

When I stopped singing, Mrs. Sawyer was gone and Irene had her back to me. I rose to leave, but she stopped me.

"Penny, I know you hurt very badly inside. Is there anything I can do to help you feel better?"

"There's nothing anyone can do. Thanks for holding my hair while I puked and for getting my water. I'm sorry." I said what I had to say and went out the front door to walk around the house so my mother wouldn't know I had been at Irene's.

Daddy was still on the couch when I went in. I passed him and went to the bathroom. I was careful not to wake him as I got a pillow, two slices of bread, and a glass of water, and returned to the glider in the back yard.

I felt someone touch my face and pat my shoulder later, and knew it must be Irene leaving to go home. Maybe she would finally kick us out and I wouldn't have to go to Edgeview without Lori.

That night, Momma charged into the bathroom while I was taking my bath. She grabbed a handful of hair close to my scalp and shook my head until I thought it might fall off.

"What the hell did you tell Lori's busybody mother about me?" She screamed, and my head felt like it was exploding. Daddy didn't come to the door to ask if I was okay.

"Nothing," I said, truly not remembering much of anything I had said that day.

"Then why does she want to take you to Chicago? It couldn't be your charming personality because you don't have one. You better tell me what you told her to make her think you'd be better off in Chicago with them, than here with your own parents?"

"She's just trying to protect Lori so she won't miss me after they move," I said.

"I don't want you talking to any of them, ever again." She watched to make sure I was going to cry before she left the room.

I turned the water back on so she wouldn't get to hear me cry. She didn't get to enjoy my pain if I could help it.

Chapter 9

The Sawyers stayed in town for three weeks after Georgia leaked the devastating news, but I didn't see them again. Irene kept in touch with Mrs. Sawyer and delivered messages to me so I would know when they were ready to leave.

It took a few days to get over my drunk, and for the news that Lori was really leaving to sink in. Irene said Lori was as sad as I was, and she sent her love. I couldn't imagine anyone feeling as sad as I did. My life was over.

I made the huge mistake of asking Daddy to intervene and allow me to see Lori before she left. He said something to Momma like 'what would it hurt'. But he wasn't about to argue when she said it would hurt Mrs. Sawyer because she'd knock her teeth down her throat if I went near any of them. I couldn't take that chance although I would have if my own teeth had been in jeopardy instead of hers.

Irene said I could slip into the shop anytime if I decided to call Lori, or just to get away. I was tempted, but afraid I'd cost Irene *and* Mrs. Sawyer their teeth if Momma caught me.

I wasted the first week sulking, and spent the next ten days on the glider writing letters. I wrote on paper bags, the backs of used envelopes, the inside of a cereal box, and stiff paper towels from Irene's bathroom. Once I had my thoughts organized on scraps, I transferred them neatly onto school paper.

I wrote one letter to the whole Sawyer family, thanking them for the fun times, the good meals I had eaten at their house, and for teaching me how to speak 'city'. I still had a lot to learn, but they had given me a good start. I sent a special thanks to Mr. Sawyer for allowing me to be a part of his pool family, and said I hoped he would be happy in Chicago, and that I would see them all again one day.

Tears dropped on the paper and made a smudge when I wrote that last part, so I had to copy the page over.

The second private letter was for Mrs. Sawyer. I apologized for making her cry, and for yelling at her. I said I wished I really could be one of her own daughters, because of all the mothers I had ever seen she was the greatest, and that included the TV mothers. I asked her to give Lori hugs from me on her birthdays and any time she was sad. I ended by telling her that I loved her too, and I was sorry I couldn't say it that day in Irene's shop.

I started a letter to Georgia, but ended up throwing it away. It wasn't right to send her an individual message if I didn't do the same for Rachel and Sue, and if I wrote individual letters to everyone, Lori's wouldn't seem special.

Aside from singing, nothing had ever held my attention as long as Lori's letter. I worked on it for a week, squinting to see through tear-swollen eyes. The more I cried, the more I hated my parents for stealing the last days I had with her.

At first, I tried to list everything that we had done together, all of the reasons that I liked her, and the things that I wanted to thank her for. But I realized it would take my whole pack of school paper to finish if I did that. I ended up spelling out the biggest things and grouping others together in categories. I specifically thanked her for not laughing at my flip-flops and for never asking to see the inside of my house. I summarized the singing stuff, thanking her for giving me confidence and for helping me decide about my name and costumes.

I wrote a whole page of things she had done to make me smile, and another page telling her what a perfect friend she was and how much I would miss her. I promised she would be my best friend until the day I died, and meant it with all my heart.

With only two days left and no stamps or envelopes, I sat on the side porch to watch for the mailman. At the first glimpse of him coming around the corner, I ran to catch him before he reached our house and begged him to drop my letters off in the Sawyer's mailbox.

"I would love to help you, but I'm not allowed to deliver mail that hasn't been processed through the postal service," he explained. He showed me a postmark on one of the envelopes from his bag, and said he couldn't deliver anything without a stamp and that mark on it.

"You're going to their house anyway," I said. "They live on Ash Street and you probably have something else in your bag for them. I'm not asking you to make an extra stop. Please, this is very important."

He looked sad. I knew he was going to reject me again when he opened his mouth so I threw myself against his chest and sobbed before he got a word out.

"This isn't really mail. They're only notes. This is my last chance to say good-bye to the only people in the whole world who love me."

He patted me on the back and said okay, he'd do it if I promised I wouldn't tell anyone. I handed him the letters and he put them in his pocket, not in his mailbag. "Okay, you convinced me. I will deliver your messages of love."

Later that day, I thought about the mailman's words. "Messages of Love" would make a good song title. Song writing couldn't be any harder than expressing my letters to the Sawyers had been, so I made up my mind to write that song. I spent the rest of the day in the glider with more scraps of paper.

My morning routine didn't change; I went to the glider every morning but I wrote songs instead of letters. A week later, as she passed me on her walk from the alley to her shop, Irene shopped and dropped a bag beside me. "I got you a few things for you," she said.

I looked up at the window over our kitchen sink. She followed my eyes and shook her head. "Penny, when was the last time your mother bothered to get out of bed before noon? Why do you let her control every thought or action you have? Take this, I promise she'll never know the difference."

I picked the bag up and Irene walked off before I looked inside. She left me three packages of school paper, two notebooks, a red folder, and a pack of Bic pens. School supplies, I thought. But when I opened the folder to write my name on the inside, I found it was more than school supplies. She had tucked a sheet of stamps, some blank envelopes, and a letter from Lori in the pockets.

Irene was right. My mother never got out of bed before noon, and I was the last thing on her mind when she finally did wake up. Still, I wasn't taking any chances. I took my new things inside, hid the bag under the couch cushion, and ran into the bathroom where I could lock the door and tear into my letter without fear of Momma catching me with it.

Lori said Chicago was very different, and she would probably like it if I was there. She shared a room with Sue now, but the room was twice the size of her old one so it worked out fine. She would continue to write and send her letters to Irene's house. Her parents and sisters sent their love.

I was a little disappointed. I expected more details from gabby Lori. I wanted to know everything about her new life, especially whether or not she had met a new best friend. And I thought she would have mentioned my letter to her after all the time I had spent writing it. Maybe the tables had turned; I had made her do most of the talking for six years, so it was my turn to do most of the writing.

***

My first day at Edgeview Junior High was much better than I anticipated. I knew ahead of time that Lori wouldn't be in any of my classes so there was no room for disappointment when I looked around and didn't find her there. On the positive side, I didn't have any classes with Beth Lincoln or any of her hateful friends.

Carrying the red folder and Bic pen from Irene, I followed my schedule and focused on finding my classes. Once in the classrooms, I wrote the teachers' names and class rules, and hoped everyone thought I was studious instead of friendless.

Almost like deja vu, someone tapped me on the shoulder in the lunch line and asked, "Are you Penny Martox from Midcity Swim Club?"

I turned to face the boy who had asked the question and didn't recognize him. "Yes," I answered. "Who are you?"

"Craig Osburn. My brother Gary worked at the club as a lifeguard. I came with him a couple of times."

I didn't remember seeing him on Teen Alley.

"Aren't you the girl that sings?" he asked. "Gary said you might be at my school this year."

I smiled at Craig and pushed my tray along the rack, waiting for the milk section because I brought a bologna sandwich from home and mile was all I planned to buy.

"I guess you could say that. I like to sing, but I'm not famous or in a band or anything."

Craig's tray was already full, with a plate lunch, a side salad that looked too brown for my taste, and a banana. "I sing a little, too," he said. "Aren't you going to eat anything?"

He would probably think I was a nerd if I mentioned the bologna sandwich so I said, "I'm not very hungry. It's probably nerves. I was anxious about starting middle school. What do you sing? Country or rock?" I felt like Lori, talking nonstop.

"I play electric guitar, so mostly rock," he said, watching for my reaction. "But I can take a little country now and then. My parents listen to country, so I'm sorta used to it."

We came to the end of the line. I picked up a carton of milk and a peanut butter cookie. He stared at my tray.

"I guess I didn't need a tray for this." I laughed, self-consciously but, by this time, didn't really expect him to make fun of me.

He shook his head. "Are you sitting with anyone, Penny? If not, we could sit together and talk about music."

I remembered Lori that first day at Midcity Elementary, bending over to stick a penny in my shoe, and was grateful that Craig Osburn was there to take her place. My heart might have broken if I had to live through that memory alone.

"I guess we can talk about music," I said, stepping to the side to wait while he paid for his lunch.

Craig lived within walking distance of me, in the nicer homes on the other side of Amelia Parkway. I had figured out a long time before that Amelia served as the tracks in our neighborhood, dividing the good from the bad. Lori told me once that the parents on the other side wouldn't allow their kids to come on our side to play.

Craig's mother either didn't keep very good tabs on where he went, or she didn't know that rule about not coming to my side, because he walked me home from school every day. When Momma wasn't around, he stayed and we sat in the glider and wrote songs together.

Momma left earlier all the time for work, often before I came home from school. She said she had to help serve dinner, or Harvey had called a meeting, or she had to pick something up from the store on the way. It was fine with me. I wished she would always leave before I came home, because then I had a couple of hours to myself, and I preferred being alone over spending time with her.

I told Lori about Craig in a letter, and even admitted that I thought he was cute and I hoped he liked me. "He isn't as handsome, or as big as Gary, but I think he's still growing. He has the same brown eyes and hair, only Craig's hair is longer. He says when he's eighteen he's going to grow it out real long, like a rock star. Right now, his dad makes him keep it above his collar and out of his eyes," I wrote.

***

On the Friday before Halloween, Craig pointed to the gymnasium as we passed by St. Luke's on our way home from school. "Have you ever been to teen club there?"

I shook my head, not sure I knew exactly what a Catholic teen club was. One time, Georgia had gone on a camping trip with a Baptist Youth Group, thinking it would be a weekend of fun things for kids. She was disappointed to find out they had meetings and read the bible at night instead of telling ghost stories around campfires and we were leery of church activities after that.

"Have you been to teen club?" I asked. "Do you go to church here?"

"I've been to teen club a couple of times. You don't have to be Catholic or go to church here. Anybody can come to teen club as long as they are between thirteen and eighteen and pay a dollar to get in. This week they're having a special dance for Halloween, and giving prizes for the best costumes.

I hadn't worn a Halloween costume since third grade, when Daddy dressed me in his black shirt and caked Momma's cold crème on my face to make me look like a witch. These days, Momma was the only one who dressed up. She was Marilyn Monroe one year, of course, a princess the next, and last year she dressed as Cleopatra. I never understood what any of them had to do with Halloween, but she claimed Harvey said men packed into the tavern just to see her costumes.

I spent my Halloweens in the bathroom with the lights off so children wouldn't come to the door and force me to apologize for not having candy to hand out.

"Are you going?" I asked. I pictured Craig dressed as a pirate or Frankenstein.

"If you want to," he said. "I thought we could go as Sonny and Cher."

My heart raced with excitement, as much over the Sonny and Cher idea as the fact that Craig might have just asked me on my first date.

"When is it? I mean, yes. I want to go, and I want to dress like Cher. But I don't know if I can. I'll have to ask my parents."

I was already plotting the escape in my head. If Momma was at work and I could get Daddy to bed early enough, I could get out. But where would I get the Cher costume?

He spit out the details quickly. "Usually teen club is on Friday but they're having it on Wednesday for Halloween. They think they'll keep us juvenile delinquents off the streets this way. My brother will probably drive us."

"I'll go, but I'm not sure yet what I'll wear. I don't have any clothes that look like Cher's."

Craig looked at me through narrowed eyes. We were in front of Irene's, getting ready to turn down the brick walk that led to my door. I had never taken Craig to my door. I had always passed it up and led him to the glider in the back yard.

"Aren't you allowed to have boys in the house?" he asked. "When it gets cold outside, will we still have to sit in the glider?"

For reasons that I didn't understand at the time, I was glad he asked those questions. Something told me I didn't have to hide anything from Craig Osburn; that he saw me separate from the things around me and would still like me even after he met my parents and saw the two rooms we lived in.

"I've never brought a boy here before. Actually, I've never invited any friend inside the house. But whenever you're brave enough, you're welcome to come inside. I warn you, it's not very nice. And neither are my parents."

I looked him in the eye instead of turning my head the way I usually did to avoid facing people's reactions. Maybe because he always looked for my thoughts, like he truly cared what they were.

"Soon," he said. "We can sit outside today and talk about our costumes. If you don't have anything, my mother might be able to help."

***

On Sunday, Momma told me she was going to dress as a go-go dancer for Halloween and needed to find white boots. I asked if she wanted me to go along to shop and help her find them. Figuring she wouldn't want to take me if she thought I wanted something for myself, I thought out my words. "I'll help you put your costume together," I said. You'll make a good go-go dancer."

"I will, won't I? I have good legs." She smiled and I almost fell over. This might go good if I didn't blow it.

"Yes you do." I complimented her legs even though I thought her thighs were too big for short skirts. "I can't wait to see how you do your hair and make-up, Momma."

"Okay, then." She actually sounded pleased. "I'll wait until you come home from school tomorrow and we'll shop together. Just hurry home because I won't have much time."

I held my tongue when hit with the urge to say it would be faster if she just picked me up from school. She probably didn't know the name of my school, much less where it was located. Embarrassing Momma wouldn't serve any good purpose.

At lunch the next day, I told Craig I would have to walk home alone because Momma was going to wait on me to go shopping. I planned to run home to make sure I didn't put her in a bad mood by keeping her waiting. If things went well, I had a plan for getting my costume. I also had a back-up plan in case things went as usual.

We had a substitute teacher in sixth period who didn't care what we did as long as we were quiet. I spent the whole period on a letter to Lori.

"I think we have a date," I wrote. "He asked me to go to the Halloween dance at St. Luke's, and he wants to dress up like Sonny and Cher. Wish me luck on getting a costume out of Momma when we go shopping later, and on St. Luke's teen club being not nearly as boring as Georgia's Baptist camping trip."

I had already signed, love Penny AKA Raven Coal, when I thought of one last thing. I added a p.s. "I think Craig will probably hold my hand when we walk over to the dance, and maybe even kiss me goodnight."

I put the letter in an envelope and stuck a stamp on the corner so I could drop it in the mailbox on my way home. When the final bell rang, I didn't waste any time going to my locker before I ran out the door and straight to meet Momma.

Chapter 10

By the time I rounded the corner onto Elm Street I was out of breath. My sides and arms ached from running two miles carrying my history and math books, and blisters had formed on my heels where fake leather rubbed bare skin. Momma waited in the car with the engine running, tapping her fingers impatiently on the steering wheel, so I didn't dare ask her to wait while I went inside for Band-Aids.

I swallowed my pain and prepared an apology for keeping her waiting, but Momma didn't say a cross word. She almost smiled, again, twice in two days. I didn't understand what was happening, or have any idea what to do with the apology sitting on my tongue.

She pulled out from the curb and started down the road. "Harvey wants me to come in early for a meeting about Halloween decorations, so we don't have much time."

I didn't have anything to say, since she was in control of the car and how fast she drove it, and I was still out of breath and choking on an unused apology.

"I think I'll go to Broadfield Manor Shopping Center since they have Fashion Shop, Kresge's, and a shoe store. Maybe we can find everything in one stop."

I couldn't believe we actually agreed for once. "If you want," I offered, "we can split up and save time. I'll go in Kresge's and look for fishnet hose and blue eye shadow, while you go to the shoe store to see if you can find boots. You do want fishnets to show off your good legs, don't you?"

She chewed on her lip while she thought it over. "Why are you doing this? Do you want something from me?"

"No." I answered too quickly. Now I either had to give up all hope of getting my costume, or admit that I had lied, in which case I still wouldn't get anything and I would have to resort to my backup plan of stealing something. I didn't like any of those options, so I thought fast and hard.

"Mom, that wasn't exactly the truth. I do want something." I liked the feeling of saying Mom instead of Momma. I also hoped she would take it as a sign that I was growing up.

"I figured that much," she said, not letting on if she noticed the new title.

"I want to learn how to be like you," I said. Flattery was the only chance I had to catch her off guard. "I'm in junior high now, and all the other girls are wearing make-up and cute clothes. I've seen some of their mothers, and they look like old ladies, not people who could dress up like Marilyn Monroe or a go-go dancer."

Her expression went from mad to proud.

"I probably embarrass you, walking around looking like I didn't learn anything from having you as my mother." It felt right, so far. "So if you want me to start fixing up a little so people won't think you didn't teach me better, I will."

She chewed her lip half off her face thinking about that statement. I waited for a response because I didn't want to spit out any more lies than absolutely necessary.

"So what are you trying to say? You want me to buy you some make-up?"

"Maybe. I don't know. Maybe just for Halloween I could try to be like you and see how it works. You know, see if you think I look good that way or something. Then, if I look stupid we can say it was just a Halloween costume."

I told her about the Halloween party at St. Luke's only I didn't mention Craig. She pulled into the shopping center and parked in front of the Fashion Shop. Before she opened the car door, she turned to look at me. She *really* looked at me, like she wanted to see me for once. I thought this might be the start of something new. Maybe she only hated little kids and now that I proved I was growing up she might like me better.

"Your appearance *is* rather pathetic. You haven't even started to develop."

"I think I might need a bra soon."

She opened her door. "Come on, we don't have time to waste blabbing."

I followed her into Fashion Shop, since she hadn't accepted my offer to split up and take different stores. She charged through the aisles, practically knocking people down, until something caught her eye. "Here we go," she said, stopping at the biggest mess in the store. "The bargains."

Women packed around a huge, square table, digging through stacks of clothing. They pushed and shoved like children, snatching things from each other's hands. My mother dove right in like there might be a diamond ring or a million dollars hidden somewhere in the pile.

I stood back to watch. Someone knocked over the metal rack that held the two-dollar price tag for blouses, pants, dresses, and underwear that were no longer in stacks by size or item. Nobody tried to fix the sign; they just shoved it around with the clothes. I was almost dizzy from watching.

Without losing her place at the table or breaking her rhythm, Momma shouted out to me. "Penny Sue, if you expect to get anything, you'd better get your ass in here and find it."

I wanted to die of embarrassment, but I wanted a Cher costume worse so I edged my way into the free-for-all. As the clothes flew around the table, I kept watched for anything glittery or bright, and ignored the regular clothes. I figured I'd just stand there and watch while they moved things, that way my hands would be free if I saw the right thing. Or to catch the metal sign if it came flying at me.

My strategy paid off when an aggressive woman to my right scooped up two arms full of clothes and left a silver mini skirt lying right out in the open. I grabbed it and backed out of the crowd.

Momma looked over her shoulder and I held the skirt up for her to see. "That's perfect," she yelled. "Now get in here and find another one for you."

Someone had cut the tag out of the skirt, but I was sure the skirt was closer to my size than hers. If I didn't find another one in her size, it wouldn't matter. I would have no chance of getting the one in my hand.

I moved back in, next to my mother this time, clenching the skirt between my knees while I searched for another one like it, hopefully in a larger size. "Mom, this was on the bottom. You pick everything up and I'll look for another one down there."

She leaned over the table, spread her arms as wide as she could, and swooped up enough clothes to open a small store of her own. I scattered what was left on the table and found another silver skirt. Someone tried to take it from me but I held on for dear life. The lady on the other side of me smacked the thief on the wrist until she let go. I thanked her while Momma dropped the clothes she was holding back on the table and we took off.

"We don't have time to try them on," she said, practically running to the check out. "These will have to do."

On the way to the shoe store, my mother paid me the first compliment I could remember hearing from her. "You're a good shopper, Penny Sue. We got two skirts for four dollars. You can't beat that for a bargain."

"Thanks," I said, grateful for any praise she could afford.

"Now let's see what we can do about boots." Her voice was playful, bordering on excited.

Things went even better at the shoe store. There was a similar scene, because it, too, was a discount, help yourself store. The customers were as rude as the ones at Fashion Shop, but there weren't as many of them.

Momma found her white go-go boots, at half price, and was satisfied. When they didn't have the boots in my size. She was ready to fight the girl who worked the register after she refused to check the stockroom for boots in my size but I stopped her. I didn't really want the boots anyway since I wanted to be Cher instead of a go-go dancer.

"It's okay, Mom," I said, grabbing her arm before she pushed the girl. "Maybe I can get some high heels instead, and you can teach me how to walk in them."

She turned to the nervous clerk. "You'd better find a pair of silver heels to fit my daughter, and give them to her at half price. If you don't, I'll tell everyone I know not to shop here. And hurry, we have other things to do."

I smiled at the girl before she took the key out of her cash register and left to find my shoes. She returned with a pair of silver sandals with platform soles. Perfect.

"Half price?" Momma asked.

The girl nodded and I exhaled.

In Kresge's, we found fishnet hose, blue eye shadow, and black crocheted vests. Momma paid, I grabbed the bag off the counter.

"Hurry, I forgot I have to take you home before I go to work," she said, as she led me down the sidewalk to our car. "Damn, I'm going to be late."

A disgusting bubble worked its way from my stomach to my throat. The strange woman I had spent the last hour with was changing back into my mother and I didn't like it. Terrified she would take my things back and be mad at me for tricking her into being nice in the first place, I said, "I can take a bus or something. I don't want to make you late."

She waited a minute before she answered, but I figured the bus idea was out when she started up the engine and drove off.

"I have an idea," she said as we pulled out of the parking lot. "I'll take you with me for the meeting, and then drive you home before my shift starts. Maybe you can help with the decorations to earn the things I bought you."

I didn't want to hang out at Harvey's Tavern, but I said sure, I'd be happy to help.

Momma put on some lipstick before we got out of the car. "Please don't embarrass me in here," she said as she dropped the tube back in her purse and blotted the excess color off her lips onto a dirty tissue from her purse. "Don't say anything you don't absolutely have to say. And, for God's sake, don't sing along with the jukebox if it's playing."

I was too hurt to be angry. "Do you want me to just wait in the car?"

"Penny Sue, are you trying to get out of helping me now? After I bought all those things for you?"

I shook my head and got out of the car, wiping a tear before she could see it. She walked a few steps ahead, giving me a chance to get over feeling hurt before she turned to face me again. I was sad to see her look like her regular sneery self.

It took a few minutes for my eyes to adjust to the dark, smoky room, so I fell a few steps further behind as Momma rushed to join Harvey and the other employees. They apparently hadn't started the important part of the meeting because they were playing around at the end of the bar, laughing very hard at something one of the waitress was saying. Momma walked around behind the bar and stood next to

Harvey, leaving me stuck out in the middle of the room not knowing what to do.

When the laughter died down, Momma apologized for being late. "I took Penny Sue to get new shoes and her feet are so small that we had to wait on the clerk to search the back room to find something to fit her. I don't think that girl will ever catch up in development."

I stood there, feeling as out of place as a flagpole in the middle of a cow pasture. Harvey looked over at me and waved, making the rest of them turn to look at me.

Grace, the redheaded waitress that Momma had complained about since the day Harvey hired her, walked over and put an arm around me. "So this is Penny Sue." She cooed like I was a toddler. "All this time and I finally get to meet you. Why, Kitty, she's as cute as a damned ladybug. You never told me she was this cute."

She made me feel stupid but at least she was nice. She pulled a chair out from the nearest table. "You sit down here," she said. "Kitty, get her a Seven-up to drink while she waits."

While Momma took her time getting my drink, the rest of them looked me over and made comments about how cute I was and how much I didn't look like my mother. I was positive Cher hadn't popped into any of their heads while they inspected me but Cher was what I was focused on to keep from having to think about what was happening.

Momma plopped my drink down on the table in front of me and said everyone could quit staring and get on with the meeting. As soon as they turned around, I slipped my feet out of my shoes under the table, positive the blisters on my heels were as big as quarters.

"Will your meeting last long?" I asked.

Even in the dim red and blue light of the beer sign hanging on the wall by my table, I could see the fire in my mother's eyes when she answered. "You made me late, so you have no right to complain about sitting here for a few minutes while I'm in my meeting."

"I'm not complaining. I thought I'd go get my math book from the car and do my homework if it's going to last awhile," I explained.

She walked a few steps toward the bar and then turned back. "Go ahead and get your book if you want."

I got my things and positioned my book so it was in the spot on the table that caught the most light, and worked my math problems the best I could without seeing the lines on my paper. I finished all twelve problems with time to spare before the meeting ended. When I had nothing left to do, I listened to Harvey.

"You girls need to wear sexy costumes. I don't want to see this place full of witches and Snow Whites, because those things don't draw crowds or sell beer. I want all of you to get busy with decorations as soon as we're through here, but don't cover up any of our advertisements or block any aisles. Stick mostly to bare wall space."

Harvey sounded like a jerk. No wonder Momma was always in a bad mood. For once, I felt sorry for her. When the meeting broke up, I went immediately to help with her share of the decorating.

***

Momma said little on the drive home and I didn't see her again before she left for work on Halloween. My heart sank when her car wasn't out front but she surprised me by leaving the blue eye shadow and black eyeliner on the back of the bathroom sink for me. I put it in the bag with the rest of my costume, and hid the bag inside Irene's door until Daddy was out of the way.

I fried hamburgers and French fries, and fixed a plate to have ready for him to eat the minute he walked through the door. "It's Halloween," I reminded him, setting his plate on the table. "I already ate, and I have your dinner ready so we can go to bed and turn out the lights before the trick-or-treaters come out."

He dropped his lunch box on the counter by the stove and washed his hands in the kitchen sink, without responding. I went to the other side of the room to pull my pillow and blanket out from behind the couch and make my bed. That should discourage him from sitting there after he was finished eating.

The first and only word he spoke to me was, "Goodnight," when he went into his room at six fifteen. What a loser. He would rather go to bed in the middle of the day than buy a bag of Halloween candy to hand out to the few brave kids who might walk around to knock on our side door.

I snuck into Irene's, changed into my costume, and carefully applied my make-up. The eyeliner was crooked and thicker than I wanted, but it wasn't too bad for a first try. Satisfied, I left through Irene's front door. Gary and Craig picked me up at the corner as planned.

"You make a pretty good imitation of Cher," Gary said. I thanked him before I giggled at Craig in his stick-on moustache.

"Are you guys going to sing "I Got You Babe"", Gary asked. "Because if you are, I might have to stick around and listen."

Craig convinced him that he could leave with no regrets because this was a costume party, not a talent show. We weren't going to sing anything.

"I'll be back at nine. Meet me right here, or at the corner if there are too many cars backed up," Gary instructed before he drove off.

Craig took my hand and held it until we got to the door and he had to take his hand back to reach into his pocket for money. "You do look good," he said. "I think you are even prettier than Cher in some ways."

My stomach did something weird. I guessed it was what people called butterflies, but how was I supposed to know that for sure?

We came in third place in the costume contest, beat out by a clown with orange hair, and a girl dressed like Tin Man from the Wizard of Oz. Craig laughed about them counting us as one. The prize was free admission to teen club for two weeks. We promised neither of us would come without the other. We never went back

Craig didn't kiss me goodnight, I think because Gary was watching. But he did hold my hand all the way home in the car so I counted it as a date. I stayed up to write a letter to Lori after I washed my make-up off, hoping that she had had her first date, too, so we could be excited about this together. Maybe she could tell me how to know if those had been official butterflies in my stomach.

Chapter 11

The temperature dropped below fifty in early November. Irene came around the back of the house and approached us, sitting on the glider. "I'm sorry, Penny Sue," she said, looking and sounding sincerely sorry, "but I need to take the glider cushions inside for the winter. The cold air will crack the vinyl."

I nodded, unable to hide my disappointment.

"You'll have to find a new writing spot for the winter. Just promise me you'll keep working so I won't feel guilty about ruining your career."

"I promise," I said, and Craig added that he wouldn't let that stop him, either. I tried to keep smiling but it was hard since this was worse than just giving up cushions. If also meant, if I wanted to see Craig outside of school during the winter, I would have to invite him inside.

We rose from our seats and Irene, looking like it killed her to do it, picked up the cushions and took them inside with her. I looked at Craig, trying to apologize with my eyes the same as I had seen Irene do, and asked if he was ready to see my home.

My hand shook when I opened the door to take him in with me, not only because I had never been a hostess before, but also because I had seldom been a guest anywhere except at the Sawyers' and Nana's houses, and those two places were just like being at home. I didn't know what guests were likely to expect. Craig probably had enough experience at being both a host and a guest to know if I did everything wrong.

"Make yourself comfortable," I said, while hanging out coats on the hooks behind the door. "Might want to take the center of the couch since the sides sink in."

I turned and waved my arm back and forth across the kitchen/living room combination. "This is it. My parents have a bedroom behind the kitchen--off limits to me--and there's a bathroom over there in the corner. The rest of the house belongs to Irene's shop."

He looked around and took everything in without showing disgust. "Where do you sleep?"

"You're sitting on my bed. When the sun goes down, I pull out my magic wand and change this into a bedroom, complete with a brass bed and fancy vanity table." I laughed, hoping he wouldn't feel sorry for me if he heard me if I made a joke of the situation. But he didn't laugh with me.

Craig was good at knowing things that I didn't tell him; so he might have guessed the part that really bothered me worse than sleeping on the couch. I was most resentful over not having a dresser, or a closet, or shift robe, or anything that normal people had for their clothes. I often wondered if I was a permanent resident, or if they might just up and ship me out to live somewhere else one night.

My dresses and blouses still hung on a door, only it was the bathroom door now instead of the pantry. I kept my folding clothes in a plastic laundry basket under the bathroom sink, covered with plastic in anticipation of the next leaky pipe.

"What about when you go to sleep?" he asked. "Do your parents have to stay in their bedroom?" I almost resented his concern for them.

I rolled my eyes, not because I found his questions or his distress ridiculous. My answers and my circumstances were the ridiculous part. "Are you sure you want to hear about my crazy family?" I asked to offer him a way out before it was too late.

"Only if you want to tell me." He popped his knuckles while he waited for my response.

"Don't do that," I said. "You'll end up with arthritis and I don't think that's good for guitar players." I sat down beside him and held his hand so he wouldn't be tempted to start up again.

"I didn't mean to be nosy." His apologetic tone made me believe he wished he hadn't asked questions. But, he could have been sorry he came inside at all, or sorry he ever met me.

"It's okay," I said. "If you're going to be mixed up with me, you'll have to find out sooner or later. My family is weird. When I was little I thought it was all my fault."

"I don't think you're weird, Penny. I like you."

He didn't seem one bit embarrassed to look straight at me and say that. I wanted to cry, and it *was* weird to want to cry because I was happy.

Maybe I didn't know how to be happy. I had the same reaction when Mrs. Sawyer tried to be nice to me.

"I like you, too," I said, although not as comfortably as he had said it, and without eye contact. "You make me happy. But there's something I need to tell you."

He tightened his grip on my hand and waited.

"Really, I wasn't little when I thought it was my fault that my family was so messed up. I still believed that when I first met you. Sometimes I still believe it now."

He looked more confused than before, probably thinking the sleeping arrangements were nothing compared to the rest of my life.

"Why would you think that?" he asked.

"It's a long story. It started when I was real little. Just about everything I did caused the adults around me to get mad at each other. If I made a mess in the house, Momma yelled at Daddy because she didn't want to clean it up. If I snuck outside while Momma slept all day, Nana yelled at Daddy for marrying Momma, and then Daddy yelled at Momma for not watching me. If I wasn't nice to Nana, Daddy got mad. If I was nice to Nana, Momma hated me. Because of me, everybody got mad at each other, and because of everybody being mad we had to run away from Crayfield and live here. I'll probably never see my grandparents or cousins again."

He let go of my hand and turned to sit sideways on the couch, facing me, with his arm across the back cushion. For a minute he looked angry. I thought I had managed to convince him that I was nothing but a troublemaker.

"Penny, all that's crazy," he said. "You were a little kid. It's not your fault they couldn't get along."

"Thanks. I'm starting to figure some of that out. I had a friend before I met you. Lori Sawyer. We were best friends for six years and never had a fight. I went to her house, even stayed overnight often, and never caused her family to get mad at each other. So I started to figure everything wasn't really my fault. At least, I didn't make people outside the family act crazy."

"See." That one little word convinced me he had confidence in me.

"I'm not finished. When Lori and her family decided to move to Chicago, I caused a big mess. My mother threatened to knock Mrs. Sawyer's teeth out. And I yelled at Mrs. Sawyer because I didn't want her to move away and take my friend."

Tears threatened to fill my eyes, but I took a deep breath and blinked them away. He put his hand on my shoulder for just a few seconds, proving he still liked me.

"You don't get upset with me, do you?" I asked.

He shook his head. "I think you're the nicest girl I ever met. I've never seen you act mean to anyone."

"Sometimes I am mean," I admitted. "Especially to my mother."

"Does she deserve it? Is she nice to you now?" he asked.

"Nobody deserves for anyone to be mean to them."

"But are things better since you moved here?"

I took another deep breath. "Depends how you look at it. Nobody fights anymore. But that's because nobody talks to each other much. Momma sleeps most of the day, and then leaves for her job before Daddy gets home from his. Most of the time she leaves before I get home from school, so I don't see her all day. Daddy comes in, eats his dinner, and goes to bed before dark."

"I guess that's better than fighting," he said. "What time does your dad get home? Will he be mad if I'm here?"

I had no idea how either of my parents would react to my having someone in the house, because I had never brought anyone in before. I didn't know how they would feel about a boyfriend either.

"He usually gets here about five-thirty," I said.

"Let me know if you think I should leave. I don't want to get you in trouble."

"We have time before anyone comes home. You can stay as long as you don't mind watching me peel potatoes." I snickered a little. "Daddy might not care if I have you in but he will care plenty if I don't have supper ready."

As we moved from the couch to the kitchen table, Irene knocked on the adjoining door and came in without waiting for me to invite her. "Hello, Craig," she said. "Nice to see you." She turned to me.

"I need to see you alone for a minute." I stood and she pulled me into her storage room.

"Did your parents give their permission for you to entertain boys in the house when they aren't here?" she asked when she had me alone.

"They never said I couldn't."

"That's not the same as saying you can. Penny, I trust you and I think Craig is a nice boy. But to be on the safe side, I think you should leave this door open when you have him in."

I thought it was none of her business, but agreed to do as she asked.

"This way, nobody can accuse you of doing anything wrong," she said. "People talk, even when they don't know what they're talking about sometimes. I'd hate for that to happen to you, or for your mother to get mad over nothing. If you keep the door open, I can defend you."

I told Craig the opened door was his escape route if either of my parents came home unexpected and he wanted out. That seemed like good news to him. After Irene's warning, I had grew fearful about how my parents would react to him being there. Daddy probably wouldn't have noticed if I brought Charles Manson in, as long as I had mashed potatoes, but Momma was another story. She was so unpredictable that I couldn't guess her reaction to anything.

We moved to the kitchen table. I peeled and Craig watched.

"Have you heard about the talent show at Edgeview?" he asked. "They have one every year around Valentine's Day and there's a sign-up sheet hanging by the main office door."

I hadn't heard, and found the news both exciting and frightening at the same time. "Are you going to be in it?"

"Probably," he said. "You have to audition to be in the show. Last year everybody who tried out got in. Want to do it?"

I dropped the potato I was paring into the pan and put the knife down. "I don't know. I wish I had the nerve to sing in front of the whole school, but I don't think I do."

Lori would have been so disappointed to hear me say that. I felt like a traitor, wasting all that encouragement she had given me.

"We have three months to practice," he said. "I thought maybe we could do something together. I'll play guitar and you sing." He sounded more excited with each word and I caught some of his optimism even though the knot in my stomach continued to grow. "It would be really cool if we put a whole band together and did one of the songs we wrote."

He kept pouring out ideas and I couldn't stop smiling. It felt strange to be scared half to death and excited at the same time. I picked up the knife and went back to work, so nervous that I cut away half of the potato with the skins. I argued with myself until the potatoes were peeled, washed, chopped, and boiling.

"Which song?" I asked. "We haven't finished writing any of them."

We had pages of half-written songs in the notebook from Irene's bag of gifts that I had dedicated to song writing. Most were ideas, or a few words that we thought would be fun to sing, and none of them anywhere near a whole song that was ready to perform.

"I like the one about running away," he said. "We can finish it in no time. Then, we'll have all of Christmas break to work on it."

"I'll do it," I said while I had the nerve. "But if I embarrass myself I'll never go back to school. I'll be a junior high drop out."

He copied what we had of the runaway song onto his history notebook and said he was going home to work on the melody with his guitar. I finished making my father's supper and served it to him when he came in but my stomach was too nervous to eat anything.

A few days later, Craig invited a wiry, obnoxious, pimple-faced guy to sit with us at lunch. "This is Billy Ranglin. He plays drums and wants to start a band."

"It's nice to meet you," I said, not sure I meant it. He brought me one step closer to the day I'd have to sing in front of everyone and the idea still made my stomach jump.

"All we need now is a bass player," Craig said.

Billy did the rest of the talking. He barely slowed down long enough to take a breath until the bell rang to announce the end of lunch period. He told us his favorite songs, without asking ours, and he bragged about his many talents and experiences, without asking ours.

According to Billy Ranglin, he was headed for big time because he had already performed in shows and bars, even got paid a few times. I wasn't anxious to believe him but Craig hung on his every word.

After lunch, Craig walked me to my locker. "Billy really has done those things. His dad is a musician, so Billy has spent his whole life around people in the business. He gets a lot of lucky breaks because his dad's friends let him sit in. It'll be good for us to be around him."

I told Craig he was starting to remind me of Lori. As soon as I said it, I missed her so much I wanted to cry. If she had been there, she would have convinced me that Craig and Billy were both exactly what I needed to make me famous, and I might have believed her.

"I'm not sure *I* want to be famous as much as *Lori* wanted me to be famous," I said. "She wanted me to sing so bad that I did it just so I wouldn't disappoint her."

"Do you want to disappoint me?" he asked.

"I don't want to disappoint anybody. But I don't want to embarrass me, either. Craig, you've never really heard me sing."

"Gary told me you're great, and I've heard you sing a little. I know you're good, Penny. If you heard some of the people in last year's show, you'd know you don't have anything to worry about."

I had learned to turn a plastic serving tray upside down and rest it on my knees to make a desk. That night, I used it to write a long letter to Lori while I was in the bathtub, where I didn't have to worry about anyone seeing me and freaking out because I was in contact with the Sawyers, even if Mrs. Sawyer's teeth were far away where Momma couldn't reach them. I told Lori about the talent show and how Craig was trying to take her place as my cheerleader, but he still wasn't as good as she was at giving me confidence. I needed her advice, and asked her to please, please, please write back more than a couple of lines.

* * *

Billy found a guy in his shop class who had been taking bass guitar lessons for over a year and brought him to meet Craig and me after school. John the bass player also sang, and wanted to join our band.

The guys met at Craig's house over the weekend to move boxes and old toys around and clean a space in the basement for their equipment. Billy's dad drove his drum set over and set it up after Mr. Osburn promised they never had water leaks. John's dad brought his amplifier.

All of the other parents were involved, and encouraging, and I still hadn't told mine about the band. I probably never would, so I had to figure out some way to get to Craig's house for practice without them.

"I have two choices," I told Craig. "Either I can come after Momma leaves for work and before Daddy gets home, but I don't see how I'll get supper made if I do. Or I could come after Daddy goes to bed, which is usually around eight."

"What about the weekends. Can't you come out on Saturday or Sunday?" he asked.

I thought about that. Momma slept most of the day, and worked on Saturday night, so I might be able to pull it off. I could mumble something about going to a friend's house and Daddy most likely would nod his head and never ask for a name. If the guys were willing to wait, Daddy usually drank himself into a stupor not too long after Momma left for work. I never saw him take a drink, and still had no idea where he hid the bottles after Irene took the cushions away, but when his chin hit his chest and he snored, I knew why.

We called our band *Coal's Crew*, so I could be Raven Coal. We rehearsed on Saturday nights. Gary and Mr. Osburn made sure I got home safely, since it was dark when practice ended. I was committed, but still as nervous as could be.

Within three weeks, we gave up on finishing an original song and chose Cher's "Bang, Bang" for the talent show. Craig bought the single so they could pick out their parts and get them perfect. I already knew every word.

My bandmates' parents came to listen to our final rehearsal the weekend before the show. Craig asked several times if I had anyone I'd like to invite. I said no. Lori and her family had wished me luck in letters. I knew that Irene would have gone if I asked, so I didn't *feel* alone.

Billy's dad was even more obnoxious than Billy, if that was possible. He tried to control everything at Craig's house. That made me not feel so bad about not knowing the rules of hosting.

While we were still in the kitchen saying no thank you to Mrs. Osburn when she offered us everything in the house to eat or drink, and inching our way toward the basement stairs, Billy's dad clapped his fat hands together and said, "Let's get this show on the road," like we should jump and do whatever he said. John's mother put her hand on her husband's arm and shook her head to keep him from saying anything.

"If it's okay," John said, "I'd like to warm up a little before the parents come down to watch."

Mr. Osburn said he thought that was an excellent idea, and told us to take all the time we needed. I started down the stairs before Billy's dad could object. My knees shook so bad from nerves about singing in front of so many people, and being afraid of a fight, that I could barely walk.

At the bottom of the stairs, John pulled a bottle of Southern Comfort out of his guitar case. "I thought this might help our nerves," he said, offering the bottle to Billy. Billy and John both took big swigs and passed it to Craig.

He didn't take any but held the bottle out to me. "Do you want any?" he asked.

I shrugged my shoulders, remembering how sick I was after I drank Daddy's Jack Daniels the night after I yelled at Mrs. Sawyer. "I don't want to get sick."

"One little swig won't make you sick," Billy said. "It'll ease your nerves and loosen you up. I heard it coats your throat and makes you sing better, too."

I took the bottle from Craig. "My nerves could use a little help." Southern Comfort didn't taste any better than Jack Daniels. It burned all the way down and made my eyes water, but at least I didn't choke. I took one small drink and passed it back to Craig. He handed it back to John, still not drinking any.

It did help, and the parents said we sounded great. So, on the night of the talent show, I took two drinks, because I was twice as nervous.

And I took two more later, to celebrate, because we were the hit of the show.

Chapter 12

The overwhelming reception we received on the night of the Edgeview Junior High talent show, and the immediate popularity upon our return to school on the following Monday affected each member of Coal's Crew a different way. John interpreted the response as proof he was a better musician than he originally thought, or than his teacher had bothered to tell him, so he severed his relationship with the guitar teacher. His head swelled so big we worried it wouldn't fit through the narrow stairwell that led to Craig's basement.

John must have had similar concerns, because he stopped coming regularly to practices. He also decided that the volume he used to fill up the gymnasium for the show was part of the success, and turned his guitar and amp to the same levels on those rare occasions when he did come to practice. When Craig's neighbors came to the door to complain, John's attitude disappointed all of us, especially Craig's parents.

"Those goofballs don't know how lucky they are to hear us every week for free," he boasted. "Someday they'll be asking for our autographs and bragging to their friends how they knew us before we were famous." He looked Mr. Osburn straight in the eye and said, "Tell them that the next time they come over to complain."

Mr. Osburn took that opportunity to sit us all down for a talk. "You won't get far in music, or the rest of your lives, if you let a little success go to your head. Regardless of what you have accomplished, you should still treat others with respect."

I interpreted that as an order to straighten up. John didn't. "They didn't show us much respect when they came over here to yell about our music."

"Let me put it another way," Mr. Osburn said. "Either you turn it down and respect my neighbors, or you won't have a place to practice."

When that talk failed to impress him, Craig and Billy threatened to replace John if he couldn't respect Mr. Osburn.

"You don't show up half the time," Craig said. When you do come, you're unprepared.

Billy chimed in with, "John, you don't show any interest in getting better. Just because we did okay in a talent show, that doesn't mean we're as good as we can get. We'll leave your ass in the dust if you don't start working harder."

"You need to take more lessons, practice on your own at home, and show up here ready to cooperate," Craig said. "It takes a month for us to learn a new song because you never know your part. That's getting on my nerves."

For once in my life, I wasn't the troublemaker. I stayed out of it so I wouldn't hurt anybody's feelings or cause any fights. Besides, it didn't matter to me how long we had to work on a song; I enjoyed singing whether I sang the same song a hundred times, or a hundred different songs one time. Practice was never a negative experience for me because it was time out of the house, doing something I loved. But, I ended up being as happy as the others when John turned his volume down and said he would start his lessons back up.

Billy, on the other hand, started out believing he was ready for the big time so the reaction of the crowd at the talent show was exactly what he had expected. His instant popularity with the girls at school was what changed him.

Girls overlooked his zits, his oily hair, his abusive personality, and his arrogance, and threw themselves at him. One day, two girls rolled around the cafeteria floor in a fistfight over which one he liked better. He had a different girl in each class doing his homework for him. Others gave him money and carried his lunch tray to him so he wouldn't have to stand in line. I couldn't picture Elvis Presley himself getting more attention.

Billy kept count of his girlfriends, including the ones he dumped the same day he picked them up, and bragged to the rest of us about them. I tore myself apart from his problems the same as I had John's, and refused to get involved when girls asked me if I could introduce them to him, or to ask advice about how to make him like them.

"I stay out of Billy's business," was my automatic response. I was sorry it rolled off my tongue so fast when Beth Lincoln asked me to put in a good word for her. If I had thought that one through, I would have told her he liked girls who wore flip-flops.

With each new girl, Billy thought he had one more reason to feel good about himself, and I had one more reason to dislike him. I could barely stand the sight of him. But Craig convinced me to ignore Billy's girl situation because he was a good drummer and someday we might need his contacts.

Craig's transformation after the talent show was more mature and productive than the rest of ours. He became more confident as a musician but, instead of taking the attitude that John had, Craig used it as motivation to become even better.

"I learned a lot just since the show," he told me. "If I continue to improve that much each year, I could be great by the time we graduate."

That took me by surprise. I had never thought of setting such specific goals, with real deadlines. Someday, maybe, was as far as I planned.

Craig practiced for hours every day, and criticized himself harshly without getting discouraged. I knew he was on track and I could learn from him, but I didn't believe in myself the way he did. Even if I had, I had nowhere to practice at home. The time I had alone was usually the hours Irene had customers, and I didn't think they wanted to hear me sing or Irene wanted to find out.

For me, the popularity was negative. If people didn't like me before the show, there was no reason for them to like me after. And the thrill wasn't about being the greatest singer or the most popular girl in school anyway. I doubted I could be either, no matter how hard I tried. I found something different.

The thrill I got from the standing ovation at the talent show was far greater than what I had experienced that day when the lifeguards and concessions workers cheered for me at the pool. The rush I got this time was addictive. I became an attention junky in search of my next fix. Applause was impersonal and not subject to the same sincerity screen as friendship.

While the students and their parents stood in the gym clapping and screaming after our performance, I was free. My history was invisible to the audience, and the noise they made drowned out the internal voice that harped at me about my role as the family troublemaker. I was free of my fear that I would never be anything more than the pitiful girl who lived in back of Irene's, and I was free of my mother's opinion of my singing. These people had obviously found something to like about my voice, if only for a few seconds. I needed that.

Following that brief period of freedom, the fact that my clothes were in an easily transportable laundry basket under the bathroom sink lost importance. I found my place in the world, and it was just as easily transportable. Things looked up for me, so much so that I actually believed my mother might acknowledge my existence as something more than a noose around her neck.

She came in and woke me from a sound sleep one night after she had closed up at Harvey's. I thought I was dreaming until I opened my eyes and saw her sitting on the end of the couch massaging her foot with both hands. "Penny Sue, wake up. We need to have a talk."

"Are you okay?" I asked. "Does your foot hurt?"

"My feet always hurt after I stand on them for ten hours," she said. "While you and Jerold sleep, I run my ass off trying to keep a room full of drunks happy enough to tip, but not so happy that they'll tear the place up or follow me home. But I didn't wake you up to talk about my feet or my tips."

It didn't sound like she was in the mood for closeness so I shifted into a sitting position in case she took a notion to swing punches.

"Do you want to tell me about the talent show?" Her voice was curiously soft. Maybe she was mad at her feet instead of me this time. The Halloween shopping trip flashed through my head, and confused me into thinking she might want to be nice again. Maybe she was going to take it up as a quarterly ritual, like making Sunday dinner.

"The talent show at school?" I stalled, hoping to get a better feel of her mood.

"No, the one at Carnegie Hall. Do you know of any other talent shows?" She dropped the foot she had been massaging to the floor with a thud and picked up the other. "Of course the one at school. Penny Sue, don't mess with me when I'm this tired."

"I'm not trying to mess with you. I wasn't really awake yet," I offered as a semi-apology.

"Some guys at school have a band and they asked me to sing with them in the show. It wasn't a big deal."

"Do you have any idea how stupid I felt when some old drunk started yapping about it at the bar? And I didn't even know what he was talking about? I didn't even know that he knew you were my daughter, so I was shocked. I made out like I did know, and that damned Grace turned me into some kind of child abuser for not going to watch you."

By then her voice was loud enough to wake the dead, which Daddy must have been because he didn't poke his head out the bedroom door.

"How do you think that makes me feel, Penny Sue?"

I took a deep breath and looked her straight in the eye because I believed whatever Craig said when he did that. "I didn't want to make you feel bad about having to work at Harvey's and miss the show, so I didn't tell you about it."

She continued to rub her foot while I wondered how missing the show did make her feel. I couldn't imagine that she cared one way or the other. Finally, she responded in a tone that wasn't the most hateful one she owned.

"Well, I want you to come down to Harvey's with me tomorrow night and explain that so they won't think it's my fault."

I wanted to ask if she would have taken off work to come hear me sing if I had told her about the show. I worked the question around in my head a couple of times but couldn't bring myself to ask it. Instead, I said I would go to Harvey's and do as she wanted, and I would be sure to tell her the next time I was in a show.

She went to bed without responding. I took that as good news. She could have said that was my last show, or she didn't want to come to the next one.

* * *

Craig walked me to the corner the next day and turned around to go back home when we saw Momma's car sitting in front of the house. I wanted to go with him so I wouldn't have to go to Harvey's and lie to half the world. He squeezed my hand and wished me luck.

"I'll go into Irene's and call you when I get back," I said as he walked off. He probably thought I offered to do that for his sake, so he wouldn't worry about me. The real reason I said it was because I knew I'd need to hear his voice to get over my anger at Momma.

When I was two houses away from my own, I heard my parents yelling. I hoped Irene would remember that it had been years since they embarrassed her in front of customers, and not throw us out. Now that I had Craig and the band, I didn't want to move back to Crayfield, or even to a house where I would have my own room. I wanted to stay right there.

"You aren't dragging her into your sleazy world," Daddy yelled. That was the most I'd heard him say in months.

"Like you care," Momma said. "All you do is sleep when she's here. You didn't even know she snuck out to be in that talent show. The only reason you're bitching now is because she won't be here to make your supper."

"You've been home all day. You should have made my supper, and hers. It's fine if you don't want to act like my wife, but you'll burn in hell for not being a decent mother to that girl."

I might have appreciated that from Daddy if he had made more of an effort to be a decent father. I opened the door and hoped my entrance would end the fight. Irene came in through the other door at the same time.

"Lucky for you the only customers I have right now are people who enjoy your sideshow," she said. "I let you go until I saw Penny walk up. Now, shut the hell up. For her sake and mine."

I smiled briefly at Irene, hoping she would read my thank you in the gesture. Momma didn't say a word to her, good or bad.

Daddy said sorry, to Irene and to me, but he never turned his eyes toward Momma. He went off to the bedroom and Momma told me to keep my coat on because we were leaving. I didn't mention his supper now that I finally realized he knew it wasn't my place to take care of him.

She was quiet in the car. I opened my social studies book and pretended to read. In my head, I was planning what I'd say to Grace, and anyone else who cared to hear my explanation for not inviting my parents to the talent show. Maybe, after I said a few words, Momma would feel vindicated and drive me back home.

"I have a lot of homework," I said, thinking that might improve my chance of getting home early and excuse me from conversation, all in one breath. It worked for the conversation part.

Again, I followed a few steps behind when my mother entered the bar, but I skipped to catch up to her once inside so she wouldn't leave me standing alone in the middle of the room. I expected things to be the same as they had been the day I went with her for the Halloween meeting, with all of the employees standing together in one place. But things were very different.

Harvey and another guy stood behind the bar loading beer into the coolers. Waitresses were scattered around the room, one of them sweeping, another washing tables, and Grace filling saltshakers. In addition to regular employees, there were several men setting up band equipment on a stage in the corner. When they saw me, everyone stopped what they were doing and started clapping and whistling.

Grace put her saltbox down and ran over to hug me. I looked at my mother's face to see if she had planned on this. She looked as surprised as I was.

I said thank you, not sure how my mother was going to react to me getting the attention. If her real reason for bringing me there had been to shame me, Grace might as well pour her salt into Momma's wound.

"Your mother never told me you could sing," Grace went on. "Where'd you learn to sing like that?"

I glanced at Momma's face again, and she looked embarrassed. "I started out singing when I was real little. Back in Crayfield," I explained, and then added some words to help my mother feel better. "Momma taught me to sing. She used to sing and dance with me in our living room when I was little and she didn't have to work so hard."

That wasn't exactly true. She sang and danced for me, but the story sounded better this way. I held my breath and waited to see if it worked.

Grace turned from me to Momma. "Are you holding out on us too, Kitty? You sing?"

Momma's expression changed from cold to warm in a flash. "I ain't sang in years, but I did used to before I got married. Jerold and his mother thought it wasn't proper enough for a Martox to sing anywhere except in church, though, so I had to let my singing go."

Either that was as big a lie as Granny naming her after Kitty Wells and Marilyn Monroe, or it was a secret nobody thought to tell me about her. I guess, since nobody ever talked at my house, there might have been a lot I didn't know about both of my parents.

While everyone was still listening, I said what I had come there to say. "I didn't tell Momma about the talent show at school because I knew she had to work. And I didn't want to embarrass her either, on account of her being the real singer in the family."

My mother smiled at me. "Next time, you'd better tell me so I can be there," she said. "Harvey, can I have off for the next talent show?"

"I think we can work that out," he yelled from the bar. "Maybe we can let her sing something tonight, so you can hear what you missed."

I wasn't expecting that, and hated the idea.

"See if those guys can play anything you know," he said, indicating by a nod that he was talking about the musicians who were setting up their equipment behind me.

I stayed where I was, silently begging with my eyes for Momma to speak up and forbid me to sing in Harvey's Tavern. She didn't say a word.

Grace shoved me in the direction of the stage. "Don't be bashful. Go talk to them. I'm sure they can play something you know."

They only played country, which was fine by me; only I hadn't practiced any country songs with my band. Before I left Harvey's that night, I sang "Your Cheatin' Heart" because they didn't know any songs by female performers, and that was the only song on their list that I knew. Fortunately, there weren't many customers there when I sang, and the employees were going to clap for me no matter how bad I sounded.

Harvey excused Momma. "Kitty, you get that girl home and put her to bed," he said. To me, "Maybe you can come back when you don't have school the next day and sing again." I smiled, positive my mother would never allow that to happen.

"You didn't sound half bad in there," she said as we walked to the car. "Maybe I can work with you a little so you don't sound so nervous when you sing."

It was dark so she couldn't see me roll my eyes. A drink of Southern Comfort would do a better job of easing my nerves than anything she could say, but I held on to the compliment. Half bad was more than I expected from her.

Chapter 13

After Momma went back to work that night, she and Harvey put their drunken heads together and came up with what they believed was a brilliant idea that would solve all of their problems. If they brought me in to sing regularly, Harvey's dropping business would pick up again. People would travel from miles away to hear the twelve-year-old singing sensation whose outstanding performance at the previously unheard of Edgeview Junior High School talent show had brought students, parents, and teachers to their feet. I would be the Brenda Lee of Harvey's and squeeze a few extra drinks out of customers

Momma stood to benefit, also. She would finally receive more attention and get bigger tips than Grace, just for giving birth to me.

I guess they counted on Daddy and me having our own reasons to welcome their plan since they didn't bother to ask our opinions before they set everything up with the band. They probably figured staying out late would excite me, and having time to himself would make Daddy not mind missing supper. They were wrong as far as both of us were concerned.

"She's still a child and she needs to stay home to study and get to bed on time for school," Daddy said. "Singing in a bar every night is your dream, Kitty, not hers."

"Use your head for once, Jerold," Momma said. "Look at Brenda Lee. She was making money at Penny Sue's age. With a little experience, Penny might be able to make money singing."

"No." He stuck with his opinion. "It's a bad idea."

Momma didn't even bother to yell. "You won't do anything to stop her. Who do you think you're fooling? Go on to your room and pass out."

"Kitty, I'm telling you. I won't allow it."

Momma laughed and turned to face me. "Do you hear this, Penny Sue? He's going to sit there and act like he's concerned about your schoolwork. When was the last time he looked at your homework?"

I didn't think the question was fair, or deserved an answer. Neither of them had ever looked at my homework that I could remember. Mrs. Sawyer had been the last adult to even pretend she cared about my grades.

"Answer me, Penny Sue." She worked up a terrible attitude. "When? When did he talk to you about anything except what he wanted for supper?"

I stared at the floor and shrugged my shoulders. I wasn't going to make eye contact with either of them and let them think I was picking a side. In my mind, neither of them was more right or wrong than the other.

She threw her last shot. "You don't care about anything except having her here to cook for you. Admit it Jerold, you don't care about either of us. You haven't cared about anyone since you got pulled away from your Mommy."

"And you just want to show her off now that you think you might get some attention from riding on her coat tails," he said. "You don't care about anyone but yourself, so you have no room to throw insults at me."

Momma won in the end because Daddy was too lazy to keep up his end of the fight. She did agree that I should only go to Harvey's on weekends after I mentioned that kids weren't allowed to work after a certain time on school nights. I added another lie to my collection. "I don't want to get you or Harvey in trouble with the authorities."

I'd still be able to walk home from school with Craig, and keep my life the same except for band practice on Saturday nights. That worked out in the end, also. The guys from Coal's Crew didn't mind switching rehearsals to Wednesday because it freed up their weekends for activities that were more important to them anyway. John chased girls, Billy let girls catch him, and Craig focused on perfecting guitar licks and song writing.

I sang one song, "Your Cheatin' Heart", each set for the first month. And I sang for free. After the band learned more songs, I sang a few each set, and repeated only when I got requests for one that I had already done earlier. Momma let me sing "It Wasn't God Who Made Honky-Tonk Angels", and "Your Good Girl's Gonna Go Bad". She put a cigar box on the edge of the stage to collect tips from people who made requests to hear them, or just thought I was good enough to deserve something for my time.

It almost seemed like an even trade-off for a while. I enjoyed the applause and unprecedented attention I received from my mother as much as I despised the atmosphere at Harvey's. While I was there, Momma fussed over my hair and let me use her mascara and lipstick. Once in a while she forgot that I was her daughter and talked to me like I was a regular person.

"That's my little girl up there," I heard her brag to a table of customers one night. I also noticed that she stopped talking and serving while I sang. She stood by the wall with her arms folded in front of her, so her hands were empty and ready to be the first to clap at the end of the song. I thanked her for that on the drive home one night.

"Don't get a big head over it," she said. "Those old geezers don't even listen to you sing. It would be downright humiliating for me if they went on talking and shooting pool after the song ended. I start them clapping so they won't forget and embarrass both of us."

She was wrong. I knew some of those people listened. There were a few who sat at tables close to the stage, who didn't talk or look away at all when I was singing. They smiled at me. One man tapped time with his finger on his beer bottle and a couple danced in their chairs. It was to them that I sang my heart out, and for them that I learned new songs. Momma couldn't take that away from me, even if she didn't want me to believe she enjoyed hearing me as much as they did.

Other than those regulars who listened, a couple of waitresses, Ella the cook, and Craig's family who sometimes came on Friday nights for fish sandwiches and a set of music, I didn't like anything about Harvey's Tavern. The drunks acted like they didn't notice I was a kid, and flirted and pawed at me the same as they did my mother. They didn't care that I didn't encourage or appreciate them the way she did, or that I was repulsed by men old enough to be my grandfather.

One of Momma's regulars--a disgusting man that everyone called Stinky Morton because of his body odor and brown teeth--

cornered me on the way to the ladies room one night. He put his arm around me and said he'd like to kiss me.

"Leave me alone," I said. "I don't want to kiss you." I tried to pull away from him but he tightened his arm around me and pinned me up against his beer belly, where I discovered that his breath was even worse than his body odor.

"Please don't," I said. "I have a boyfriend."

"I won't tell him. What he don't know won't hurt him," he said, pulling me closer until my back felt like it might break. "One little kiss won't hurt."

I lowered my head, sickened by the smell and the thought of him kissing me, but he grabbed my chin and forced my head back. He pried my lips apart with his tongue, and poked it in mouth.

True to his word, one kiss was all he wanted. He released me after he had accomplished his mission. I ran into the bathroom and puked, and refused to leave until someone brought my mother to me.

Momma locked the outside door so no one else could come inside while we talked. "Dry your face and don't cause a scene, Penny Sue. He's a big spender and a generous tipper. One little kiss isn't the end of the world."

I remembered his tongue in my mouth and gagged again. My mother's disappointing reaction didn't help any, either. It might not be the end of the world to her, but it was the end of my feeling safe at Harvey's. It was the end of my thinking Craig would be the first one to kiss me that way. It might have been the end of me wanting to kiss anyone ever.

"Straighten up and walk back out there like nothing happened," she said. "Don't embarrass me, or you'll live to regret it."

Grace knocked on the door. "Is everything okay in there?" She yelled through the door.

Momma glared a warning at me. "Yes," I answered. "Just a minute and we'll be out."

Momma wet a paper towel and wiped the tears off my face without another word. She tossed the towel in the trash, handed me her lipstick, and walked out. If ever I deserved a hug, that was the time, and I wouldn't even have minded if it came from her.

After Momma stormed off, Grace came in. "I'm fine," I said, trying to scoot past her before Momma missed me and came back to see what was keeping me.

"Don't feed me that pack of lies," Grace said. "George Hazelup told me he saw Stinky Morton giving you a hard time. That son-of-a-bitch. If any man puts his hands on you again, you knee him right in the balls and then you come get me. In fact, you should get me or Liz to come with you when you need to use the restroom."

I thanked her and left before I caused her any trouble with Momma.

***

By the time I started high school, my emotions had hardened toward my mother and I had decided I didn't mind if Craig slid his tongue down my throat. I knew Momma only pretended to like me because it was good for tips, and I didn't care anymore because I didn't like her either. Craig liked me because I was me, and that was all I needed at the time.

My relationship with my father had diminished to absolutely nothing. I don't think he ever ate supper again after I stopped putting a plate in front of him, but I didn't carry any guilt over his failing health or unhappiness.

"I hate both of them, and all of my grandparents too," I wrote in a long, depressing letter to Lori one night when I was too drunk to see the lines on my paper. "I can't believe I spent my whole life thinking I caused them trouble and heartache when the truth was none of them cared about me or each other to begin with."

I called them terrible parents, and meant it. I knew it wasn't my fault that the adults in my family made poor choices. I asked them to return Granny's station wagon and Pappy's socks. I begged them to mail Christmas cards if we couldn't go back to visit. They chose not to do those things, and they had chosen to marry one another for who knows what reason. None of it was my fault.

I knew those things in my mind but emotionally couldn't move past wondering what I did to make them not love me. I asked the same question of Irene and Craig. "What is it about me that makes my parents hate me?"

"It's their loss," Irene said. "Maybe they never wanted to have kids. I can't think of any other reason because you sure don't do anything to ask for them to treat you so bad."

Craig's answer was less generous. "They're mean, nasty people who don't deserve you. Someday, I'll take you away from that house and you won't have to put up with them."

I started out needing one drink at the beginning of the night. Before long, I needed one before each set. Grace and Harvey understood my need to have a drink or two before I performed. Harvey left a bottle of bourbon behind the toaster in the kitchen, where I spent most of my time when I wasn't on stage. Ella, the cook, thought the bottle was for her. When she turned her back, I took my sips, and she took hers while I was on stage.

Grace carried a bottle of rum in her purse and shared when she walked me to the ladies room. So even without the drinks I snuck from Momma's beers when she wasn't looking, I was well taken care of. Eventually, I carried my own bottle to supplement what the others provided and drank most of it before my ride home with Momma at the end of the night.

My tip box collected a steady amount, providing at least ten dollars a night, after Momma took out gas money for driving me to and from work. The bandleader saw her counting out the money one night and decided it was time to change the rules. From then on, he added the tips in with their regular pay and gave me an equal cut. I took home eighteen dollars a week.

After working nearly the whole school year, I decided it was time to speak up for myself and confronted Momma. "It's not fair. After I give you two dollars for gas, I'm set back at least four dollars a week. You would be driving there anyway, without me."

"You're never happy with anything," she said. "What do you need money for? I pay the rent, and I buy the groceries. I bought the car."

"That's what you're supposed to do. You're the mother," I said.

She backhanded me across the face, reminding me that being the mother held other privileges that I hadn't thought about when I opened my mouth. "Don't ever sass me again, you ungrateful little bitch."

I tried not to listen. "You Ain't Woman Enough to Take My Man" filled my head, but it wasn't enough to block her out completely. For a while, her hateful words mixed in with the attitude in my song.

"I never wanted to marry your dad," came through loud and clear, followed by "and I sure as hell didn't want a baby to hold me back. I had plans for my life and this ain't it, thanks to you."

Unable to listen to any more, I opened the car door and jumped out at the next stop sign. If she got out of the car she'd have to chase me down. I knew I could out run her tired old feet.

But I didn't have to run. Momma went on through the stop sign and left me standing on the corner, without looking back. Fortunately, it wasn't cold, and I wasn't too drunk to walk.

Chapter 14

I walked a few block before I spotted a pay phone in front of a gas station and stopped to call Craig's house. Gary answered. "I'm stranded," I told him, trying to control both the thick tongue that finishing off the bottle of rum in my purse had left me with, and the tears that the rum hadn't erased.

"Penny, what are you doing out alone this late?" I heard someone enter the room he was in and hoped it was Craig and not one of his parents.

"It's a long story. Got in a fight with my mother and couldn't stay in the car with her. I jumped out and didn't know who else to call. Is Craig awake?"

Gary said for me to hold on. I heard him tell Craig I was crying and making no sense. To me he said, "Talk to Craig while I get dressed, and we'll come to get you."

Craig took the phone. "Are you okay?"

I broke into heaving sobs when I heard his voice. "I'm tired. Disgusted. Sad. Craig, she didn't even look back. She took off without me and never looked back."

"I can't understand you. Calm down and tell me where you are." He spoke slowly and sounded worried. "Gary's dressed now and we're ready to walk out the door."

I didn't know exactly where I was but thought I remembered a corner we had passed shortly before I got out of the car. "I'll meet you at 'Sixth and Oak'," I said and had to repeat it three times before he understood me.

"Be careful, Penny. We're on the way." Before he hung up, he said he loved me. That was the first time I had heard those words spoken to me since Mrs. Sawyer said them the day I yelled at her.

After hanging up, I wilted to the ground. I crossed my arms over my knees and buried my head in my arms, and cried even harder. Why did he have to say that and ruin everything?

"Take it back." I yelled into the air because he wasn't there to hear me. I forgot I was supposed to walk to Sixth and Oak and stayed right there on the ground at the gas station.

Dusty Springfield's voice kept me company until the sun came up. *"You don't have to say you love me, just be close at hand. You don't have to stay forever, I will understand. Believe me. Believe me."* I couldn't decide which felt worst, my head, my heart, or my back. I searched my purse and didn't have anything left in it to kill the pain. I did have a few dimes left, but it was too early to call Craig's house again and I couldn't remember Irene's phone number.

Vague memories of the night before came back, so muffled by the hangover and sadness that I wasn't sure how much had really happened and how much was a nightmare.

One thing I knew for sure, though. Craig said he loved me. I wasn't worthy, so I didn't want the responsibility of having to live up to that. Craig—my new best friend—was a good person. He didn't drink or cause trouble for anybody. He deserved a girlfriend who was normal and didn't need a drink to sing, or to sing to keep from thinking. He deserved someone better than me – someone like Lori.

Craig wasn't just my best friend; he was my only friend. I'd probably never see Lori again. She might not even be a nice girl anymore for all I knew. She didn't write enough for me to know.

The tears started again, almost a relief because my eyes felt like they had sand in them. *"Mr. Sandman, bring me a dream. Make him the cutest that I've ever seen."* Craig's face popped into my head and I choked on tears that had backed up clear down to my chest. I had *the cutest* but couldn't straighten up enough to deserve him. I was a disaster.

I had to get out of there but home was out of the question. I never wanted to see my mother again. I used another dime to call information and get Irene's number.

"I'll be glad to come after you, but you have to tell me where you are," Irene said, without one hint of anger or disappointment in me. "Penny, put the phone down and walk to the nearest corner, or find the owner's name on the door of the gas station. There are lots of gas stations in town. Somehow, you have to find out which one you're at."

I turned to see if I could find a name on the door, and spotted a boy with a newspaper bag crossing the other side of the lot.

"Hold on, Irene. There's the paperboy. I'll ask him." I put the phone down and called out to him.

"Can you help me please? Do you know the name of this street?"

He came to where I stood and looked at me suspiciously. "How'd you get here if you don't know where you are?"

I didn't want to tell my life story to this guy. "It's a long story. Please, just tell me what street I'm on." I could see the number 922 on the door.

"Stratton Avenue," he said.

I thanked him and returned to the phone. "922 Stratton Avenue," I told Irene.

"You stay right where you are," she said. "It'll take me about twenty minutes to get there. Don't go anywhere until you see me."

"Please hurry," I said. "I need a bathroom real bad."

Irene told me to go to the side of the building and try the bathroom door. "Sometimes they leave them open at night. But don't go anywhere else," she ordered again. "And be sure to lock the door if you go inside. That's not the best neighborhood to be stuck in alone."

I walked around to the bathroom, considering something that I had never thought about before. Could this neighborhood be worse than the one I lived in? All that time, I had believed we *were* the wrong side of the tracks and nothing could be worse.

The door was unlocked but I wasn't home free. Pigs had been there before me and left a repulsive mess, on the sink, on the floor, on the seat, and even on the wall. My stomach jumped into my throat when the odor hit and I rushed back out, scrubbing the hand that I had used to open the door against my pant leg.

I leaned over at the waist to inhale deep breaths while my stomach settled, only to find that my bladder wouldn't wait. I stood up straight, drew in a huge breath and held it, and ran back in to relieve myself.

Nana taught me early to line public toilet seats. I used paper towels because there was no toilet tissue, but still wouldn't sit. I did my business as quickly as I could, shuddering and gagging the whole time. When finished, I stuck my head outside for another clean breath, went back and washed my hands, and came out with two wet towels to use on my face and teeth.

The paperboy stood in front of the building with a smile on his intruding face.

"What are you doing here?" I screamed at him, sounding just like my mother. "You scared me half to death."

"Excuse me for trying to be nice. I thought you might need some help since you didn't know where you were," he said.

"I'm sorry. Thanks. My friend is coming to get me, so I'll be fine."

"I'll wait with you." He decided on his own without asking me first, so there wasn't much I could do except let him stay.

"You look sick," he said.

"I am. You might not want to get too close."

He smiled. "I don't think your kind of sick is catching. You look kind of young to be drinking. My name is Phil, in case you're wondering."

"Thank you, Phil, for worrying over me, but I really don't need a lecture right now. I need a drink, and before you start in on me again, you'd drink too if you had my life."

"Do you have a name?"

"Penny."

"Penny, you might be right. Maybe I would drink if I had your life. I'm sorry you're so sad."

I wanted Phil the paperboy to go away and leave me alone, but he was too nice for me to say that to him. He looked at me like he might cry or something.

"I'm okay, really. I'll get my life straightened out."

"That's how you need to look at things," he said, sounding too cheerful. "Your life might stink right now, but you have your whole life ahead of you so it could still turn around if you play your cards right."

I looked at him while I let that soak into my half-drunk brain. "What are you? A philosopher or something?"

"No, that's something my grandmother always says to me when I feel sorry for myself. I thought it might help you."

"You get sad too?" I couldn't picture that since he hadn't stopped smiling since I met him.

"If I'm not careful. My old man's a drunk and my mom is sick. I deliver papers and cut grass in the summer to try and help her out.

Sometimes I get sad. Heck, sometimes I get mad, too, but neither does much good."

I saw Irene's red Mustang inching up the street and waved her down. She brought a smile to my face, but mine wasn't as big as Phil's. Irene was probably as old as my mother, and she drove around in a Ford Mustang, wearing bell bottomed jeans and halter-tops like she was eighteen. She kept her hair and make-up current instead of sticking in the past like my mother.

"Thanks for waiting with me, Phil. And tell your grandmother I said thanks for the advice."

He waved at Irene and wished me luck.

Irene examined my face. "You look like hell. What happened to your lip?"

"Momma busted me. That's why I got out of the car. That wasn't the only reason, but it was the final one."

"Want to talk about it?" she asked. But she changed her mind about the question before I answered. "First, do they know where you are, and are you going home?"

"I never want to go back, and they don't care where I am," I said. "She never even looked back, she just drove off and left me here."

"We need a plan. I can't drive without a destination. I'll take you anywhere you want to go, or we can sit in the park and talk," she offered. "I'd take you to my house, but I'm afraid your mother would have me arrested for kidnapping or something."

"Anywhere? You'll take me anywhere I want to go, for real?"

Irene laughed. "Within reason. I have a tank of gas and the whole day free."

"Is Crayfield within reason? How far is it, do you know?" The idea sprung into my head when Phil mentioned his grandmother. I wanted to see Nana and Pappy, and ask why they never came looking for me so they could tell me things like Phil's grandmother said to him.

Irene hesitated a few seconds. "What the hell. It's less than three hours and we have all day."

Three hours. We were only three hours away and hadn't been back one time in eight years.

***

I bored Irene with my life story on the way to Crayfield. I told her about the cut in pay at Harvey's, and the man who stuck his tongue down my throat, and how Momma never took up for me.

"I love to sing more than anything, Irene, but I'm sick of that place. I never get to go to teen club or the movies or any place with kids my age. I'm stuck in a stinky bar with old men every weekend. And they never let me sing anything but country. I like country best, but that's not all I like. And Craig never gets to have a date because he's stupid enough to love me and I'm sitting at Harvey's."

Craig! He was probably worried sick about me. I asked one more favor. Irene pulled over at the next phone booth we saw so I could call Craig and tell him I was on the way to my grandmother's house.

After my call to Craig, I dozed off. Irene woke me with a loud cheer when she spotted the Crayfield sign. "We made it, Penny. Wake up."

My stomach tied in knots. I was hung over and starving. I was nervous about how my grandparents would react to my surprise visit. And I had no idea where to find my grandparents' house.

I broke the depressing news. "Irene, I don't remember where they live."

"No problem. In a town this small we shouldn't have any trouble finding them." Irene slowed the car down and turned into a service station. I wondered how people like Irene and Phil managed to stay so cheerful about everything and decided I'd ask her when I felt better.

She shut the engine off and smiled at me. "Before we go anywhere or do anything, we have to get you cleaned up a little. You really are a sight."

She reached into the back seat and picked up a bag. "I brought a few things," she said. "Something in your voice told me you might need them," she added with a wink.

Irene had packed a toothbrush and toothpaste, a bar of soap and a washcloth, a hairbrush, deodorant, and a tie-dyed t-shirt. "I knew my pants would be too long, but the shirt ought to work for you."

"Someday I'll pay you back for everything you do for me." I couldn't look at her when I spoke because I knew I'd cry again. I was humiliated remembering the times she had rescued me, and spent money on me. And I was sure my parents had never paid her back.

She put her hand on my arm. "Honey, let's get one thing straight. You don't owe me anything. I have something to say, and I hope it won't offend you."

"Say it." I braced myself. I deserved whatever she had to say.

"I don't like either one of your parents and would have thrown them out years ago if I could have kept you in my life any other way. I feel strange for saying this, but I've always wished you could be my daughter instead of Kitty's. I would treat you better."

"Did Mrs. Sawyer tell you to say that to me?" I couldn't believe two other women could want to be my mother when my own mother didn't like me. That seemed impossible.

"Heavens no. I thought that long before I ever met Mrs. Sawyer. The first time I laid eyes on you, I thought you were the prettiest little thing I'd ever seen. Since I'm a stylist, I fell in love with that long, black hair, and wanted to brush it and put it in braids. And I wanted to see you in cute little dresses, with some sparkle in those big blue eyes. No, way before Mrs. Sawyer came long, I thought you were the prettiest, sweetest little girl ever put on this earth."

"But I'm not so pretty today."

"Yes you are. You're still beautiful inside, and once you go in that bathroom and clean up, you'll be beautiful outside again."

I sniffed because I didn't have a tissue. Tears were pouring and my nose was about ready to follow. I opened the car door, but hesitated before I got out.

"Irene, can I have a hug?" It wasn't such a brave request. I knew she wouldn't mind.

Ten minutes later I came out of the bathroom feeling like a new person even if I did still look like death warmed over. "I held a cold rag on my eyes for as long as I could stand it, but it didn't help the swelling very much," I told Irene.

She pulled the visor on my side of the car down to reveal a mirror, and handed me her cosmetics bag. "Go for it," she encouraged. "I have good news. The guy inside the station gave me directions to your grandparents' farm. We're five miles away."

Irene drove carefully so I could apply make-up to hide my hangover and my tears. Just as I closed the cosmetic bag and flipped the visor up, I spotted our old barn house.

"That's it! Irene, that's where we used to live."

"Honey, that's a barn." She pulled off the side of the road and stopped the Mustang. "Are you sure? Did you live in a barn?"

"Yes." I giggled. "Pull up a little. On the other side, you'll see where they made a porch and put on a regular door. They made it up like a real house inside. I had my own bedroom in there. Nana's house is on the other side of that field," I said, pointing.

She inched the car up the road slowly, until we could see the front of the barn. Everything looked the same as I remembered, broken screen and all. Then I saw the drop off, where Momma had parked her old car. I remembered that day through the perception of a near adult instead of the excitement of a child who wanted to drive.

"She tried to kill me!" The words slipped out with no planning on my part. "Momma tried to kill me."

Irene shifted into park. "What are you talking about? Maybe I shouldn't have brought you here."

"No, it's okay. Everything makes sense now. I can hate her for real, without feeling guilty."

We stared in silence for a minute before I figured Irene was wondering what I got her into and how she could get away from the crazy. "Drive on over to Nana's house. I'm glad to have seen the truth, but I don't want to sit here staring at it all day."

Pappy stood up out of the rocking chair on the front porch when he saw the Mustang come down his drive. He put his hand up to block the sun from his eyes while he twisted his face around and tried to make out who was in the car.

"Do you want me to stay here with you, or just drop you off and come back for you later?" Irene asked. "Your call."

"Stay, please. I'm scared."

She parked next to the porch and we got out of the car. Pappy walked over to the end of the porch and asked if he could help us. Irene looked at me and smiled.

"Yes, sir," I said. "I thought maybe you'd listen to me sing a song." I started right in, singing Brenda Lee's version of "I'm Sorry".

He hobbled down off the end of the porch and hugged me. "Penny Sue, if you aren't a sight for sore eyes." He nearly choked on the words. His voice dropped so I couldn't tell if he was talking to himself or to me. "You're all grown up and still as pretty as a picture."

"Where's Nana? Oh, I almost forgot, this is my friend Irene." I pulled her forward to meet my grandfather. "She drove me all the way up here to see you."

Pappy said it was nice to meet her, and thanked her for bringing me. "Let's go inside and surprise Gladys. She'll be so happy to see you."

Nana sat at the end of the kitchen table. "Look who came to see you, Nana," Pappy said, pushing me closer to her. "She doesn't get around well," he whispered. "You go over there to her."

I walked to the end of the table and hugged my Nana. She was half the size I remembered her, and her hair was cut off shorter than Granny Treeton's. She let me out of the hug, held my face between her hands to look at me, and cried. She managed between tears and blubbering to say, "You're beautiful, Penny Sue. You look just like your daddy. How is he?"

I couldn't tell her the truth. "He's fine. He works at the gas company, reading meters at tall buildings in town."

"I don't have much use for hearing about him, or your Momma, since they ran off and never came back. So sit down and tell me all about Penny Sue."

"Gladys, where are your manners?" Pappy asked. "Let these girls—that's Irene, by the way--sit down and catch their breath before you start drilling them with questions. Can I get you something to drink?" He presented the offer to all of us, including Nana. Something was wrong.

While Pappy got glasses and poured lemonade, I asked to be excused to the bathroom. It was exactly as I remembered, bright and soft, and clean. I closed the door and sat on the rug, taking in deep breaths of Nana's talcum powder aroma while I looked at myself in the mirror on the back of the door. In all these years, nothing had changed.

If one more person told me how pretty I was, I just might start believing it. Even with my tired, swollen eyes and dirty hair, I looked a little bit pretty. Wasn't all Irene's make-up, either. If I asked, Irene would probably cut my hair up to my shoulders so I could tease it and wear it in a flip like everyone else.

I scooted closer to the mirror and studied my face. Had Daddy really looked like me? Nana would probably drop over dead if she saw the wrinkles in his skin and the faded look of his eyes. And the gray hair. He hated the gray hair. He looked older than either of his parents.

Irene tapped on the door. "Did you fall in, Penny?"

I reached up to open the door, and moved back to let her in. She looked upset about me sitting on the floor, until she saw my smile.

I pushed the door closed so she could see the mirror. "This was my favorite place in the world when I was a little girl. I loved to sit on the rug in Nana's yellow bathroom." I took a deep breath. "Smell it? Isn't it nice? It always smells the same."

"It is nice," she said. "I was afraid you were in here crying or something. I'm glad you're reliving pleasant memories instead."

I looked in the mirror. "Do you think I look like my dad?"

"That's a loaded question, Penny. I think you have his coloring and his features. You probably look like he did when he was healthy."

"You think he's sick now? Oh, Irene, I think Nana's sick too."

"Why don't we go back out there and talk to Nana and Pappy while we have time. We can talk about your dad later, on the ride home."

When we returned, Nana and Pappy had moved to the living room. Nana was sitting back in a new reclining chair with her feet propped up. Pappy sat in the rocking chair right next to her.

"Sit over there on the sofa and tell me all about yourself," Nana said. "We've got a lot of years to catch up and I want to hear everything."

I didn't want to tell her everything, so I carefully weeded out the ugliness and there wasn't much left. "I'm starting high school soon. I've been on the honor roll since third grade." That part made both of their faces light up.

"I still sing. I'm in a band with some boys from school. We call ourselves Coal's Crew and we perform in the talent shows at school. The lead guitar player is my boyfriend. His name is Craig. We rent from Irene. It's a small place, but we don't need much with just the three of us, and it's on the right side of the tracks, Nana."

Nana folded her hands and looked at Pappy but she was talking to me. "Pappy said you sang a little piece for him out front. Maybe you can finally do your concert on the porch while you're here. How long are you staying?"

Nana's face went long and she reached for Pappy's hand when I said we only had a few hours. "It's three hours back," I reminded her.

"I was hoping you'd stay over at least one night. You're both welcome to stay as long as you like," Nana said, using her sad eyes to plead with Irene as she spoke.

Irene winked at me. "I need to get back tonight or my husband will have a hissy fit. But if Penny wants to stay a few days, I can leave her and come back on Wednesday to pick her up again."

I couldn't believe Irene was offering to use another day off to drive back to Crayfield for me.

"I didn't bring any clothes," I said.

Nana looked me over. "I believe you can wear Wanda's clothes, but Gwen way outgrew you. And maybe Pappy will run you in to Sears on Monday and get some things. We owe you a few birthday and Christmas presents."

Irene must have read my mind. "I'll tell your parents where you are, and I'll call Craig if you want."

I stayed, knowing my mother would be furious, especially since I'd miss a night at Harvey's. At that point, I didn't care because I didn't ever want to go back.

Irene stayed long enough to meet my aunt, uncle, and cousins, and to eat dinner. When it was time for her to leave, she asked me to come out to the car with her so she could hand me the bag of things she brought. She also took her cosmetic bag out of her purse and put it in the bag. "I have plenty more at home," she said, when I shook my head.

"Have a wonderful time, Penny. Enjoy these people and don't think about anything at home while you're here."

I nodded. "Gladly."

She hugged me and said she'd see me on Wednesday. As I watched her drive away, I decided she would be my mother from then on, in my heart at least.

While we washed dishes, Wanda told me that Nana had been operated on for cancer of some organ in her stomach. I think she explained it better than that, but I didn't want to listen. "She's doing better and getting stronger every day," was the only part I wanted to hear.

Nana said little about my parents while I was there, but Pappy talked about them while he drove me to Sears for three new outfits.

"Your dad broke Nana's heart, but that's neither here nor there as far as how we feel about you," he explained. "Nana cried for a straight year after you left. I tracked down an address, since we never could hook up with a phone number for you, and she wrote I'd guess somewhere near a hundred letters, to no avail. I reckon your Momma tossed them out unopened. I just want you to know we've always loved you and we missed you, Penny Sue."

"Did you miss your socks?" We both laughed over his socks. "I worried about that and begged Daddy to turn the car around and bring them back to you. He said you'd go to Sears and buy new socks."

"Is your Daddy really okay?" I heard a lump in Pappy's throat when he asked. I didn't want to tell the truth and make him carry any more sadness than he already had.

"I think so. He likes his job, and he's never sick or anything."

Pappy clamped his lips together and nodded his head up and down until I figured his neck must be tired. Finally, he stopped bobbing and sort of changed the subject. "Penny Sue, remember one thing as you grow up. You get back out of life exactly what you put into it. Remember that."

I said I'd keep that in mind, and I did. That and the message from Phil's grandmother. I kept them both stored together in the back of my mind, proud to have started a collection of wise things adults had said to me – even if Phil's grandmother's message had come indirectly through him.

Chapter 15

While in Crayfield, the only time I thought about my parents or my home, or missed Craig, or craved a drink, was when I sat up alone at night, after the bedtime ritual. I created a little ritual of my own. I helped with dinner and then, when it was time to do the dishes, and they insisted I was company and shouldn't work while I was their guest, I would say, "I'm family." Then, Pappy would give in without too much fuss. They sat at the table and talked to me while I worked. Shortly after the dishes were dried and put away, he'd push his chair back and announce that they were old and needed to turn in early.

Right on cue, Nana followed with the same instructions every time. "You just make yourself at home, Penny Sue, and don't worry that you'll disturb us if you play the television or make phone calls. We don't hear much of anything these days."

Then he'd finish up the conversation. "Do the same as you would do at home. Help yourself to anything in the refrigerator."

The routine ended when my grandparents went to sleep. What I did afterwards changed according to my mood.

The first night, I thought I was anxious to sleep in a real bed, in a real room with four walls and a door, in a real house that didn't smell like hair products or stale alcohol. I aimed to drop into the bed and fall straight off to sleep, making up for the drunken waste of the night before.

Unlike the rest of the house that looked smaller than I remembered, and slightly disappointing, Nana's spare room excited me more than it ever had. Having had sons, Nana went a little crazy and made up a room fit for a princesses for her granddaughters to sleep in when we stayed over. I walked into that prissy room—as unchanged as the bathroom--with the flowered wallpaper, Priscilla curtains, feather pillows, and plastic flowers on the dresser, and picked up the silky gown that Pappy had left for me on the pillow. Suddenly, sleep was out of the question. My body was tired but my mind raced from one thought to the next, none of them comforting despite the coziness of the room.

My parents would be furious with me for leaving. Craig would be hurt, or disappointed at least. Harvey might fire me. Did I care? About any of them?

I put sleep aside and went to the bathroom, where I found the expected bottle of bubbles behind the curtain. While the tub filled with water, and the air filled the combined aroma of talcum powder and bubble bath, I rinsed out my underclothes for the next day. Before I opened the linen closet door, I knew there would still be three nails on the inside of the door to hang my things on while they dried.

Steam rose from the tub, so I eased into the water a little at a time, until my body adjusted to the heat and I could lie back and rest my head against the wall without screaming. The water was therapeutic. It pulled the tension from my aching muscles, the misery from my broken heart, and washed the stink of Harvey's Tavern from my skin and hair, replacing it with the smell of Gardenia bubbles.

Solitude replaced the void of everything familiar. New thoughts introduced themselves. Four people loved me—Nana, Pappy, Irene, and Craig. That night, for a few minutes at least, I believed I loved me too.

I stayed in the tub until the water turned cold and my skin shriveled, and then I put on Nana's gown and went to sleep in the feather bed. I sprawled to all four corners and slept like a log until Pappy came home for lunch the next day.

Things weren't quite the same the next few nights. I wasn't sleepy when my grandparents "turned in" at eight, so I sat in their living room with nothing to do but think. I focused on the difference between the way my grandparents treated one another and the way my parents related to each other.

After a few nights of listening to Nana and Pappy repeat the bedtime routine where they so comfortably finished one another's thoughts to form one complete one, I wondered how my father felt switching from that to living in a house with a wife who wouldn't be able to guess one of his thoughts even if she cared enough to try. He must surely miss having love in his life.

I didn't want to go back and live in my home where one day people screamed insults at one another and then no one spoke again for days. Nor did I want to stay where I was. Nana and Pappy were more anxious to make me feel at home than my parents were to make a home for me and I appreciated them, but life in Crayfield would be more boring than home. I would miss Craig and music, and Irene, too, if I stayed.

I worked myself into being angry with Craig over him saying he loved me, and causing me to think I would miss him if I stayed to escape my life. His words changed everything by putting me in a role of bad guy again. Love hurt, and now that he loved me I would have to hurt him. That was the last thing I wanted to do, and the one thing I was certain I would do.

Lori probably wouldn't understand. She would say I was lucky to have a boyfriend who loved me. As far as I knew, none of the people she loved made a habit of hurting her. She thought love was good.

I found paper and a pen in the drawer by the stove, right where they had been when I was a child and Nana pulled them out for me to practice writing my name while she worked in the kitchen. I poured my fears into a letter, only to realize after hours of writing that I couldn't send that letter to Lori. It wasn't fair for me to taint her view of love, or to make her think I felt burdened if she and her mother still loved me. I tore the letter into tiny pieces and put them in the trashcan on the back porch.

I tried talking to Nana the next day. She had experience with love hurting on account of what had happened between her and Daddy. But thinking that I was too young to worry about 'that kind of love' distracted her. Love was love to my way of thinking, but I didn't try to explain that to her.

"Penny Sue, my advice is that you need to wait a long time before you get mixed up with any boy," she said. "Finish school. Travel. Work on a career. Do what you can to learn what you really want before you settle in with a man. Have you talked to your Momma about this?"

I hadn't expected her to mention Momma, especially without calling her a name, and I was surprised that she would think I'd talk to her about anything as serious as love.

"She wanted me to drive off the cliff. Remember that?" I threw the question out before I thought it through, and felt bad after I saw the hurt expression on Nana's face.

"Do you remember it?" she asked.

I looked away and nodded, wishing I could take the whole conversation back and never discuss love with her.

"I don't know what Kitty was thinking that day, or any other day for that matter," Nana said. "She probably wasn't thinking at all, because she was a very confused girl."

"Why?" I wanted answers now that the conversation started. I wanted someone to explain my crazy mother to me. I wanted Nana to call her the spawn of Satan or something.

"I think her biggest mistake was in chasing after boys before she was ready to accept the responsibilities or consequences of catching one. And that's all I have to say on the subject." Nana meant it. She ended the conversation immediately.

I spent my last night thinking about what Nana had said, and wishing I had a sip or two of rum to ease the headache her words had given me. I decided Irene was the best person to ask about love. I would wait and ask her opinion on the drive back.

Pappy stayed home from work on Wednesday so he would be there to say good-bye when Irene came to pick me up. That's the excuse he gave anyway. I thought his real reason he wanted to be there was to protect Nana from being too lonely after I left.

I promised my grandparents I would come back to see them again as soon as I could drive, or when I saved enough for a Greyhound bus ticket.

"And if necessary, I'll bring her back," Irene offered.

"You have the address and phone number in the meantime," Nana reminded me. "Be sure to call and write, Penny Sue. We don't want to lose you again."

Irene wrote her address and phone number on a piece of paper. "You can contact Penny through me," she said, handing the paper to Nana. "She doesn't always get her mail at home so you might want to write her at my address."

Nana held on to Irene's hand. "Thank you, dear. I'm comforted to know that Penny Sue has a friend like you." She stopped talking and studied Irene's face like she was memorizing every line. "You're a nice lady, Irene, not at thing like Kitty."

Irene hugged Nana, then Pappy, and then came over and put her arm around my shoulders. "I'm the lucky one in this deal. Penny is the daughter I've always wanted, and a great friend, all rolled into one beautiful young lady. I'll make sure she gets back here soon."

I hugged Nana and Pappy and managed to get out of there before a new river of tears broke loose. Irene had a tissue ready in her pocket and handed it to me before we got to the car.

"Did you have fun?" she asked as we drove off. "I think you made them happy with your visit. They seem to love you very much."

"Yeah, they do. And now I run off and leave them again. Irene, love is so confusing. Does it always have to hurt? I tried to talk to Nana about it but she wasn't much help."

I repeated the earlier conversation for Irene, and she offered her thoughts on the subject. She didn't try to talk me into or out of loving Craig or my parents. She said the most important thing was how much I loved myself, not how much I loved Craig or how much he loved me.

"That's true about every relationship, Penny. How you feel about yourself affects your ability to love others and to accept the love they offer you. You have to love yourself first."

"The other night, after you left and my grandparents went to bed, something important happened to me." I watched her face and drew the courage to continue when the corners of her mouth turned up a little. "I thought about what you said about wishing you were my mother, and about how happy my grandparents were to see me. For a few minutes, I loved myself."

"Only a few minutes?" she asked. "You need to keep on doing that."

I took a deep breath. "Irene, I have a lot of problems. I can't love all of me until I work them out. I really don't think I can." I got to talking so fast I didn't need all of the breath I had drawn in to spit those words out. I exhaled the rest and inhaled some more and held it while I waited to hear what she had to say about my problems.

"You'll always have problems. Everyone does. Real love is about caring for someone despite the problems. Maybe that's even the best love because it takes strength. It would be easy to love a perfect person or to receive love if you were perfect."

Craig was perfect. Maybe that's why I stuck to him, because it was easy.

"Think about it, Penny. Would you stop caring about me if you knew that I cussed like a sailor at home and when I'm with other adults?"

I laughed out loud. "That's not a real problem, Irene. Is that the worst thing you do?"

She giggled with me, but got serious again when she answered. "It's the worst thing I'm going to admit to you, kiddo. It's something that I don't like about myself, and it embarrasses my husband. The point is, he loves me anyway."

"And you love yourself anyway?" I asked, knowing the answer.

"You got it. If I hated myself because of it, I wouldn't be able to accept the love that Ralph offers me. I wouldn't believe I deserved his love, so I'd reject him whether that was my intention or not."

She had hit one nail on the head. I hated myself because of the drinking. And I didn't want Craig to love me because then I would either have to stop drinking or feel guilty when I did.

"What if Ralph didn't like cussing, and you didn't see anything so wrong with it?" I asked. "Would you still feel guilty for cussing, or for letting him love you?"

She looked at me from the corner of her eye and frowned. "No fair asking hard questions like that. Give me a few minutes to think this one over."

We rode the next few miles in silence. I figured she was stretching her brain for an answer so I tried to think up one of my own. Did people have to agree about right and wrong if they wanted to love each other? I was still confused when she pulled off the road, into an empty parking lot.

"This place is closed down," I said, pointing to the for sale sign on the door of the small store.

"I know," she said. "Have you ever driven a car?"

"Nope." I didn't count the time I almost drove off the cliff, because all I had done was turn the key over. "I don't have a learner's permit yet. I'm only fifteen. Besides, Momma says she won't let me get my permit until I can buy my own car anyway. That's one reason I was so upset about getting my pay cut. I'll never save up enough for a car now."

She opened her car door and told me to get out and switch places with her.

"For real?" I squealed like a child. "You're going to let me drive?" I ran around the car before she could change her mind.

"Only in this empty parking lot," she warned. "You can't take my baby out on the road."

I drove around the parking lot, jerking the car because I didn't have the feel of the gas pedal. I went fast one second and slow the next. Irene laughed and said I was doing fine, but she probably had whiplash. Before we left, she made me pull into a parking space and back out, over and over until I had the car perfectly between the lines.

"Not bad at all," Irene said when we switched back to our right sides of the car. "That wasn't bad at all for a first try."

I thanked her, for the compliment and for letting me drive.

"Now, if you quit drinking before your next birthday, I'll help you get your permit and learn to drive." She drove off without looking at me.

Irene proved what a great friend she was again when we got back in town, although for a while I didn't understand what she was doing. First, she stopped at another phone booth and handed me a dime without asking if I needed it. "Call Craig and tell him you're back," she instructed. "Your parents may not let you out for a long time and there's no use in him worrying over nothing."

Craig made the mistake of letting me know how excited he was to hear my voice. The only way I could protect him was to hide my own feelings about talking to him again, which surprised me by being a heap more excited than I'd ever been to hear his voice before.

"I'm really glad you're home," he said. "I missed you but I hope you had a good time. And I have a new song that I can't wait for you to hear."

"I don't know if I'll make practice tonight," I said. "Even if Momma goes to work, Daddy might be mad enough to stay up and yell at me or something."

Craig said he understood but added that he would wait for me at the corner in case I got out. "Try to call me from Irene's later if you can't make it," he asked. "I'll want to know how things went when you got home."

Irene parked in her usual spot in the alley behind the shop and turned the engine off.

"They're going to be very upset with you for running away," she said, as though every nerve in my body didn't already know that. "And rightfully so, Penny. Keep that in mind. Your mother was wrong when she didn't defend you, and she was wrong to hit you and leave you stranded on a street corner in the middle of the night. Hell, she's wrong about damn near everything she does, but that doesn't make it right for you to do crazy things, too."

I felt betrayed. How could Irene turn this around and act like she was defending my mother?

"Do you want my advice?" she asked.

"Sure." I didn't, but I figured she'd give it to me anyway since she wanted to be my mother.

"You need to go in there and admit what you did wrong. Say you're sorry and that you learned something from this experience. You did learn something, didn't you?"

I stared her straight in the eye and reviewed what I had learned. "I learned that I was right all along, and that my mother will never take up for me no matter what anybody does to me. I learned that my mother tried to kill me when I was little. I learned that my Nana sent letters that my parents never told me about, and that my parents kept me away from people who loved me, but didn't bother to love me themselves. You think *I'm* supposed to apologize to *them* for that?"

"Is that all you learned? I'm disappointed," she said.

That pretty much summed everything up for me. Irene was like my real parents, turning on me when I needed her most. I fought hard to be strong, but a huge tear leaked out to show me I was no better than they were; I even betrayed myself.

I reached for the door handle, prepared to leave the car and walk off into nowhere. I wanted to just walk until I was too tired to go any further and then sit down and die, probably in the parking lot of a closed up Shell station on the other side of town. With my luck, another preaching paperboy would come along and try to convince me that life was good.

Irene grabbed my arm and handed me another tissue. I was about tired of her thinking she knew every single thing I needed or thought, but I took it from her anyway.

"Hold on a minute. We need to finish our conversation before we go inside," she said.

"It's Wednesday, Irene. You don't work today."

"I don't plan to work. You don't think I'd let you walk in there to face them alone do you?"

More tears fell. I wiped at them with my tissue. "I wish I would have stayed in Crayfield," I said. "I don't want to go back in there. No offense to your property, but I wouldn't care if I never saw this place again."

"No offense taken. I think the reason you feel so desperate right now is because you still haven't admitted the good things you learned."

I sighed. "Tell me what they are if you think you know. I sure can't think of anything good."

She held my hand while she told me; probably thinking it was the motherly thing to do. It embarrassed me and I hoped nobody would walk past and see us.

"I think you learned how loveable you are, and how many people do love you. And I think you found out that love does feel pretty good when you allow yourself to accept it. And I think you may have learned that there's a big world outside this house. In a few years, you'll be free to explore the world and decide what you want, instead of being restricted by their choices."

"Maybe," I said.

"It's only a few years away, Penny. You don't have to like them, or believe they are right about anything. All you have to do is play by their rules for a little while longer. Hang on until this inning is over because there's a lot more game left after it. I'll be around. And you have Craig. Complain to us all you want, but keep your nose clean at home."

I nodded. Maybe I could do it if she helped me. "Okay," I conceded, figuring I would regret it but Irene deserved a favor. "I'll tell them I learned a lot."

Daddy was in his semi-comatose state on the couch and Momma was in the bathroom teasing her hair when we walked in. Daddy didn't bother to stand up or speak, but he tried to smile until Momma came flying out of the bathroom and screamed at Irene.

"Get out of my house, bitch," she ordered. It seemed pretty funny to me because Irene was the owner of Momma's house. Also, Momma wasn't wearing a blouse and her bra strap was twisted. I bit my cheeks and gathered courage.

"Please don't yell at her," I begged. "None of this was her fault. She drove all the way up there this morning to bring me back home."

"She shouldn't have taken you there in the first place," Momma yelled. She turned, shaking her rat-tail comb in Irene's face. "I could have you arrested, you know. That's what I ought to do."

"If it will make you feel better, you're welcome to borrow my phone to call the police," Irene responded calmly. "I think it might do more good to sit down and talk about what made Penny decide she needed to get away for a few days."

Daddy opened his mouth like he wanted to say something, but changed his mind, again, when Momma shot him a hateful glare.

"Listen," Irene said. "I don't want any trouble. I apologize if you were worried when she didn't come home that next morning. I'm sure you must have thought about all of the horrible things that might have happened to her after you left her on the street corner in the middle of the night. It must have been painful to imagine those things."

Daddy rubbed his eyes with his index finger and thumb, and coughed. Momma threw her comb at him and called him a sucker, but he didn't look up. Daddy had lost his will to fight a long time before that happened.

"I didn't mean to worry you," I said, to break the silence and move things along so Irene could get out of there. "I was mad over Pete dividing up the money different, and took it out on you instead of him. I learned a lot." I looked over at Irene to see how I did and she winked.

"You *learned* a lot," Momma mocked. "How sweet. You run off for four days, come back in here all enlightened, and I'm supposed to get over it, huh? Try again. You've got a lot left to learn, and I'll teach you."

I bit my lip and held my breath. Momma wasn't even warmed up yet; I sensed a huge fight coming. Irene must have sensed the same thing. She stepped up and put her hands on my shoulders.

"Kitty," she said, "I can't tell you how to run your life."

"You got that straight." Momma interrupted.

"Hear me out, please." Irene had extraordinary self-control, I learned right then, because she delivered a strict message in a calm voice. "I can't tell you how to run your life, but I can promise you this. If you ever lay another hand on this child, allow another old drunk to abuse her, or leave her on a street corner in the middle of the night, you'd better be prepared for the fight of your life. After I clean up the street with your sorry ass, I'll drag you into court and fight for guardianship of your daughter. Don't push me."

That was the first time I ever heard an adult fight without raising her voice, and it was far more frightening than Momma' screaming. I didn't breathe or blink an eye.

Daddy spoke up. "That's fair enough. Thanks for bringing her home, Irene, and we'll see you soon."

Irene squeezed my shoulder and turned to leave. "You know where to find me if you need anything," she said to me on her way out the door, loud enough for Momma and Daddy to hear.

Momma stormed back into the bathroom and slammed the door, complaining that because of me she was going to be late. I stood in the middle of the room feeling as out of place as I had felt standing in Harvey's the night of the Halloween meeting.

I thought about the Princess bedroom at Nana's and tried to imagine how it would be to have a room like that to run into right then. As it was, Daddy was sitting in my room, on my bed, and I had no place to run. I turned to go sit at the kitchen table, where I couldn't feel his pain mixed in with mine, but he asked me to sit down. I knew he meant on the same side of the room with him.

"We were worried," he said. "We didn't know what happened to you when we woke up Saturday morning and you weren't here."

You didn't know, I thought. And you probably didn't even wake her up to ask if she knew where I was because you're afraid of her.

"I couldn't call," I reminded him. "I knew you wouldn't go in and answer Irene's phone even if I tried."

"How are Nana and Pappy?" he asked.

"Sad. Old. Nana's sick and doesn't cook or pour lemonade any more. They miss you."

He closed his eyes and dropped his head.

"Did you know they sent letters? Nana wrote a hundred letters."

He shook his head without looking up.

"Did you know Momma tried to make me drive off the cliff?"

"Nana exaggerates."

"I remembered, Dad. Nana didn't have to tell me anything."

Momma came out, wearing a blouse this time, and said she'd deal with me later. "Harvey was furious when you didn't show up Saturday night. I covered and told him you were sick with a stomach virus and you'd work this week without pay to make it up to them."

She picked up her purse and walked out the door.

"I hate her," I admitted to Daddy. "I'm not working for free."

He told me to play along and he'd pay me whatever I was supposed to earn, then went to his room. I didn't want his money. I wanted the money I rightfully earned, from the band members at Harvey's.

Craig practically jumped up and down and cheered when he saw me walking toward the corner. I forgot that I wasn't supposed to encourage him, and ran to meet him half way.

"How'd it go with your parents? I can't believe you got out tonight," he said.

I gave him the condensed version. "I hate my mother and I'm glad my father is a pushover."

He sang the new song he had written for me as we walked to his house. I didn't listen, because it was a love song and I knew he had written it to me.

I was free, at least until Harvey's closed and Momma came home. I tried to set my mind on the freedom. That, and the hope that John would bring me a new bottle of rum and slip it in my purse when Craig wasn't looking.

Chapter 16

I stayed in touch with Nana and Pappy after I returned from my visit in Crayfield. Since my parents never mentioned them again after the night I came back home, I assumed they weren't in favor of a renewed family connection and kept my communications secret. I called my grandparents from Irene's phone on the first Sunday of each month. They sent weekly letters to me at Irene's house.

Nana's health continued to deteriorate, although she never complained about anything to me. Pappy sent separate letters to tell me about her. He and Wanda both reported that no matter what the doctors said about Nana's physical condition, they knew her spirit had improved when I reunited with the family. She was already planning what she would wear to my high school graduation.

"Wanda and Gwen want to ride down there with us and stay over for a few days," Nana wrote. "We need to plan early to make sure they don't call Gwen in to work at the hospital any of those days, so you need to send us the date as soon as possible. We need a list of hotels, too, so we can make reservations. And Pappy wants to hear you sing one night while we're there, so we might ought to stay in a hotel close to where you sing. Let me know if we should make reservations or buy tickets for that."

I stuck the letter in my biology book instead of answering her right away. The school board had set the date of graduation before our senior year started, but I wasn't sure I wanted Nana to come. What if Momma and Daddy decided to go, and Nana ran into them? It might cause her to have a heart attack, or a broken heart when she saw how old and thin he looked. And what kind of family made their relatives stay in a hotel when they came to visit?

Even worse, the last thing I wanted was for them to see how unglamorous my singing career was at Harvey's Tavern, or that Momma served drinks in a sleazy bar. Nana didn't belong in a place like Harvey's, not even for one night to hear me sing.

"Maybe we can book a gig somewhere else that week," Craig said. "Somewhere more suitable for your grandparents, and then they can hear Coal's Crew instead of Harvey's band. Maybe you won't even be working at Harvey's anymore. Do you plan to stay there after graduation?"

"That's six months away," I reminded him. "You know I don't plan that far ahead. Anything could happen between now and then."

I put my hand in his lap, hoping to distract him before he started into a lecture about maturity and responsibility. Craig had been acting more like a parent than a boyfriend, and it was playing on my nerves.

He ignored my hand. "Six months isn't so long, Penny. We need to plan ahead. What do you want for Coal's Crew? We've outgrown the annual talent show performance and should be playing teen clubs and weddings. We ought to start working on connections to get into real clubs, where we can make a name for ourselves. And what about us? Do you want to stay here and sleep on the couch forever, or think about how we can afford to get married and get you out of here?"

Craig didn't understand why I hated plans. For me, they never worked out. If I planned on making Coal's Crew a hit, then Billy and John would probably quit. If I planned on getting married, Craig would most likely stop loving me. That was my pattern; plans turned into disappointments. As long as I accepted what was, if something good came along it was a pleasant surprise. I liked things my way, and Craig wanted to plan out every move for the rest of his life.

"Craig, why can't we just make out or something? Why does everything have to always be so serious with you, especially on Wednesday when Irene isn't here to open the door? Come on, we have a little time alone."

I encouraged him to my way of thinking by teasing his neck with my tongue.

"No fair." He protested insincerely before he kissed me. By that time butterflies in the stomach were old news to me and I could easily identify the difference between the ones that popped up before a final exam and the ones Craig gave me. I had experienced new feelings that made the butterflies seem like nothing. And I had discovered that a tongue did wonderful things as long as it belonged to Craig instead of Stinky.

I also knew how it felt to turn warm and wet between my legs, and to hold my breath and wait for Craig to make every nerve in my body tremble with excitement. I thought I hated Craig the first time he made me feel that way. We were in his basement, cleaning up after band practice. Gary was the only person left in the house and he was waiting upstairs in his room to drive me home before he and Craig went to meet their parents at the VFW to celebrate their grandfather's birthday. Neither of them was anxious to go, so Gary wasn't going to bother us. Craig got the idea we could have some fun before we went upstairs.

When I lost control of my body for the first time, I ran up the stairs and out the door, thinking I would never want to see him again. I believed he had taken over control of my heart, my mind, *and* my body, and I was lost forever. If love hurt, then I figured lust must destroy, because at the moment there was nothing left of me. I was a trembling, thoughtless mess, gasping for air.

Craig and Gary tracked me down and made me get in Gary's car. By the time we reached my street, my breathing had returned to normal and I could think again. I decided it wasn't so bad after all if my body could go to that place and then return to normal again.

Each time after that got better, and I decided that feeling was my favorite – right after applause.

"It is fair," I said between kisses. "You teach me about responsibility and in return I make you feel good. Shut up and feel good, Craig." The next time I broke away for air, I added a comment. "All work and no play will ruin your life, Craig Osburn."

"And all play and no work will do the same to you," he warned, as he released my breasts from the bra I had finally matured enough to need.

When Daddy came through the door an hour earlier than usual, Craig was on his knees in front of the couch, circling my nipples with his tongue. I was in that special place where Craig was the only thing in my world, and didn't notice that Daddy had come in until he pulled Craig up and threw him across the room.

"I guess this explains a lot," Daddy said, looking at the floor while I fixed my bra back in place. "I blamed your mother for clogging up the toilet with rubbers, when it really was you. I thought she was lying on you."

Craig stayed over by the bathroom door when he spoke. "No, sir. Those didn't come from us. I shouldn't have done what you just caught me doing, but Penny is still a virgin."

Technically that was the truth, although I felt like something really tainted now that Daddy had seen me. Craig and I figured it was okay to do anything so long as one of us still had our pants on. That way, the two most important parts never touched and I stayed a virgin.

"He's telling the truth, Daddy. I promise we didn't flush anything down the toilet."

Craig looked agitated with me. "It's not a matter of flushing anything. We've never used them to begin with because we've never done that. We don't have any rubbers to flush or throw away anywhere."

Daddy shook his head like he was trying to clear out his brain. I listened to see if I could hear whiskey sloshing around in there.

"Sit down, boy. I need to think this over."

Craig pulled a kitchen chair over into the living room instead of sitting next to me on the couch. I decided that was a good idea because I really wanted him to hold my hand right then and that probably wouldn't have set well with Daddy.

Daddy flopped down in his chair and rubbed his forehead with the tips of his fingers. "I came home with a headache. This isn't helping."

I looked at Craig, but he wouldn't meet my eyes with his. My instincts told me to run through the door into Irene's because I was about to be in the middle of something I wouldn't want to see. But I couldn't leave Craig stuck with it alone.

"If the condoms weren't yours, whose were they? Have you had anyone else in here?" I think Daddy would have been happy at that moment to hear that they belonged to anyone other than Momma, including me.

"I've never had anyone in here other than Craig. Never since we moved here, I swear. Maybe someone slipped in here from Irene's while we were gone sometime."

Daddy shook his head again, slower this time. "Nobody came in from Irene's to flush a bunch of used rubbers down our toilet, Penny. You know better." He sat still for a minute. "Penny Sue, you'd best not lie to me. This is serious."

I raised my right hand. "They didn't belong to me, or any of my friends, I swear to you."

Craig finally looked me in the eye when Daddy snorted and drooped like a man who had lost everything. I looked around the room and realized how little he had to lose in the first place. I actually felt sorry for him, because Momma was truly the best thing he had and that wasn't saying much.

"I'm not through with you two," he warned. "After what I saw you doing, I'm not sure I believe you. Even if the rubbers weren't yours, we need to get other things straight."

Craig took a deep breath. "I love Penny, sir. I plan to marry her when we're out of school and I have a decent job."

Irene's door looked more inviting than ever.

"You go home, boy. I'll talk to you after I clear things up with my wife and get rid of this headache. Don't let me catch you in this house again without an invitation from me."

Craig said yes sir and walked to the door. He turned to me before he opened it. "I'll see you in school tomorrow, Penny." I watched him leave. He turned when he was on the porch to blow me a kiss before he walked away.

Daddy went to his room without saying anything more to me, and didn't come out the rest of the evening. My stomach was too nervous for food so I soaked in the tub and went to sleep early. It was a good thing.

All hell broke loose when Momma came in from work that night. She and Daddy fought in their bedroom for a long time, then they moved into the room where I slept. I figured she would drag me into it sooner or later, but kept my eyes closed until that time came.

"Wake up, you lying bitch." Momma must have spent the whole night's tips to get that slur. "You won't get away with this."

I sat up quickly then, and slid my feet into my house shoes so I'd be prepared to run if she started swinging. Irene had installed a lock on her side of the dividing door, which she left unlocked for me. One punch and I would run in there and lock myself on the other side.

"Tell your dad the truth so he'll get off my ass and let me get some sleep," she said, waving her arms and throwing off her already wavering balance. She stumbled forward a couple of steps, filling the air with the stale beer and cigarette stink that she had worn home from work. "Tell him those were your condoms and then we'll deal with you and Mr. Stud later."

I hated her for dragging Craig into our filthy life. I didn't care who she screwed or how many condoms she flushed down the toilet. I did care if she lied about Craig and called him names.

I looked Daddy straight in the eye. "They weren't ours."

"She's lying, Jerold." Momma didn't take her eyes off me. "She's afraid of what you'll do to her little boyfriend if she tells you the truth. Don't be a fool and let her get away with this."

"I did catch them in the act," Daddy said.

"In the act of what? We were both fully clothed only my shirt was pulled up. You don't need condoms for that."

"You got here too soon is all," Momma said to him. "If she pulled her shirt off for him, no telling what else she was fixing to pull off if you hadn't come in when you did."

Daddy sat again, totally defeated. It was the best fight he had put up in years, but he caved before he won it.

"Penny Sue, the boy said he would marry you. I expect you to hold him to that, and soon. We won't be waiting until school is out and you're already pregnant or something." He finished what he had to say and went back to bed.

"I'm not through with you," Momma told me. "I'm not even started. How dare you try to make him believe those things belonged to me?"

"They weren't mine. That's all I know and all I told him," I answered. "I never said a word about you, he brought that part up."

"Your Daddy believes marriage is the only answer, and he also thinks it has to last forever. That's why I'm stuck in this mess. Well, you made your bed, Penny Sue, and now you get to lie in it."

"I didn't make any bed, Momma. I haven't even had a bed since I was seven years old. I'm not the liar in this family, and I won't lie to cover for you. Who is it? Harvey?"

I ran for Irene's door knowing she was too drunk to chase across the room and stop me before I got there. She charged forward and tripped over the corner of Daddy's chair just as I slid into Irene's and locked the door behind me.

***

Irene came to get me, and I apologized for calling her out at four in the morning.

"That's what friends are for, Penny." She handed me a tissue but for once I didn't even need it. "Don't worry about me, just tell me what's going on."

I told her the whole story. "We weren't doing anything, Irene. Daddy knows that."

I spent the night at Irene's and she drove me to school the next morning, making jokes about ours being the first shotgun wedding she'd heard of where the bride wasn't pregnant. I didn't think anything about the situation was funny.

"He loves you, Penny. Craig seems positively head over heels in love with you. It could be worse. Do you love him?"

"Yes and no," was my honest answer. "I guess I love Craig as much as it's possible for me to love anyone. I know he's just about perfect, and I should probably be happy. But I'm not. We don't have any money and I don't want to get married and live with his parents."

She winked at me. "Have I got a wedding present for you! Let me play mother-of-the-bride and everything will be fine, I promise."

"But I don't want to get married," I protested.

***

I got married anyway, a month later at the courthouse, with Irene and Craig's family in attendance. Mrs. Osburn and Irene cried. I was too numb to show any emotion after hiding in a stall before the ceremony to kill a pint of vodka.

Momma and Daddy didn't make the ceremony because they were busy moving. That was Irene's wedding gift. She waited until Daddy pushed the marriage into a reality and then she took me with her to make the announcement.

"I would have thrown you out six months after you moved in, if it hadn't been for Penny Sue," Irene told Daddy. "So I'm doing it now. I'm throwing you out now because you ruined the plumbing with your condoms. You have a week to get out."

Irene gave Craig and me one year of free rent if we agreed to keep the shop clean for her and the yard work done. She called us resident managers.

Harvey rented Momma a room over the tavern. Daddy reluctantly agreed to go with her on account of he didn't believe in divorce. Irene laughed and said Harvey could plug up his own plumbing for a while.

Craig's family had a small reception for us in their basement, and invited his relatives and a few of our friends. Nana wanted to come but she didn't feel well enough to make the trip and Pappy wouldn't come without her.

Nana and Pappy sent us a full set of stoneware dishes and stainless steel silverware. Other guests gave us enough basics to survive. We got two sets of sheets, some towels and washcloths, glasses, pots and pans, and a toaster. Wanda sent a crocheted tablecloth from her hope chest. Momma and Daddy gave us nothing.

Mr. Osburn hired Craig to work after school and on weekends in his carpet store. He worked the sales floor during the week, where he explained boring things like grades and depths of carpet and padding to customers. On Saturdays, he helped with installations. I missed having him walk me home from school, and the hours we had spent on music, but there was one part of married life that I really did enjoy. Sex was much better without our pants on.

Without my job at Harvey's, which I gave up the weekend after the condom discovery, I received no applause. Sex moved into first place on my list of favorite things to do. When Craig was too tired, which was most of the time, I drank to keep from missing all of my favorite things.

I had written to Lori about the wedding as soon as I knew there was no way for me to escape. She didn't write back. Weeks after the big day, Craig tried to make me feel better by saying that she may have been out of town, or the letter could have been lost in the mail, but my feelings were hurt all the same. When her response finally showed up months later, it did little to make me feel better.

"Congratulations. My family wishes you a lifetime of happiness." That was it, except for a p.s. at the bottom of the page. "Be sure to name your first daughter after me."

Luckily, Craig was at work and the shop was closed when I dropped the letter and screamed. Babies were out of the question. I had to get my singing career off the ground before I wanted to even think about having children.

While I waited on Craig to come home from work, I turned my anger into energy and moved every piece of furniture in the house so it wouldn't feel like the same place I had lived with my parents. I threw out the dishtowels that Momma left behind—probably by accident since I didn't think she wanted to help me out in any way—and covered the couch and chair with the spare set of sheets.

I called Gary from Irene's and he agreed to help me surprise Craig. We moved Daddy's old chair out from the wall a couple of feet and Gary drove Craig's amplifier over and put it in the empty space. Now, Craig could practice his guitar and finish writing our songs when Irene's shop was closed, and I could get ready to start my career and stop thinking about babies.

Chapter 17

My husband and my landlord/surrogate mother were the only members of my family present when I graduated high school. Craig's mother—who still hadn't given me permission to call her anything more personal than Mrs. Osburn—tried unsuccessfully to convince me that Craig's relatives were there for me as much as for him. A few brought cards and gifts for me, but I knew most of his family would have a hard time picking me out of a crowd if he wasn't standing beside me. The rest of them resented me for making Craig marry me before he was ready.

If only they had known us better they would have seen that he was much closer to ready than I was. After Irene offered us a place to live, Craig never had a second thought about getting married. It had been his plan all along, the same as singing had been mine.

Irene, as my wanna-be-mother, had offered to pay for my graduation announcements, but I didn't see much need for wasting her money. The printing company didn't offer individual orders, and it didn't make sense to order twenty-five when I only needed five – one for Nana and Pappy, one for Uncle Bobby and his family, one for the Sawyers, one for Irene, and one for me to keep.

If I had still worked at Harvey's, I might have hung an announcement on the front door for my fans to see. As things turned out, I figured Momma would have snatched it down the minute she spotted it.

It warmed my heart to know that my family back in Crayfield had wanted to see me graduate enough to look into travel arrangements and hotel reservations. But when the time came, Nana was too frail to make the trip and their plans fell through. Wanda had to cancel the hotel room and the Winnebago they had planned to drive Nana in so she could sleep on the road.

Nana was barely able to get out of bed, according to Wanda's letters. She and Gwen took turns staying over in the princess bedroom to help Pappy care for her, and to keep things done around the house. When I talked to Nana she never let on that anything was wrong.

I kept my Crayfield family on my mind while I got ready for graduation so I wouldn't feel sad about my parents not coming.

Craig knocked on the bathroom door. "Hurry up in there. It's about time for us to leave."

I opened the door to check the clock on the television. Just as I suspected, we had thirty minutes left.

Since I had let Irene cut my hair, it took me twice as long to get ready for anything and Craig couldn't get used to the change. I had to curl, tease, smooth over, and spray. He wasn't much happier about the change I had made in my make-up, going from almost none to the complete deal with foundation, eye shadow, eyeliner, lip liner, lipstick, and blush.

"You were beautiful before," he said, almost every day. "Why mess with a good thing?"

"To make it better, same reason you practice guitar," I answered. "To keep from being bored, or boring. For fun. Because I want." I ran down the list. "Do I need a reason? You'll have to rework your master schedule to include my primping."

I went into the shop where I could comb my hair over and call Nana at the same time.

"You be sure to tell Irene to take lots of snapshots for me." Nana repeated that request several times during our conversation. "And tell Craig to give you an extra special hug for me and Pappy."

I promised I'd do both, wondering when I would start including Craig's name in every request as though we were one person with combined thoughts. Had Nana and Pappy always done that, and predicted each other's sentences, or did that start after they got old and had spent too much time together?

"Now that you're out of school maybe you can come back for another visit, and bring Craig and the gradation snapshots."

"We'll do that as soon as he gets a few days off work. Nana, he works so hard. It seems like I never see him anymore unless he's sleeping. I hope that changes now that school's out."

128

"Penny Sue, you be careful," Nana warned. "Don't get bored and take it out on him. It sounds to me like you got a good man, and he's trying to be a good provider. Keep your hands and mind busy and your heart light, and your marriage will be healthy."

I had the feeling Nana wanted to say more on the subject, but my time was running out and Craig was standing at the door waiting on me. "I need to run, Nana. I wish you were here."

"I do too, sweetie. You try to get up here soon to visit," she said again. "Pappy has a big surprise for your graduation present."

Before I hung up, I told Nana I loved her. The words came out surprisingly easy, considering I hadn't said them more than a few times in my whole life. Maybe it was getting easier for me because of having Craig say them to me so often.

"Pappy has a graduation present for me," I told him on our way to the car. "Nana says it's a big surprise."

"Any idea what it could be?"

I tried to imagine. "The first time I went down there, he took me to Sears and bought me three outfits to make up for missing birthdays and Christmases eight through fifteen. They sent each of us a sweater, and an electric skillet for Christmas, and I got the Dust Buster for this birthday. I can't decide between a dress and a vacuum cleaner. What do you think?"

Craig laughed. "I don't have a guess, Penny. Are there any kitchen things we don't have?"

After we guessed a few more items, he pulled off the road, blocks before we had reached the auditorium.

"What are you doing? I'm sure we can find a closer parking space than this," I complained.

"I'll move closer before we get out of the car. I just want to talk to you for a few minutes before we go in," he said.

I tensed up, expecting another lecture about planning for my future, or more questions about my hair and make-up. But I made up my mind before he started that I would control any smart-ass responses that came to mind. Nana's warning still sat fresh in my mind and I wanted to keep a healthy marriage, whatever that meant.

"Penny, this is a special day for you, even if you don't plan on getting a job or going to college. You worked hard to get through school and stay on the honor roll. I know you hate it when I try to act like your dad or something, but I think somebody needs to say how proud they are for all you've done."

I felt the familiar sting rolling up behind my eyes and knew tears would ruin my make-up if I let them loose. "Thanks, Craig. But I really don't need anybody bragging on me."

"Penny, I'm proud of you and I want you to hear this even if you don't think you need it. I brag on you all the time, to my family, to the guys at school, and now to the guys at work. I brag on your grades and your singing, and I tell them how pretty you are and how good you cook, and how much I love you. I'm glad you married me."

I wanted to tell him how much I appreciated what he said, and that I was glad I married him too. But I couldn't push my words past the huge knot sitting in my chest. I also wanted to tell him that I was almost over being afraid of love, because his love really didn't hurt. I wanted to say I loved him as easily as I had said it to Nana a few minutes before. But nothing got past the knot.

The only peace I had known in my life had come after Craig married me and took me away from my parents. For a while, I confused the peace with boredom. It felt like there wasn't much left when the fire went out in my stomach and I stopped keeping a song in my head to drown out everything I didn't want to hear.

Then, after I figured out that Craig had given me a good life, and I wasn't supposed to have the fire or need the song, I went back to being afraid that my love would end up hurting Craig. He had given me everything and I had nothing to give him in return. I wanted to tell him those things. I truly did.

The best I could work up was a little smile, and even then I couldn't look him in the eye when I delivered it. I planned on telling him everything later, when it didn't matter if I cried my make-up off.

Craig started the car again and moved it to the auditorium parking lot. He didn't look at me before we got out of the car, or reach for my hand as we walked to the building. I wanted to run back to the car and wait there until the ceremony was over, but Irene was inside somewhere waiting to see me receive my diploma. I couldn't let her down.

Mrs. Osburn invited Irene to their house for the family party immediately following the graduation. I offered to ride in her car in case she had forgotten how to get there, and Craig didn't try to talk me out of it. He also forgot to kiss me good-bye before I left with her.

Irene was excited. She talked non-stop about being proud of me, and how this was the beginning of my real adult life, so I just let her go on instead of bringing her down with my problems. She stayed by my side at the Osburn's house while Craig made the rounds to talk to cousins and family friends that I didn't know well.

When Irene was ready to leave, Craig and I walked out with her. "I'm going over to Billy's party for a while," he said. "Do you want to go with me, or have Irene drop you off at home?"

In all the time we had been married, Craig had never mentioned going anywhere without me, and it hurt my feelings that he did on our graduation night. "I want to come with you," I said. I went to hug Irene good-bye.

She whispered in my ear. "You haven't smiled at that boy all day. Straighten up. It's his special day too."

There must have been a hundred people at Billy's party, from little kids to great-grandparents. His parents supplied a keg of beer in addition to a bar in the basement stocked with more alcohol than Harvey's. For the first time in our lives, Craig drank more than I did. And he ignored me while we were there.

Mr. Ranglin's friends came prepared with their musical instruments, and they talked me into singing. At first I said no, unless Craig and Billy sat in with the band, but Craig told me to go ahead. I killed another glass of beer and a shot of bourbon and then took the microphone without hesitation. I had missed having an audience.

The women came down from the kitchen and living room, and children came in from the yard when the music started. They clapped and whistled and shouted out the names of songs they wanted to hear. I tried to find Craig in the crowd to see if he wanted me to keep singing or turn the microphone over to someone else, but I couldn't find him. Billy brought me another beer and I decided it was easier for me to sing to strangers than talk to them, and kept on singing.

The alcohol and applause turned the room into a blur and my emotions into mush. I would have sung any song, and all night long to keep that euphoria going and avoid the hurt I had carried into Billy's house with me, but the musicians tired and wanted a break.

Billy took my microphone and handed me a fresh beer. "I need to find Craig," I said, downing half the beer in one swallow. "Have you seen him?"

"He was upstairs the last time I saw him," Billy said. "He's such a bore, Penny. I can't believe you married him. He doesn't know how to have fun."

I finished my beer and pushed through the crowd, aiming to find Craig and see if he was having fun, or if he wanted to leave. Billy's mother grabbed my arm and took me to meet his aunts. I tried to answer their questions. How long had I been singing? Did I sing out anywhere so they could come hear me again? Was I interested in singing as a career?

I finally broke away and started up the stairs to look for Craig, hoping everything I had said to the aunts made sense because my tongue was thick and my head spinning. Half way up the stairs I had to sit down and refocus. Where was Craig? I needed him to help me walk.

Billy found me sitting on the steps and handed me another beer, which I said I didn't want. "I need to find Craig. Help me up the stairs, Billy, I can't walk."

He pulled me to my feet and held me while I half-walked, half-crawled up the stairs. At one point I slipped and his hand ended up between my legs when he caught me. We both laughed, but I decided it wasn't funny when he put his hand there again on purpose – and I admitted to myself that it felt good.

"Help me, Billy. I need my husband," I said, trying to mean it. "Stop playing around and help me find him."

He sat me in a chair at the kitchen table. "Sit still, Penny. I'll find Craig and we'll be right back."

I was too drunk to do anything other than stay there. My limbs were so heavy they felt paralyzed, and my eyelids drooped. I leaned my head back against the wall, planning just to rest my eyes until Billy came back with Craig but I dozed off.

"Come on, Penny." Billy pulled on my arm. "Wake up. I found Craig and you aren't going to like this."

I heard Billy's voice but needed a few more minutes to focus before I could react. My eyelids refused to cooperate when I tried to open them.

"Craig is passed out on the couch in the den. He won't wake up," Billy told me. "You have to pull yourself together and get him up yourself."

"I can't. I can't move Billy. Go wake him up for me. Please."

Billy pulled me out of the chair, touching everything he had no business touching. In my half-conscious stupor, his fingers sent electricity shooting through my body. Zit-faced, obnoxious Billy Ranglin aroused me. I wanted to puke. How could my body betray me, and Craig, that way?

"Stop it, Billy. I want Craig."

He pinched my nipple and got in my face with his beer breath. "Admit it, Penny. You like it."

I shrugged his hand off my breast, but couldn't find my balance to take the rest of me away from him.

"Admit it and I'll take you to Craig. Look what you did to me," he said, grabbing my hand and rubbing it against his erection.

"If you don't get out of my face I'll puke all over you," I warned. The bubbles were working their way from my stomach to my throat.

"If you puke on my mother's carpet we're both dead," he warned. "Hold on."

Billy led me into the bathroom and held me around the waist while I leaned over the toilet and lost six beers and who remembered what else. He moved his hands up from my waist to my breasts, and pressed what was left of his erection against my butt. I puked until my stomach and my throat were raw.

Mrs. Ranglin came to the bathroom door and told Billy to go wake Craig. She ran water on a washcloth and wiped my face.

"It looks like somebody had too much to drink," she said, not sounding too upset in my opinion. I was glad I hadn't puked on her carpet, but it seemed she shouldn't want me staggering around and throwing up in her house anyway.

"We'll get you home," she promised. "Sit down and hold this rag on the back of your neck for a few minutes."

Mr. Ranglin and one of his friends managed to get Craig up, and both of us into the back seat of Mr. Ranglin's car. "I'll drive you home and you can come back for your car tomorrow," he offered. Billy had to tell him where we lived.

I slept most of my drunk off and woke somewhere just short of consciousness, wanting Craig to hold me and erase the day before from my memory. Singing was out of the question, and there was only one other thing I knew to do that would make me stop thinking.

I snuggled up to Craig's back and reached across his hip to stroke him and get him ready. He turned on his back and pushed my hand away. I tried again, this time running my tongue down his stomach while I stroked him. Again, he pushed me away.

He didn't open his eyes or say anything, so I convinced myself that the alcohol still controlled him and he hadn't purposely rejected me. Maybe he really was still asleep.

Carefully, to keep him from pushing me away before I had him where he couldn't resist, I eased down between his legs and put my mouth on him. He grabbed me with both of his hands under my arms and pulled me back up on my pillow. "Leave me alone, Penny. I'm trying to sleep."

The rejection made me more determined to prove this was a mistake. "Craig, please wake up. I need you."

He turned his back to me and kept his eyes closed.

"I love you, Craig. Please don't do this to me."

He continued to ignore me. Memories of Momma never giving up on her harping and Daddy acting like he didn't see or hear her popped into my head. I didn't want to be like them, but I told myself this was different. Craig's feelings were hurt and I had to keep on until I showed him that I loved him. I was scared and needed Craig to prove he still loved me. This was necessary, not insane.

I crawled across him and lay on the other side where he would be facing me if he opened his eyes. "Craig," I whispered. "I need you to love me. I'm begging you to wake up and love me."

He rubbed his face and moved over to my side of the bed to get away from me, but he did open his eyes and stare at the ceiling. "Penny, I don't think you know what love is," he finally said.

At least he responded. I stayed where I was and stared at the ceiling with him. "Maybe I don't, since you're the only person who has ever loved me. Maybe I don't understand any of this, Craig, because I lived with a married couple who never acted like the cared about each other. I don't know how to do this."

He ran his fingers through his hair and I ached with jealousy. I wanted them in my hair, or on my body.

"I lied. Nana and Pappy love me, and they love each other. I have seen love, but I still don't know how to feel it or show it. Maybe there's something wrong with me."

He didn't say anything, so I checked to see if he was still awake. His eyes were glued to the ceiling.

"Why won't you touch me? Right now I need you to hold me. I want you to make love to me. Please, make me feel your love."

"Penny, you've got everything all mixed up. I told you how much I love you on the way to the graduation ceremony and you didn't feel a thing. I don't want to hold you right now because what you want isn't love. It's sex. You've almost convinced me to believe like you do – that love hurts and it's not worth the pain."

"You were making me cry. I didn't want to talk then because I would have ruined my make-up. The pictures would have turned out ugly. I wanted to tell you later, but you passed out. And now you won't let me."

He turned his head and looked at me, but still made no attempt to touch me. "I'm listening now. Tell me how much you love me without touching me."

"I love you. I'm glad I married you. I'm happy with you and I would brag on you, too, if I went anywhere to talk to people."

He shook his head and closed his eyes again. "That sounds empty. Thanks for trying though."

I took a chance, turned on my side and put my hand on his chest. He moved it. I took my pillow and went to the couch.

The next time I woke, I was in a panic, remembering Billy's hands on me the night before. I wanted to believe that had been a nightmare but the memory became clearer as the fog of my drunken sleep wore off.

I liked it. I remembered enjoying the feelings I had when Billy touched me. How was that possible when I hated Billy and I loved Craig? It must have been the drinks.

I went to the bathroom and brushed my teeth before crawling back in bed next to Craig where I felt safe, even if I couldn't feel loved.

Chapter 18

When I woke for the third time, Craig was gone. My heart raced in fear until I heard the plucking of electric guitar strings being played without an amplifier. Maybe he didn't hate me after all, since he tried to play quietly while I slept.

Or, maybe Craig was just so nice that he respected the comfort of people he didn't even like. Billy and John came to mind. He was always considerate of them and I knew he didn't really like them. Or, he could be like Daddy, and think good men stayed married no matter how much they hated their wives. There were many possible explanations for him to be unplugged other than he loved me.

I wasn't ready to leave the bed and find out which it was. I stared at the ceiling again, this time allowing tears to run from the corners of my eyes and drip onto the pillow. I let them flow freely until I was forced to turn over to keep them out of my ears.

Craig was finally interested in music again and I couldn't join him. No matter what he had on his master plan, Coal's Crew was history for me. I never wanted to see Billy Ranglin again.

The fact that Craig had chosen that morning to pick up his guitar again could have come out of several different reasons. Maybe he was sorry he hadn't played at Billy's party and got the urge after he got home. Or maybe he wanted me to see that he would still play, just not when I wanted to sing. Or he could have been using his music the way I did - to ease his pain and clear his mind.

For the first time in months, I pulled a song up in my head to stop everything else from crashing around in there. My chest ached, mostly from having to hold my song inside again.

"Penny, are you okay?"

I opened my eyes to find Craig sitting on the edge of the bed, wearing a worried expression. I nodded but the tears continued to pour, making me look like a liar or an idiot.

"You scared me," he said. "I couldn't wake you."

"Sorry. I was thinking." I closed my eyes again. He stayed, but didn't touch me or wipe my tears away.

"Do you want to think in the car for a while? Dad gave me a long weekend for graduation so I don't have to work until Wednesday. I could take you to Crayfield to see what Pappy's surprise is."

"Now?" I asked without opening my eyes.

"If you want. Pack some things and we can go for a few days. It might make you feel better."

I wanted to throw my arms around him and say thank you, but I couldn't. What if he pushed me away again? Then I wouldn't want to go anywhere.

I got out of the bed, carefully avoiding any contact with him, and opened a drawer in the dresser that I was still excited to have. "Are you going to stay with me when we get there?"

"That was my plan, unless you don't want me to."

"You can stay if you want," I told him, hoping with all my heart that he would want to, and that I wouldn't have to explain to Nana how I managed to run off a husband in less than a year. I stacked my clothes on the foot of the bed and told him I'd go call Nana while he got his things ready.

Craig said little while we ate breakfast, and even less when we got on the road. His silence set my nerves on edge but I couldn't think of anything to talk about and I couldn't go to sleep. I sang nearly every song I knew, in my head, and waited a couple of hours into the drive before I found the courage to say anything.

"If you're sorry you married me, Craig, I won't make you stay. I don't want to turn you into my Daddy."

He stared at the road ahead and breathed hard.

"If you're planning to leave me in Crayfield, I wish you'd say so now," I asked. "Give me a chance to think what I want to say to Nana about it."

"Penny, what's wrong with you? Why are you acting so crazy about everything? I tried to talk to you yesterday and you didn't want to talk. So now I try not to talk to you, and you want to talk but you don't say anything. I'm confused about a lot of things but I'm not ready to leave you. I'll let you know if I ever get to that point."

"Why wouldn't you touch me? Why'd you push me away? Craig, I needed you."

Again, he sighed, heavily. "You pushed me away first. You shut me out emotionally. Penny, I tried to tell you how much I love you and you completely closed me off. I'll be honest, you made me so mad that I didn't want to look at you, much less touch you after we got to the graduation. And that's why I drank so much later."

"I guess I'm just not good at love," I admitted. "I don't know how to let you love me and I can't tell you how I feel about you. I want to, I just don't know how."

I didn't remind him that I had tried to show him the only way I knew how--with my body—and he wouldn't let me. I just let the subject drop.

"Tell me what to expect when we get there. Will we have a bed to sleep in?"

I told him about Nana's spare room, and that I was sure Wanda or Gwen—whoever's turn it was to sleep over—would gladly let us have it for a few days. To ease his mind more, I promised my grandparents weren't anything like my parents.

The whole family—Nana and Pappy, and Uncle Bobby and Aunt Janet, and Wanda and Gwen and Gwen's boyfriend, Cody--waited for us on the front porch. They started waving as we passed the pond and didn't stop until they ran to help us out of the car.

I didn't have to introduce Craig. They grabbed him up and hugged him the same as they did me.

"Come inside everyone. Let's let Nana sit down," Pappy said. He helped Nana in the door and ushered her to the recliner. "Make yourself at home, Craig. Penny Sue can show you where to drop your bags, and where to find the bathroom if you need to get in there after your long drive."

I took Craig and our bags, which were literally grocery sacks since we didn't own luggage, and showed him the princess room. While he placed the bags in the corner by the window, I flopped back on the bed and stretched out with my arms over my head.

"You can't believe how huge this bed felt to me after sleeping on that couch all those years. I remembered this bed, and this room, from when I was little. It was almost like a wonderland to me." I rambled on and on, forgetting that Craig and I were barely speaking except for strained conversations about everything wrong with our marriage, and that there were people waiting in the living room to see us.

Craig leaned over the bed and kissed me. He didn't touch me with anything except his lips. The kiss was gentle but passionate, and it sent my whole body into a tingling spasm. I caught his eyes with mine, to see if he was doing that to tease me. But I saw love there, as plain as anything, and for an instant that love touched my heart.

He straightened back up. "You'd better show me where the bathroom is now, and give me a few minutes."

I led him to the yellow room, stuck my head in long enough to inhale a memory, and left him.

"Why, Penny Sue, that boy's handsome enough to be in the movies," Nana said when I walked back into the room alone. "And he seems nice enough too."

"Yes," Pappy agreed. "He seems like a fine young man. Are you happy with him?"

"Happier than I've ever been," I answered honestly.

"Stop talking about the poor guy behind his back," Gwen said. "He's probably nervous as all get out coming here to meet all of us as it is."

"Mother baked a cake for your graduation," Wanda said. We would've planned a bigger party if you would have let us know sooner that you were coming."

Craig walked back into the room and sat on the floor in front of my chair, copying Cody, who was sitting at Gwen's feet. Craig turned to the side and put his arm across my leg, looking like a husband who was comfortable touching his wife.

My heart beat too fast, and I breathed too hard. Nana and Pappy asked a string of questions, which I left for Craig to answer so I could concentrate on my breathing.

"What do you want," Craig asked, looking up at me so I'd know I missed a question that I was expected to answer. I bit my lip like I was thinking, and he rescued me.

"Eat first, or see your present first? Come on Penny, make up your mind." He said it playfully.

I put my hands on his shoulders, hoping he wouldn't pull away in front of everybody. "How hungry are you? Can you wait a little longer before you eat so I can see my surprise?"

"Pappy, why don't you take them to see the surprise and we'll get dinner on the table while you're gone," Nana suggested.

Craig jumped up and took my hand to help me out of my chair. He kept holding it after I was on my feet, and kept it all the way out to Pappy's truck. I felt fourteen again, learning again how butterflies over Craig holding my hand felt. Only the feeling didn't stop at butterflies, and the handholding wasn't going to satisfy me for long.

Instead of circling around to drive out the road, Pappy cut across the field. I pointed out the barn house to Craig.

"That's where I lived when I was little. It was a real house inside, at least that's the way I remember. Was it Pappy?"

He chuckled. "Your memory is fine, Penny Sue. It was a real house then, and it's even better now. Look at the door."

"A screen! Somebody fixed the screen." I laughed. "Now what's the biggest disgrace in Crayfield?" I asked.

He got serious. "I reckon that's your Daddy, Penny Sue. He hasn't ever called to check on his mother."

Pappy pulled the truck up next to the barn house porch and shut his engine off. "Here we are. Happy graduation, Penny Sue and Craig."

I looked at Craig and then at Pappy. "Where? What?" I was afraid to believe what I hoped he was saying, but it turned out to be the truth.

"Nana and I want you and Craig to have this property. Even if you don't want to live up here full time, we hope it will bring you back to visit more often. And when you have little ones, there'll be plenty of room. Look."

He pointed out the fence that he had put up at the drop off. "That's Nana's big idea."

"Thank you." Craig said it first.

"Yes, thank you. Pappy, are you sure? This is too much. A card with a ten dollar bill would have been enough."

"I gave Wanda and Gwen each five acres when they graduated. Yours is a little under three acres, but it has the house."

I hugged him. "This is the nicest thing anybody ever gave me, Pappy. Can we go inside?"

He handed me the key. "You two go in and check things out. I'm going to run up to Jake's and gas up the truck. I'll come back after you before those women get feisty over their supper sitting out too long."

"I can't believe this," Craig said, as I unlocked the door. "A house. They gave you a house for graduation."

"Us," I corrected. "He said it was for both of us, Craig."

I pushed the door open slowly, afraid negative memories might overwhelm me when I looked inside. Nothing looked the same. The rooms were smaller than I remembered, but much brighter and more inviting.

The living room and kitchen were visible from the front door, and had new, yellow paint. It wasn't a bright yellow like Nana's bathroom, but warm, mustard shade that matched the couch. Someone had switched out the furniture we had left behind, replacing it with newer used furniture.

"This looks like Aunt Janet," I told Craig. "I'll bet this was her furniture and curtains."

Wherever it came from, the furniture was still nicer than what we had in Irene's furnished apartment. Momma and Daddy had never replaced one item in that apartment in ten years.

Craig walked into the kitchen and opened a cabinet door. "Penny, they left dishes and everything in here. It looks like someone lives here."

There was a small hall off the kitchen, with a bedroom on each end and a bathroom between them. I walked into the hall and stood at the door to my old room. In place of the iron cot I had used was a double bed, covered with a red and white quilt. Everything in the room was red and white. My black patent leather shoes were the only things left from my old life, sitting like little trophies on the dresser.

Craig walked up behind me and put his arms around me. "Are you okay?" He whispered the words in my ear, preserving the peace I had found, and sending chills down my spine at the same time.

With my back still toward him, I pressed my body close to his and pulled his arms tighter around me.

"Can we sleep here tonight?" I asked.

"It's your house. I guess we can, unless we're needed to help with Nana."

Pappy pulled up out front and tapped on the horn. I turned in Craig's arms, to face him before he let go.

"Thanks for holding me. I've never felt happier in my whole life than I do right this minute."

He kissed my forehead. "I haven't either, Penny. Come on, before the women get feisty."

Pappy confirmed my guess; the furniture had come from Aunt Janet's house. "That woman changes the furniture in their house more often than I change undershirts. Bobby says she keeps Sears in business. She already furnished a place for Wanda out of her leftovers, and will for Gwen, too, if she ever moves out on her own. I think she has her eye on marrying Cody so she might be going out soon."

We thanked everyone when we got back to Nana's house, Aunt Janet for the furniture, Nana for the dishes and decorating ideas, and everyone who had anything to do with the painting and cleaning.

"I'm planning to stay here tonight," Gwen said. "So you two can go over and stay in your house if you want. But there's no TV or telephone."

Craig embarrassed me by saying we wouldn't need a TV or telephone. I laughed with everyone else. I hoped he meant that, because I still felt the effects of the earlier kiss on Nana's feather bed.

I helped Wanda and Gwen clean the kitchen after supper, while Craig answered more questions in the living room. Then we all sat and talked until Nana looked worn out. Craig retrieved our bags from the princess room, Nana told us to come back for breakfast since there wasn't any food over there, and we drove across the field.

The idea of going to our own house, even if it was an old barn, excited me but my heart was racing for a different reason. My body ached for Craig. I would either be the most excited, or the most disappointed woman in Crayfield that night, depending on whether my husband acted like his real self or the mean, touch-me-not he had been the night before. The anticipation had me dancing in my seat.

"Craig, are you aiming to let me touch you tonight? I can't wait much longer to know the answer to that question."

"You don't like plans, remember?" His face didn't give anything away as he turned the car off and reached into the back seat for our bags.

I ran ahead to unlock the door and turn on the lamp I had seen just inside the door earlier. The room was even cozier at night, and on another night I would have wanted to sit on the couch to enjoy it. That night I didn't want to waste any time. I was ready to run straight to bed.

Craig carried the bags to our room and I followed on his heels and jumped on the bed before he dropped them on the dresser next to my old shoes. He found the switch on the bedside light and sat in the chair beside the nightstand to take his shoes off.

"I like this room," he said. "It looks more like you than the one at home."

I smiled and turned the quilt back, unable to believe that he wanted to sit in the chair and talk about the room when all I wanted was to get him out of his clothes and into the bed.

"It looks like me because Nana knew what I'd like. Red was my favorite color when I was little. She remembered that all these years."

"You never told me your favorite color," he said. "Mine might be red, too, now that I've seen this room."

"Good, we have something in common," I said, stepping out of my pants and reaching for the hooks on my bra. "Come on, Craig. Are you just going to sit there all night?"

He stood up, but didn't give any indication that he was in a hurry for anything. I walked across the mattress on my knees, naked, and reached out to pull him over to the bed. He took a step forward and sat on the side of the bed, fully clothed.

I reached for his belt buckle, but he grabbed my wrist and moved my hand away. Tears sprang to my eyes before I could stop them. He couldn't do this again. My heart would break and other parts would suffer even worse.

He pushed me gently back on the pillows. "Don't cry, Penny. I won't hurt you. Just relax for a minute."

"Craig, I've waited all day. I can't relax now." I tried to remember how much was left in the bottle in my purse. If he rejected me, I would go into the bathroom and drink myself numb.

He shifted his weight off the bed and I breathed easier, but he only repositioned himself to face me and sat back down.

"Why are you doing this?" I tried not to sound angry.

He leaned forward. "Don't touch me, Penny. Trust me. Lie back and relax, and don't touch me."

Before I protested, he came forward and kissed me the way he had at Nana's house earlier. He spread light kisses over my face and neck, and then came back to my mouth, all without touching me with anything but his lips.

My body reached out for him, but I kept my hands glued to the mattress and closed my eyes. I considered pulling up a song to distract me, but decided against it. Instead, I thought about what I wanted him to do to me.

He held his mouth a fraction of an inch from mine, where I could feel the warmth of his breath, and talked to me. "Tell me what you're thinking, Penny."

"I'm thinking I might have to hurt you if you don't give me what I want soon."

He kissed me harder, using his tongue this time. "Tell me more," he asked. "Tell me everything you're thinking."

"I want you in me. Damn Craig, you're driving me crazy. I want you to get out of those clothes and love me."

I raised my hand and he pushed it back down.

"Love you? Don't you think I can love you with my clothes on? Don't you think I loved you all day? Didn't you feel any of my love?"

"I think you love me, Craig."

"I *know* I love you, Penny. I even think you love me. But you don't know it."

He kissed me again. I pushed his words out of my head and thought only with my body. "Please, Craig."

"Please what? Tell me what you want. For once, Penny, think about yourself."

"I want to come. My whole body aches from wanting you. I want you to make me feel good. I want you to make me forget everything I've ever known and think of nothing else except how good I feel with you."

Craig gave me everything I asked for, without letting me touch him.

"It's about you this time, Penny. It's about you learning the difference between love and sex, and about you understanding that you don't have to earn either from me because I want to make you feel good every way I can."

Later, he held me while he fell off to sleep. I stayed awake for hours, thinking how crazy and unfair life was. I deserved love from the parents who didn't care one thing about me. I didn't deserve this much love from Craig, because I didn't know how to return it and because I had allowed my body to be excited when Billy touched me.

I especially didn't deserve Craig's love because I wanted to sneak away from him and find a drink, even after what he had just done for me. I wanted to be too drunk to remember that I had forgotten, for ten long years, to have favorite colors, or favorite foods, or favorite television shows and had settled for accepting whatever I got.

Chapter 19

We left town promising we would be back the next time Craig had two days in a row off work. I might have agreed to stay in Crayfield forever if Craig had a job there, or if they had a real club or show where I could get a singing job. Having family around to spoil me and to eat meals with brightened my spirits. What happened with Craig in Crayfield affected more than my spirits.

For weeks my heart beat fast and my mind stayed fixed on Craig every time I thought about those nights we had spent in our red and white bedroom in the barn house. On the second night, he had decided that it didn't have to be only about me anymore.

He let me touch him that night, and we made love until we were both too exhausted to move. Then we started up again the next morning, and made an excuse to go back over to the barn house while Nana rested after lunch. I couldn't get my fill of my husband. He said he would need another vacation when we got home just so he could rest up.

I figured sex was good for music, too, because Craig played his guitar every night after we came home from Crayfield. He even put some music to the songs in our notebook that he hadn't touched in months. Because he seemed so happy, I couldn't work up the nerve to tell him what happened with Billy on the night of our graduation. Instead, I told him I had taken a special liking to country music.

"It's what I started out on," I explained. "I sang Loretta Lynn songs when I was a little bitty thing. And I sang country all that time at Harvey's, so I have those songs ready."

Craig said he would do whatever made me happy. "Since we're closer to Nashville than New York anyway, this is probably the best thing for you."

Billy and John weren't interested in playing country, so they decided to look for another band. They left the name of Coal's Crew for me if I wanted to use it for my next group.

Craig made up signs to put on the music store bulletin boards: female vocalist and husband, lead guitarist, seek members for country music band. Within a week we were practicing with a new group.

We lucked into three guys--Boomer on drums, Tommy on bass, and Tinker on keyboard--who had worked together for over a year with another female vocalist. They already knew a few of my songs. We also picked up Mike, a fiddler who claimed he had played on Printer's Alley in Nashville a few times and could pick out any song the first time he heard it. Boomer and Mike sang, although neither wanted to be a front man.

I decided to use the name Raven with this group. Craig said he wouldn't object if I used Coal instead of Osburn, because Raven Osburn didn't sound as good as Raven Coal.

"Maybe I need an alias too," he teased. "We sound like the seven dwarfs or something with Boomer, Tinker, and Raven."

We got together every night for the first few weeks to practice in Boomer's garage. Boomer drove a Sterling beer delivery truck in the daytime, and kept a well-stocked refrigerator in the garage. After rehearsals we sat in lawn chairs, drank beer, and talked business.

The new group didn't like the name Coal's Crew since a group of kids had already used it before. We decided on Raven Coal and Friends. Craig liked the idea of using my full name, even if it wasn't my real name.

After we decided on the name, Tinker set his beer on the ground and chewed his fingernails until Mike finally asked if something was eating at him. "If you aren't happy about the name, speak up now," he said.

"It ain't the name. These nightly rehearsals are causing problems between me and Sharon. She's on my ass constantly about not spending enough time with her."

Boomer told him to dump Sharon and that would solve a lot of problems, but the other guys gave in and decided two nights a week was enough. We only had three sets of material ready so I didn't agree. But,

I didn't raise a fuss over it because Craig thought it was important for everybody to get along.

After we cut back, I missed the beer almost as much as the music. Craig and I continued to practice, just the two of us, most nights at home.

Craig surprised me by having our own phone line run into the kitchen. "Irene has done enough for us already," was his reasoning. "We can afford a phone now that I'm working full time and we'll be making money with the band soon."

After we got our phone, I told Irene to lock the door from her side when she left at night. "We have friends drop by a lot now, and I don't want anybody slipping over to your side by accident."

The part I didn't say, and that I liked most about the situation, was that I didn't need to escape anymore. I was safe with Craig.

The first call I answered on our new phone came from Tinker. "Hey girl, are you the same teen-aged wonder that used to sing at Harvey's Tavern on weekends?"

I laughed. "I don't know about being a wonder, but I'm the fool that sang at Harvey's every weekend while I was still in high school. Harvey found out I made a hit at my junior high talent show and figured if the kids liked me, his drunks would too."

"The Captain over at the Langly Street VFW was one of your fans at Harvey's. He wants to hire us as the house band for the Friday and Saturday night dances over at the post. Wanna do it?"

"Yes! I want to sing anytime, anywhere," I reminded him. "If the others agree, I'll do it."

"Don't you want to ask Craig first?" he asked, laughing at how quickly I had responded.

"Craig wants to do whatever I want," I told him, without thinking how tired Craig was after installing carpet on Saturdays.

We took the VFW gig, with only enough material to cover three of our four sets. If anyone noticed, they didn't complain. "We had a request to repeat a song we did earlier," became a standard introduction for many of our songs. Boomer also killed a few minutes of each hour with jokes and announcements.

The job was fun. The VFW patrons were nicer than the regular drunks at Harvey's had been, and they left bigger tips even though the post paid us a regular salary and gave us free draft beer while we worked, without asking our ages.

What I enjoyed most was the enthusiastic audience. They clapped and they danced, and I felt like I was at a party instead of work. Before long, I got requests and wasn't lying when I said someone had asked to hear the same song over. We weren't background noise the way I had been to many people at Harvey's. Even the guys at the VFW bar stopped talking and turned to watch me sing. We were the reason many people came to the post, and the crowd grew larger each week.

With music back in my life, a barn house and family in Crayfield, and a husband who never complained about much, I was about as happy as I could be. I tried to think up ways outside the bedroom to show Craig how much I loved him so he would be happy, too. I cooked his favorite food, folded his boxer shorts into little squares the way his mother showed me, and massaged his back after he worked hard.

And I hid most of my drinking from him so he wouldn't worry about me so much. He never knew about the bottle I kept in the back of my Kotex box.

Tinker's girlfriend, Sharon, started dropping by while the guys were at work. She acted like she was doing research on me sometimes, asking personal questions that I didn't want to answer. One night she even followed me around the club during my break to dig into my private thoughts some more.

"Are you ever sorry you got married so young?" she asked.

"Craig's a good husband," I told her, taking a mug of beer from Charlie the bartender and gulping it down so I could finish it before my break ended.

"That's not what I asked. He may be a good husband, but you're still young. I see the way men look at you. If you were single you could have your pick, or play them against each other and get everything you want out of them."

"I guess I don't want much," I said, "because that thought never entered my mind." I decided then that I didn't enjoy Sharon's friendship in the least.

"I make sure Tinker knows I always have my eyes open," she bragged. "If another guy comes along and shows me something better, I'll drop poor old Tinker like a hot potato. Knowing that keeps him on his toes and gets me what I want."

"What do you want?" I still resented her for making him cut back our rehearsals. It wasn't my intention to give her what she wanted so she'd stay around.

"I need lots of attention. I want flowers and dinners in nice restaurants. And, of course, flattery and gifts. What girl doesn't? Check this out," she said, flashing a diamond ring in my face. "I told him to put a ring on my finger or he wasn't getting any more sex, and I wouldn't accept anything under a caret."

The ring was beautiful. I switched my beer mug to my right hand so she wouldn't be staring at the thin, gold band on my left hand.

"So you're engaged? When's the wedding?"

"Probably never," she admitted. "Like I said, I keep my eyes open for something better. If Tinker thinks I want to spend the rest of my life in dumps like this so he can earn a couple extra dollars, he's got another thought coming."

"Sharon, music isn't about money." I started to set her straight but Craig strummed his guitar strings to remind me that they were back on the stage waiting for me. I sat my mug on the bar and ran, leaving Sharon as ignorant as she started out.

I kept my eye on her the next set. She didn't return to the table where Mike's wife and Boomer's girlfriend sat. She stayed at the bar, touching the men while she talked, and flirting. She danced with several of them and stayed on the floor to talk longer when the song ended, right in front of Tinker's face.

On the way home I asked Craig if he had noticed the way Sharon acted and what he thought. "I can't believe she does that right in front of him," I said. "She told me she probably won't marry Tinker and she's fishing for somebody better, but she asked for that big ring anyway."

"It's not our business," Craig reminded me.

"What if I did things like that to you? What if I told your friends I was keeping my eyes open for someone better, aiming to dump you if another man offered to buy me stuff? Wouldn't you want someone to tell you?"

"Not if I couldn't see it for myself." He answered too fast, leaving me to believe he had thought the question out before I even asked it. "Sometimes people love somebody enough to overlook things that outsiders don't understand. It's Tinker's business to decide how much he loves her and what he'll put up with."

"I think what she's doing is wrong," I told him.

"Do you want to talk about Sharon all night, or hear my good news?" he asked.

"I'm done. Tell me good news."

"Channel Twelve is coming to the post to film us while we play next Saturday. They're doing an ad for the annual picnic. Are you ready to sing on TV?"

I forgot all about Sharon and Tinker. "Yes! Oh my gosh, Craig, this is so exciting. We really get to be on television?"

"We won't be on long," he said. "Probably not even a whole song, but it's a chance for you to be seen."

I was already sorting songs in my mind, trying to decide what to sing. Maybe Irene would fix my hair that night and help with my make-up. My stomach churned so that I could barely control my excitement. I leaned across the seat to kiss Craig's cheek. He held my hand the rest of the way home and listened to me repeat, "I can't believe it," over and over.

By the time we got home, I was wide awake. Craig was ready to drop over dead after working all day and playing music half the night, so I kissed him and sent him to bed. I went to soak in a bubble bath and unwind.

By the time the bubbles melted and the water turned cold, I had decided on "Me and Bobby McGee" as my television debut song, and jeans and a halter-top with western boots and hat for my costume. My mind and body felt relaxed as I patted myself dry with the towel, and I thought I was ready to curl up next to Craig and drift into a night of pleasant dreams about singing on television.

As I turned to leave, and faced the full length mirror that I had hung on my bathroom door in an effort to duplicate some of the magic of Nana's yellow room, I couldn't resist the opportunity to rehearse. I held an imaginary microphone and practiced facial expressions and dance moves to the words of the song.

The excitement that I had shut down with my bath returned to chase away sleep again. I wore my towel to the bedroom, dropped it on the floor, and snuggled up to Craig's back. He kept on sleeping, without acknowledging my naked body pressed against his flesh.

I tried to sleep with him but my mind still ran off on other things. Focusing on a song wouldn't work to clear my head that time; it only made things worse.

I needed either sex or alcohol. Craig didn't respond when I kissed the back of his neck, so I went to the bathroom and emptied the bottle in the back of the Kotex box.

Chapter 20

Irene planned her whole day around getting me ready for my TV appearance. While she cut layers in my hair, curled it around plastic rollers, manicured my nails, applied a peel-away mask to my face, and then fluffed curls out under the brim of my hat, she announced my debut to every customer in the shop. Some promised to come to the VFW, either in hopes the camera would catch them in the audience, or to show support.

When she finished with me, she and her husband followed us to the post so she could refluff and spray my hair, and touch up my make-up in the women's room at the last minute.

"Break a leg," she wished, kissing the air beside my face so she wouldn't leave her lipstick on my cheek or smash my hair. "I hope that's what I'm supposed to say to a singer and not something like break a neck or sprain a vocal cord." She hugged Craig and blew a kiss at the rest of the guys before running out to join her friends at the front row table that they had been saving since before we arrived.

The crew from the TV station told us to perform the same as we would if they weren't there. "We'll turn the cameras on when we're ready. Pretend you don't know we're here, and you'll look natural."

They actually filmed the whole song, but warned us they would only show part of it on the air. "We'll cut clips from it," the announcer explained. "Then we'll show a little of the interview with you and some shots of the audience. We may get some dialog from them too, but rest assured we'll only use positive comments if we do that."

"When will it be on?" I asked. "I hope it isn't while my husband is at work."

"It'll air twice during the news on Monday," he told us. "Once during the six o'clock spot and again at eleven, unless a major story breaks in the meantime and bumps you."

Craig came home early that day so he would be there for both programs. I made hamburgers, French fries, corn on the cob and baked beans, and we turned the TV around to face the table so we could watch it while we ate but my stomach was so nervous I could hardly force my food down.

"Are you sure it's on the right channel?" I asked, after the local sports and the weather both aired, and it seemed time was running out.

Craig took a few steps toward the TV to check the dial, and my face came on the screen. He ran back to his seat and grabbed my hand.

They showed the best part of my song, and then cut away to keep the camera on each of the guys for a few seconds. Craig looked like a professional, picking out his part and then nodding at Tinker so the cameraman would turn to him.

Next, they showed me answering questions about how long we had been together as a group, and where people could come to hear us. I invited everyone in the TV audience to come to the picnic, and to come to the weekend dances, wondering where they'd put them all if they showed up.

Craig squeezed my hand and winked, like he was proud of me. "You're on the way, Penny. Raven, I mean. I feel it in my bones. This was a big break."

"Look!" I interrupted. "It's Irene."

"I'm so proud of that girl. She has overcome some huge obstacles in her life, but she plugged ahead with her goals in front of her, never complaining. She had very little help or encouragement from anyone. She's a hard worker who deserves great things." After she said that, she turned directly to face the camera and waved.

"Come on out, people. Support this local girl and help her get to Nashville where she belongs," she said, like a professional announcer.

The crowd screamed and cheered as the camera panned the room and settled on Charlie, standing behind the bar. "She's the best singer anywhere around here, and she packs the house every weekend," he said, raising a mug of beer in a toast. "Come early if you want a table."

My eyes filled up. "I can't believe they said such nice things about me. Everyone was so nice."

"They aren't just saying that to be nice," Craig told me. "You really are great. They told the truth. I was worried about your song choice, but it ended up working out fine with the country look."

I pushed my plate aside. What little appetite I had disappeared the second Irene's face had appeared on the screen.

"You know what, Craig? I just realized that Irene really has been like a mother to me, and I don't think I've ever told her how much that means to me."

"It's not too late to tell her," he said. "We have a phone if you want to call her."

"I'll call after I clean up the kitchen." I needed a few minutes to remember everything and plan out how I wanted to say it.

Craig offered to help with the dishes but I chased him off to the couch where he wouldn't disturb my thoughts. He picked up his guitar to practice the song he had been writing, and I started on the dishes, rehearsing my lines to Irene in my head while I worked.

I forgot every word I had practiced when Craig called out to me. "Your mother just pulled up out front. Did you know she was coming?"

I grabbed the towel and dried my hands, watching her come up the side of the house as I walked toward the door. "She's alone. I wonder if something happened to my dad."

He tried to ease my mind. "She probably saw you on TV and wants to congratulate you."

"Not my mother. She'd never do that and you know it."

She came down the sidewalk in a huff and pounded on the door until I opened it. She charged past me before I could ask what she wanted. My first inclination was to push her back out and lock the door. No doubt, she wasn't there to be nice.

"I have half a mind to smack you," she growled at me. "But I think I'll save that for Irene."

Craig leaned his guitar against the wall and stood up to face Momma. "You won't smack anybody around here." He said it firmly, but without yelling, just like Irene. "Mrs. Martox, I think you owe Penny an apology for barging in here with that tone. You haven't even told her why you're upset."

"She knows why I'm upset," Momma said, looking at me instead of Craig. He had the good sense to put his guitar in the case and slide it behind the couch in case she went on a rampage.

"No, I don't know why you're upset," I said, resenting her more as my excitement drained. That meant I was letting my mother control me on one of the most exciting days of my life. "I'm not sure I want to know, Momma. I'm busy tonight and don't have time for this."

She snorted and rolled her eyes. "You don't look busy to me. Weren't you washing dishes? I think they'll wait."

Craig came over and put his arm around my shoulders. "Penny doesn't need any trouble tonight. If you want to visit without causing trouble, you can sit down. If you can't be nice, I want you to leave now."

"Who do you think you're talking to, punk? Don't try to boss me around because you'll find out I'm more than you can handle."

"This is my home and my wife," Craig said. "I'll do what I have to do to protect them."

He squeezed my shoulder and I knew he aimed to make me feel good and to chase Momma off before she got the best of me. But I couldn't stop it when more resentment came forward. I wanted the pleasure of chasing her off on my own. This was my first opportunity to face her as one adult to another.

Momma ignored Craig and tore into me like he didn't matter. "How could you let that woman get on the TV and spread those nasty lies about me? Irene did this to get even because she never liked me. She's nothing but a butt-in and a lying bitch."

Momma didn't take a seat or leave. I wondered if she even considered this causing trouble, since it was about as nice as she ever got. I smiled at Craig so he would know that I wasn't aiming to let her swipe my good mood out from under me.

"Momma, Irene didn't mention your name one time, and I didn't hear her tell any lies. How did you like my song?"

"You didn't bother to mention that I taught you to sing in the first place, or that Harvey gave you your start," she accused. "Oh no, Penny Sue was selfish as usual, acting like she got on the TV all alone. And what kind of song was that? You think you're too good for country now? You can't get above your raising, Penny Sue."

"Did Daddy see me?"

"See what I mean?" she asked Craig. "Even when I point things out to her, she can't stay on anything but herself for one second. I can't believe I raised such a spoiled brat."

I laughed. "You didn't raise anybody, Momma. Whatever I turn out to be—a brat or a famous singer—you don't need to take any responsibility for it. You have to actually do something for or with a kid to raise her. I don't remember you doing anything."

Her head shook and her mouth drew up in silence for once, while she worked out what she wanted to say next. "Considering how I never wanted a kid to begin with, you ought to be thankful I took it in my heart to keep you at all. Gladys Martox threatened to run off with you. She took you off to her house aiming to keep you away from me for good. I rescued you from the old goat and brought you up here so I could keep you."

I stared at her, wondering why she had done it.

"I gave up everything for you," she reminded me again.

"I'm sorry you did that because Nana loved me more," I told her.

She searched for something to bring me down. "You ruined your Daddy's life too. He's never been happy up here."

"You can't pin that on me. You ruined Daddy's life, or maybe he ruined it himself by staying with you instead of taking me back to Crayfield like he should have."

Momma waved her arms for emphasis, but her words still rang pathetic in my ears. I knew I had finally held my own with her, maybe even beat her at her own game.

"I think you should come to Harvey's tonight and make another apology. Besides making me look like a fool, you ignored all the people that put it in your head you could sing anyway. That ain't no way to pick up fans."

"I'll think about that," I told her. Craig frowned at me. "You go on down there and wait. I'll come along as soon as I come to the understanding that you're right."

She put her hand on the doorknob but turned back to say one more thing before she left. "You tell Irene she'd better hope I don't run across her anywhere because I'm liable to take her apart piece by ugly piece."

She walked out and slammed the door. Craig shook his head. "That woman has some serious problems, Penny. She never one time said a word about how good you sounded, or how pretty you looked."

I shrugged my shoulders. Momma was already gone from my mind. "I wish they could pick up Channel Twelve in Crayfield so Nana and Pappy could see me. I'm going to stay up to watch it again. Does that make me conceited?"

He shook his head and pulled the guitar back out. "As far as I know, there's nothing conceited about you, Penny. I'm staying up with you."

Irene called me before I got around to calling her. "You looked great! And you sounded even better," she added. "I'm so proud of you."

I giggled. "Thanks, Mom. I looked good on account of all your hard work on my face and hair."

"That's not entirely true," Irene said. "You're a beautiful girl with no help from me."

"Irene, I've never told you how much it means to me that you act like a mother to me. Thanks." The words weren't enough, but I didn't know how to say it any better. "I guess if I ever have a kid, I'll need you to teach me how to be a mother."

"Thank you, Penny. You've made my day." She sounded like she might cry, and for a second I thought I had messed up another adult life. "I think you have enough love and experience to be a great mother with no help from me, but I would like to be a grandma."

"It's a deal," I said. "Just don't get in a hurry about it because it'll be a long time. By the way, you looked great on TV too. Thanks for what you said."

"I meant every word of it," she said.

With the good stuff out of the way, I told her about Momma's surprise visit. "Craig thinks she has serious problems. I agree. Maybe she's crazy and can't help being such a bitch."

"What about your dad? Did he have anything to say?" Irene asked.

"Come on, Irene. You ought to know he didn't come with her. They haven't done anything together in years. If he saw me on TV, he hasn't let me know and probably never will. I think his problems might be more serious than hers."

Irene said she had to go because dinner was ready. "I'm going to watch again at eleven. Enjoy your moment in the spotlight, Penny. And don't let Kitty bring you down. Don't pay any attention to her threats against me. I almost wish she would come at me once so I'd have an excuse to give her what she deserves."

Craig put his guitar down again and came over to the sink with me. Instead of picking up the dishtowel, he stood behind me with his arms around me.

I finished my work quickly and turned in his arms to face him. "I'm happy Craig. Truly happy. I think I'm about to get over my parents. I don't care much what they do or don't do. You and Irene make my life good.

He pulled me to him and kissed me. "We have time to celebrate before the eleven o'clock news," he suggested.

I led him to the bedroom, thinking the day couldn't get any better, unless maybe he dozed off quickly after the news so I could have a drink to finish the celebration.

Chapter 21

My mother disappeared from my life again as quickly as she had dropped back into it. The excitement of the TV spot wore off, and life returned to normal, except for the occasional person who came into the club and recognized me. One man asked for my autograph.

We didn't return to our barn house until mid-August, when Craig's dad gave him the whole week off. August was the worst month of the year in his business, because people spent their money on vacations and back-to-school clothes. The installers appreciated the drained budgets of their city, because it was also the hottest month to haul carpeting in and install it.

By then, Craig was exhausted from working six days and two nights a week. All he wanted when he finally hit the bed at night was to fall off to sleep as soon as possible. I suggested the farm hoping a week there would revive him. I wanted a repeat of the first time we had stayed there, when our sex life had been the most exciting ever.

If Craig took interest in me again, maybe I wouldn't stay up half the night drinking myself into a stupor. I needed more alcohol all the time to put me out, and it was getting harder to sneak my drinking money out of the budget without Craig asking where it had gone.

I packed two bottles in my make-up bag, hoping I wouldn't need them, and we drove to Crayfield on Sunday. We arrived in time to eat at Nana's house, with Wanda and Gwen.

While Wanda and I cleaned the kitchen, Craig sat in the living room with my grandparents and fell asleep in the middle of Pappy telling him about Uncle Bobby opening a second hardware store in town. Wanda motioned me to come look at Pappy covering Craig with a crocheted afghan even though it was about a hundred degrees in the house.

Wanda whispered good-bye and said she'd be back in a few hours, after she took care of a few things at home. I lifted Craig's feet and slid in under them on the end of the couch.

Pappy sat back in his chair and spoke quietly to me. "Penny Sue, I think that boy works too hard. He's thinner than he was the last time you were here, and look at the circles around his eyes. That's not a good sign."

"I feed him," I answered defensively, while examining my husband for signs of weight loss. "He works six days for his dad, and plays music on the weekends. I've tried to get him to give up the Saturday carpet installation, but he likes the overtime."

Nana's weak voice surprised me because I thought she was sleeping. "Are you working, Penny Sue?"

How could she take Craig's side over mine? I felt betrayed. "I sing on the weekends," I said. "And I keep the house clean and cook the meals."

"With no children and only two rooms to put in order, I don't reckon that takes up all of your time, does it? Maybe you should work part-time and take some pressure off that boy to put in those overtime hours."

"Careful, Nana," Pappy warned. "Don't get mixed up about who you're talking to. This here's Penny Sue."

I didn't understand his warning. Nana seemed clear-minded to me. Was he trying to tell me she was confused?

"I know, Claude. She's not Kitty. But I won't sit back and watch her turn into her Momma if I can help it. She does have the woman's blood running through her, remember."

He patted Nana's hand, and smiled at me. My thoughts ran off in different directions. Surely Nana didn't think I was like Momma. I refused to be like her. If Craig was thinner, it wasn't my fault. I cooked a good meal for him every night.

"I guess I'll take Craig over to the house and put him to bed," I said, gently shaking his shoulder to wake him. "He'll be fine after gets a good night of sleep."

"That place will be stifling after being shut up so long. Why don't you sleep here tonight? Tomorrow we'll air the house out and get some fans over there," Pappy suggested.

"Wanda won't mind if you take the bed in here," Nana said.

"We'll be fine over there." I wanted to get away from them and sort out the confusion they threw on me. "We're used to the heat. We don't have a window or a fan in our bedroom at home." I shook Craig's shoulder again, with more energy this time. I wanted him to support my decision to leave, but he didn't budge.

If he was going to sleep this early, I wanted to be where I could stay up without disturbing anyone, or where I could drink without alerting anyone. I wouldn't be sleepy for hours.

After another round of shoulder shaking, more violent than the last, Craig straightened up and folded the afghan. "It might be easier to just stay here tonight, Penny." As an apology for falling asleep and a plea for me to hurry and let him get back to sleep, he added, "I guess the drive really wiped me out."

Careful to hide my rising panic, I promised him that easy wasn't an issue. "I'm not a bit sleepy, so I'll drive over there and carry our things in. You can go straight to bed and I'll unpack and straighten up while you sleep."

Nana motioned for Pappy to help her out of her chair. "We'll go on to bed and let you two work out your plans," she told me. "Whatever you decide is fine by us."

Pappy stared at me while he helped Nana out of the room, and called over his shoulder when they were out of sight. "If you decide to go over there, take that extra fan from the bottom of the pantry. Don't let Nana's gruff words upset you. Her resent isn't really meant for you."

I said thanks and Craig stood, knowing that my mind was already set on leaving. He went directly to the car without saying a word to me. I went to the pantry for the fan, said good night to Nana and Pappy, and drove Craig across the field to our house.

He walked through the stuffy house and crawled into bed, without opening a window, turning on a light, waiting for me to bring in his toothbrush, or kissing me good night, and he still hadn't said a word. I tossed possibilities around in my head while I carried our bags inside and opened windows. He might have been upset because he wanted to sleep in the big house where it was cooler. Or he could have been coming down with something. The circles under his eyes might indicate a cold.

I hoped he was tired, so he would be over it the next day. Upset or sick might last for days and ruin the vacation, along with my plans for a sexual reawakening.

I left the clothes in the living room so I wouldn't disturb Craig, and unpacked the small bags, putting our toothbrushes in the rack and our other toiletry items in the medicine cabinet. It felt like home – everything in place and my husband sleeping through my needs.

Nothing in the house reminded me of the early days I had spent there. It was as though time had exorcised that part of my life, along with my parents, from my mind and heart. The spare bedroom was empty. I peeked in, thinking one day we might fill it with music equipment, and moved on to the kitchen. Without groceries, there wasn't much to do in there. I checked to see that the appliances worked, and before I flipped the light switch to leave the room, it dawned on me that someone paid to keep the utilities running when we weren't there.

How naïve had I been not to think of the utilities, or upkeep on the property all those years, especially in the months since it had been ours? Someone mowed the grass and paid the bills. Nana and Pappy must have thought I was an ungrateful brat when I didn't think to thank them.

At the risk of hurting Nana's or Aunt Janet's feelings, I quietly rearranged the furniture in the living room. I preferred the couch against the interior wall so I could sit on it and look out the picture window at the field during daylight hours. Also, with it in that position, I could sit on the end to drink and Craig wouldn't catch me off guard if he walked in on me.

That reminded me that I had bottles under the couch cushions at home that I needed to get out. I usually did that on Sunday night, and carried them to the alley for trash pick-up on Monday morning.

Physically exhausted but mentally wide-awake, I collapsed on the couch with an unopened pint of Bacardi rum, the drink least likely to alert Craig's nose. The bottle was empty before my eyelids felt heavy.

I stripped my clothes off and dropped them on the floor in the hall to keep from waking Craig, and scooted my feet across the floor until I found the edge of the bed. Craig stirred when my weight hit the bed beside him, but he didn't wake.

The air was close and hot as an oven, so I stayed on top of the sheets and turned away from Craig so he wouldn't smell my breath. I hoped sleep would overtake me quickly, before I started tossing and before the disappointment of not making love in our red room set in. My body was too numb to want him, but he still played on my mind.

If he was mad, I hoped he slept it off.

Thoughts raced, and sleep escaped me. What if he stayed mad all week and didn't want to replay the last passionate weekend in the house? I had already drunk half of the booze I had packed. Wanda could probably get more, but I didn't want to ask her if I could avoid it.

I had to know what to expect, or I'd never get to sleep. I rolled over onto my back and my hand found Craig's. I laced my fingers between his. He didn't respond.

"Are you awake," I whispered.

"I'm trying not to be. Go to sleep, Penny, it's late and I'm tired."

"Please talk to me, Craig. Tell me you aren't mad."

"I'm not mad."

"You sound mad."

"I will be if you keep talking," he warned.

I tried to convince myself that he wasn't already mad, and that it would serve me best to keep quiet and sleep. But I had no control.

"Craig, who pays the utilities?"

He pulled his hand away from mine and huffed. "Go to sleep, Penny, or I'll move to the couch."

"Will you hold me? I promise I'll be quiet if you just hold me."

"No. This scene is getting old, Penny. You're drunk and it's too fucking hot in here." He sounded more disappointed than angry. "Just go to sleep. Please."

I took my pillow and went to the couch, knowing I'd never get to sleep if I stayed in the bed. Craig seldom mentioned my drinking, but when he did it was like a knife in my heart. Did he think I *wanted* my body to be unable to sleep without a drink? I envied his ability to close his eyes anytime he wanted and be asleep within seconds. I envied the way he could play music and believe in himself with a clear mind.

Craig deserved so much more than I was giving. He should have been living in a dorm somewhere, partying between classes instead of working his ass off to support a loser wife. If I had any courage or decency about me, I'd divorce him and set him free.

In a drunken haze, I lay awake until I saw the sun peek over Nana's house the next morning, planning Craig's escape. I would find a job when we went home and earn my independence so he could be free of me one day. The hard part would be convincing him that I didn't love him and I wanted out. That wasn't the truth, but it was the only way my plan would work. He had to believe that he was leaving for my benefit.

Craig slept through my shower, and a loud, unsuccessful search through the kitchen cabinets for something to eat. My stomach couldn't wait much longer so I decided I'd let him sleep, and go for food alone.

Wanda's car was still in Nana's drive. I left a note for Craig to tell him I was going for groceries, and drove over to see if Wanda would go with me.

"Thanks for rescuing me," Wanda said as we pulled onto the highway. "It's always hard to break away from them and this morning they used you as an excuse to keep me even longer. Pappy was sure you'd be over for breakfast, dying to see me."

"I did want to see you," I told her. "I could have found my way alone, but was happy when I saw your car still here and thought you might ride along to keep me company."

Actually, I was afraid that with too much time alone, I would lose the nerve to follow through on my plan.

"So Craig's still sleeping? Did you keep him up all night, or was he really that worn out when you got here?" she asked.

The plan started without much effort, although I felt like a traitor as soon as the first word was out of my mouth. "I didn't have anything to do with it, believe me. I stayed up all night, alone. Like most nights. I think I married the one exception to that male testosterone epidemic I've heard so much about."

"That's too bad," Wanda said, sounding as though she had personal experience that made her understand. "I'll bet that makes you sorry you got married."

"We were too young," I told her. "He only married me because of pressure from my parents. It was probably a mistake for a lot of reasons."

A couple of tears slipped out before I could catch them. They made my story believable, but damaged Craig more than he deserved. I was sure Wanda thought he was a jerk to let me down.

She tried to give me hope. "Maybe he'll perk up. It sounds like he does work a lot, and he seems to love you. Maybe he really is just tired."

"He works because he wants to," I lied. "To keep from spending too much time with me."

Wanda shed a few tears of her own and I felt like a heel. "I'm so sorry for you, Penny. First you got stuck with jerks for parents, and now this."

She stopped and put her hand over her mouth. "Forgive me. I shouldn't talk bad about your parents. That just slipped out because I'm sad for you."

"Don't worry about hurting my feelings. You can say whatever you want about my parents. I try not to be anything like them and I didn't ask to have them as my parents, so I don't take responsibility."

"Did you know Nana hired a lawyer once, to try and get you away from them? She wanted to bring you back and raise you herself," Wanda told me.

"I didn't know." And I wasn't sure how to feel. "Thanks for telling me. I thought everybody in Crayfield forgot me until that time when Irene brought me back to visit."

"We never forgot you. I'm glad you're coming back now, so we can get to know you again."

I smiled at my cousin, sorry that I had to be dishonest, so she wasn't really getting to know me at all. I reminded myself that my dishonesty was necessary for Craig's future happiness. Someday, when I knew her better, I could explain the truth to Wanda.

I parked in front of the market, beside the only other car in the lot, and we went inside. As I pulled a cart from the corral, I told her that I wasn't planning to get much, so it shouldn't take long.

"Want to come over to our house for lunch?" I asked. "That way we can talk without an audience. I'll send Craig out to explore the property with Pappy."

"Sure," Wanda said but she sounded unsure.

"Did you have other plans? We can do it another time if you'd rather."

"No, I don't have plans," she said. "I'll see if Mom will get Nana's lunch and eat with her."

I stopped in the middle of the aisle, disgusted with my ignorance. "I'm not thinking, Wanda. I'm sorry."

"Mom won't mind," Wanda said quickly. "Can we invite Gwen to join us, though? Her feelings might be hurt if she's left out."

"Yes, of course." That made it a celebration of sorts, and led me to a great idea. "Wanda, you're twenty-one, aren't you? Let's buy a bottle of wine, or champagne to celebrate."

She directed me to the liquor store after we left the grocery. I convinced her to buy wine for lunch, and champagne for me to use later to try and seduce my husband. Poor Wanda. I wondered how many other people had manipulated her as easily as I had.

We had chicken salad, potato chips, and olives for lunch. I drank two glasses of wine to every one they had.

Wanda giggled. "You'd better watch it, Penny. You'll be tipsy if you keep up at this pace."

"Maybe that's what I need," I said, faking a wobble to the refrigerator for the chocolate ice cream I had bought for desert. They exchanged grins when I worked up a slur in my speech.

"Thanks you two, you've taken my mind off my problems. I'm so happy to spend time with you."

Wanda explained that I hadn't realized the effects of wine and was sleeping off a headache, to excuse me from dinner at Nana's house. Craig ate the leftover chicken salad and pouted, while I finished off the wine. I had the champagne safely hidden in the vegetable bin, under a stalk of celery and a bunch of radishes. At least I had learned something from my parents.

On Thursday, our last day in Crayfield, Craig finally spoke to me with kindness in his voice again. We had washed the dishes and Nana was nodding off in her chair. "Are you ready to go home, Penny? Wanda tells me you have a bottle of champagne and some big plans waiting."

My heart skipped. Could he be seriously considering what I had wanted more than anything at the beginning of this trip? The long-term plan could wait until we went back home, if that was the case.

"I'm ready any time you are," I said, trying my best to ignore the satisfied look on Wanda's face.

While I brushed my teeth and removed my clothes, Craig lit candles—courtesy of Wanda and Gwen—and brought the champagne to the bedroom.

That night was better than any of the others we had spent in our little home. Better than any other night in my life. I drew as much love from him as I could, knowing it would have to last the rest of my life.

When things settled down and we turned to go to sleep, he pulled me close and asked, "Penny, why are you crying?"

"Tears aren't always a bad sign," I answered, thinking that mine were a combination of pure happiness and the pain of knowing I'd never have it again.

Chapter 22

Craig didn't let on if he noticed the difference in me after we returned from our trip. He didn't complain, and he didn't do anything to move in closer and fill the space I put between us. He let me drift away from him so easily that I almost wondered if he had the same plan in mind.

Ignoring my husband wasn't all that hard to do. It almost came naturally after watching my mother treat my father like he was invisible for most of my life. It killed me to purposely take on her behavior but I had to give her credit; she had been the perfect example of the worst possible wife.

Most nights I waited until Craig came home from work before I took my bath. I soaked for hours in bubbles, sometimes refilling the tub several times before I came out. Often, Craig went ahead and made our dinner because he was too hungry to wait on me.

He also did the laundry when he ran out of clean clothes for work, and he mopped the kitchen floor after I left a sticky mess in front of the stove for over a week. He never complained about what I hadn't done, or what he had to do to make up for my shortcomings.

Irene noticed the changes, even if Craig hadn't. "What's wrong with you lately? Penny, you're letting everything go, including your appearance. Aren't you feeling well?"

She had come in through the door from the shop and caught me off guard for this inquisition. She sat down on the couch uninvited. I felt attacked.

"Look at this place," she criticized, eyeing the breakfast dishes on the table, and the supper dishes in the sink from the night before.

When I failed to respond, she continued. "I've never seen it such a wreck, not even before your parents turned housekeeping over to you."

I turned my back to her, afraid of her ability to read my mind. "I've been tired lately. And maybe a little down in the dumps." Both statements were true, but I knew I had no reason to feel sorry for myself since I had purposely planned to bring everything crashing down on myself.

"Maybe you should see a doctor," she suggested. "Do you know why you're depressed?"

"I think it's over the music," I said, still unable to face her. "I'm afraid I'll never get anywhere. We don't work on any new songs because Tinker only wants to practice one night a week, and nobody with good connections will ever see me at the VFW. I'm in a dead-end."

"Your time will come." She tried to sound optimistic. "You're still young, Penny. Is that all that's bothering you?"

"Yeah, that's all." I mumbled and yawned, hoping to cut the conversation short.

She came over to where I was half-heartedly dusting the TV with my bare hand, and hugged me. Before she left, she took my chin in her hand and forced my head up until my eyes met hers.

"I don't think you're being honest with me, but that's okay," she said. "I'm always here for you. Remember that if you change your mind and decide you don't want to suffer alone."

I thanked her and waited until she had gone to the other side and closed the door between us before I ran to the bathroom, where she wouldn't hear me cry. The Kotex box sat on the front of the shelf, and I was certain I hadn't put it there. I was careful about that. Craig must have found my hiding place, and had probably tattled to Irene about my drinking and that's what caused her to come in and attack me. To hell with both of them. They weren't any more honest than I was if they were sneaking around in my personal things behind my back.

My pulse quickened, pounding blood into my head. Betrayal was the last thing I had counted on from either of them. They turned out just like the other pathetic losers in my life - my parents, Harvey, and even Lori, who had stopped writing after I married Craig.

Screw all of them. I dumped half a box of bath crystals in the tub and reached for the Kotex box while the tub filled. If they had taken my bottle, or the bag of valiums that Sharon had given me the last time she stopped over to whine about Tinker's failure to deliver the moon to her on a silver platter, I would have to hate them.

I pulled the pads out of the box and reached to the back. The bottle was there. So was the baggy of pills, and most significantly, so were the same ten pads that had been there since before our trip to Crayfield six weeks earlier.

I returned the pills and pads, and sank into the water to drink the rum and clear my mind. I intended to drink until there wasn't one thought left in my head.

When Craig came in from work three hours later he found me passed out in the tub, shriveled like a prune in cold water.

"Penny!" The panic in his voice broke my heart. I wanted to respond, to tell him that I was okay and ease his fear. But my body wasn't taking orders from my brain. The heaviness of my drunk had taken control of me. The best I could do was lift my eyelids for a fraction of a second. Even then, my eyes didn't focus, so I didn't know if he had seen my response.

He tried to lift me out of the tub but all he managed to do was get his clothes and the rug drenched. When he realized that he couldn't pull my waterlogged, dead weight over the side he released the stopper to drain the water and carefully rested my head against the back of the tub.

"I'll be right back," he said, and ran to get Irene.

"I was over here earlier, and she acted strange then," I heard Irene report as they came through the living room. "I've been worried about her for weeks, but she seemed more despondent than ever today."

"Holy shit," she said, when she saw the bathroom. "Did she make this mess?"

"No, I did trying to get her out," Craig admitted, positioning himself to reach under my arms and carry the top half of my body. "She has acted weird since we came back from Crayfield. Irene, I think she might be pregnant. I've tried to ignore her moods, and I don't complain because she's too tired to do anything. I wanted to give her time to adjust, and to tell me the news.

Irene sounded excited when she responded. "Do you really think she's pregnant? That would explain a lot of things."

"The same old Kotex box has been here forever. I dropped the toothpaste off my brush and it landed on the box, months ago. I noticed the toothpaste on the box the other day when I was searching through the cabinet for shoe polish. It's the same old box and it's still full," he reported.

They lifted me out of the tub. Craig sat on the toilet and held me while Irene wiped me dry with a towel and wrapped my robe around me. Then they carried my limp body to the bed and left me alone.

Craig thanked Irene. "I hate that you had to see her this way," he said.

I had succeeded in becoming such a total embarrassment to him that he had to apologize for me. It wouldn't be long before he would be happy to see me disappear from his life.

"Craig, her drinking is a big problem. If she really is pregnant that makes it even worse. I think it's about time for us to confront her about the drinking," Irene said.

His voice caught in his throat. "You're right. But I don't want to make her think we've ganged up on her. One of us should do it. You, or me?"

"It may be better for me to be the bad guy," Irene said. "It was my idea, and there's no point in making her angry with the one she has to live with."

My head cleared just enough to let their conversation enter and cause an explosion. Irene had overstepped her role as my make believe mother. If she wanted to control someone's life, she needed to have a kid of her own and leave me the fuck alone.

And what kind of pervert was Craig to sit around counting Kotex pads? I couldn't be pregnant. I hadn't thrown up one time. We had only had sex a few times in the last few months. I hadn't gained any weight.

He was wrong. They were both crazy. And they needed to mind their own business

But all my rationalizing didn't change the fact that I had forgotten to take my birth control pills with me when we went to Crayfield.

I heard Irene leave and waited, with my eyes closed, for Craig to come through the door and tell me how embarrassed or ashamed he was. But he didn't come near the door. The last sound I heard before going to sleep was him moving quietly around the kitchen to make his own supper.

The house was dark and silent when I woke. The clock said eight-ten, and I had no idea whether it was day or night. I hoped it was morning, and that Craig was gone to work so I wouldn't have to face him.

The hope was gone when I opened the door and saw him sitting on the couch, staring into space. "Why are you sitting in the dark?" I asked, turning the lamp on beside him.

He looked at the floor. "I didn't want to wake you."

I wanted to smack him for being such a fool. How could he be nice to me after all I had done? He should have slammed the pans on the stove when he had to make his own meal because I drank myself into a coma. He should have played his guitar, or watched the television to pass the time instead of sitting silently in the dark.

Most guys would have demanded answers or delivered ultimatums. Not Craig. He didn't know the first thing about how to protect himself from a crazy wife like me. He was just like my father.

"I was passed out, you fool. A sliver of light coming under the door wasn't going to wake me. A damned parade marching through the living room wouldn't have disturbed me."

He winced, obviously feeling the sting of my insult, or pain over the carefree way I had announced my drunken state without shame. I knew he tried to hide my drinking, from himself as much as from everyone else. That's what made it so easy for me.

He sighed. "I saved your plate in the oven. Hamburger and macaroni and cheese."

"What's wrong with you?" I shouted at him. "You ought to be mad, not nice. Why can't you act normal?"

"Normal? Penny, what's normal to you? Getting drunk and fighting? No matter what I do, you can't be happy. What do you want?"

I took my plate from the oven, pretending to ignore his questions because I sure couldn't answer them honestly. In my heart, I wanted to tell him that he was the nicest person I had ever known, and that I didn't deserve him. I had no idea what normal was; I just knew it wasn't me.

"Are you going to answer my questions? When you get through with those, I have an even bigger one," he said.

I rolled my eyes and answered with my mouth full. "I'm not in the mood to play twenty questions tonight, you'll have to find someone else."

He came and sat across table from me. With a tight jaw, he spoke very slowly. "Penny, I'm losing patience. I don't know what your problem is, but it's getting old. If you won't talk about it, you can't expect me to make it better."

"Congratulations, Craig. You're getting closer to normal now. Maybe you'll work up a real emotion when you hear this. I don't want you to make it better."

I focused on my hamburger, knowing that the hurt or anger that must be on his face at that moment would destroy me and my resolve to follow-through with my cruel plan.

He scooted his chair back, sending lightning bolts of pain through my head with the scraping sound of wood against wood. He stood beside the table until I finally looked up at him, and then he spoke.

"I hope you figure out how to make it better on your own then," he said calmly. "I hate seeing you this miserable."

He returned to the couch and picked up his guitar. The plan told me to yell at him before he strummed the first chord, but I couldn't do it. Being mean took a lot of energy, and I had used all of mine.

I carried my dishes to the sink, planning to leave them until morning. Tears poured as soon as my face was away from Craig. Crying seemed to be my normal. I didn't want to let him see so I filled the sink with water and washed the dishes.

My thoughts jumped from one thing to another, refusing to settle on any individual problem long enough to sort it out. Each miserable situation flashed up long enough to attach to the ones before and after it, and collect like a chain around my neck. The weight of that chain sent me to the floor, where I landed on my knees, in a pile of aches and tears.

Craig threw his guitar on the couch and ran to my side. "Are you okay?" he asked, reaching to help me up.

I smacked his hand away, buried my face in my hands, and leaned my head against the metal door on the cabinet. "No, I'm not okay. Craig, I think my brain exploded," I sobbed. "My head hurts so bad I can't even think."

He went to the bathroom and returned with a cold rag and two aspirins. "Hold this on your forehead and I'll get you a glass of water," he instructed.

I did as he said, and tried to cooperate when he pulled me up and offered to help me to bed. My legs, locked into place by the weight of the chains, refused to move. He picked me up and carried me. I buried my face in his neck to block the light and reduce motion.

Craig eased me onto the bed. He fluffed my pillow and positioned it under my neck, and pulled the sheet up over me. Then he kissed me gently on the head as he tucked me in.

"Let me know if you need anything," he whispered.

"I need you to hold me," I whispered back, angry with myself for ditching my plan when I was getting so close to having it right.

Chapter 23

Craig forgave me for every rotten thing I had done but I couldn't forgive myself as easily. I did move the guilt of my plan to a back row in my theater of self-loathing, however, once I admitted that I was pregnant. I couldn't forgive either of us for that devastating condition.

Craig and Irene didn't share my feelings. They couldn't have been more excited. 'Daddy' and 'Granny' spent every spare minute camped in the living room discussing names, and planning schools, and deciding how this child would look, talk, and be raised.

Craig's mother even took an interest in me. She called every day and dropped by often with lunch, claiming she wanted to make sure I ate properly. I knew she really wanted to make sure I wasn't drinking while Craig was at work.

All of them, along with Craig's dad and brother, brought in trunk loads of toys, blankets, books, highchairs, infant seats, clothes, and bottles that they had either found on sale, or in a garage sale, or received as a donation from someone whose child had outgrown it.

The less I thought about the baby and how it had affected my body and life the better. But there wasn't room to walk through our house for all the junk they had brought in to remind me, so my nerves were on edge constantly.

Sharon was the only person who understood my disappointment. She suggested abortion but, by the time I had admitted that I was pregnant and made an appointment with a doctor, it was too late for that. She stopped whining about Tinker and devoted her negativity to my condition for a few months. I learned not only to tolerate, but also to appreciate her.

Several times I thought about calling my mother. I knew she would have understood my disappointment, since she had felt the same about me. The only reason I didn't call her was that I thought it might give her too much pleasure to know that some other rotten kid was paying me back for the mistake of my own birth.

The VFW let us keep our gig until two weeks before my due date, and then asked us to allow another group to take our place through the summer. The guys said they didn't mind, and that they welcomed the break. I minded. If I couldn't perform for three months, I was afraid I would lose my mind, as well as my voice. Singing was the only part of my life that was tolerable.

According to my doctor and Mrs. Osborn, I had an easy pregnancy. I was never sick, didn't gain much weight, and wasn't terribly uncomfortable until the last few weeks. My misery was emotional, not physical and they didn't see that. I had planned to enjoy sex as much as possible during the pregnancy because I doubted I would ever want to do it again afterwards. Craig decided he was afraid he'd hurt the baby after the sixth month and forced me to live all that time with no music, no booze, and no sex.

The delivery wasn't so easy. The pain started while Craig was dressing for work, on June 12. He called Irene, even before he called his dad to say he wouldn't be in to work, and wanted to rush me straight to the hospital.

"It isn't time yet," I tried to convince him. "The doctor said to call when the pains are seven minutes apart. After that, I won't go to the hospital until he tells me."

That wasn't good enough for Craig. He wanted to do something immediately. I sent him to pack my toothbrush and gowns, and asked him to fix a breakfast that I never intended to eat, just to keep him busy until Irene got there to take care of him.

My water broke at noon, I arrived at the hospital at two, the doctor went home for dinner at six, and my stubborn son wasn't born until after midnight, by which time I wasn't sure I ever wanted to see him, or Craig, again. They moved me to a regular hospital room around three, and all I wanted to do was sleep.

"Your family has been here all night," the nurse told me. "Don't you want to let them in for a few minutes before they go home? I promise I won't allow them to stay long."

175

"I need sleep," was my final answer. "I'm too tired for guests."

She agreed to tell them, but I could see that she thought I was unfair. She stopped at the door to ask if that included my husband.

"I don't want to see anyone," I snapped.

Craig and Irene arrived the minute visiting hours started the next morning, bringing flowers, balloons, a teddy bear, and an outfit for the baby.

"He's gorgeous!" Irene's voice surely carried to the next block. "Penny, he looks just like you with that full head of black hair. I reserve the privilege of giving him his first haircut."

I smiled. I had declined the opportunity to feed him during the night, so I hadn't seen my son since they took him to the nursery to clean him after birth.

"He's perfect," Craig said, leaning over to kiss my hair because I turned my head away from him before he could kiss my lips. "The nurse said I can stay in here when they bring him for a feeding. Can I give him his bottle, Penny?"

"Sure," I said, thinking I'd be happy if Craig wanted to give him every bottle.

"We watched him through the nursery window for thirty minutes before we came in here," Irene told me. "He's by far the cutest baby down there. He opens his eyes wide and looks around already. I think he's going to be a smart one, too. What's his name?"

I looked to Craig for the answer. I hadn't thought about names but knew he had given it plenty of thought.

"Think he looks like a Jason. Jason Craig Osburn. Do you like that?"

I nodded. Jason sounded like a fad name to me. I knew hundreds of parents had already named their boys Jason that year, but it didn't matter to me.

"How do you feel, Penny? You had a long labor," Irene reminded me, as though my body didn't remember. "Have you been out of bed yet?"

"They got me up this morning, after the last of the spinal wore off. I don't feel so good yet," I admitted. "I'm tired and sore."

"We're going to take care of you," she said, and patted my hand like that was going to fix what ailed me. "I've already called Judy Lanterfield to take my customers so I can help you out for a couple of weeks while Craig works. I'll make sure you get plenty of rest."

I smiled, but didn't have the energy to talk. If she cared so much about my wellbeing, I wished she would leave and let me go back to sleep. The nurse had already warned me that she'd be back later, to take me to the shower and check my stitches. And the nursery would bring the baby to me, and the doctors—the obstetrician, the pediatrician, and the anesthesiologist—would visit. Someone would be in to pick up my menu selections and carry out my breakfast tray, and another someone would teach me how to bathe and dress my baby. Sleep was the last thing anyone seemed to want on my schedule.

Irene read my mind again. "I'll let you get started on your recovery now. I just wanted to drop in a minute to say congratulations, and I love you. I'm leaving now so you can get some rest, but remember you can call if you need me."

I let her hug me and said thanks for everything. I kept forgetting that Irene wasn't responsible for my pregnancy, or my marriage, or any other rotten thing in my life, so I shouldn't take my anger out on her.

"Give Jason a big kiss for his Granny Irene when you see him," she ordered on her way out. "Craig, you can call too if you need anything."

Craig pulled his chair up close to the bed and held my hand. "Thank you, Penny, for a perfect son. I love him already, and I love you twice as much as before for bringing him to me."

I smiled through tears. He loved me twice as much, and I was mad as hell at him. Nothing ever changed for us; I was always the one who couldn't deliver my end.

"I called your Nana. She said congratulations, and she loves you – same from Pappy and everyone in Crayfield. She doesn't think she can make the drive when Wanda and Gwen come to see him, so she wants us to come visit as soon as Jason can travel."

"Thanks for calling," I managed to force out.

"I called the guys in the band," he added. "But I didn't know how you'd feel about your parents, so I didn't call them."

"Good. I don't plan to tell them. Craig, I'm sorry but I really need to sleep. Do you mind?"

He wanted to sleep, too, but wouldn't go home and miss his chance to hold the baby. He moved his chair to the corner, leaned his head against the wall, and settled in.

On the third day, the doctor discharged me from the hospital, with my son and a box of formula. Craig made an early trip to the car to take the flowers and gifts, so when they took the baby and me down in a wheelchair he walked beside us carrying my overnight bag and the formula.

"Irene is waiting for us at the salon," he told me, when he saw how inept I was getting into the car. "She'll help out so you can rest when you get home. Mom said they'll come over after Dad gets off work tonight, but to call if you need her before then."

I leaned my head against the seat and tuned out his voice. I didn't care who came over, or when they came, as long as they poured their attention on the baby instead of me. I wanted to go to bed and wake up again when this whole nightmare ended. I felt as much like a mother as I did the Queen of England. I wasn't born into either role.

Craig carried the baby inside and put him in the bassinette that his mother had scrounged out of her attic and recovered, and then he went back out to carry my things in from the car. I crawled into bed and closed my eyes before he got back.

In the hospital, Craig had driven me crazy staring at the baby. He started up the same thing at home, after wheeling the bassinette from my side of the bed to his so he could sit on the edge of the mattress and watch. The kid did nothing, but he held Craig's attention until Irene came in.

"Anybody home," she called from the door.

Craig wheeled the baby out to meet her. "Penny's asleep. I'll keep him out here so I won't have to disturb her when people come in."

"Good idea," Irene said. "This little guy seems to be able to sleep through anything. Can I hold him?"

They sat on the couch, probably side-by-side and cooed and gooed and discussed every inch of his perfect little body. "Is Penny doing any better," Irene asked after she had run out of body parts. "Has she called him by his name yet?"

"Not that I've heard," Craig answered. "She hardly says anything at all, Irene. She didn't say one word on the way home. She went straight to bed, and didn't show any interest in Jason at all. I don't know if she has changed a diaper other than the one that the nurse watched her change before discharge."

"I think it's fairly common for new mothers to be afraid of their babies, and to go through a period of depression. It's called baby blues, or something like that," she explained. "We have to be patient and help her through this."

I tried not to listen. Neither of them understood. They couldn't help, and I doubted they had the patience to outlive my depression.

Sharon provided the help I needed. She stopped by while Irene, Craig's parents and brother, and the neighbor from across the street were all there, so nobody missed her when she slipped into the bedroom to visit me.

"I replenished your Kotex box," she whispered. "Ten valiums and a half pint of Southern Comfort. I'll come back one day while Craig's at work and bring more. You were smart not to breast feed."

"Thanks, Sharon. You're a life-saver," I told her. "They sent me home from the hospital with Tylenol. That wasn't going to get me far."

"The baby's cute. I know you aren't thrilled about being tied down like this, but you did a good job, girl."

I smiled. That was a big compliment coming from Sharon. Everyone carried on about how cute he was, and I honestly thought he looked like a shriveled old man. I hadn't been around many new babies, so I guessed that must be natural from the way they all reacted.

Craig had tried to get me to walk to the nursery to look at the other babies while I was in the hospital. If I didn't want to see my own, I sure wasn't interested in the others. I wished I had after they all made such a big deal about his appearance, so I could compare him to the others for myself.

After Sharon left, I ventured out of the bedroom and shuffled through the crowd to get to the bathroom. Craig and Irene both jumped up to help me, but I said I was fine. I took three valiums while I was in there, slurping water from my cupped hands to wash them down.

The mirror on the door haunted me. My face was as disgusting as my flabby stomach, with circles under my eyes and a puffy jaw line from the excess weight that hadn't disappeared when the baby was born. The doctor had cautioned me against any heavy exercise right away, but I'd never be in shape to perform without it. How could someone so small have destroyed so much of my life? It didn't seem possible.

My mother must have felt the same way when I was born and had never changed her heart about me. As much as I wanted it not to be true, I had to admit that I was just like her. Too sad to cry, I took a deep breath, and walked out into the crowd.

Irene jumped up from the couch. "Penny, I gave Jason his bottle at four because you seemed to be sleeping so soundly that we didn't want to wake you. He'll probably be ready to eat again in a few minutes. Want to sit here, and I'll fix the bottle for you?"

"I'm not very comfortable sitting yet," I explained. "I'd rather go back to bed if that's okay with you."

Craig got up to walk me to bed and said he'd feed the baby. I slept, or pretended to sleep, until everyone left. Craig brought the baby and my supper to the bed. He planned my meal so that I'd be finished eating before the baby wanted his next bottle and forced me to feed him while he washed the dishes.

It was the first time I had been alone with the baby. Without an audience, I was more comfortable but still didn't feel an overwhelming urge to cuddle or kiss the baby, the way Craig seemed to feel every time he held him.

Craig returned, camera in hand, to capture me burping Jason. He took a few shots, and then asked if I wanted him to get a diaper for me. I said no thanks, and handed the baby to him so I could go back to sleep.

Chapter 24

My son was six months old before I learned to control my anger and admit that I loved him. By then, his face lit up and he reached for Craig the instant he came into sight. After Craig, Irene was his next favorite person, followed by Gary and Mrs. Osburn.

He wanted little to do with me unless he was hungry or wet, and I was the only person in the room. That was understandable, since I had passed him off as long as someone else was willing to take care of him.

It was as though a shade had been drawn over the window between us, and I hadn't seen him clearly for all those months. And then one day the shade was raised and everything I had missed before suddenly became perfectly clear. Clear and shocking.

Jason was down for his afternoon nap when the truth finally came to me. He was in his crib, on the far side of the bedroom where Craig slept, and I peeked in as I walked past the door to get a sweater off the rack by the front door. He looked peaceful, sprawled on his back with his arms up beside his head, vulnerable, like he trusted me to protect him from any monsters that might come in after him.

I ran around the foot of the bed and snatched him out of the crib to hug him and apologize for the months that I had missed. He cried, understanding only that I had interrupted his sleep and nothing about my change of heart or how happy he should be that I wasn't going to stay like my mother.

I carried my baby into the living room and cuddled him close on my shoulder, the way I had seen Craig do, and rocked him back to sleep. That was a first. Craig was the rocker, unless one of Jason's Grannies happened to be around to take his place.

I whispered in the little ear so close to my face. "I'm sorry, Jason. Please forgive and trust me to make everything up to you. I didn't understand what I was doing, to both of us."

I begged his forgiveness until he finally curled his little body comfortably against mine and went to sleep. Instead of rushing him straight to his crib as I usually did the minute his eyes closed, I continued to hold him while he slept.

When his breathing grew regular, I pulled him away from my shoulder and rested his head in the crook of my arm to study his face. Finally, I saw in him what Craig must have seen all those times when he sat beside the bed to watch his son sleep, or in front of the infant seat to stare at his face while he played. Jason's face *was* perfect. He looked helpless and innocent, and his life depended on my love and protection.

Each beautiful little feature on his tiny face perfectly combined to form a miniature replica of Craig, only with my hair and my long fingers. Maybe he would use them one day to play guitar like his dad, or piano.

I gasped, startling him for a second, but he calmed down when I resumed rocking. He was the perfect combination of Craig and me, created in the red and white room that Nana had decorated in the house that Pappy had built. Nothing could be more special than this baby.

And no one could less deserve to be Jason's mother than I did. He should have been born to someone who had planned to have him, and who would have worshipped him from the moment of conception instead of shunning him the way I had. I hugged him closer repeating my apologies and promises.

"I'm ready to be your mother now," I promised. "I'll never act like Momma again. Never." It seemed an easy promise to make, since I had never wanted to be like her in the first place.

After putting Jason back in his bed to finish his nap, I went to the bathroom to flush everything I had stashed in my box. I didn't think I'd ever want to numb myself or look for ways to avoid my husband or my son again.

While Jason slept, I mixed up a meatloaf and peeled potatoes. Craig had turned into a decent cook, but still hadn't tried anything beyond the basics. He hadn't had his favorites in months, since I had quit cooking.

I left the potatoes soaking in salt water on the back burner, and took a bottle of formula out of the refrigerator to get ready for Jason. For once, I was anxious for him to wake.

It was Friday, Jason's night to stay with Craig's parents while we worked at the VFW. I wanted to pick him up when we got off, instead of waiting until morning like usual. We could slip into his parents' house and remove him quietly, without waking or inconveniencing anyone. I needed to spend every minute I could with my son, until I was positive he would be able to forgive me.

After strapping Jason into the highchair for a feast of formula and Gerber's strained green beans, I noticed how crowded our place had become. As I shoveled spoons full of baby food into his mouth, trying to keep up with his pace so he wouldn't fret between bites, I took inventory of Jason's things.

The highchair filled the space between the pantry and the cabinet when not in use, blocking the doors to both. There was barely space to walk through the living room with the playpen and rocking chair in there. There was no place left to put a Christmas tree, and Jason had to have a tree for his first Christmas.

He would need his own room soon. I wouldn't allow him to sleep on the couch and store his clothes in the bathroom the way I had, and I wanted him to have toys that didn't fit in a shirt box under the couch.

Irene wouldn't have any trouble renting our space if we moved. The other duplexes on the block rented as quickly as they vacated. I knew she would support my opinion that we needed a bigger place because she wanted the best for Jason.

I'd ask her about it when she came in to see the baby before she went home at the end of the day. With that thought, I realized how much I would miss having her on the other side of the door. Irene had been the most constant person in my life. Jason would miss her too, if he didn't get to see her every day.

She could still keep him on Saturday nights. And we could start making big Sunday meals, the way Nana had before she got sick. Then, Jason could see everyone he loved all together, at least once a week.

While I wiped Jason's hands and face with a washcloth, I tried to get him to talk. He made sounds, but they didn't mean anything. "Ma Ma," I said, dramatically enunciating the syllables, with my face close to his so he could watch my lips. He didn't say Momma, but he put his hands over my mouth and giggled. That was almost as good.

Irene came in before Craig. "It smells good in here," she called. "What are you cooking?"

"That's a meatloaf you smell. I'm going to mash potatoes and make green beans and a salad to go with it if you'd like to stay."

She reached for Jason and said Ralph would have already started dinner, otherwise she would have loved to stay. "I just came in to give my boy a hug before I leave," she said, squeezing Jason while she scattered kisses over his head. "He's growing up so fast, Penny. Can you believe he's already six months old?"

It seemed like a perfect time to discuss space after she made that comment. "Irene, I thought about the same thing earlier. He'll need his own room soon, so he can have a place to keep a dresser for his clothes, and a toy box. I'd like to get him a rocking horse, but there's nowhere to put one in here."

"A rocking horse, you say?" Irene smiled and looked from me to Jason. "You're concerned about room for a rocking horse and a dresser?"

"And a Christmas tree. I can't let Jason grow up the way I did. Irene, living here was good for me because I wouldn't have had you if we didn't. But I was embarrassed, never having a bed or a dresser or closet for my clothes. I never brought friends here. I don't want Jason to feel that way and the difference is, if we move away he'll still get to see you. I'm not like Momma."

"I see that. Penny you aren't anything like your mother. I'm glad you finally realize that."

"So am I," I admitted. "I think I realized a lot of things today."

"Good. Now, about space. I've given that some thought myself. If you want to stay here a little longer, I'm ready to give up the storage room to Jason. We'll need to remodel a bit, but it'll make a nice room. We can move the door to the other side and open that room up to your apartment.

My thoughts spun out a cute room real fast, with bunk beds, a rocking horse, and lots of toys.

"Actually, that room is bigger than your bedroom. You and Craig could move in there and give Jason your room," Irene offered.

"Where will you keep the dyes and towels?" I asked, hoping she had a great idea so I would be able to accept her offer without feeling guilty. That room had been full for as long as I could remember, with things Irene used often.

"I've been ready to cut back on my business for a long time, Penny. I don't need the money, and I don't enjoy the work the way I used to. Louise told me last week that she's giving up her station in a couple of weeks. I can eliminate her chair and vanity and build a supply cabinet in that space. I'll put a shelf over the sinks for towels, and everything will be fine."

"It's perfect for us, if you're sure you don't mind," I said.

Irene shook her head. "Not at all. Semi-retirement sounds great, now that I have a grandson to spoil. Maybe I'll be ready for full retirement by the time you have the next baby and you can have the whole house. Just don't do it real soon."

Craig found us in the storage room when he came home, planning the changes. He hugged Irene when she explained what we were doing.

"You have been so great to us. Thanks." He took Jason from Irene's arms and put him on his shoulders. "What do you think, big boy? Do you like your new room?"

I envied Craig's ability to carry on real conversations with Jason, even though he didn't understand a word.

"I'm out of here," Irene announced. "Enjoy your dinner and feel free to come in here to measure or plan, or work if you get the time and energy."

I ran to the kitchen to finish dinner so we'd have time to draw out the renovation before we went to the VFW.

"Do you think Jason is old enough to eat mashed potatoes?" I asked Craig when he followed me to the stove. "I think I'll go light on salt and pepper so he can try them."

"What happened here today?" Craig was confused, but happy. "Welcome back, Penny. You seem like your old self."

I mashed harder, wishing he wouldn't make a big deal out of things. I didn't want the pressure of his excitement, or of having to live up to anyone's expectations. I hadn't exactly succeeded at keeping one man happy, and now I had two of them to worry about. It wasn't going to be easy, especially if he watched over me.

"I feel a little better today," I said calmly, trying to deflate the significance of my change. "I have energy for a change."

"Maybe you're finally over being pregnant," he said. "I think the pregnancy and the long delivery took a lot out of you. As much as I would love to have a bunch of little Jason's running around, I'm not sure you should have any more children. Penny, I never want to see you suffer like that again."

He sat at the table and played with Jason while I finished making the salad and wondered if that meant he would like to have more little Jason's with someone else. "Will you put Jason's highchair at my end of the table tonight?" I asked. "I want to feed him his first real food."

Jason liked potatoes. We laughed until my sides hurt at the faces he made while he gummed his food and reached his hand out for more before he had swallowed the last bite.

Craig washed the dishes while I packed Jason's diaper bag. He said he'd call his mother to warn her that we'd pick Jason up before coming back home because she'd take the news better from him than from me.

"He's our son, so she'll have to agree," I reminded him.

We had time to measure the storage room and the window for curtains before we left. Both of us agreed it would be best to move Jason into to the bigger room, since he would have toys, and eventually friends over to play in his space. I already pictured the room in blue, with stars on the walls and red rugs and bedspreads.

***

Tinker told me I sang from my heart that night. "I was beginning to think you had lost it, but you haven't," he told me at the end of the last set. "I don't think I've ever heard you sound better."

Sharon agreed. "I wasn't even bored." Usually I hate sitting here but tonight it wasn't so bad. Penny, you really do have a great voice, I just don't understand why you waste it on country music."

Their compliments eased the last of my fears. I could be a mother and still sing. Why had I thought that having Jason meant my life was over? That was more of my mother's thinking, and made about as little sense as anything else she had said or done.

I waited in the car while Craig went into his parents' house to pick Jason up, but I changed him and tucked him in when we got home. Finally, I felt like a real mother. The Mrs. Sawyer type.

Chapter 25

"I'll take vacation days and stay here with Jason," Craig promised. "This is an opportunity you can't pass up."

I wrapped my arms around myself and squeezed, partly because I had stopped begging for hugs and maybe a little like an exaggerated pinch to see if I was dreaming. "I can't drive to Nashville alone, Craig. I've never spent a single night alone in my life, and I don't want the first time to be in a hotel room in a strange city." I agonized aloud. "Why can't you and Jason come with me?"

After seeing an ad for a country music contest in Nashville, Irene had snuck a tape recorder into the VFW and recorded me singing. She sent the tape, a completed application, and the twenty-five dollar entrance fee in without asking me first, like I had been before the first talent show years before.

"I could kill you!" I cried, half-heartedly. I was scared to death but excited at the same time.

"I entered you as a solo vocal," Irene said. "The guys in your band thought your chances of winning were better that way because the contest people will hook you up with studio musicians and judge you only on your vocals."

"Craig, you knew about this?" I couldn't believe he didn't say a word to me.

"He knew you'd do exactly what you're doing now – think of excuses why you couldn't go. And he knew you'd want to take the band but it's better this way," she assured me. "Penny, I've seen you become increasingly discouraged over the last year. You need to get out of the

VFW and expose your talent to people who have the power to move your career forward."

I moved Jason's tricycle out of the way so I could sit on the couch and think. He hadn't been away from me overnight since he was six months old. We were working on potty training, and he needed consistency. Everyone told me two was too young to train a boy, but he seldom had accidents and I wanted to prove them wrong. My son was special.

"What would I sing? And how long would I have to stay there?" I didn't think I could do it, but wanted the information before making the final decision.

"You'd have to be there on Thursday to rehearse with the musicians, and then compete on Friday. It would make sense to drive down there on Thursday morning and come back Saturday. That's not so long." Typical Irene encouragement.

After Craig offered to take off work to stay with Jason and work on the potty training, I didn't have a good excuse left not to go, other than I was a big chicken. I said I'd do it if they promised not to be disappointed when I didn't win.

***

Sharon came by for the first time in months. She had finally concluded that no other man would put up with her constant whining and inability to hold a job or carry on a conversation about anything other than herself, and married Tinker. Their wedding was much like ours, meaning no one was invited. She still complained, but about different things. Now she whined about Tinker's clothes on the floor, and that he woke her when she wanted to sleep.

"Tinker told me about the contest," she said, after she had run out of things to complain about. "Are you going to do it?"

I said yes, and admitted that I was afraid to go alone. I also told her that I feared I'd lose confidence in my singing if I didn't win the contest, more because I thought she wasn't interested enough to laugh at me than because I expected advice or sympathy from her.

"I think you should do it," she urged. "If I could sing like you, I'd do whatever I could to get out of the VFW and into some real money. I'll go with you." She threw that last part in as an afterthought.

I hadn't thought of asking anyone other than Craig to go with me. "Would you really do that? I thought you hated country music."

"I do," she said. "But I love excitement. This could be fun Penny, just the two of us on a road trip. And you could win some big money, or at least be seen by someone younger that those old geezers at the post. Think of the opportunity."

Nashville was where I needed to go if I ever hoped to make it big in country music. I knew that. For a long time after Jason was born, I had almost forgotten about my dreams. Once Irene found the contest, they returned quickly.

"Let me think about it," I said. "If you're serious about going with me, I may take you up on the offer. Irene already paid my entrance fee so I can't hardly back out."

Craig and Irene wouldn't let me out of it once they heard that Sharon wanted to go along. They each set out on separate missions. Irene searched for the right outfit and a new hairstyle, and Craig looked for a song that would showcase my voice and range.

Gary brought me a four-leaf clover and a rabbit's foot and told me I didn't really need either. He had believed in my talent since that first day when he had heard me sing on Teen Alley.

* * *

I decided to spend the weekend before the contest in Crayfield. We hadn't been there since Jason's second birthday party, and I thought the encouragement of family, as well the inner peace I always found in the country, would prepare me for the nerve-wracking event.

Nana put forth her best effort to make over Jason, but it was clear to see that she would rather have been in bed. Wanda said she spent most of the days sleeping, sometimes in her recliner but more and more often flat in the bed. Pappy looked older, and very tired, but refused to complain. He took Jason for long walks outside. I watched them through the window and it appeared that neither of them ever stopped talking. I was sure Pappy was telling him the names of all the trees and plants.

Gwen and Wanda came over to the barn house after Nana was in bed for the night, to listen to me practice my song for the contest. Jason sat in Gwen's lap and clapped for me.

"I can't believe my own cousin is going to be a big star," Gwen said. "Will you thank us on TV when you accept your first country music award?"

I laughed. "Sure I will. But don't plan your life around that happening. This is just a little contest. Not anything major."

"But it could lead to something bigger," Craig added. "It's an opportunity to work with Nashville musicians, and to be heard by producers. Penny, important people sponsor these contests looking for new talent."

Unsure my legs would hold me, I flopped down, cross-legged on the floor. "Craig, nobody told me that part before. I thought the thousand dollars prize money was what I was shooting for. Now I'm really scared."

Wanda moved to the floor with me and took my hand in hers. "Penny Sue, you don't have any reason to fret over this. You're as good as anybody on the radio. I just don't see how you could possibly lose."

Jason had fallen asleep in Gwen's arms so Craig took him to his toddler bed in what I had once intended to be a music room.

"I agree with Wanda," Gwen said. "If I didn't have to work and help with Nana, I'd drive to Nashville to watch you win."

"You're nice, but you're my cousins so you aren't exactly objective." To protect feelings, I quickly added, "I appreciate your confidence in me just the same."

A flood of emotions, mostly gratitude, washed over me when I looked at them. They should have been free to enjoy their nights and weekends, and chase their own dreams. Instead they took care of Nana. I never had to take a turn, and that wasn't fair since I was a granddaughter the same as they were.

"Okay girls, here's the deal," I announced. "With your encouragement I'm going to win this contest. And then I'm going to get a recording deal and make real money. And when I do, we're all going to do something special, like take a big trip somewhere. And when this contest is over, I'm coming back to take care of Nana for a week so you two can have a break."

Craig smiled at me from the doorway. "I don't want to intrude on the girl talk, so I'm going to bed. I'll see you in the morning." He leaned over to kiss me goodnight before adding, "You might be more comfortable if you sit on the furniture instead of the floor."

We laughed and moved up to the couch, but Wanda got serious again as soon as Craig had left the room. "Penny Sue, your offer is really nice but you don't have to worry about staying with Nana. We're used to being over there. We don't mind."

"But we still want you to come spend a week," Gwen added.

"Right. Listen, I have a good idea. Are you through practicing now that Craig and Jason are going to sleep?" Wanda asked.

"For tonight," I said. "But I'll start back up in the morning."

"Why don't we ride in town to Leo's Bar and Grill? We actually have live music in Crayfield now," she bragged. "Maybe they'll let you sing a few songs. Will Craig care?"

I went in the bedroom to catch him before he was too deep into his sleep and ask if he would mind if I went to Leo's with my cousins. He said to have fun, and asked me to move Jason into the bed with him so he'd hear him if he woke.

Leo's was smaller than the VFW, had pool tables instead of a dance floor, and was packed from wall to wall. The music was too loud and the customers too drunk. And there was nowhere for us to sit. My first thought was to turn around and get out of there, but Gwen had already spotted a friend and run off to talk to him.

"I know the drummer," Wanda said. "He was in my class. When they take a break, I'll ask if you can sing. You come with me so you can tell him what songs you want to sing."

I nodded, figuring I'd ruin my throat if I tried to answer loud enough for her to hear. I secretly hoped the band wouldn't know anything I could sing. Their timing was off and I wasn't comfortable singing with musicians I hadn't practiced with. Realizing that made me more anxious about the contest and using studio musicians who would recognize how inexperienced I was.

The guitar player took me outside to plan my songs, where we could hear each other speak and so I could sing a few lines of each song for him to figure out which keys to play them in. "If we miss your modulation, cue me with a thumb up and I'll kick it up," he said as we walked back inside.

Wanda handed me a beer and we waited for my turn to sing. The only alcohol I had touched in the last eighteen months had been a glass of champagne on New Year's Eve, which was practically a requirement at the VFW. I tossed around the idea of telling Wanda that I didn't like beer, but ended up drinking it rather than hurt her feelings or embarrass her.

The absence of a dance floor didn't discourage Gwen. She danced a slow song with her friend, in less than the space between two bar stools. Wanda saw me watching. "Poor Gwen. Since Cody quit her, she gets a little carried away if any man shows her a little attention."

The band paused for the drummer to announce that I would sing a few songs. The games and noise continued as though no one heard or cared. I put my empty mug on the bar, said so long to Wanda, and squeezed through the crowd to make my way to the stage. My stomach jumped into my throat while I adjusted the microphone to my height. This could be the biggest disaster of any performance in my history.

The band started my first song "I Fall to Pieces" in the wrong key, but stopped when they realized the error.

"What'd she do, forget the words," a drunk shouted from the bar. A group of men laughed.

I smiled, wishing I had about six more beers in me, but it was too late for that or to back out of singing. Gripping the microphone tightly, I listened to the intro and tried to pin down the tempo the drummer might finally settle on.

The first line was shaky because I wasn't sure where the band was going, but they pulled it together and I found my way. I saw Wanda watching anxiously at the side of the stage and forgot the rowdy bunch at Leo's. I sang to the cousins who believed I would win a CMA.

When the song ended I was still focused on Wanda. She screamed and clapped, and looked proud to know me. I realized she wasn't alone. Nearly everyone in the place had stopped what they were doing to clap for me. Someone shouted, "More, sing another one".

I scanned the bar and found Gwen, standing on a chair whistling through her fingers like a man. Her friend held her around the waist to keep her from falling.

I sang four songs, with the reception growing louder and more energetic after each one. They seemed to have forgiven the wrong key problem at the beginning and became real fans when I sang "Blue Kentucky Girl".

I thanked the band, the audience, my cousins, and Leo for allowing me to sing, and returned the microphone to the stand. As I left the stage, the drummer filled the audience in on the fact that I'd be in Nashville the next week, and my new fans screamed for me again.

The bartender asked if I'd prefer a mixed drink instead of the beer someone had asked him to bring me. I asked for a shot of Jose Cuervo, but stopped after one, even though five people had paid for another.

"You ought to pass those on to Gwen," Wanda told me. "She'll go broke at the rate she's putting them down tonight."

"I'm sorry." I wasn't thinking, partly because I didn't know too much about having guys buy drinks for me. "I'll tell him I've changed my mind. What does she drink?"

She looked at Gwen, sitting in her friend's lap, and shook her head. "Never mind. It looks like she's had enough."

Before we left Leo's, I signed autographs on napkins and matchbook covers, and one on a five-dollar bill. I was embarrassed over the drummer's misleading announcement about Nashville and the attention I received as a result, but didn't know how to explain without making him look stupid so I let it go.

We had a hard time dragging Gwen out. She wanted to ride home with her friend but Wanda insisted she was too drunk and made her come with us. I was quiet on the way home, wondering if Gwen behaved this way often. Maybe I inherited my addictions.

Craig and Jason were sleeping soundly when I went in, so I slept on the couch. I fell right off to sleep. With the help of the beer and tequila, and the reactions of the crowd, I didn't worry for a minute about the contest.

Chapter 26

Sharon forgot that this trip was for me and took over the plans. She decided she would drive her car to Nashville and I would ride with her. And we would share a hotel room, and find something 'not country' to do while we were there. I let her plan all she wanted, but made my own reservations because I wasn't sure I trusted her to follow through.

"You can pretend you're already a star and I'm your chauffer or personal assistant," she offered. "I'll take you anywhere you want to go and carry your bags for you."

Craig liked the idea because I wouldn't be alone, and he wouldn't be stranded without transportation while I was gone. I wasn't thrilled about being at Sharon's mercy, but agreed it was best that I wouldn't be alone.

The drive up there was easy. We started out after the morning rush hour, to avoid traffic and give me a couple of hours with Jason before I left. That still gave us plenty of time to stop at the outlet malls we would pass along the way.

"I love your new haircut," Sharon said, as we tried on western hats in a discount boot store. "Do you think Irene would cut mine the same way? If so, I'll buy a hat."

"I'm sure she will if you ask," I answered, wondering if she cared whether I wanted her to have the same haircut as mine, or if she realized the cut would look different with her natural curls instead of my poker straight hair.

Sharon bought teal colored suede boots at half price, and a black hat with a matching teal feather glued to the band. Satisfied that she had found the perfect country look for herself, even though she wanted nothing to do with country, she drove straight through the rest of the trip without stopping at any of the other outlets or malls even though I had told her that I needed to buy earrings to go with my costume. I convinced myself that it was just as well; I should save money for the things I wanted to get for Jason's room.

With map in hand, I directed Sharon to the Swingin' Door Motor Inn, which had been listed in the contest entry packet as an alternative to the expensive host hotel.

"It's only three blocks away, I had argued when Craig told me to stay in the expensive hotel and charge it to the MasterCard.

"Penny, I don't want you walking the streets alone while you're down there," he insisted. "I'll worry about you."

I convinced him that the host hotel wasn't worth the extra hundred dollars a night and I would be safe since Sharon promised to do everything with me. I wouldn't be walking the streets alone. He conceded.

Sharon's face fell when we pulled into the parking lot at the Swingin' Door.

"For God's sake, Penny. This dump looks like a rent-by-the-hour flea bag," she cried. "I expected valet parking and porters, not outside doors and flashing neon lights."

"It's not that bad," I argued. "It's well lit and it looks clean."

She waved her arms in the air and acted like her life depended on changing my mind. "Come on, this is supposed to be an exciting trip. We can't stay here."

"We can pull the car right up to the room," I said. "So we don't need a valet." I didn't remind her that she had volunteered to carry my bags.

I counseled myself on patience. I was excited about the contest and this was her vacation, so things like the hotel and carrying bags weren't as important to me as they were to her. Still, I thought she was making a big deal about nothing and hoped I could persuade her that we could have just as much fun at the Swingin' Door as we could anywhere else.

"Didn't Craig say it was okay to use the credit card?" she asked. "Do you really want to stay in a dump like this? It probably has rats."

I knew she would drive me crazy if she didn't get her way. "Maybe we can ask to see a room before we decide," I suggested. "As long as we have what we need, I don't think an inside hall is worth a hundred dollars. Is it that important to you?"

She huffed, opened her car door, and got out without answering. When I didn't jump out as quickly as she had, she rolled her eyes and slammed her door. Then she adjusted her purse on her shoulder in a move that reminded me of my mother, and I knew I was facing a hard time.

I got out of the car and followed as she stormed down the sidewalk and into the small office. Once inside, I pushed past her and went to the counter, hoping she'd stand where she was and pout quietly while I did the talking. The small man behind the counter didn't look any happier than she did, and I wasn't anxious to be thrown out on account of her attitude.

"Hi. I'm Penny Osburn and I have a reservation. I'm in town for the Miller Country Music Contest." I smiled big enough to make up for the hateful look on Sharon's face, thinking that might draw him out of his solemn mood.

"Unfortunately, my friend also made a reservation at another hotel," I explained despite his stony expression. "We would like to share a room, so I'm hoping to convince her that the rooms here are as nice as those in her expensive hotel. Will you show her the inside of one of your rooms?"

He stared at me like he didn't believe I had asked such a question. I leaned across the counter to whisper. "Please. I really need to stay here for good luck. This is where my husband and I spent our first night together, so the place is special to me."

That made him smile. "Sure. I'll walk y'all down to 106 and let you check it out. We renovated that room after a water leak so everything's new."

Sharon rolled her eyes again when I smiled at her, but I refused to let her change my mind without at least taking a look first.

I noticed our guide's name badge as he opened the door to 106 and stepped aside to let us go in before him. "My grandfather's name is Claude," I told him. "You're the only other Claude I've ever met. This has to be a good sign."

The newly renovated room still smelled faintly of fresh paint. There were two double beds, covered with lavender-flowered spreads and topped with matching pictures on the wall above the headboards. A round table with two chairs sat in front of the windows, with armed chairs for each of us in the corners of the room.

"We give you free cable TV, local phone calls, and a continental breakfast in the meeting room behind my office in the morning," Claude announced proudly.

Sharon looked around and nodded. "It's not as bad as I thought it would be," she admitted. "It looks a lot better inside than it did out."

I walked back to the office with Claude to register while Sharon backed the car into the parking space in front of our door and carried our bags in. Claude returned my credit card and smiled, like a grandfather instead of the grumpy man I had first met.

"I'm glad things worked out with your friend," he said. "You girls be sure to keep the door locked, and let me know if you need anything."

I thanked him again and he wished me luck in the contest.

Sharon claimed the bed closer to the bathroom and put my bags on the one by the window before I returned. "I hope you don't mind," she said, emptying her suitcase into a drawer. "I get scared close to the door."

I didn't mind, although I thought she should have asked me before she took over the room that I had reserved and paid for. To assure myself some control, I claimed the first shower.

"I need to get ready for my rehearsal with the musicians," I reminded her when she looked like she might argue. "Now that I'm actually here, I'm getting nervous again. I hope a shower helps me relax."

She continued to empty her bags, lining cosmetics and hair supplies across the top of the dresser.

"Sharon, I don't know if I'm ready for this. I'm scared."

"Sure you are." She tossed the words at me without thinking. She was through with cosmetics, and had pulled her new boots from the box to inspect them more carefully.

I took jeans and a long-sleeved tee shirt to the bathroom. Irene had helped me decide what to wear, saying that the jeans flattered my long legs and the outfit looked neat and comfortable, and was appropriately western without looking like a stage costume.

When I came out after my shower, Sharon looked up from the movie she was watching on cable. "Is that what you're going to wear?" Her tone clearly said she didn't approve.

"Yes. Don't you like it?"

She didn't answer, so I sat on the bed to do my make-up and think my way through a rehearsal. When I was ready, I closed my eyes and pictured the choreography I planned to do with my song.

"Are you okay," Sharon asked.

"I'm fine. I'm practicing in my mind," I answered, without opening my eyes.

"I thought you were doing some sort of yoga or something. You've practiced for weeks, Penny. If you aren't ready now, you'll never be. Why don't you try and have some fun while you're here? I'd think you'd be relieved to be away from your husband and that baby for a few days, and you'd want to party while you have the chance."

I wished I hadn't agreed to bring her with me. If I had come alone, I would have been able to stand in front of the mirror and practice the way I wanted. My clothes would be in drawers instead of stacked in a chair because Sharon had brought everything she owned and used both drawers. She played on my nerves already and we hadn't been there three hours yet.

"Sharon, I came here to win a contest, not to party or run away from my husband and son. I need to stay focused on winning. I'll lose my courage if I'm not careful."

She turned to watch a love scene in her movie, but I kept talking.

"I'll feel terrible if I don't win at least enough to cover my expenses and pay Irene back for the entry fee."

She rolled her eyes, again, and I wished they would get stuck that way. "Loosen up a little, for Christ's sake. You didn't ask Irene for anything. I happen to know how this whole thing went down. Irene brought it up on her own. You don't owe her, or Craig, anything. This won't put you in the poor house, so relax."

"That's easy for you to say. You aren't the one getting ready to sing with musicians you've never laid eyes on before. Sharon, this is a big deal to me," I reminded her. "It's not just about Irene and Craig and the money. I want to win this for me, so I'll know if I'm really any good or not. This determines my future."

She reached into her purse and tossed two bottles at me - a glass bottle of rum and a pill bottle full of Valium. "Do what you gotta do. Just promise me you aren't going to mope around and bore me the whole time we're here. I can't take that."

I left the bottles on the bed where they landed, grabbed my shoes and purse, and walked down to Claude's office.

"Are you happy with your room?" he asked.

"The room is fine," I assured him. "The roommate is the problem. Is anyone using that meeting room? I need a place to practice."

"Come on back," he said, motioning me around the end of the counter. He opened the meeting room door and let me in. "You have forty-five minutes before I need the room back."

At first I rehearsed the song in my head and used the privacy of the room only for my choreography. Claude opened the door and poked his head inside.

"I can't hear a thing. You're gonna have to sing louder than that if you want to win," he coached.

"I was afraid I might disturb you, or people in the other rooms," I admitted.

"Ain't nobody going to hear you except me. Go ahead and practice while you got the chance. You won't bother me none."

I looked at him and tried to imagine that he was Pappy standing there. "Thanks. Do you want to help? Will you watch me one time and tell me if you think my movements look good with the song?"

He nodded. "I sure will. Show me what you can do, little girl."

I went through the whole song, self-conscious at first but warming up after I saw him smile. When I had finished, he thought for a minute before offering his opinion. "I've been in this town long enough to have a good ear for country music," he said. "You've got the voice and the look. I'd say you have as good a chance at winning as anybody."

I thanked him, not sure exactly what he meant by as good as anybody, and if that was good news or not. "Is there anything you think I need to work on?"

He rubbed his cheek and studied me carefully. "I'd say the only thing you're lacking is faith in yourself. You have to believe you're good enough to win, even if you don't win."

"This is my first contest. I'm scared."

"Well you can't let them know that. There's one thing you gotta remember," he said. "These things ain't always about who can sing the best. Sing from your heart and make them think you've already won, by your attitude. That's all you can do, and remember that the outcome of this won't mean a thing about you as a singer."

"I'll try to remember all of that," I promised. I felt guilty about lying to him about spending my first night with Craig in his motel. Claude was honest with me and deserved the same in return.

"Sing it again, this time like a star," he said.

I did. I pretended I was doing a concert for thousands of fans who loved me enough to buy tickets to see me. I imagined Craig, Jason, Irene, and Nana, Pappy, Wanda, and Gwen, all of them sitting in the front row, screaming and cheering for me.

Claude clapped and whistled when I finished this time. "You got it girl. You go down there and sing like that and they'd be fools not to pick you." He stared at me for a minute then said, "One more time, then I need to get back to work."

I sang it once more for him and he said I was ready. I practiced a couple more times after he went back to his counter, to be sure, and felt confident when I walked out of the meeting room.

My scheduled time to rehearse with the band was still an hour away. I decided to forget Sharon, and walk over to the host hotel and find the room so I wouldn't get lost at the last minute. After orienting myself, I went to a sandwich shop for soup and tea, finishing in time to touch up my lipstick and hair before I went to the rehearsal.

Anxiety hit big time in the elevator. My knees turned to mush and my heart raced. I called up Claude's words in my head and took deep breaths.

Luck was with me. When I opened the door to the rehearsal suite, I found a receptionist and three other contestants sitting comfortably on sofas instead of the room full of anxious musicians that I had expected.

"Welcome. You must be Penny," the receptionist said.

"Yes. I'm Penny Osburn. I'm scheduled to work with the band at seven," I said, in what I thought was a professional voice.

"You're in the right place at the right time. I'm Madeline, and it's my job to make you comfortable. Have a seat. I have a couple of forms for you to sign." While she got the papers together and put them on a clip board, she asked, "You're singing "Til I Can Make It on My Own", aren't you?"

I confirmed my song and she looked relieved.

I sat on a love seat, next to a girl who could have been Tanya Tucker's twin, and Madeline handed me a clipboard with the forms. "We're running a little behind schedule," she said. "You're up next, but it could be another thirty or forty minutes before they finish up this session. You're welcome to sit here with us, or leave and come back if you want."

"I did mine this morning," the Tanya Tucker look-alike told me. "The guys are really nice. I came back because I want to change my bridge. I'll sit here all night if I have to, waiting on a chance to talk to them."

Madeline smiled. "I really can't promise you anything," she told the girl. "But you're welcome to wait."

I decided to wait there. My nerves jumped from one extreme to the other. Madeline and the other contestants were friendly and encouraging. For the most part, I felt relaxed, until I thought about going into the adjoining room with professional musicians who had been working all day with amateur singers. Waves of anxiety hit as I thought about how tired they must be, and how good the other singers might have been.

My stomach turned completely over when Madeline finally said, "Okay, Penny, they're ready for you."

I sucked in as much air as I could, through my nose and mouth at the same time, and blinked away a tear that had popped up out of nowhere.

"You'll do fine," Madeline promised, and squeezed my shoulders. "The guys are great to work with."

I knew she was right the second I walked into the room. Brian, the keyboard player, acted as host. He shook my hand, introduced the other guys, and led me to the microphone. "Just relax, and remember that this is a rehearsal." He adjusted the microphone to my height as he talked and positioned me behind it. "Now's when we all make our mistakes and figure out how to fix them before tomorrow."

"We need to do a quick sound check and adjust your levels, so talk to us, Penny. Tell us a little about yourself and then sing the chorus of your song. Take the mike off the stand if you want. Do what makes you comfortable."

I hesitated before I took the microphone in my hand. "My name is Penny Osburn. I'm married to Craig, and we have a two-year-old son, named Jason. I love to sing. My husband plays lead guitar and we write songs together."

I'm an idiot, I thought, and I sound like a robot. I have no life and no confidence. Words rolled around in my head, but none of them seemed worth spitting out.

"Sing your chorus for us," Brian prompted. "Try to hit the same levels you'll use on stage."

I sang better than I had talked. What a relief.

"Excellent," Brian said. "One more time on the chorus and then we'll try the whole song with music."

The musicians played my song perfectly the first time, and I sang it well enough to feel good about my performance. Brian kept eye contact with me most of the way through, smiling and nodding encouragement.

"I think we've got it," the drummer said after our first time through the whole song. "You're going to put us back on schedule Penny Osburn. Thank you."

"Yes, you are very easy to work with," Brian agreed. "But let's try it once more, to be sure we've all got it."

I sang it better the second time, and remembered to add my choreography. When I finished, the guitar player took his guitar off and placed it on the stand. Brian came out from behind his piano.

"You have a great voice, Penny, and good stage presence. Work on your confidence a little, and you'll do fine tomorrow," Brian advised. "We'll see you then. Good luck."

I said thank you and went back to Madeline's room, where I wished the others good luck and said I'd see them tomorrow.

On the way back to the motel, I decided to call Craig from the payphone in the office. I didn't want Sharon to hear my conversation because I knew she wouldn't share my excitement and my feelings would be hurt. I was disappointed to find that Claude was gone for the day, and a younger man was behind the counter.

Craig answered on the first ring.

"I only have a couple dollars in change, so I'll have to talk fast," I said. "Rehearsal was great. I was nervous but I still did well, and we only had to go through the song twice. I think I can do this. How's Jason?"

"Jason is fine, but he misses you," Craig said. "I knew you could do this, Penny. You go in there tomorrow and win this thing. You deserve it."

"I wish you were here." The words, and the fact that I meant them, probably surprised me more than they did him. "Next time you have to come with me."

"That's a deal, Penny. Next time I'll be there. I love you, and good luck tomorrow."

Sharon was gone when I got back to the room. She left a note on my bed, saying she was bored and went out to do some sightseeing. The rum and Valium were still on my bed, so I moved them to the dresser beside her hairspray and turned the TV on.

With twenty channels to choose from, I couldn't find anything that held my interest. I was stuck on the thought that Claude and Brian had both seen the same problem. I needed confidence. I didn't appear relaxed because I wasn't. All the pretending and imagining that my fans were with me didn't help. My insecurities still showed.

I couldn't go home without the thousand-dollar prize. Craig would be disappointed, although he'd never say that. My mother would find out somehow and rush back into my life just for the chance to use it to hurt my feelings. Wanda and Gwen would be heart-broken. I had to win.

I took two valiums from Sharon's stash and put them in my wallet just in case I needed them the next day. I drank a fourth of the rum, and filled the bottle back up with water, hoping Sharon would never notice. I only wanted something to make me relax and didn't want Sharon to believe I was back in that habit again.

I didn't know when Sharon returned, because the next time I spoke with her was after I woke the next morning.

"My head is splitting," she cried. "If I sit through a whole day of country music, I'll want to commit suicide. Please don't make me go."

"We don't have to stay the whole day," I reminded her. "The part for solo singers only lasts four hours."

"That's as good as all day to me," she said, settling back into bed.

"Fine. Don't go." I picked the bottle up from her dresser and headed for the bathroom, where I soaked in a hot bath without bubbles and drank half of the watered-down rum. I felt much more relaxed by the time I sat down to do my make-up.

Sharon had turned the lights and TV off to create a recovery zone for her hangover. I took a mirror and my cosmetics to the table in front of the window and parted the drapes an inch to let some light in.

"Damn, Penny! You're killing me with that sunlight," she yelled.

I gathered my costume and cosmetics, slammed the door hard enough to bounce Sharon out of her bed, and went to the office.

"The meeting room is in use," Claude apologized.

"I need someplace to get ready. It's a long story," I told him.

He grabbed a key from the drawer. "Come with me," he said, and led me to an empty room. "Try not to mess anything up, and hurry."

In ten minutes, I changed, did my face and hair, and swallowed the two Valiums. I stayed in the room long enough to run through the song once in front of the mirror and then headed to the hotel, waving at Claude as I passed his office window.

All twenty-five contestants were ushered into a room backstage, where we were asked to sign more forms and draw an envelope from a box.

"Don't open the envelopes until I tell you to," Madeline instructed. "Each one contains a number between one and twenty-five. That number will determine your order in the competition. After everyone has arrived and signed in, you'll open them together and give me your numbers. You'll then be allowed to return to the auditorium to watch. Just make sure to return here two numbers before yours comes up."

The Tanya Tucker look-alike had already opened her envelope and announced that she was number two. "Being second sucks almost as much as going first, but it doesn't matter. They wouldn't let me change my song after I waited all that time yesterday. This whole thing is rigged," she complained.

Madeline tried to console the girl, and assure her that she had the same chance as everyone else. I gave her the same talk that Claude had given me the day before but it didn't make her any happier.

I drew number twenty. I thought that was perfect because I would be able to listen to most of the others before I had to go backstage, and I wouldn't have to wait long after I sang to hear the results. The drugs and alcohol kept me from being nervous.

I sat in the front row, where I could smile and encourage the others until number seventeen finished his song. Then I went backstage to get ready, and rehearse in my head while the two before me performed.

When my turn came, I walked out with energy and confidence. I pretended I was in concert, the way I had when I sang for Claude. In my heart, I sang for Craig and Jason and Irene, and in spite of Momma. I gave my performance one hundred percent of my talent.

Brian winked at me as I exited the stage. I knew I had won, long before Madeline came out on the stage to announce it.

She called me forward and handed me a trophy and a check. I accepted, with no emotion. I was numb from the chemicals. The applause meant nothing because he people didn't know me or really want me to win. I forced a smile and squeaked out a weak thank you.

"I think our winner is in shock," Madeline said into the microphone. "Let's give her another round of applause while she pulls herself together."

I still couldn't feel a thing. The roar of the audience sounded like it came from a distance, but I managed a bigger smile. I waved to my audience.

Madeline held my hand. "I need to talk to you backstage, to explain what comes next," she said. "So don't run off."

I didn't know anything came next. I thought they could hand me a check and it would be over. I realized then that I should have read the papers before I signed them.

Brian shook my hand as I walked out. "I had you picked as the winner from the first time I heard you sing. Congratulations Penny, you did a great job."

"Thank you," was all I had to say. My mind wandered, then faded, and I couldn't pull it back in. One Valium would have been enough.

Madeline pulled me into a small room. "We won't keep you long. I just need to go over a few things. You do the Grand Ole Opry a week from Friday. We'll make the hotel arrangements, but you'll have to get here on your own. A man by the name of Jackson Elliott will be in touch this week about the club dates. Congratulations again. I think the judges made the best choice for once."

Grand Ole Opry? Club dates? The words didn't register. I couldn't let on that I didn't understand, so I smiled and asked if there would be something in writing. "I'm too excited to remember all of this," I explained.

"I'm sure you are," Madeline said. "Yes, we'll send you a schedule by mail. Also, I'll call you on Monday, when you're settled back in at home."

I walked back to the motel office to see Claude. He was registering a new couple, but looked up when he saw me come through the door.

I nodded my head and smiled.

"First place?" he asked.

I nodded again.

"Woo hoo!" He explained to the new couple. "This little lady just won the Miller contest. First place. Wait until you hear her sing. She'll blow your socks off."

The couple congratulated me, and the woman asked for my autograph. I signed their receipt, and wished I could feel the excitement.

"Thanks, Claude. You made me do it," I said, before going to my room. "I'll never forget you."

Sharon was out again, this time having dinner with a man she had met the night before. "Don't say anything to Craig if you talk to him," she wrote in her note. "He'll tell Tinker and then my life will be shit."

I called Craig, not intending to waste my breath or my money talking about Sharon. "I got first place," I said, as soon as he answered. "First place, Craig."

"You don't sound very excited." I could hear in his voice that he was disappointed, maybe worried. He took a long breath and came back sounding excited enough for both of us. "Penny this is great. I knew you would do it."

"I guess it hasn't had time to sink in yet. I was too nervous to pay attention to everything they said to me. Craig, I have to come back. I think I'm going to be on the Grand Ole Opry."

"You think? Penny, you need to find out. This is great news."

"They'll call me on Monday, and send something in the mail. I already got the check. A thousand dollars, Craig. I won a thousand dollars."

"Did you call Irene? She'll be more excited than you are."

"I didn't call anyone before you," I told him. "You can call Irene, so it won't be long distance. Kiss Jason for me. I'm going to hang up and go to bed. I'm beat."

"You ought to go celebrate. Get Sharon to take you out somewhere nice."

"Thanks, but I'm too tired. We can celebrate when I get home," I said. I hung up the phone and fell asleep almost immediately, still wearing my costume.

Chapter 27

We made it home without killing each other, only because we were both too hungover to pull up the effort a good fight required. We didn't stop at any malls, or even for lunch, although I had a thousand extra dollars in my purse. My mind, when I could think, was on the future. I was on the way - one step closer to making a real career out of singing. Sharon never let on what she was thinking about.

The front porch of Irene's salon was decorated with balloons and a huge 'Welcome Home' sign. Sharon dropped me at the street and handed me the keys to the trunk so I could get my bags--apparently taking back her promise to serve as my personal assistant--and drove away without saying good-bye, thank you, or congratulations.

I spotted familiar cars parked up and down the block – Irene's Mustang, Gary's Cougar, Mr. Osburn's Cadillac, Boomer's old Nova, and Tinker's over-sized van. I wondered if Sharon would return for my surprise party when she got home and found Tinker missing, or if Tinker would leave when I showed up without her. I was almost sure enough to bet my whole check on Tinker leaving.

I felt too bad to entertain or to draw up the energy to act excited, so I hoped everyone would see how tired I looked and leave as soon as I walked in. Maybe they had been waiting all morning and would be ready to go after they congratulated me.

They yelled surprise when I opened the door. Craig and Irene nearly crushed me with hugs, and Craig quickly traded the bags in my arms for Jason. The house had been cleaned and decorated with crepe paper streamers and posters made from paper bags and markers. My favorite said, 'Look Out World – Here Comes Raven Coal', and hung over the couch.

Disappointment showed on Tinker's face when I walked in without Sharon but he managed to keep his voice cheerful. "Where's Sharon? Didn't she see my van out front?"

"I don't think she saw much of anything," I tried to explain. "She had a terrible headache on the drive home. I think she was in a hurry to get to your house and take something."

Tinker grinned. We both knew that Sharon carried a small pharmacy in her purse at all times, so my excuse was a joke.

"I guess I should run home and check on her then," he said. "I'm proud of you, Penny. You can tell me the details later. I want to hear all about those musicians down there."

Jason wouldn't let go of my neck, so Craig brought a kitchen chair over for me to sit on in the living room side where everyone else was. They bombarded me with questions.

"I'm not sure what all I won," I said, honestly. "They gave me a trophy and the check right there, on the stage, but there's more. I was too nervous before the contest to pay attention to what anybody said. Afterwards, I was too excited to understand. Someone will call me on Monday to explain it all to me again."

Mrs. Osburn drew her lips in a tight line and eyed her husband with a suspicious glare. I pretended I didn't notice that she doubted me, but Craig leaned forward to block my view of his mother. I wondered how often he had protected me and I hadn't noticed before.

"That's understandable, Penny." Craig defended me, but I believed his message was more for his mother's sake than mine. "I remember how I felt the night the TV crew came to the post. I was too nervous and excited to concentrate on anything other than my guitar parts."

Boomer backed us up. "I was the same way. The important part is that you remembered your song and got it right, Penny. Congratulations."

"That's right," Irene chimed in. "We're so proud of you."

I didn't want to hear about anyone being proud of me, especially Irene. She was the one person who had noticed my year of sobriety and complimented me on the changes in my life. The truth would hurt Craig as much as her, but she would probably feel more betrayed.

"There's no call for you to be proud of me," I said. "If you think about it, I was born with a good singing voice. It's just something

I came by naturally, not something I did on my own. I feel lucky, not proud."

"Don't sell yourself short," Gary said. "You worked hard to develop your voice, and to learn all those songs. I can't get the words straight to one song all the way through, and you know hundreds."

I smiled, and silently accepted credit for that part.

"I remember the first time I heard you sing. It was at the pool, Penny. Remember that day? You were so shy. It took a great deal of courage for you to overcome those feelings. Accept your compliments. You deserve them."

I appreciated Gary's support, and the fact that he had expressed it in front of his mother.

Craig agreed with his brother. "She still gets a case of stage fright every weekend before she performs."

Craig turned to me and talked like there wasn't a bunch of people listening. "I heard the fear in your voice when you called me before the contest. I thought you might back out and come on home. But you didn't."

"How *did* you manage to overcome your fear down there, Penny?" Mrs. Osburn asked the question so everyone else would think she was concerned, but I suspected she knew the truth and wanted me to squirm in the hot seat over it.

"Sharon helped. And an old man at the motel gave me some helpful advice. He reminded me of my grandfather. His name was Claude, the same as my Pappy's," I explained.

Mrs. Osburn looked disapprovingly at Craig, but directed her question to me. "Penny, don't you know it is dangerous to run around an unfamiliar town, picking up strange men? Women traveling alone are extremely vulnerable to all sorts of cads."

"Claude was the desk clerk at the motel, and harmless," I told her. "I didn't pick him up, although I might have been able to if I had tried. He didn't weigh more than a hundred pounds, and he was about seventy years old. He was a nice man who wanted to help, and he didn't ask anything in return."

"Well you were lucky," she said, not sounding at all relieved to me.

Craig stood up. A piece of me wanted him to tear into his mother for tormenting me. The rest of me knew that I deserved her doubt.

"I have ham and potato salad," he announced. "From the deli. Is anybody hungry?"

"I'm starved, but I think I'm even more tired," I said, shooting Craig a pleading look.

"It's Jason's nap time. He just waited up to see you. Why don't you take him in our room and rest with him for a while," Craig suggested. "You can eat later."

I welcomed the escape, and waited while Jason made his rounds to kiss everyone night-night and ran back to me. Irene and Craig both kissed me as well, and wished us a good nap.

Jason snuggled close, with his arm around my neck and his head on my shoulder. He fell asleep within seconds, but I lay awake, haunted by guilt.

I didn't deserve this celebration, or the pride that Irene and Craig and Gary expressed in me. Still fuzzy around the edges and shy of complete focus, my brain understood what my heart wanted to forget. I didn't have any right to appreciate an accomplishment that I received while under the influence of a failure. The two canceled each other out and left me with nothing. Empty. That explained the numbness when I heard the applause in that auditorium in Nashville.

I would never know now if I was good enough to win that contest straight. Maybe my voice was good enough to compensate for the lack of confidence. Maybe not. I had cheated myself, and those who believed in me, of the truth. The next time I took the stage, I'd know nothing new and would still face the same insecurities I always had.

Sleep stayed just out of reach, no matter how desperately I fought to grab it. Still, I was relieved to be behind a closed door, where Mrs. Osburn couldn't search my face for clues, and where I didn't need to avoid eye contact with Irene to hide my shame.

Jason came through for his Mommy. He slept until the last guest went home. Craig came into the bedroom to check on us. I closed my eyes because I wasn't ready to face him yet. He tiptoed back out quietly.

Craig deserved peace. That was my final decision. He had told me once that he wouldn't want anyone to tell him what he didn't see on his own. Unless he saw me using, I would never betray his wishes and tell him. He couldn't see what had happened while I was gone, so this scene was over. Correction - the whole play was over I'd never use again.

I slipped out of the room and left Jason sleeping. Craig lay on the couch with his hands behind his head and his eyes closed. I crawled on top of him and buried my face in his neck.

"Don't move," I whispered when the muscle in his arm tensed. "Please stay where you are and hold me."

He shifted, only enough to make both of us more comfortable, and wrapped his arms around me. I found sleep, as soon as he said he loved me.

Later Craig said I must have been in a coma, because Jason woke from his nap in a cyclone and I slept right through hours of his running and yelling. They had eaten dinner, he had bathed Jason and put him in his pajamas, and I still hadn't opened my eyes until he brought Jason over to kiss me goodnight.

"You'll be up all night after sleeping this long," Craig predicted. "You slept so soundly that I didn't want to wake you. Didn't you sleep at all in Nashville?"

"I didn't sleep at all. It wasn't a fun trip, Craig. I'll tell you all about it when I'm over wanting to kill Sharon."

He shook his head. "We should have known she'd be trouble. Poor Tinker puts up with that every day."

"Poor Tinker has a choice," I reminded him. "So do I, and I'll never choose to go anywhere with her again. Now, about staying up all night," I changed the subject. "I hope to stay awake, but not up. Are you ready to celebrate?"

"Aren't you hungry? Penny, you haven't eaten since you came home."

"I'd rather have you than food," I told him.

"You can have both," he offered. "Why don't you run a bubble bath while I make your plate? I'll feed you while you soak."

"I'm glad I married you," I said, halfway to the bathroom.

We celebrated until Craig reminded me that he hadn't slept all day like I had, and that one of us would have to get up at seven with Jason. "I think Jason missed you more than I did. He'll probably want all of your attention for the next few days.

"He'll get my days, but promise you'll want my nights. I missed this while I was away."

He reminded me that I hadn't been gone long enough to miss him before he pulled me close and fell asleep holding me. Again, my guilt kept me from sleeping. I couldn't depend on Craig to make love to me every time I wanted a drink, because no man had that much energy.

I needed something else to offset the cravings. For the first time in years, I pulled the words to a song up in my head to keep me from thinking. "*I beg your pardon, I never promised you a rose garden*". It helped, but it wasn't enough.

I got up with Jason at seven because I was still awake, wishing I had never heard that song. I put him in his highchair with a cup of apple juice to keep him quiet while I made oatmeal and toast. The longer I let Craig sleep, the better my chances would be of dragging him into our room for some fun during Jason's nap.

Irene called while I washed the breakfast dishes. "Do you feel like company? I want to hear about the trip since you didn't tell us much of anything yesterday."

I apologized for ignoring her the day before. "I want to see you, and tell you about the trip, but would you mind waiting until dinner? Irene, I was away from my husband for a couple of days and I'm hoping to catch up a little while Jason naps."

She laughed. "I guess I know where I fit in now. Of course I'll wait. Penny, I'm actually very pleasantly surprised to hear that there's that much fire left in your marriage."

"Great. Meatloaf at six. Bring Ralph if you want. He avoids us too much, and it would be nice if Jason had a Grandpa to go with his Granny Irene."

Irene's comment brought me down again and played on my mind while I mixed up the meatloaf. Why was she surprised? Did she know something that I didn't; like that Craig was tired of me? "*I beg your pardon, I never promised you a rose garden, along with the sunshine there's gotta be a little rain some time*". I guessed it could work both ways. Craig had never promised me a rose garden either.

"You mean to tell me last night wasn't enough for you?" Craig didn't sound particularly interested when I attacked him the minute Jason was out. "Are you trying to kill me?"

"Come on Craig. You're young and healthy. I missed you." He gave up without much of a fight when I promised I'd be on top and do all the work.

Irene came to dinner alone; Ralph had a poker game. I told her and Craig about the contest, and filled them in on how Sharon had ditched me after she took over the room. Neither of them was surprised.

"Claude, the old guy in the hotel registration office, turned out to be my best friend while I was there. Madeline and Brian were great, but Claude made the real difference. If I ever get rich and famous, I want to help him retire."

A new wave of guilt washed over me in the middle of my story. "I forgot to call Nana and Pappy to tell them I won."

"I called them right after I called Irene," Craig reassured me and laughed. "Gwen was there, so I'm sure the whole county knows by now."

For their sake, I was relieved. They would never know that I hadn't thought of them when I should have. I would, however, and I didn't deserve their love and support.

"Did Sharon stay drunk the whole trip?" Irene asked.

The subject made me uncomfortable. "I'm sure she did plenty of drinking when she went out at night."

"That's probably why she didn't invite you to go with her," Craig said.

I felt Irene watch for my reaction. I rolled my eyes in true Sharon fashion and said I didn't want to talk about her any more.

Chapter 28

I got up with Craig on Monday morning so I'd be alert and prepared when the call came in from Madeline or the man she had told me about. At times, I wasn't sure there really was a man, and feared he was something I dreamed up during my altered state.

What if I had dreamed all of it and there wasn't anything more than the check? I wished I hadn't mentioned the rest to anyone because I was going to be embarrassed if the call never came.

I took a deep breath. I was going to hope for the best and be prepared just in case. I placed a pen and note pad on the counter near the phone and planned to write down every word of the conversation so I wouldn't be confused again.

Jason had been my shadow all day on Sunday and started Monday clinging to me again, so I went into his room to work. I rearranged what little furniture he had—the toddler bed, a four-drawer chest from Craig's old room, and a toy box that Gary had found in a yard sale—moving his bed away from the wall that adjoined Irene's shop. I put the toy box on the far side of the bed where the mess he often left around it wouldn't be visible from the living room when we had company.

He worked with me, pushing his tricycle into the corner where Craig always put it at bedtime, and he ran his hand over the quilt on the bed to straighten it. My son wasn't a baby any more. Soon, I would be free to do what I wanted because he wouldn't require all of my time or attention. I'd be able to get my notebooks out and write, or sleep late if I wanted, or have a career. Did I know what I wanted?

On the other hand, he would learn more about life and see my faults. So far, Craig and I were perfect in his eyes. Craig would remain that way, since he had no faults. I would never measure up as long as he compared me to his father.

"Jason, I'm going to the kitchen now," I said as I unplugged the vacuum cleaner and rolled the cord. "Do you want to come with me?"

He shook his head no and pushed a plastic truck across the bed.

"Okay then, I'll see you in a little while." I picked up the vacuum and left his room.

He screamed for me before I got across the living room. "Mommy!"

I ran back into his room, where I found him in the same spot I had left him in.

"Are you okay?" I checked his fingers to see if he had hurt them on the truck, but found nothing. He returned his full attention to the truck and stopped crying. I left the room again, and he screamed again. We repeated this routine a couple more times before I lost patience.

"Jason, I need to wash dishes and mop the kitchen floor. You can come with me if you want, or you can stay here and play by yourself with your toys. You can't keep screaming for me."

He ran across his room and I thought he had decided to go with me. Instead, he put his arms around my legs and screamed, "No, Mommy."

I walked to the kitchen with him hanging on my leg, and tried to pull him loose to sit him in the highchair with a cookie. He wouldn't cooperate. When I had pried him off my leg, he bucked and kicked, refusing to sit in the chair.

"Jason, please stop. I need to get my work done." I pleaded. He screamed louder. "Are you hungry? Do you want a cookie?" I tried to find something to please him. He shook his head and smacked the cookie out of my hand. "Are you tired? Sick? Do you want to ride your bike?"

Nothing appealed to him. He wanted to hang on my leg. I picked him up and carried him to the couch, where I sat him down forcefully.

"You sit here while I do my work. I don't know what you want."

He screamed louder, but stayed on the couch. I went to the kitchen, filled the sink with water, and loaded the dishes. He continued to scream, and was still screaming when the dishes were dried and put away. I wanted to scream with him by that point.

Irene knocked on Jason's bedroom door. The salon! I hadn't worried about disturbing customers since my parents moved out. I picked Jason up and took him with me to open the door.

"Is Jason okay?" Irene looked worried until he reached for her. He stopped crying as soon as he was in her arms.

"He's spoiled," I explained. "He wants me to carry him around and I can't get anything done. He's screaming like that because I won't hold him all day."

"He missed you when you were gone, Penny. He's probably afraid you'll leave again if you put him down."

"So I'm supposed to cart him around all day?" My voice had risen without my meaning for that to happen, but I couldn't hold it back. "What about when I do leave again? Should I pretend that's never going to happen? He has to learn."

Irene coddled my whimpering son while she lectured me. "He's a baby, Penny. He doesn't understand all of this. You should be more patient with him."

I snatched Jason away from her and he screamed again. "I'll keep him quiet so he doesn't bother you," I said, and closed the door in her face.

Jason and I sat on the couch together until lunchtime. My resentment toward him and Irene grew by the second. How could she chastise me in front of my son? How could he jump into her arms like I had abused him? Why were they ruining my life? I couldn't stay tied to a two-year-old, or a wanna-be-mother.

Madeline called while Jason napped, convincing me that it was possible for at least one thing to turn out right in my life.

"Are you over the shock, and settled back in at home?" she asked.

"I'm not sure about either," I admitted, and followed with a nervous laugh that I wished afterwards I hadn't let out.

"Don't get too settled," she warned. "Your schedule for the next few months will be crazy."

I grabbed the pen and pad before she continued. "You'll do the same song you sang in the contest at the Grand Ole Opry next Friday night. You'll go on around nine-thirty." My heart raced so that I almost missed the next part.

"We have a room reserved for you at the Opryland Hotel. You can bring your husband, and have a nice time on us. Dinner Friday night and breakfast Saturday morning are included."

I tried to write every word.

"You still with me, Penny? You aren't saying much."

"I'm here. I'm writing," I explained.

"Good. I'll run through all of this for you, but we'll still send you a schedule by mail. Stop me if I go too fast."

"Okay, I'm ready," I said, stilling my shaking pen and my heart.

"We want to push as much of this as possible through before the holidays and bad weather set in, so you'll start traveling right away. We don't want you on icy roads. You have ten dates, all in medium sized clubs, in the Midwest. Driving time for you should max at around nine hours."

Craig will kill me. That was the only thought in my head, yet Craig had seldom even raised his voice to me.

"Do I bring my band?" I knew that was out of the question for Tinker, but wasn't sure about the others.

"No. Brian will put together musicians."

"What about my husband? He's my guitar player," I reminded her. We had discussed that in the waiting room before my rehearsal.

"Penny, you'll have plenty of time for that later. This tour is for you, as a solo artist, backed by our musicians. That's what you did in the contest, and that was in the contracts you signed. Your husband is welcome to travel with you, but he won't be part of the group this time."

"I understand." I was ashamed to admit that I hadn't read the contracts. I didn't even know I was signing contracts.

"You'll do two clubs in Indiana, one in Indianapolis and one in Jasper. Then there's Ohio, Columbus and Cleveland. You do Moline, Illinois, and then come through Missouri. Three stops in Missouri, one in Nashville, and then you wind up doing one date in Owensboro, Kentucky. You'll get a lot of exposure, which is important for any career."

"And I have to drive myself to those places?" It was impossible, even if I bought a car with the thousand dollars.

"You can ride in the bus with the band if you want to leave from Nashville. Or you could fly, if you are willing to pay airfare."

"If it's okay, I need to talk the travel details over with Craig," I told her.

"Fine. I look forward to seeing you again, and to meeting your husband," she said, and rushed off without asking if I had any questions.

What would I wear? Who would keep Jason? Would they pay for hotels and food? How many songs did I sing at each place? Questions flooded after I hung, and I imagined Craig would have plenty more when he came home.

I put a roast on and took Jason outside to play until it was time for Irene to leave. Not only did I owe her an apology, I needed her advice, and maybe her help. Madeline made it sound like I had no way out of this deal so I needed rides and babysitters and costumes. I may need a place to live if Craig threw me out.

Craig came home before Irene left. He took over in the yard with Jason, and I ran inside to catch Irene and ask her to come in and talk while I finished up dinner.

"Are you feeling better?" She sounded the same as usual; not upset with me.

"I'm sorry about earlier. I have too much on my mind, and it was unfair for me to take it out on you and Jason." My voice cracked and Irene handed me a tissue.

"Tell me what's wrong, Penny. I know you and something is heavy on your mind." Her kindness made me feel guilty and that made me cry harder.

"I can't let Craig catch me like this," I said, planning to rush to the bathroom if he walked in. "I'm not ready to tell him anything. I need to talk to you first, and we don't have time right now to go over everything I have to say."

"How long will your dinner take?" she asked. "Maybe the two of us can slip away for a while tonight."

"Thanks, Irene. I'll need about forty-five minutes to finish up cooking, eat, and clear the table."

"I'll tell Craig that I need you to help me find a dress for a wedding. You come over after you're finished here. Now, change that look on your face or he'll know I'm a liar."

I laughed and hugged her, and watched through the window as she stopped to talk to Craig and Jason. Craig nodded, so I knew she had cleared my escape.

When I finished eating, Craig told me to run on and meet Irene, and he would clean up the table and watch Jason. I kissed them and rushed out before he suspected that anything was wrong.

Irene took me to Frisch's, where one of her regular customers worked as a waitress and sat us in the backroom that she normally reserved for large parties. "You'll have plenty of privacy here," she promised. "Take your time, and let me know if you need anything."

When the waitress left, I slapped my notes down on the table between Irene and me. "My life went completely crazy, Irene. I'm an idiot. I signed contracts in Nashville without reading them first, and now I'm committed to all of these shows."

She looked at the schedule and whistled. "That's a lot of traveling. And Craig knows nothing?"

"I told him I might have the Grand Old Opry show, that's all."

"Tell me everything you know, Penny. I'm lost."

I filled her in as best I could with the details. I couldn't take my band, not even Craig, and I didn't know about costumes, and I either had to drive myself, or leave from Nashville with the band members.

"Do you at least get paid for this?" she asked.

"Three hundred dollars a show."

She looked over the list again, counting shows. "That's four thousand dollars including the thousand you already got? Not bad."

"Think back over what happened earlier today, Irene. Jason already couldn't deal with me going away one time. What's going to happen when I leave him ten more times? And you know Craig won't want both of us to go and leave him. So how will I get there? And what about my band, and the VFW?"

"You do have a lot to think about," she said. "Before you get too discouraged, let's think this through. We'll figure out something."

"I don't think Craig will be happy," I said. Actually, there was little thinking about it; I was positive he would hate this. What I didn't say was how badly I wanted to go, whether Craig and Jason were happy with it or not. Once I heard the details, and had an hour to mull it over, I realized this was really a dream come true for me.

"Irene, this is a great opportunity." I said it carefully, testing for her reaction before I let on whether or not I thought it was an opportunity I deserved or intended to keep.

She kept her eyes straight on me, like she had never seen me before, and she needed to memorize how I looked. She had a hard time settling on which expression she wanted to wear while she studied me, but I kept mine the same.

Her eyes squinted up like she was in pain, and then she softened up and smiled a little. Just when I thought about smiling back, she closed her eyes and bit her lip. Finally, she drew a deep breath but blew it out without any words on it. Then she smiled again.

I blinked a couple of times and tried to find a smile but couldn't get one to come forward. I probably shouldn't have dumped my problems on Irene this time because it appeared I had made her crazy.

"You can yell at me if you want," I finally said to break the silence.

She held my hand across the table. "I don't want to yell at you, Penny. I want to figure out how you can do this without hurting yourself or your family. You're right. This is a great opportunity."

"Are you serious?" The excitement that I had fought off for two days finally overtook me. I shook, like it was the dead of winter and somebody stuck me outside without my coat.

"We'll work this out, Penny. I can keep Jason if Craig wants to go with you. Or I can travel with you if he wants to stay with Jason. Somehow, this will work out."

Irene followed me home and came in to help me break the news to Craig. His emotions were almost as mixed up as hers and mine. Irene repeated her offers for him to hear, and I told him this was important to me. We volleyed back and forth, talking so fast he didn't have a chance to let a thought settle.

He said he'd call the guys about Friday night, and asked for a few days to think about the rest.

I knew I was going, regardless of what he thought. It could be my last chance, and I wasn't giving it up. Not for Jason or for Craig.

Chapter 29

Craig saved his objections until after we had talked to the band members and heard back from the Captain of the VFW. The guys in the band, who all worked full-time jobs in addition to playing music, welcomed the break and offered to do what they could to help me get ready for the road.

"You guys are great, and I promise I'll be back after I do these ten jobs," I told them. "This will be an opportunity for all of us because it could open doors for our future."

The Captain hired the dishwasher's sons to fill in while I was on the road. Tinker said that would make the regulars appreciate us more than ever when we came back. He had heard Moe's boys and thought they were terrible.

As far as our budget was concerned, Craig and I came out ahead. The VFW paid six hundred dollars for the two nights, so we each took home one hundred dollars. Even if I paid for meals and gas on the road, I'd still make more in one night than Craig and I normally made for two.

With those things settled, there weren't many obstacles as far as I could see. Craig thought up a few. "Penny, Jason would be miserable on a ten hour drive, and we can't both run off and leave him every weekend. Not even with Irene. I'll go to the Grand Ole Opry this weekend, but I need time to think about the rest. I think I should stay here with Jason."

I said that was fine, counting on Madeline to talk him into more when we got to Nashville. Unless he brought it up first, I didn't mention the subject other than to tell him that Irene had agreed to stay at our house with Jason on Friday night.

As it turned out, Brian spent more time with Craig than Madeline did in Nashville. The two men became buddies when they joined forces to talk me through my last minute fears before the show.

After the show, Craig, Brian, and Madeline said I was great, and they were excited about how much the crowd had screamed and clapped for me. But I knew everyone had to have seen my knees knocking together while I was on stage.

Madeline took me to a back room to talk business while Craig helped the musicians tear down equipment and carry it out to the truck. Madeline filled me in on costumes and what to expect in the clubs that she had booked. Brian made Craig an offer that he couldn't refuse. That night, after we had toured the hotel gardens and listened to the harpist in the lobby, Craig told me all about it while we got ready for bed.

"Brian said he will pick you up in the tour bus, since they will be coming through our way. I told him I'll drive you to an exit along his route to make it as easy as possible for him."

"Do we have to talk about this now?" I asked, disappointed that they hadn't included me in their discussion but not ready to address it. "We have a free night in a beautiful hotel, no baby, and we don't have to get up early. Can't we have fun?"

He pulled his lips tight, the biggest sign he ever gave that he was upset. "Penny, I don't get you sometimes. I thought this whole deal was fun for you. Isn't it what you want?"

"Yeah, I want this, but can't we talk about the plans on the way home? I'd rather do other things now."

"Brian said he'll watch over you, Penny." He climbed into bed, still talking as though he hadn't heard my objections. "He won't let anything happen to you while you're on the road or in those big nightclubs."

"Great. Now are you satisfied? Can you forget about it at least for tonight?" I turned the light out on my side of the bed and snuggled in close to him.

"I'm tired, Penny. I worked nine hours today, drove another three hours, spent the next three at your show, helped Brian carry equipment, and walked all over this hotel," he reminded me. "I'm ready for sleep."

My feelings were hurt, and I was angry with myself for being that selfish. "How about if I promise to drive home tomorrow and let you sleep?" I asked.

"I had hoped you would do that anyway. I'm too tired to do anything else tonight, Penny."

I kissed his cheek, said goodnight, and turned away from him.

"Don't be mad," he said. "I can't help it if I'm exhausted."

"I'm not mad," I assured him. "Go to sleep. I'm fine."

I wasn't fine. I was wide-awake, horny, excited about traveling in a real tour bus, and I wanted a drink to celebrate. Craig had rushed me past all of the mini bars that were set up in the hotel gardens. I envied the other couples who sat on benches along the trails, leisurely sipping wine and toasting one another. Scenes like this told me how scared he was of my drinking, even if he never verbalized it.

I tossed around while Craig snored, until a streak of independence hit me. I was an adult, old enough to do what I wanted and old enough to buy a drink if I wanted. I slipped out of bed, took ten dollars from his wallet, and went into the bathroom to cover my gown with jeans and a tee shirt. After propping the door opened with a shoe, I raced to the nearest mini bar for two shots of Jose Cuervo and returned before anyone happened by and saw the opened door.

Craig never knew I was gone, and the drinks helped me sleep. When he woke me early, hoping to make up for the night before, it was my turn to be too tired. I stayed in bed until checkout time, and he went downstairs for the free breakfast.

A thunderstorm changed Craig's mind about letting me drive home. He didn't trust me to drive in the rain. That was fine with me; I closed my eyes and let him think he was protecting our lives, hoping he'd remember to tell Brian that I needed extra 'watching over' when the weather was bad.

Not one person in the world took me seriously. At twenty-one, I was still a burden to everyone who cared about me. My husband arranged for a sitter to watch over me. Irene offered to take over my role as a mother because she had seen me fail with my son and figured he was better off without me around. My grandparents gave me a home, knowing that, otherwise, I would wind up like my parents, never owning one. I caused so much trouble for my parents that they married me off the first chance they got.

They would all be better off without me. And I might grow-up without them. I would at least be free to make decisions on my own, and to have a drink when I wanted.

The first decision I made on my own was to take three hundred dollars of my winnings out of the savings account that Craig had put it in. I didn't tell Craig that I wanted to spend the money, and I didn't ask Irene to help me shop for the costumes I intended to buy with it. I didn't even ask Craig for the car when I was ready to shop; I announced that I was taking it and would be back later.

"If you need something, I'll go to the store for you. Or Jason and I can ride along if you want," Craig offered.

"No thanks. I want to be alone for a while." I kissed them and walked to the door. "You guys have fun. I won't be long."

I walked through the main corridor at the mall without entering any stores at first, just enjoying my independence. In my head, I marked off the stores I wanted to return to later, then erased them with "*I beg your pardon, I never promised you a rose garden.*"

Craig and I had both gotten what we deserved. He knew that I was nothing but trouble and married me anyway. And I wasn't even pregnant. I knew he wanted to protect me, and that I'd never make him happy, and I married him anyway. Neither of us had any right to expect a rose garden.

I wanted to sing since I learned to talk - long before I met Craig. It was my oldest memory and the only dream I had. He knew that. He also knew that I drank before he married me, and that I was sick of having people manipulate me. Did he rescue me from my parents, only to control me himself?

I stayed in the corridor until I knew I could walk into a store without taking any of my controllers with me, not even in my mind. I went in without Momma's criticism of my skinny legs and flat chest. I left Irene's love of western wear behind, and forgot Craig's favorite colors and styles. I took my free mind and walked through a whole store waiting for something to catch my eye. I hoped to learn Penny Sue's taste, finally.

I didn't look at price tags. If I found what I liked, I intended to buy it even if it took the whole three hundred dollars I had marked for my costumes. If I needed more than that, I'd charge it and go back to the savings account to pay it later. My new attitude drew attention to me. Sales clerks seemed eager to help me.

"Are you looking for something in particular," a girl who appeared to be about my age asked as I wandered through a small boutique that I would normally have passed by because it looked expensive.

I laughed. "No, just the opposite. I'm looking for nothing particular. I'm open to anything today."

"May I help?" she asked. "This is the fun way to shop."

I nodded, so she stepped back and studied me carefully. "You'd look good in just about anything. You're so thin."

That was the first time anyone had made me feel good about being thin. She said it like I was lucky, and she didn't seem to hate me because I was lucky.

"I have something I want you to try on," she said, rushing to the back of the store like she couldn't wait for me to see it. I followed at her heels, caught up in her excitement.

"We only ordered one of each size in this, so you won't see someone else in it everywhere you go," she explained. "Many of our things are unique. Here," she said, pulling the outfit from a rack.

I was a little disappointed because it didn't look like much on the hanger. The top was shapeless, and hung in a narrow strip over the pants, which were draped across a hanger. I liked the color. It was somewhere between royal and navy blue.

She grabbed my arm and pulled me toward the fitting room. "Go in there and try it on. I think it will be perfect with your hair and eyes."

As soon as she closed the door and left me alone, I read the inside tag to confirm what I suspected. One hundred percent silk, dry clean only. I had never touched real silk that I could remember, much less covered my body in it. Nervously, I removed the outfit from the hanger and put it on.

The pants fit snugly, from the hip-hugger waistline through the knee, and then flared at the bottom. The pant legs hit the floor, but would be perfect with heels. The top, cut in the same style, fit closely through the shoulders and bodice, and flared at the bottom of the sleeves and at the waist. There were only four small buttons, covered in the same silk fabric, so it was open at the bottom and a bit of skin showed between the last button and the top of the pants.

I stared at myself in the mirror, turning to see it from all angles. I loved it, and thought there was something familiar about the look. Maybe Dusty Springfield wore it?

225

"Hurry up. The suspense is killing me," my salesclerk called, knocking on the door to rush me.

Afraid the clerk's eyes wouldn't reflect what I thought I saw in the mirror, I held my breath and opened the door. She pulled me out of the fitting room and made me model the outfit in the aisle so she could get a good look.

"It's perfect on you." She squealed and clapped her hands. Another customer stopped scraping hangers across a rack to look. She agreed, adding that the color made my blue eyes jump right off my face.

"I'll take it," I said, still not knowing the price.

I went back into the fitting room to change into my old clothes and came out carrying my silk outfit. The salesclerk took it from me and began wrapping it in tissue paper instead of stuffing it in a paper sack the way they packaged my things where I usually shopped.

"Are you going to wear this for a special occasion?" she asked as she placed the tissue wrapped items in a silver shopping bag.

"Sort of." I told her about winning the contest and having the ten club dates as a result. "Do you think this is okay to wear on stage?"

"It's perfect. Oh, how exciting. I may have just helped a future star," she told a co-worker who had joined her behind the counter. "What's your name," she asked, "so I can listen for you on the radio."

"Raven Coal." The words came out as naturally as if that had always been my name.

"Cash or credit, Raven?" she asked, punching at the cash register.

"That depends. How much it is." I held my breath and waited.

"One twenty-six, with tax."

"Cash," I said, relieved. At this rate, I could get another costume and a pair of shoes. I paid her for the blue outfit, thanked her, and then told her I might want a second costume if she thought she had something else that might work.

She thought for a second and came up with a red skirt and black blouse. "Both pieces are on sale today. You could get the whole outfit for eighty dollars."

I walked out of the boutique with my independence, both outfits, a new fan, and ninety dollars still in my wallet. Before leaving the mall, I spent forty of those dollars on black heels that would match both costumes. Without caring who was watching, or how silly I looked, I danced in those shoes, right there in the store, and bought them, knowing that they'd be comfortable on stage.

To celebrate, I stopped at Jim's Liquors, a tavern/liquor store combination, for a shot, and a pint of Bacardi.

Jason was in bed when I got home. Craig sat on the couch strumming his guitar without the amplifier. "Did you have a good time?" he asked, without putting the guitar down.

"I did," I admitted. "Craig it felt good to have a little time to myself. Want to see what I bought?"

He asked me to try both outfits on for him, and told me I looked beautiful. As I walked across the living room in the blue costume, I remembered why it seemed familiar. Lori had designed the same pattern for me years earlier. That was the first time I had thought of Lori in a long time, and I wished I could tell her what was happening in my life.

"You're going to be a hit, everywhere you go," he said.

I believed him.

Chapter 30

Craig scheduled another vacation day to see me off, and to stay with Jason. He told me not to worry about breakfast, we would eat as a family when we got to the restaurant where he had arranged to meet and deliver me to Brian and his band. His obvious pleasure in making all decisions and organizing my life struck a nerve in me.

"We'll probably have to get Irene to drop you off next time," he said. "Dad won't want me to take off every Friday for this."

A second nerve reacted. "Are you always going to work for your dad?" The question had been on my mind since we graduated, but always before I had thought it wasn't my business to say where I thought he should work. It was my turn to organize his life. "Don't you ever think about getting out on your own?"

He looked surprised by my questions. "I never really gave it much thought," he admitted. "Dad pays me enough and he lets me off for things like this. Besides," he added, "we're on our own. We have our own place, and we raise Jason without any help."

"Enough? Is that all you want out of life?"

Now he looked hurt. "I didn't know it bothered you. What do you want that you don't have?"

"Independence." The word shot from my mouth without any thought beforehand. "I don't want your parents or mine—including Irene—controlling anything we do, or keeping tabs on us. And more money wouldn't hurt either. We could buy a house one day, or a second car. Maybe we could take a real vacation once. I've never been anywhere on earth except Crayfield, Nashville, and here. Wouldn't you like to go to Florida, or Mexico?"

He nodded, but his eyes were far away. He wasn't agreeing with me, he was killing time until a logical discouragement came to him.

"Don't you want a nicer house?" I asked, refusing to let him off the hook without an answer.

"I never really thought about it," he repeated.

"Well, think about it," I ordered like I wouldn't consider an option. "Think about those things while I'm gone, Craig. Where are we headed? Or do you want to stand still for the rest of our lives?"

A white truck pulled into the parking lot and Craig pointed when Brian got out on the driver's side. "They're here," he said, obviously relieved to end our conversation.

I wrapped the last wedge of my club sandwich in a napkin and shoved it in my purse. It wasn't exactly the tour bus I had expected, but I was glad they had come to pick me up.

"Give me the keys and I'll get my things out of the car while you pay the bill," I offered, enjoying my take-charge attitude.

He handed me his keys and unbuckled Jason from the highchair. "I'll be out in a minute. Please don't leave without saying good-bye."

* * *

After I kissed Craig and Jason, and Brian promised Craig he would take good care of me, Brian opened the passenger door for me to climb in the truck. While he carried my bags to the back, I continued to wave good-bye to Jason until they had pulled out of the parking lot and he could no longer see me.

Inside, the truck wasn't as disappointing as it had appeared from the outside. The driver and one passenger (me for this trek) had over-stuffed captain's chairs up front, with a table between them. Between those chairs and the wall that divided the cab from the back of the truck, where the equipment was stored, there was a living area with a padded bench seat that went all the way across, another table, and a chair on the side that didn't have a sliding door.

Brian drove off as he made introductions. "That's Keith passed out on the bench back there. He plays bass. He's been out like a log since we left Nashville, and if we're lucky, he'll stay that way the rest of the trip. He never shuts up when he's awake."

"This is Phil on my side, the drummer, and Link behind you. He'll cover lead and steel. There's a refrigerator under the table they're playing cards on if you get thirsty. And this is Penny," he told them.

"Raven," I corrected. I had called Madeline the day after my shopping spree to clear it with her. She said she would notify the clubs of the name change, but warned me that I would have to stick with it the whole trip. "I am prepared to stick with Raven."

I told Phil and Link I was happy to meet them. Link nodded in my direction, still studying the cards in his hand and Phil said likewise.

"We changed the group a bit," Brian explained. "Instead of the fiddle, I brought Link along. He'll cover all of the same leads as before, switching instruments, so we do it with less people.

I had never been in the room with a live steel guitar player, much less sang with one. I hoped it wouldn't throw me off. I did a quick rundown of the instruments I'd never seen – banjo, mandolin, steel guitar.

"Music is music, right?" I tried to sound optimistic and secretly hoped Brian would verify my belief.

"What'd I tell you, guys?" he asked. "She has a great attitude." He reached behind the seat for Phil to slap a five on his hand.

"Yes, Raven, music is music. You just sing your little heart out and remember when to come in after the leads, and everything will be fine," Brian coached.

"Your seat lies back if you want to sleep," Link told me. "And any time you get tired of sitting and want to stretch out, just let me know and I'll swap places with you. We have sleeping bags in the overhead if Keith keeps on hogging the bed and you want to lie down flat on the floor."

I thanked him and looked at Brian from the corner of my eye to see if he had anything to add. His eyes were on the road and his thoughts with them. I noticed how handsome he was from the side, even though his hair was nearly gone on top. I decided he had plenty enough in his ponytail to make up for what he was missing up front.

Before Brian, or anyone else, noticed that I was staring at him, I reclined my seat halfway and turned my head. Physical comfort might override the emotional shock I felt when I realized that I was taking off with a truck full of strangers.

The next thing I knew, Brian was waking me from a sound sleep. "We're thirty minutes outside of Indianapolis. The guys need a pee break so we pulled off. Do you need anything while we're here?"

I oriented myself, a little embarrassed about falling asleep and missing everything that had gone on around me. "Will we have a dressing room at the club?" I asked. "Or should I get ready here?"

"We'll either have a room, or you can get ready here in the truck," he explained. "This rig has a generator, so we have lights, cold drinks, and air-conditioning, even when the engine is turned off. We'll probably end up spending the night in here. If not tonight, most likely on the Missouri or Illinois gigs. Madeline is kind of tight about springing for hotels on these short trips."

I didn't really need the bathroom but decided to go inside while we were stopped. I took my purse with me and took a swig from the rum bottle while on the toilet. I brushed my teeth and hair before going back to the truck.

"You're fast," Brian said from the back. "Link is driving the rest of the way. Want to come back here with me and we'll map out the show?"

I picked up my purse, returned the seat back to a sitting position, and moved to join Brian. Keith sat in the front with Link, and Phil helped us plan the song list.

"You only have to do one song each set according to your contract," Brian explained. "Madeline gave us your song list and the tapes Craig sent, so we have charts to work from. It'll be a little rough the first time through, but we'll be fine." He must have seen the disappointment in my expression, because he asked if I wanted to do more. "It's up to you. Just remember the money stays the same."

"Did you make charts for all my songs?" I asked. "How many did I send?" Which should have been a stupid question, but wasn't since somebody else took charge and sent them for me.

He pulled a folder out of the overhead and opened it. "There were eighteen total on the list," he said. "Only six on the tape. We made charts for the six, but we can probably wing a couple more."

He and Phil looked over the list. Phil put a checkmark beside the songs that he knew. Brian read off the songs that Phil knew, and put another mark beside the ones that they all knew. We added four to the six they had charts for.

"Okay, that's ten," Brian said. "We can repeat the songs from the first set again on the last set, because the same people aren't usually there for both."

"If they are, they're too drunk to remember," Phil pointed out.

"We do five sets. Do you want to do three songs a set?" he asked.

I said I did, and he worked out the song lists to accommodate. "We'll bring you up after the third song in each set. Pay attention and be in place about halfway through the song before yours."

We passed a sign that said five miles to Indianapolis and my stomach jumped with excitement instead of fear. I couldn't decide if the Grand Ole Opry show had cured me of my stage fright, or if Brian's confidence made me feel more comfortable than I had ever been before.

We didn't have a dressing room at the club so I changed into my blue outfit in the truck while the guys unloaded equipment from the back. After they set up the stage and I downed two strawberry daiquiris, they changed in the truck and I went to the women's restroom to redo my make-up and drink my rum.

As soon as I had finished my first three songs, my excitement turned into disappointment. Counting the bartenders and waitresses, there were nineteen people in the club. One of them clapped after I sang Linda Ronstadt's "When Will I Be Loved". I wished I were back at the VFW, or Harvey's even, where the audience at least noticed me. Where there *was* an audience.

I left the stage and ran to the restroom, where I stayed while the guys finished their set. I wanted to stay there until two o'clock when we could leave, but Brian came after me.

"Brian, this is the women's room," I said. "You can't come in here."

"I'm here, so I guess I can if I want." He chuckled. "I locked the door so no one will come in and be shocked to see me."

So much for my independence and confidence. I felt like a child now that he had come after me. I stared at the floor and waited for him to tell me how unprofessional I was.

"I like your outfit. The color is great on you," he said.

"Thanks," I mumbled. "I'm sorry I ran off. I felt stupid sitting out there after nobody even clapped."

"Pen, I mean Raven, this is how clubs are," he explained. "Probably eighty percent of the people are only here to drink or pick up somebody to take home later. They wouldn't care if the club played a radio, and they don't know talent when they hear it. The clubs pay us to draw the other twenty percent, and so they can charge a cover."

"The VFW is packed every weekend. I guess I expected the same here."

"In another hour, you won't be able to walk through this place, trust me. For some reason they don't come out until late. Don't take it personally. It's the same everywhere, no matter who's playing."

Someone banged on the door and yelled for us to open up.

"You go first," he said, pushing me ahead of him. "I don't want to scare her."

The place wasn't full yet, but at least there were a few people sitting at tables and a couple more on the dance floor. He was right, they were dancing to the recorded music coming through the house speakers like they didn't care if there was a band or not.

Brian took my hand and led me to a table in the corner by the stage. "This table is reserved for the band. It might be safer to stay here where we can keep an eye on you when you aren't on stage."

"I won't run away again," I promised. "You don't have to watch over me."

He squeezed his cheeks between his thumb and index finger, and I smiled because I thought he looked cute, like a little boy, that way.

"Let's get this straight," he said. "I'm not worried about you running away. I believe you're more professional than that. I'm worried that one of these creeps will give you a hard time if he sees you wandering around here alone, especially in that outfit."

"And you don't think I can take care of myself," I added.

"I didn't say that. Actually, I think you could. But I don't want to see you in that position. Call me old-fashioned, I guess. I want to protect my ladies."

"Old-fashioned," I teased. "But thanks. I'll be careful."

While I waited for my cue song, I thought about the conversation. I had never been in a fight in my life, yet I felt able to defend myself. Maybe it was because I had spent so much time dreaming about beating my mother to a pulp. Or because I had watched her pummel my father and figured if she could, so could I. Or maybe it was because I had twenty years of anger stored inside and believed I could turn that into power, under the right circumstances.

My second set went better. People on the dance floor made eye contact with me and smiled, and they clapped after each song. I drew energy from them, and wished I could stay on the stage after my songs were over. A drunk at the bar and Brian must have had the same thought as me. The drunk yelled 'more' when I put my microphone back on the stand, and Brian called me over to him.

"Do you play tambourine? There's one in front of the drums if you want to stay up here."

"Where should I stand?" I asked. I had never touched a tambourine but didn't think it could be that hard.

He used his head to point to the space between his keyboard and the drums.

Phil grinned when I picked up the instrument. "Now they've got something to look at," he called out.

Each set was better than the last. My performance improved in direct proportion to the number of people in the room.

During the break before the last set, Keith sat down next to me at the band table instead of rushing to the bar for a drink as he had the other sets. "Son of a bitch, I thought Brian was full of shit when he told us about you. But he didn't exaggerate a fucking bit. You're a hell of a singer."

I thanked him, after I figured out that he had complimented me somewhere in the middle of his cuss words. "I started out a little nervous," I said. "But each set got easier."

Several people came to the table to say that they had enjoyed the music, and to ask where I was from and when I would be back. One lady said it would be better if I sang more, and couldn't believe me when I told her that I had only met these musicians a few hours earlier so we didn't have many songs worked up.

Brian was right. I repeated my first set again in the last hour and received a completely different reaction. One whole table on the right side of the stage stood up and screamed after I sang, "Rescue Me".

Instead of staying on stage while the band finished out the final set, I jumped down and went to the bar for my free drink. I felt Brian's eyes on me the whole time. As the bartender pushed my shot over to me, he said I had more free drinks coming if I wanted them. "Brian told me to put anything you want on his tab, and several fans have asked to buy you a drink."

"Then I'll have two more of these," I told him. "Charge them to the fans."

He brought the drinks and leaned across the bar to speak quietly. "I told you about the fans because it was the right thing to do. May I suggest that you let Brian pay for these instead? Some of these guys around here think they have a right to expect something in return if you take their money."

I told him to hold on while I went to get my purse from behind Link's amplifier. I paid for my own drinks.

"At the risk of ruffling your pretty little feathers," Brian said later, "I'm going to ask you to sit here with this bouncer while we change and pull the truck up to the door."

I rolled my eyes, mostly over the pretty feathers comment.

"I know, you're a big girl and you can take care of yourself," he said. "But I've seen some people in here who even I wouldn't want to meet in the dark. Please humor me on this. I'm not in the mood to fight, even for your honor."

The bouncer backed him up. "There are some crazy fuckers in here. Better safe than sorry, I always say."

I sat at the table, where the bouncer could see me, and drank another shot, this time charged to Brian.

Brian surprised me by bringing my bag when he came back in. "I thought you'd be more comfortable changing inside," he said.

"Shows what you know about women," I replied. "Apparently you've only visited the women's room at the beginning of the night and never at the end. I'm not dragging these pants across a wet floor."

I picked up my bag and started toward the door.

"Wait!" He called after me, but I kept walking.

He laughed when I tried to open the truck and found the door locked. I looked away while he opened it, and went inside without looking at him. After changing my clothes, I finished off the rum in my purse and curled up on the bench to wait while the guys loaded their equipment in the back of the truck.

I didn't wake until morning. Keith and Phil had the front seats, reclined into sleeping positions. Link was in a sleeping bag on the floor, under the backs of their seats, and Brian was asleep in a chair, with his head leaning over on the table. I had the bench to myself.

Brian looked up as soon as he heard me move and put a finger to his lips. He wrote me a note. "Keith is sleeping off a killer headache. Let's give him a little more time."

"Craig will be worried to death," I wrote back.

"I called him last night, he's cool," he answered.

"Do you want the bench for a while?"

"I'm fine. We shared it most of the night."

I dropped the pen on the table and laid back down.

Chapter 31

Jason was napping when I called home from the payphone at Jerry's, so Craig stayed with him and sent Irene to pick me up. While we waited for her to arrive, I asked Brian to get my bags out of the truck so they could take off. He stood beside me, refusing to leave me alone until she arrived.

As he transferred my bags from the back of the truck to the trunk of Irene's car, he gave her a full report on his babysitting job. "She was great, a little nervous the first set but we worked it out quickly." He talked about me like I couldn't speak for myself, or I wasn't there. "She'll be great on the road. She slept like a rock, on a narrow bench in the truck. Never complained or asked for a thing."

Irene took it in like a proud mother. "Thanks for taking care of her and bringing her home safely. I'm glad I got to meet you."

"Aren't you supposed to pay him now?" I asked. "Or does he babysit for free like you do?"

"She's a feisty one." Brian smiled. To make things even worse, he tousled my hair. I hated him at that moment.

"What's the matter? You don't have any hair of your own so you have to abuse mine?" I asked.

"Penny!" Irene blushed and turned her head away. "She didn't mean that. What's wrong with you, Penny?" She turned back to face Brian and rambled on, saying she didn't understand what had come over me and, "I've never heard her be rude to anyone before."

"Why are you apologizing for me, Irene?" I asked. "I'm an adult, and quite capable of speaking for myself."

I looked from her to him, and back again, waiting for one of them to speak.

"Does this mean you aren't going to hug me good-bye?" he asked, squishing his face between his fingers again.

"I hadn't planned to anyway," I said. "Call me this week and we car work on the song list. Good-bye." I walked away from him and got in Irene's car without looking back. She followed right behind me.

"Whew," Irene sighed after she had said good-bye to the guys and joined me in the car. "I guess I missed something big. Do you want to tell me about it?"

"Okay. Yes, I do. I don't need people talking for me, thinking for me, or watching over me. I swear Jason has more freedom than I do. Irene, I'm twenty-one years old and it's about time everyone treated me like I'm an adult."

"Did he give you a hard time?" she asked. "If this isn't working out, we can talk to Madeline and try to get it straightened out. You can probably get out of that contract if there are big problems."

I smacked my forehead. "It's not only Brian. It's everyone. Before we left, Craig made a deal with Brian to watch over me while we were gone. You just apologized for me, like I'm a child. My parents controlled me for seventeen years, even when they didn't watch over me. Then, they turned me over to Craig, who treats me like I'm his child instead of his wife, and you're acting more like a mother the older I get."

She pulled into a Blue Boar Cafeteria parking lot and turned the engine off.

I laughed. "I'm not *this* old. I don't need cafeteria food yet."

"Let's get something to eat and talk this through," she said. "I don't want you going home in this mood, and I'm not sure I understand the problem yet. Do you mind? I'm hungry."

I called Craig to tell him that I was okay and would be a few minutes longer. He sounded disappointed until I told him that Irene was hungry and wanted to stop. Then, it became a good idea.

I was too mad to eat, so I got lemonade and watched her eat an assortment of over-cooked, dried out vegetables.

"First, I'm sorry," Irene said, and took a break to blow on her steamed carrots. "I'm not good at this mothering stuff. I never meant to compromise your independence, or embarrass you. Second, Craig and I love you and want to protect you for that reason, not to control you or make you miserable."

I added a packet of Sweet'N'Low to my drink and stirred while I thought about my answer. "I know you love me. I love both of you too. And I know neither of you deliberately tries to hurt me, but it still makes me feel terrible when you treat me this way."

"Let's make a deal," she said. "From now on, you tell me everything I do that makes you uncomfortable or pisses you off. That's the only way I can learn to correct the problem."

I said I needed more lemonade and went for a refill instead of waiting for our server to come around to refill glasses. I walked slowly, and went to the back of the line so I'd have time to think. I didn't understand why her words upset me. She had finished her vegetables and was working on a slice of coconut cream pie when I slipped back into my side of the booth.

"Thanks for what you said," I offered, in a neutral tone. "I know it was a very nice thing for you to say, but for some reason it made me angry. I'll get over it."

"Thank you for the honesty," she said. "Want a bite of this pie? It's delicious."

"Not with lemonade. Thanks anyway."

I turned my glass in circles while she finished her pie and left a tip on the table. "Does that mean we're ready to go?" I asked.

She shrugged. "Unless you want to sit here and say thanks to each other all day. It's up to you."

I slid out of the booth and led her to the door. We didn't talk until she pulled up in front of the house to let me out. "I can get my bags in alone," I told her.

She turned the engine off and handed me the keys to the trunk. I kissed her cheek when I returned the key. "Irene, I love you. I need time to think about a lot of things. Please don't be mad at me."

There weren't any streamers or posters this time, but Craig and Jason met me at the door and acted like I had been gone for twenty-four days instead of twenty-four hours. Craig took my bags and handed Jason to me.

"He cried for you last night," Craig reported. "I had to bring him in our room and let him sleep with me."

I hugged Jason close to me and looked at Craig over his head. "Why did you tell me that?"

His smile faded, and he didn't respond.

"Why?" I asked again. "Did you want to make me feel guilty for leaving him to do something that was very important to me? Or did you think it would make me feel good to hear that my son was unhappy? And why did you smile like you thought it was good that he cried?"

"Penny, what's wrong with you? Why are you twisting things around like this?"

"You think it's twisted? Answer the question, Craig. Why did you tell me that? Let's get to the bottom of twisted."

He sat down in his chair and scratched his head. I thought of Brian's balding scalp, but quickly returned my attention to Craig when I noticed that he looked ready to cry. I almost wanted to take my questions back.

"I wanted you to know that Jason missed you is all," he finally said. "I wasn't thinking any deeper than that. I guess I thought it would make you feel good to know that you were missed, but I swear I never thought that you'd be happy because he was sad."

I nodded. "I know, Craig. You didn't think about how I would feel. You thought about Jason, and how you wanted me to react, but not about my real feelings. I know you weren't thinking anything mean, because you never do." I should have stopped there but couldn't. "You just plain don't think. The point is my feelings matter and people need to think about them."

"You already told me that. And last night I thought about what you said before you left. You're right. I need to look for another job, and move this family forward. I don't want to sit still. I'm going to do that, Penny."

I closed my ears to him and turned to a mental song. He talked for a good twenty minutes more and I didn't hear a word. This wasn't the time for him to say what I wanted to hear yesterday.

"I'm tired, Craig, and I haven't had a bath. I'm going to soak in the tub for a while and relax."

"If you want to wait until later, I'll join you after Jason goes to bed.

"If I had wanted to wait until later, I wouldn't have said that I was going now, would I?" I left without looking at the wounded expression I could picture without peeking.

I heard Craig dial the phone while the water filled the tub, and knew he was calling Irene to compare notes on how crazy I was acting. If I had tried, I probably could have heard the conversation. Instead, I went over my songs and blocked out all sounds, including his voice.

I pulled up nearly every song I had ever known, and imagined how each would sound with Brian's band. Gradually, my thoughts moved from Brian's band to just Brian, the man. Had he really shared the bench with me the night before, and I didn't feel him there? Probably not. He would say anything he could think of to upset me. He had done it the whole trip, but what he had done in front of Irene was plain unforgiveable.

If I didn't like him, and didn't want to forgive him, why was I wasting my time thinking about him? Nothing made any sense.

Craig knocked on the bathroom door. "Are you okay in there? It's almost time for Jason's bath."

I doubted that Jason would suffer any serious consequences if he stayed up a few minutes late one night, or if he missed his bath altogether. But I didn't argue. I pulled the plug and surrendered my haven like a good little girl. And I wished I hadn't finished off the Bacardi because I would have gone straight to the bedroom to do so while he bathed Jason if I still had it.

"Look how clean Mommy is," Craig mocked. "She took a nice long bath."

Jason giggled and ran past me to throw his plastic boat in the tub.

"I'll turn his bed back and get it ready," I offered, to let Craig know that I expected him to bathe his son. I sat at the table with my old notebook and made a song list for Brian while I waited on them to finish in the bathroom. Then, I carried Jason to his room and tucked him in.

"Stay here, Mommy." He held onto my neck and wouldn't let go.

"Jason, I'm staying at home tonight. I'll sleep in my bed with Daddy, and I'll be here when you wake up in the morning. Sometimes I need to go away, like I did yesterday, but I promise I'll always come back."

When I came out of Jason's room, Craig was waiting at the door. "Do you think he understands that?" he asked.

"He might," I answered. "I don't know. But I do know that he'll never understand what I don't tell him, so I'd rather try than not. One day he'll get it."

"That makes sense," he admitted. "Maybe one day you can start explaining things to me and I'll get them too."

I turned the TV on and stretched out on the couch. Craig sat across the room and stared into space. I fell asleep before long. I don't know what he did, until he carried me to bed at eleven.

"Are you sleeping?" he asked.

"I was," I whispered back.

"Do you feel like waking up?" He curled in behind me and kissed the back of my neck.

"Not really. Craig, this time I worked long hours, and I'm worn out."

He stopped kissing me, but stayed close, with his arms around me "Did you get to sleep? Brian said they gave you the bed on the truck, and that you were already asleep when he called."

"The bed was a bench in the back of a truck, and I don't know exactly what time he called you but it had to be sometime after three in the morning," I complained. "Craig, how many times have you pulled this too tired routine on me, and expected me to understand?"

"But I was really tired." He huffed and loosened his hug.

"So am I. I was on the road for twenty-four long hours. The club was wild. I was nervous. I'm stressed out of my mind over the song lists. Why are you doing this to me?"

He rolled over onto his back. "Usually you want me, especially if it has been a few days. What's different tonight?"

My defenses kicked in. What did he suspect? "I'm tired, I told you. What are you insinuating?"

"Nothing." He answered too quickly.

"Please don't lie to me, Craig. Say whatever is on your mind and get it over with."

"You drank too much last night, didn't you?"

I didn't know whether to laugh or cry. I thought he was going to accuse me of being with another man, but it was only the drinking that bothered him. Craig probably didn't think any other man would want me.

"We got a free drink at the end of the night," I said, leaving out the others. "Go to sleep, Craig."

He didn't say anything more. I kept my eyes closed, but was still awake when the sun came up. I had sleepless dreams, about Brian, and about Irene and Craig. Brian kissed me with those cute lips that he habitually scrunched between his fingers, and then teased me about it later. Irene practically killed herself trying to please me, but I wasn't satisfied with anything she did. And Craig spoke to me in a language that I didn't understand. Real nightmares were more pleasant.

I had a hard time facing Craig the next day. No matter what our problem was, I knew it wasn't that he didn't love me, or because he

241

didn't try to please me. I should have left him before Jason was born. No, I shouldn't have married him in the first place, because I knew he deserved more than I could give.

I felt guiltier over my imagined kiss with Brian than I had over the real-live incident with Billy Ranglin on our graduation night. Maybe because this one didn't repulse me. It played on my mind most of the day.

After Jason went to bed that night, Craig sat next to me on the couch. "Do you want to tell me about the trip?" he asked. "Are you upset with me because I didn't go?"

I rested my head on his shoulder. "No, Craig. I'm not upset because you were right. One of us should stay with Jason whenever possible."

I told him about the trip from beginning to end, leaving out the drinks and the possibility that Brian had slept next to me on the bench. "Kind of boring, huh?"

"It sounds like you were a hit. Brian said you got a standing ovation."

"I forgot that part. It was only one table that stood up. It wasn't such a big deal. But they did like me, Craig. And I loved it once I got over the shock of the empty first set. This is what I want to do."

He pulled me close and kissed my head. "I know that, Penny. This is what you have to do, not just what you want to do."

"How is it going to work, with Jason?" I asked.

"I'm still thinking about that. Penny, it will all work out somehow. Finish these ten gigs as planned and we'll see what comes next."

Neither of us was too tired that night. Craig wore himself out and went on to sleep. I stayed awake again, thinking about Brian and hating myself.

Chapter 32

By Tuesday, my brain was worthless from lack of sleep. Madeline called to ask what I had done to poor Brian and my heart jumped into my throat. Had I pushed him too far? So far that he had complained to Madeline and jeopardized the rest of my club dates?

"I'm not sure what you mean," I said, hoping she would volunteer information to help me understand how to talk my way out of the mess I had created. I would apologize—grovel even—if necessary.

"Brian is a difficult man to win over," she explained. "I've had several singers quit, complaining that he was impossible to please. And I can't tell you how many phone calls I've had to make to smooth over hurt feelings and problems with him. But, honey, he's totally smitten with you. He says you're the greatest thing since Brenda Lee, who he says is your idol, and he's throwing your name all over Nashville. Raven, that is. He's using your new name."

"I don't know how I managed that," I admitted, relieved but confused. "I was afraid he didn't like me, so this is a surprise."

"Trust me, he likes you. He asked me to call and get your updated song list from you. How soon can you get it to me?"

I told her that I had already worked on it and she held on while I went to get the notebook and read the new list to her. She promised to pass it on to Brian, and said he would be in touch with me soon.

I replayed the conversation until what little was left of my brain scrambled. What did she mean by he was smitten with me? And if he liked me so much, why had he asked her to call instead of calling me himself?

More importantly, did I want this balding, middle-aged man to be smitten with me? Was this about music, or something else, and were we in agreement on that point?

I told Craig that I thought I was coming down with a cold that evening, so he took Jason to visit with his parents and let me rest. I went to the phone a couple of times, thinking I should just call Irene, tell her the whole situation, and ask her advice. But each time I picked up the phone, I changed my mind before I dialed. She loved Craig.

I couldn't think straight about anything on Wednesday morning, and wanted a drink to calm my nerves. There was a liquor store less than six blocks from the house. I could have walked it if I didn't have Jason. Even if I hadn't been afraid that he would tell Craig, I knew he would want me to carry him most of the way and I wasn't up to that.

Shortly before lunch, I looked out the kitchen window and noticed Irene's car parked by the alley. There was hope after all. I went into the shop through the door in Jason's room.

"Why are you here on a Wednesday?" I asked. "Is something wrong?"

"Nothing serious," she said, pulling permanent rods from her customer's hair. "I accidentally booked two perms at the same time for tomorrow, so I called one in today. Everything okay with you?"

"I was sick last night and I'm not feeling much better today. I'm mostly dragging around getting nowhere," I complained.

"Have you taken anything?" Irene was too predictable for her own good.

"There's nothing here to take," I explained. I'll go get something after Craig gets home with the car."

She offered to go for me if I gave her thirty minutes to finish up, but I made a big deal about not wanting to be a burden. I was worse than I burden; I was a dishonest manipulator.

"Take my car and go. You can leave Jason here with me," she offered.

I sat Jason in a dryer chair with a stuffed gorilla and a storybook, got Irene's keys from her purse, and promised I'd hurry back. At Walgreens, I bought aspirin, cough syrup, and Bacardi.

The bottle wouldn't fit in a tampon box, so I stuck it under a couch cushion this time, disappointed that I wouldn't be able to get to it as easily as before. I'd have to do my drinking only while Craig worked or slept.

Craig pampered me that night since I still felt sick. He fixed dinner, and encouraged me to take my medicine and lie down after we ate. "You need to be well before the weekend. I heard that club in Jasper is huge. Boomer played there once."

"Yes, Madeline mentioned that when she called," I told him. "Are you planning to go there with me?"

He shrugged, unconvincingly. "Penny, I thought we agreed that I should stay with Jason."

"We did. I'm sorry I brought it up," I said, hating myself again for setting him up. "Honest, I'm not upset. I won't ask you about going anymore because I know you're right about Jason and you would go if you could."

He hugged me and made me feel worse.

"Did I tell you that we got rooms in Jasper? The club is part of a big hotel, and they provide rooms for band members who come from out of town. Madeline didn't know if the guys would want to stay over, but at least I won't have to dress in the truck this time."

"That's good news." He sounded relieved. "Penny, I'd rather know you are in a hotel than a truck. It's safer. One of the things that bothered me about these jobs was the idea that those guys planned to drive back at the end of the night. It would be different if they had a driver who hadn't worked all night."

"Did you tell Brian that? Is that why we slept in the truck last week?"

"I don't know if my opinion influenced their decision," he admitted. "But yes, I did tell him what I thought."

He ended the conversation by telling me to get some rest, and left me alone in the bedroom. I rested my body, but my mind continued to race. Could Brian resent me because my husband had butted in and forced him to sleep over in Indianapolis? He'd had two days to contact me about the song list. Why hadn't he called to tell me whether or not they were adding any songs to the list for next week? Why would he say those nice things to Madeline about me, and then ignore me?

When he hadn't call on Thursday, I drank half of the rum. I finished it off on Friday morning, using the same excuse.

An hour after I threw the empty bottle in the garbage, I went back out to get it. Our next scheduled trash collection wasn't until Tuesday. That left the weekend for Craig to take out the trash and discover the evidence. At first, I put the empty bottle in my purse, intending to toss it out while I was away. Later I took it back out to make room in case I got a full one. I ended up stuffing it back under the couch cushion.

Irene came in to ask if I had heard from Brian.

"No, he's so inconsiderate." My tone was nearly a scream. "I'm packed and waiting, but still no word."

"I'm here," she reminded me. "Calm down. Whenever they call I'll drive you to meet them, and I'll stay with Jason until Craig gets home."

"Irene, you don't think they would ditch me with no warning, do you?"

She shook her head. "I wouldn't think so. Listen Penny, if worse turns to worst and the plans were mixed up, I'll drive you to Jasper. Give it another hour and then call Madeline."

The phone finally rang at three, ten minutes before the hour was up. Phil was on the other end, not Brian.

"Are you ready to go?" His voice was cheerful, but I was too disappointed and frustrated to respond the same.

"I'm ready, but it will take a few minutes for me to get there. Nobody called to tell me what time we were to meet," I explained.

"The wires got crossed somewhere," he said, still pleasant. "Didn't Madeline let you know we'd pick you up at your house this time?"

I tried to keep the frustration out of my voice. "No, she didn't. I've been sitting here all day, worried that I had missed my ride."

"I apologize, Raven. Calm down, honey, we're right on schedule and everything is cool. We'll be there in ten minutes. I've already got you circled on my map."

I put my bags by the door and scribbled a note to Craig. With two minutes to spare, I went to the medicine cabinet for a swallow of cough syrup.

When the truck pulled up out front, I kissed Irene and Jason, and carried my bags out. Jason didn't cry, because he was with Irene and knew he was in for a good time.

Link got out to help with my bags this time, and then he crawled into the back of the cab to leave the passenger seat for me. Phil sat in the driver's seat.

I turned to say hello to everyone, and spotted Brian in the chair at the back table. He responded with the least amount of enthusiasm of any of them.

"Jasper is less than four hours," Phil told me. "We'll get there in time to check into our rooms and have dinner. There's a lot of good eating in Jasper, but none better than right there in the hotel."

I didn't care about food. I hadn't eaten much in the last week and nothing appealed to me then. "Do we all get our own rooms?" I asked.

"They usually double us up. Don't worry, though, you'll always get your own room since you're the only female."

I thanked him and reclined my seat, planning to sleep until we arrived at the hotel.

Brian harassed me less than five minutes after we had pulled away from my house. "Hey, Sleeping Beauty. Don't you think we should work on set lists before you doze off?" I decided Madeline must have lied to me.

I flipped my seat back into the upright position and turned to face him. "Since you didn't bother to call, I assumed we would do the same songs that we used last week."

"Take a little advice from a friend and never assume," he warned. "It's dangerous. Why don't you come back here and look at what we've got ready."

I sat on the bench and worked on song lists with the guys, avoiding eye contact with Brian as much as possible. We added a fourth song for me in each set. Since I liked to stay on stage, they mixed my songs in with theirs this time.

"You're almost earning your cut of the check this time," Brian teased. Keith laughed alone.

We were assigned three adjoining rooms. Brian and Phil shared a room on one end, Keith and Link on the other, and I was in the middle where everyone could watch over me. Phil tried to carry my bags to the room but I took them from him.

When the door closed, I realized it would be the first night I had spent alone in my life. I could do anything I wanted in the privacy of my very own hotel room and nobody would ever know. I wouldn't let my resentment toward Brian spoil another second of my time.

I pulled the drapes tighter so there was no possibility of anyone peeking through the crack, double checked the locks on the doors, and sat my bag in front of the inside door that connected me to my band, for added security. After years of sleeping on the couch, followed by sharing a bed with Craig, the two double beds in my private room made my heart race.

Despite the lectures I had given Jason about the danger, I kicked my shoes off, and climbed on the bed that was further away from the windows, and jumped until I knew I'd giggle out loud and give myself away if I didn't stop. When the excitement settled I unpacked my bag, happy to have a dresser all to myself even if it did only have one drawer.

As I lined my cosmetics on the counter in the bathroom, someone tapped on the adjoining door. "Who is it," I called.

"Since only two of us live here, you have a fifty-fifty chance if you want to guess." It was Brian's voice.

I opened the door and he charged through. "Everyone else went down to the buffet about ten minutes ago. Are you about ready?"

"Nobody bothered to tell me the plan," I complained. "Just like nobody told me you'd pick me up at the house, or what time, or that you had worked up more songs. You should have gone with the others. I'm not hungry."

"Sure you are," he said. "Come on, I'll escort you to the dining room." He offered his arm to me like the gentleman I didn't think he was.

"No, I'm not hungry. Why does everybody think they know more about me than I know about myself?"

"I can't speak for everybody, but I know you're hungry because I heard your stomach growl in the truck." I understood the expression shit-eating-grin then, because that's what I saw on his face. "It's your business if you want to starve yourself. Just don't mess up tonight because you were too stubborn to come to dinner. Then it will be my business."

Defeated, I slipped my shoes on and grabbed my purse, but I didn't take his arm. When I stepped out into the hall ahead of him, he still hadn't moved.

"Why are you so impossible?" I asked. "You rush me out and then just stand there. Do you enjoy irritating me?"

He picked my room key up off the television. "You might need this, unless you were planning to enter through my room. Want me to bring it for you?"

Without answering, I stomped toward the elevator. He caught up, dramatically sticking my key into his pocket so I'd notice.

"I'll just hold on to this for you." He smirked.

The elevator door opened and we entered, avoiding eye or body contact. "One please," he ordered, and waited for me to push the button even though it was on his side. I didn't move. We stood there until the elevator buzzed before he laughed and pushed the button.

"Try to control yourself when we get off the elevator," he warned. "Remember, the people you pass in the halls and in the dining room may be the same ones you sing to tonight. Be careful with your image."

"Thank you, Daddy." I sneered, but as much as I hated to admit it, I was grateful for the warning and the advice. Without it, I might have made a fool of myself at dinner. As it turned out, I put a smile on my face as soon as the door opened again and shared a pleasant meal with the band.

Brian stayed with me through the buffet line, pulled my chair out at the table, and went back after the napkin that I had forgotten to pick up. He laughed easily and often during the conversation, and stayed with me after the others guys finished their meals and returned to their rooms.

I expected him to stop talking after they left, but he didn't. "Did you have a good week?" he asked, like an interested friend who hadn't spent the last few hours doing everything possible to annoy me.

I smiled, so anyone watching would have thought that we were happy together, and spoke softly. "I think you are insane. I've never met anyone more confusing, or confused, than you. I had a miserable week and I hope yours was the same." I continued to smile sweetly, never taking my eyes off his.

My words had no effect on him. He kept a smirk on his face and ran a hand over his head. "I hope your misery wasn't the result of worrying about that rude comment about my hair, because I never gave your comment a second thought."

"I never gave you a second thought," I lied. "Except when Madeline called to do your work for you."

"You thought about me the whole week. Don't lie, Raven, it isn't attractive. Why were you miserable thinking about me?"

I wiped my mouth on the napkin and laid it on the table. "I'm ready to go," I said. "I need to start getting ready."

"Enjoy yourself." He smiled but didn't attempt to get up.

I took a deep breath and blinked back tears. "May I have my key?"

"If you'll give me three minutes to smoke a cigarette, we can walk back together," he suggested.

I sat back in the chair and waited.

* * *

Brian went to the club early to meet with the sound and light people. I walked over later with Phil. The crowd loved me. I felt their energy and it was like the old times when the applause made me forget my problems. I didn't think about Brian, or Irene, or Craig, or anything that had gone wrong in my life. After my fourth song in the third set, I refused to stop.

"Do "Misty Blue" again," I called out to the band. Phil counted off the beat and the guys fell right in. When I finished that song, the club manager called me to the side of the stage and said he wanted to talk to me at the end of the set.

Brian caught my arm before I left the stage. "What did the big man want?"

I shrugged, too elated to let him bring me down. "He wants to talk to me. I guess I'll find out soon."

He pinched his face and rubbed his head. "Trust me without flying off the handle," he started. "It would be best if I went with you. Or Phil, if you don't want me."

"Do you really think I need a constant baby-sitter?"

"No. Do it your way, Raven. Just be careful if you go alone."

I pulled my arm away and went to meet the manager.

"I like what I see, and obviously my customers agree," he said, drawing himself a beer from the tap. "Can I get you something?"

I ordered a shot. "Thanks for the compliment, and the drink. I'm having a good time here."

"Since I booked this through Madeline as part of the contest tour, I know this isn't your permanent band. Do you have one?" he asked.

I told him about my band, and that my husband was my guitar player and co-writer on songs.

"I'd like to book you in here for a whole weekend. We have live music Thursday, Friday, and Saturday. Interested?"

My first instinct was to say yes, the sooner the better so I could get out of the VFW. I drank my shot and gained control. "I'd have to talk it over with the band. What does it pay?"

"Pays according to what you bring," he said.

I stopped him before he went into details. "Will you give me your number so I can call you next week? I need to get back now."

Brian left his seat at the end of the bar to follow me back to the band table. He put a shot on the table in front of me before speaking. "Did he offer to book you?"

"Yes. He asked if I have a regular band, and said he wants me for a whole weekend."

"What did you tell him?" He nodded at the still full glass in front of me and motioned toward the stage with his head.

I took the shot and stood up to go back to work. "I asked him for his number and said I'd get back to him."

He stepped up on the stage ahead of me and offered his hand to help me up. "You're a smart girl, Raven. I think you're going to be okay."

I banged the tambourine that set without looking to the right. The less I saw of Brian the better. He was purposely driving me crazy, nice one minute and a jerk the next. I almost missed my cue trying to figure him out instead of paying attention to the music.

We all walked together from the club back to our rooms. The guys changed clothes and went back to load equipment. I stayed in my room alone, and wished I had something to drink.

To take full advantage of my private room where I could do anything I wanted, I stripped my clothes off and left them on the floor – one of Momma's many pet peeves. With the remote in hand, I jumped from one bed to the other, flipping channels when I could make a connection. Even with hotel cable, there was nothing worth watching at four in the morning.

I gathered all four pillows and propped them behind me like I was a naked princess, only when I clapped my hands no one came to serve me. Thoughts of Brian came back quickly to push my imagination aside. As my mood deteriorated, the desire for a drink increased.

Maybe I could call room service and order a drink. But that would mean I'd have to get dressed. And getting dressed meant I needed a bath. No, a shower. I had almost forgotten that I had a real shower in my hotel room, something I would never have at home if we didn't buy a newer house.

My mind jumped from crazy thoughts to crazier thoughts, and I couldn't find a song to replace them. For a minute or two, I wished Craig had come with me because I could have used him to distract me. Used him. After the thought accidentally jumped into my head that way, I realized that that was exactly what I did to him. Poor Craig. He seemed to enjoy it. Did that make it right?

I heard the guys come down the hall and say good night to each other before they went into the rooms on either side of mine. A short time later, someone knocked on my outside door.

The guys would have used the adjoining doors. Who else would be up this late, or know that I was there? I wrapped the bedspread around me and crept slowly toward the peephole in the door.

As I stood with my eyeball almost touching the door, still unable to see anyone, the pounding started again.

I jumped back, shaking so badly that I had to hold on to the wall to keep my balance. I inched down the wall to Brian's door and tapped lightly.

"Someone's at my door," I whispered when he appeared. "I can't see who it is, and they won't stop knocking."

He stepped past me and walked to my door. "Who's there?" He asked the obvious question that I had forgotten.

"Room service," came the answer.

"Did you order something," he asked.

I rolled my eyes and huffed. "If I had ordered something, I would have put clothes on and answered the door instead of calling for you."

He led me into his room. "Don't get grumpy. I had to make sure. Wait here."

He returned to my room, closing the door between us, and answered my outside door. The deliveryman was nowhere in sight, but he had left a bottle of Jose Cuervo by the door.

"You can come back now, here's your visitor," he called, holding the bottle up for me to see.

"That's weird, Brian. I didn't order it. I thought about it, but didn't. Who would know what I drink, besides you guys?

"Anyone watching you at the bar," he answered.

I eyed the bottle, ready to open it. He held it tightly while he picked up the phone.

"I'm in room 342," he said. "Can you find out who just made a delivery to this room? I was in the shower and didn't tip."

He waited for the person on the other end to check, and then thanked him. He shook his head. "I'm glad you didn't answer that door," he said.

I sat on the foot of the bed, still wrapped in the spread. "Where's Phil? Could it have been him?"

Phil left as soon as we loaded the truck. One of his lady friends picked him up and they're headed for Chicago."

He walked around the room and picked up my clothes while he talked. "Looks like you undressed in a hurry."

"I was being defiant," I admitted. "While I had the chance I did all sorts of things that I've always wanted to do but didn't have the nerve. I threw my clothes on the floor and jumped on the bed naked."

He threw his head back and laughed out loud. I couldn't help but laugh with him.

"Drop them," I ordered. "This room will be a total mess before I leave here. In a little while I'm going to brush my teeth and leave toothpaste in the sink, and I might pee and not flush the toilet. Or maybe I'll skip all that and just drink what's in this bottle."

"I don't think that's a good idea. The bottle should be tamper-proof, but why take that chance?"

I hadn't thought of that. All I knew was I wanted a drink, and I was saying things that I didn't want to say, even without the drink.

"Come on," he said, guiding me into the bathroom by my shoulders. I want to watch you leave the biggest toothpaste blob you can in that sink. I'll skip the unflushed john though."

Suddenly I became self-conscious about my silly mood. Why was I telling him my secrets? No doubt, he would make fun of me later.

"I think I can probably live without the toothpaste experience."

"Oh no you don't. I came over here to rescue you, so you have to entertain me in return."

"You refused the drink," I said. "I don't have anything else to offer. Sorry."

He mumbled, so low that I barely heard. "You have a lot to offer."

My body betrayed Craig again. I needed to get away from this man, quickly. "Thanks for rescuing me, Brian. I think I should shower and get to bed now. I've had a long day."

"Will you be okay? Why don't you leave this door open so I'll hear if your admirer comes back?"

"I wish you hadn't put that thought in my head. Now I'll never get to sleep without that bottle."

"Hold on." He walked back into his room. I pulled my gown from the drawer, but didn't have time to put it on before he returned so I grabbed the spread again.

"I don't have a drink, but this might help your sleep problems," he said, lighting a joint.

"I've never smoked pot before." My pulse drummed in my head, making me almost dizzy. "I've never smoked anything."

"Then take it easy or you'll choke." He held it to my lips and coached me. I choked, but managed to hold smoke in my lungs on the second try. By the fourth hit, I had forgotten to hold the bedspread closed, and the load had lifted off my mind. I waved him off when he offered me a final hit off the stub between his fingers.

"Feel better now?" he asked.

In response, I fell back on the bed, completely relaxed. The bedspread was under me instead of around me, but I didn't care.

"You've lost your robe, my dear," he said, reaching across me to fix it. His fingers brushed my side and sent warm waves sloshing through the most sensitive parts of my body.

"Oh my God." I wasn't sure the words had come out until he leaned over me and smiled.

"Still want that shower, or would you rather wait now?" he asked.

"Wait," I whispered, wondering how he made his voice tickle my ears that way. When I opened my eyes I realized that his mouth was on my ear, I giggled at my lack of orientation.

"Are you relaxed? Do you think you can sleep now?" He pulled back, and I thought he was leaving.

"Please, don't go," I asked.

Pot had the exact opposite effect on me as alcohol. Instead of replacing sex, it made me want it more. On some level, I knew what I was doing was wrong, but that didn't stop me.

Chapter 33

Ohio was the next state on the itinerary. Madeline arranged for us to drive to Columbus on Thursday evening so we would have time to rest between the drive and set-up, and the performance. We would still stay in the hotel again on Friday, because it would be too late to drive back and too cold to stay in the truck, even with sleeping bags. It seemed more practical and cost-effective to hire an extra man to drive and move equipment, but I didn't suggest that to her. I planned to ask Brian's opinion later.

Madeline called to tell me the arrangements early on Tuesday. I waited until Wednesday night to tell Craig. My 'cold' conveniently lingered until I was sure I could look my husband in the eye without crumbling.

"Maybe your mother can watch Jason while Irene works on Friday morning," I suggested. "She always complains that she doesn't see him often enough."

"What you're forgetting about Mom is that she wants to see Jason with one of us present, that way she doesn't actually have to do anything for him," he reminded me. "She only watched him while we worked the VFW gigs because he came at bedtime and Dad and Gary were around to help her take care of him."

"Don't you think she'll watch him a couple of hours if you tell her it's important to you?"

"If nothing else," he said, "I'll stay home with him on Friday. I'll use my vacation time one hour or one Friday at a time if that's what it takes. We'll work this out."

I wanted to scream. Why couldn't he stand up for himself about anything? Why not tell his mother that he needed this favor and would be disappointed if she refused? Why didn't he tell me that the plans were unacceptable, or that finding a sitter for Jason was my responsibility? Just once, I wanted him to challenge me, the way Brian did.

That was the difference, carefully whittled into a three-word sentence. Brian challenged me. He made every part of me feel alive, and that was dangerous. In contrast, I felt like I had no life with Craig.

Brian respected my right to decide if I wanted to drink or smoke pot, or talk to a club manager without him. He wanted to watch me experience everything, including emotions. In one night, he had made me laugh, cry, scream, and relax. Maybe love and hate. And he jumped on the beds with me.

After spending the biggest part of four days in bed with my eyes closed, I still couldn't picture Craig jumping on the bed, with or without me. I had replayed my time with Brian a hundred times over, in my dreams and in full consciousness. I had tried to figure out what I could change to make my relationship with Craig the same as my relationship with Brian and decided it was impossible.

Craig let the conversation die when I stopped talking. I closed my eyes and watched another rerun of the trip.

Originally, I was devastated when I woke in the same bed with Brian. My first thought was that I had succeeded in following in every one of my mother's misguided footsteps. I didn't want to face him but he left me no choice. When I finally opened my eyes he was propped on his elbow, staring at my face. I turned my head away but he turned it back. When I met his eyes, the pained expression in his reflected the way I felt.

He drew a breath. I expected him to say that it had all been a mistake. We could pretend it never happened and return to our normal lives, tormenting each other on weekends until the tour ended. I braced myself, knowing the words would sting, but that he would be right.

"Raven, I don't know what to say. This is unforgivable," he started. "We wasted three perfectly good beds, and Madeline will still have to pay for them."

I laughed, probably much harder than necessary to compensate for the tears that poured from my eyes.

"We don't have much time before the guys start hounding me to get on the road," he warned. As he spoke he reached over and pulled the covers off the extra bed in my room.

"Come on," he said, moving to the other bed.

We jumped for a few minutes, touching the ceiling with our hands, kicking our legs in the air like cheerleaders, and turning in circles, first individually and then in each other's arms. Finally, he pulled me down on the mattress and dropped light kisses in a straight line from my head to my toes.

He led my quivering body to his room, where we repeated similar choreography on each of his beds.

My heart raced. I caught myself before the disappointment of coming back to reality sent me into convulsive sobbing that might never end. When I looked across the room to see if Craig was reading my mind or body language, he wasn't even looking at me. So, I let the memories flow.

Link knocked on the door and called in to Brian. "Are you up?"

"In more ways than he needs to know," Brian whispered. "Yeah, I'm coming," he yelled back to Link.

I stifled a giggle and ran from his room to mine, silently closing the doors between us. Unfortunately, I wasn't as successful in closing the internal door that would separate him from the hold he had over my body.

With trembling hands and liquid knees, I stuffed my clothes and cosmetics back in the bags they had come in. I packed and dressed in less than five minutes and sat on the end of the bed to wait for my next cue.

Brian banged on the door. "Come on, Sleeping Beauty. We don't have all day."

I opened the door and said good morning to Keith and Link, but shot Brian a sneer. "I've been up for hours, waiting on you to tell me when we were leaving. Thanks to you, I've probably missed breakfast."

Keith said he had a box of donuts in the truck that he would share.

I frowned at the covers that were hanging off the beds and strung across the floor. "It looks like you had a wrestling match in here."

"What I do in my bed is none of your business," Brian said. "But you're welcome to fantasize if you want."

I begged my body to conceal what it felt, as I had done the last few days every time Craig looked at me. Clueless, Link intervened on my behalf.

"Easy, Brian. That was rough man, even for you." He turned to me. "Raven, he's always an ass in the morning. Don't pay any attention to him."

"I'll get my things and meet you guys in the hall," I said, as I opened the door to return to my room – my first private room where I could do whatever I wanted, and I ended up not doing it alone after all.

Brian and Link took the front seats. Keith hogged the bench again and I snuggled down in a sleeping bag on the floor, where I slept until Craig and Jason came out to meet me at home.

"She's been asleep since we pulled out of the hotel garage," Link told Craig while I folded the sleeping bag and returned it to the overhead compartment. From that comment, Craig had assumed that the cold had got the best of me.

"Do you feel better today?" Craig asked. "It looks like you have a little color back in your face, and you're out of bed. Those are good signs."

Craig fussed over me like he would have Jason, telling me to rest, bringing me fluids and medicine, shushing anyone who spoke above a whisper. I hadn't used a single tissue with my feigned cold, yet he coddled as though I were recovering from major surgery. Should I appreciate his concern, or resent his denial? Was it unfair to want my husband to treat me like an adult and see through my lies?

Nothing made sense. More and more, I knew I was like my parents and felt sorry for Craig because he was stuck with me. At other times, I compared his refusal to see me to their neglect, and wallowed in self-pity.

At least they had walked away and left me to be what I wanted. I resented him for being too nice, them for not being nice at all, and me for thinking about it. Half of the time I hated myself for giving them the power to control me. The other half I hated myself for letting them down. Hating myself was the only consistent part of my life.

"Penny, are you okay?" Craig sounded worried. I opened my eyes and sat up. "You were whimpering, like something hurts."

"I'm fine. I must have dozed off and had a bad dream."

"Are you sure you'll be able to make this weekend?" he asked. "You're supposed to leave tomorrow night."

I convinced him that I would be fine. I would get my things packed the next morning and I could sleep again in the truck. "I really don't have to do much for my three hundred dollars," I reminded him. "A few songs each hour is all I'm committed to. I should be able to handle that."

The Cleveland trip wasn't as dramatic as the one to Columbus had been. The hotel wasn't as nice. It was a one-story building with outside entrances, no dining room, and no adjoining doors.

The club was mid-sized and the crowd more sedate. I took advantage of the offer to sit out except for my four songs in the middle of each set. Since the band didn't have a designated table, I spent my breaks sitting at the end of the bar where the waitresses gathered when they weren't busy. They kept me company and the bartender gave me two free drinks a set. I stuck to Senor Cuervo, my trusty old friend.

Keith disappeared every break, probably running to the truck to smoke what he couldn't smoke in the club. Link joined me part of the time and mingled the rest.

Brian spent every break practically molesting the same woman. He sat at her table, bought her drinks, and danced with her. I looked over once and saw her rub his head. At least I didn't have to resent being watched over, since he never even looked my way.

Because the hotel was four blocks from the club, the guys took an extra set of cloths so they could change in the restroom and start tearing down equipment at the end of the night. I sat in the same seat I had occupied during my breaks and talked to the bartender while they loaded the truck.

As they carried the last load past me, I heard Brian ask Link if he was sober enough to drive. "I'm going out for a while if you don't mind driving the truck back."

Link said he was fine to drive. Brian lagged behind to hand me a napkin after the other guys walked away. There was a message written on the napkin—open your door in thirty minutes—but I didn't see it until after he was gone.

I heard him outside my door but didn't open it. How crazy did he think I was?

A few minutes passed before the phone rang. I wanted to ignore it, but realized that it could be Link checking on me since he knew Brian was out, or Craig calling to say that something had happened to Jason. I picked up and it was Brian.

"Why didn't you open the door?" He didn't sound upset.

"What do you think I am? Crazy? You spent the whole night snuggled up to someone else, went off with her for a quickie I guess, and then you expect me to welcome you here? Forget it, Brian."

He laughed. "Raven, she was our cover. The guys will expect me to be with her when I don't show up tonight. Link won't suspect anything. Open the door. I'm cold and my hands are full."

I let him in. He had a bottle of wine in one hand and a dozen roses in the other.

"You wasted your money on these," I said, hugging the flowers to my chest. "I can't take them home so they'll be tossed out in the morning."

No one had ever bought flowers for me before. I wished I could save one.

"The smile on your face is worth the price of the roses. We'll have to drink this from the bottle, or the plastic hotel glasses," he said, opening the wine.

"The bottle is fine with me," I said. "My Momma warned me not to get above my raising."

"So you were jealous of Linda, huh? She's not my type. Just so you'll know. I don't like bottled blonde, or crude."

"I wasn't jealous. I have no right to be jealous," I admitted, more for my benefit than his.

"That's right. You have a husband."

I realized that I didn't know the first thing about his life. In another of the extremes that were popping up constantly, I knew every detail of Craig's life but nothing about what was in his heart or mind. I thought I understood Brian's heart, and I was figuring out his mind. But I knew nothing about his life.

"What do you do the rest of the week, when you aren't traveling with us?" I asked and then turned the bottle up, killing a good quarter of it in one drink.

He took the bottle from me and explained that wine shouldn't be taken in shots or guzzles. "I do the same thing most people do. I shower, wash dishes, mow the lawn, and watch a little TV."

I tried to sip from the bottle on my next turn and dribbled wine down my chin. "Be serious. I don't know anything about you. Are you married?"

"That's the kind of thing I would have told you. I'm not married and I don't have any communicable diseases." He took another drink. "I don't have children or pets, although I love animals. I've never been in jail and I'm not wanted by the police or the IRS."

I took the bottle and moved up the bed to lean against the headboard. He followed. We sat side-by-side and talked until the bottle was empty.

"Are you tired?" he asked.

"I'm getting that way. My eyelids are heavy, which is unbelievable since I was in bed by seven every night last week."

He looked puzzled, so I explained how I had let Craig believe that I was sick so I could avoid him. "I needed time to figure all of this out. Brian, I've never done anything like this before. Before you, I never willingly kissed anyone except for Craig."

"Is it okay if I stay here tonight? I should have cleared it with you before, but I didn't come up with this great idea until Linda grabbed my ass and presented the opportunity."

I complimented his resourcefulness and said he could stay. He put the wine bottle in the trashcan and sat on the side of the bed to remove his shoes. I pulled my jeans off and threw them on the floor beside the bed.

"Still enjoying the defiance?"

"It isn't defiance anymore," I explained. "I've moved up a level so now I'm asserting my independence."

"You sure think straight for a skinny girl who can drink most men under the table."

"Imagine how brilliant I'd be sober," I teased, wondering if he meant for his comment to be a compliment or an insult.

"I *have* imagined. Raven, I believe there's a lot more to you than most people know. I'm anxious to try and pry it all out of you."

We slid under the sheets and talked until I couldn't hold my eyes open. He agreed that it would be more cost-efficient to hire a driver, but we promised each other we'd never suggest it to Madeline.

Chapter 34

Moline, and the first two dates in Missouri, were about the same as Ohio. They had medium-sized clubs, cheap hotels, and nothing exciting. Even though I received positive responses everywhere we went, I still hadn't met an audience that appreciated me more than my regulars at the VFW, who, I'd been told, were looking forward to my return for their New Year's Eve dance.

I remembered what Brian had told me in the women's restroom after my first disappointing set in Indianapolis. Most of the people in these clubs weren't there for the music. With that in mind, I reverted to the attitude that I had way back when we practiced in Craig's basement, and sang only for me. It didn't matter if I sang the same songs every night, or twice in one night sometimes. I called up all of my disappointments before I went on stage and sang them out of my body before the night ended.

Brian managed to orchestrate circumstances where no one should notice that he snuck into my room at least one night on each trip. The guys played along, although I doubt we fooled anyone. They conveniently, or discreetly, never came to my door or called my room when he was there.

Some nights we talked all night, sometimes we made love, and sometimes we did both. Regardless of what we did, I treasured every private moment with him. I decided that I liked pot more than alcohol, and discovered that it was much easier to hide at home. I walked around with a joint—sometimes two or three—tucked in my bra, and no one knew.

St. Louis was the last stop in Missouri, and the nicest place on the schedule. The hotel was top quality, with a formal dining room, weight rooms and a spa, an indoor pool, and several game rooms. There were malls and other nice restaurants within walking distance.

A booking agent approached me in St. Louis and said he could book me in clubs from the east coast to as far west as Colorado. I took his card.

The downside of the trip was that I realized that my time with Brian would end soon. "Next week could be the last," I told him when we were alone in the Jacuzzi. "Craig and Irene both want to come to Nashville for our last booking. We'll have to make Owensboro extra special."

"They have a pool and game room in that hotel too, but the rooms aren't nearly as nice as these," he said.

"I'm not talking about accommodations," I said, with rising disappointment after his comment.

"Raven, you aren't going to freak out over this are you? You knew all along that this would end and you'd go back to your husband and the VFW job."

"I'm already freaking out. I stayed stoned all week and I'm not sure I watched Jason as closely as I should have. Brian, I want more. I'll be crazy if I'm stuck in that house with no one but Jason to talk to and nothing bigger than the weekend at the VFW to look forward to." My disappointment turned into hysteria. "I thought this trip was my first step toward the big time. I built new dreams around this."

He rubbed his head, a habit that I had come to love and would miss. I told him once that he would probably still have a full head of hair if he hadn't rubbed it away.

"Do you think I should contact that booking agent?" I asked.

He held his hand up. "Hold on, Raven. I can't tell you what I think you should do about anything. I'm emotionally involved now. My motives aren't honorable at this point, so I should keep my opinions to myself."

"Pretend you're my agent and you're in charge of my career, and you have no other interest in me." I begged with my eyes. "Or pretend you're my father or my husband. What would you tell me then?"

He kicked at the water. "My wife wouldn't spend weekends on the road with someone else."

"Are you telling me that you would control her? That you'd stand between her and her dreams?" I kept the final question-- that she would be better than me?--to myself.

"Not at all. I'm telling you that I'd make sure she was so happy with me that she wouldn't want to be with another man. And I'd move her to Nashville where she could make the right connections. I'd give up every job I had and my home to travel with her and watch her grow if that was her choice."

I let "Stand by Your Man", one of the first songs I had ever learned, roll around in my head so I didn't have to hear any more, or digest what he had already said.

"Raven, are you okay?" He found my hand under the water and squeezed it.

"I've had enough heat. Can we go back to the room now?" The song wasn't working and I needed a smoke. I had to get out of there, where no one could see me, before the tears started.

We changed into dry clothes in separate locker rooms and met at the door to walk to the elevator together. The only conversation we had was to exchange benign comments so the people around us wouldn't think we were rude.

He stopped in front of my door, holding his gym bag between us like a shy boy on a first date, and asked if I wanted him to stay or leave.

"Thank you," was my response.

"You're welcome, but that doesn't answer my question." He smiled, mostly with his eyes.

"I want you to stay." I said, opening the door.

He followed me in without checking first to see if any of the guys had come out a door or around a corner to catch him going into my room. When the door closed he dropped his bag and held me close, where I'd have to look him in the eye.

"What were you thanking me for?"

My tears broke loose. "For this," I said, pointing to my face. "For making me happy enough to cry. For letting me care enough about you to cry over the mere thought that you'll be gone soon. Most of all, for asking what I wanted instead of telling me what you thought I needed."

"You are very welcome," he whispered.

I buried my face in his chest and sobbed. He held me close and massaged my back until I finished. He never said *don't cry*, or *it'll be okay*, or *let me fix you*.

"Crying with you is better than anything in my real life," I said, as I walked into the bathroom for tissues. "How crazy is that?"

We got cheese crackers, candy bars, and Cokes from the vending machines and napped instead of going to dinner. He put a cool washcloth over my eyes to draw the swelling out.

I lost myself in the music that night, brushing up on old coping skills that I'd soon need again. My version of Dolly Parton's "I Will Always Love You" brought tears to my eyes, and the three front tables of people to their feet. I hoped I would remember that exact feeling later, so I could describe it to Brian. The overwhelming conflict of knowing that others loved me most when I was miserable would make a perfect blues song. Maybe he would help me write it.

I hung around and talked to the guys while they broke the equipment down, sitting on a speaker cabinet, rolling cords while we talked.

"I think you outdid yourself tonight," Phil told me. "I thought you were good the first night I heard you, and you've gotten consistently better each week. This trip has been good for you."

Keith stopped what he was doing to agree. "You're a hell of a singer, girl. You ought to be doing something better than these hotel lounges."

Link said he thought he might cry when I did "I Will Always Love You". "The first time we worked on your set lists, I told Brian it would never work. Nobody could go from "Rescue Me", to Tammy Wynette and Dolly Parton, but I was wrong. You can sing anything and they love it."

I thanked them and looked to Brian for his contribution. He continued his work without a response, never looking up although I knew he must have felt me looking at him.

"Maybe you guys can help me," I said. "I'm sad that this is almost over, and don't know what to do next. Do you think I should hook up with a booking agent and go on the road for real?"

Link was quick to respond. "Road work makes people old before their time. It's a hard life and you have to turn hard yourself or it will kill you. I'd recommend taking a different route."

Phil agreed with Link. "You get exposure out here, but I'm not sure it's worth the tradeoff. I think you should work on a good demo tape and pitch it out to record labels. Forget the booking agents for now."

"Ain't you got a kid?" Keith asked. "This road ain't a very good life for a mother. Music in general ain't."

I thanked them for their input. "Keep me in mind?" I asked. "If you have any ideas later, or hear about anything that could help me, I'd appreciate it if you'd let me know."

Brian didn't say much at all until we were in the hotel room. "Did the guys help you out tonight? It's always wise to get opinions from as many people as you can, Raven. You need to hear different perspectives."

"I don't know how much help it was. I think I'm more confused now than I was before. Do you have any pot? I'm out."

While he rolled the joint, he told me he agreed with what the guys had told me.

"Which part?" I asked.

"You are great. You get better every week. Life on the road sucks, and it's no life for a mother."

"You do pay attention. Sometimes you look like you're a million miles away, so I never know."

"I don't miss anything."

We took our clothes off and smoked the joint under the sheets, with four pillows behind us.

"I wish I could stay right here in this bed with you forever," I told him.

"Raven, you'd better be careful. You have to make it through two more weeks of this tour. They'll be hard weeks if you get yourself all worked up now. Take things a day at a time."

"You sound like Craig and Irene, telling me how I should feel. Screw that, Brian."

He chuckled. "I'd rather screw this," he said, stroking the inside of my thigh.

As much as I wanted to hate him for not saying what I wanted to hear, I couldn't resist his offer. I rolled over on top of him and helped myself to what I wanted, with a surge of emotional power that could have supplied New York City.

I fell into rhythm with the pounding in my head, angry that the pot hadn't done an effective job of numbing my thoughts, and hissed at him through clenched teeth. "I love you. I hate you. I need you. My son needs me."

"Raven, stop." He asked gently, and I ignored him.

"I thought you were different," I cried, without missing a beat.

He pulled me close and tried to hold me down. "You're hurting me, Raven."

I pulled out of his embrace and continued until the drum in my head died out and my song was over, and then I collapsed on the bed beside him.

He wrapped his arms around my shoulders and cuddled me like the baby I behaved like. "I thought I was different too," he said. "What's going on here? You weren't with me just then. What was that?"

"That was Penny Sue Martox, the me you haven't had the misfortune to know," I said "Since you brought out the other side of you, I thought I'd return the favor."

"Is Penny always this angry, or hurt?" he asked.

"Always," I answered. "For as long as I can remember."

"How about Raven? Is she angry?"

"Look, this is crazy," I said, pulling away from him to lean over and grab my tee shirt from the floor. "You're making it sound like I'm psycho and you're the shrink or something. You have two sides yourself."

"I don't think you're crazy." He moved to a sitting position with his back against the pillows. I pulled my shirt over my head and settled in beside him. His arm went around me as automatically as Pappy and Nana finishing each other's sentences.

"I think you are complex, and troubled, but not crazy. Raven, I don't think you ask for, or deserve the sadness you know. You didn't answer my question. Is Raven angry?"

"When she needs to be." I felt foolish talking about myself in third person. "Brian this is crazy. Talk about something else."

"Where do you want your career to go?"

I laughed. "My career? I sing in a dump for a hundred dollars a weekend. Old war veterans sip beer, turn up their hearing aids, and listen, between war stories. Some of them don't remember their own names, but they clap for me and put tips in my jar. The dishwasher's sons replaced me, and I'm sure the same old men are clapping for them and dropping dollars in their jar. This trip was a lucky break, only because I won that contest."

"That wasn't a lucky break," he assured me. "I heard your competition and you won because you blew the rest of them out of town. Tell me what you think of yourself as a singer."

"No. You're making me uncomfortable," I said.

"I'm trying to make you comfortable with the truth. The only way you'll get anywhere is by first admitting the truth." He hugged me. "I won't push if you don't want to talk about it."

Things couldn't get any worse than they already were so I drew up the courage to tell him the truth, certain that my life would end if he laughed or disagreed with my beliefs. "I think I'm a great singer. I have a good voice, good range, and great emotion. I need more confidence because I don't want to talk to the audience. And I need to work on my dancing because I'm still awkward about that.

"Do you want to make this a career?"

"I don't want to," I told him. "I have to. I'll die without it."

"I promise I won't let you die," he said. And I believed he would keep that promise.

* * *

Irene came up with what she thought was a great plan. She'd go to Owensboro instead of Nashville. That way, she would be at home to watch Jason when Craig went to Nashville with me.

"After I thought it over," she explained, "the first plan wasn't very smart at all. One of us would have had to stay at the hotel with Jason and would miss the show. This way, we both get to see you perform."

She beamed at me like she had delivered the best news I could possibly want. I was dying inside, but I smiled and nodded while she went on with the details. "You know how Ralph is. At the last minute he'll say he can't go because there's a ballgame or poker party he can't miss. If he decides not to go, I guess I'll just stay in your room and save the cost of our hotel room."

Songs popped into my head, several at a time, to block her words. I would surely hurt her feelings, or choke her, if I listened and responded.

"Are you listening to me?" Her hands were on my shoulders, gently shaking me.

I shook my head. "No. I'm not listening. Sorry."

The truth felt good to me. I looked her in the eye to see if it had affected her the same way.

"Penny, please talk to me. Whatever it is you can tell me."

I dropped my eyes but she took my chin and pulled my face up so I'd have to look at her again. "Your happiness is important to me.

You haven't been happy for weeks, and it shows. Talk to me or I can't help you."

I had to tell her. Otherwise I may never have another minute alone with Brian. I'd never get to kiss him good-bye, or thank him the way I wanted. But how could I dump that on her?

"I've smelled the evidence Penny, if that's what you're afraid to tell me. This isn't a lecture and you won't get one from me. I'm just telling you so you'll know. The smell of smoke lingers in your hair and clothes even after you've washed them."

"Has Craig said anything to you about it?" I asked.

"Not a word. He acts like everything is fine."

"Don't you think that's strange? Irene, I feel like I don't even exist here. He doesn't care what I do, what I think, or what I want."

"He cares, he just doesn't want to upset you."

I took a deep breath and pulled up the courage to finish what I had started "I need more than that, Irene."

"You've found it, haven't you?"

I nodded.

"Brian?"

I had been so careful not to even mention his name around her. "How did you know?"

"I knew that first day when I picked you up at Jerry's and you insulted him," she said. "I didn't know at that very moment, but I figured it out later, after I came home and thought about it."

"I didn't know then," I told her. "I thought he was a jerk."

She shook her head. "The jerks are always the ones. They wake-up parts of us that we didn't even know we had, and then we need them because we don't know how to satisfy those parts without them. Don't worry. I'll get my own room in Owensboro, with or without Ralph."

"You won't try to stop me?"

"You're a big girl, Penny. Only you can decide what's best for you. Whatever that is, I'll be on your side."

Craig dressed Jason up like Sonny Bono and took him to trick-or-treat, proving he was the most unimaginative man on earth. I stayed at the house to pass out candy to the few kids who ventured back to our door, and thought about Irene's advice between knocks.

"Jason needs a little sister to be Cher," Craig hinted when they returned. He would have had more fun if he hadn't been alone."

"He'll have to make some friends then," I said, and slipped back into my own thoughts. I wondered who Irene's affair had been with, and whether or not she regretted it.

Chapter 35

Irene had pegged the situation perfectly. Ralph backed out on her at the last minute when one of his buddies called an emergency poker game at his house. I rode in Irene's car instead of the truck to Owensboro, but we stayed in separate rooms as planned. She said she couldn't cancel her reservation on such short notice and was going to have to pay for the room anyway, but I knew that wasn't true.

She didn't waste much time on small talk before she got serious and asked if I was in love with Brian. I told her the truth; that second to music he was the most important thing in my life. If that wasn't love, it was something better.

She kept her promise and didn't try to tell me what she thought was best for me. We crossed into new territory in our relationship. We were adult friends, more loyal to each other than to our spouses, or she to mine, as I had always believed before.

The club in Owensboro was more like a concert hall than a dance room, with tables butted all the way up against the biggest stage we had seen yet in a club. Irene sat at a front row table and screamed for me after each song. I joined her at the table during my breaks. She bought me two drinks, in addition to the freebies the management allowed me.

Brian sat with us during one break. He told Irene that I had spoken of her often, and with a lot of love, and won her heart with no effort. In return, she bragged on me the way an ordinary mother would if someone had opened that same door and offered her the opportunity.

Almost immediately after I went to my hotel room that night, Brian showed up at the door, announcing that he had hired Keith to load his share of the equipment so we'd have an extra hour together. We spent that hour staring at and touching each other, memorizing what we wouldn't have any more after that trip. He held me and we talked.

He told me about his dreams, both for himself and for me. He planned to spend more time in Nashville, doing studio work and expanding his publishing company. He expected me to become a superstar so he could at least see me on television occasionally, and maybe even work with me in the studio someday.

I laughed at that part, wishing desperately that he had said he wanted to see me in person, or for any reason other than professional. I would have done anything he asked. Sadly, that included leaving Craig and Jason. But he didn't ask.

As the truck pulled away from the hotel on Saturday morning, Irene put her arm around my waist and held me up. When I hadn't eased up on my crying a few hours later, she called Craig and Ralph to tell them we were staying another night in Owensboro.

"There are a few things I want to see while I'm here," she lied. "I talked Penny into staying with me."

I turned my room key in at the front desk and moved my things over to Irene's room. She decided we should order dinner from room service, split a bottle of wine, and have a bitch session.

"You never went to slumber parties when you were young, did you?" she asked but didn't wait for an answer since she already knew I hadn't. "Well, we're going to have a slumber party tonight and cry about boys."

We splurged on dinner. I had prime rib and she ordered lobster. We moaned and cried over Craig and Ralph and Brian, and the man she missed from her past but wouldn't identify. After dinner I soaked in the tub and smoked a joint while she went for a swim. By the time we went to bed, we were exhausted from purging demons.

The drive home was quiet. We were talked out and sleepy. She came to the house and spent her days off with me the next week. On the days that she worked, she came in frequently to check on Jason. I wasn't offended because I smoked myself into a fog so I wouldn't have to think.

Craig pretended all was well and talked constantly about the upcoming trip to Nashville.

"It's only a two hour drive," I said. "We don't need to stay overnight. Craig, I'm sick of hotels."

"Whatever you want," he said, hiding the disappointment that I was sure he must have felt after planning the trip for weeks. "I thought you would want to spend some time with Madeline, and maybe celebrate the end of the tour with the band."

"Craig, you call it a tour like it was a major concert deal or something. I played a lousy club circuit, only I did one night instead of the usual two or five. They didn't believe in me enough to book me for the whole week. It's nothing to celebrate."

"Then maybe we can celebrate getting our life back to normal," he offered. "You're right, it may be best to come back home, to our own bed."

The 'our life' part penetrated my fog and suffocated me. That's how Craig pictured us – as two people sharing one life. And it seemed to me that he sucked up most of the life when we were together. I wanted a life of my own.

I didn't want to celebrate with him because I didn't want to return to our normal existence. The thought of sex with Craig repulsed me. He hadn't shown any interest for at least a month and I hoped things would stay that way.

On second thought, Craig had seldom initiated sex; that had been my job. I was the one who really changed over the last month, not him. Back when I wanted sex with Craig, it was usually for all the wrong reasons.

It hit me hard, as the truth about myself always did. I had done the same thing to Brian when we were in St. Louis. He asked me to stop. He said I hurt him, but I didn't listen.

I wanted to leave Craig alone to fantasize about the revival of our life, while I found someplace to smoke until my brain cooked. But I only had one joint left and didn't know where I'd get more when it was gone. Sharon was my only drug connection and I hadn't heard from her since the day she dropped me out front and skipped my welcome home celebration.

She would be at the New Year's Eve dance with Tinker, but I couldn't wait that long. I decided to call her sooner, using the excuse that it would be easier for everyone involved if we had talked out our differences before we met in a group.

One problem led to another as I tried to think through the fog. Even if Sharon wanted to talk to me and knew where to get what I wanted, how would I pay for it? Brian had indirectly supported my pot smoking. He had paid for my meals and entertainment on the road, and I used my food allowance to buy pot from Keith.

I was back where I started—out of pot, disgusted, broke, and wondering if I wanted to call Sharon now that I realized she may be of no use to me—when the phone rang. I let Craig get it so I could retreat further into my depression without his distractions.

"That was Tinker," he said when he returned. "He and Sharon want to go to Nashville for your last show. Would you care if they ride with us, and Tinker and I switch off driving? You'll probably be tired after working."

I took that as a sign that fate had conveniently intervened to tell me that I was supposed to be a pothead. At that moment I believed the money situation would resolve itself as easily as this one had. "I don't care."

"I told him I'd have you call Sharon tomorrow to work out the details. You can make an excuse if you want," he said.

Sharon came through for me. She didn't mention our previous trip to Nashville, nor did I. She said she had a friend who could get anything I wanted, but I had to give her the money before she picked it up, and roll her a joint when she delivered it to me.

I recovered from my foggy depression long enough to drive Craig to work on Thursday so I could keep the car to shop for groceries. He was excited that I had shown some initiative, and handed over the checkbook willingly. I carefully planned budget meals, forfeited my lunch and snacks, and squeezed out enough for a bag of pot. I took the money to Sharon before I went home and she said she would deliver the pot on Friday.

The guys rode together in the front seat, putting Sharon and me in the back to 'catch up'. Craig made a bathroom stop halfway, where Sharon delivered the pot and a bottle of Bacardi. The rum was a nice gesture, so I didn't tell her that I preferred tequila and pot to rum and pills those days.

Since we didn't get a hotel room, I changed into my costume in a storage room backstage. Sharon, Craig, and Tinker waited at a table near the back of the room, because Sharon didn't want to sit close to the speakers. At least she didn't wear an earpiece attached to a tape player in her purse, the way she often had at the VFW.

I had planned to change quickly and then sit with them until show time. But Madeline changed my plan when she pulled me aside to talk before I escaped the back room.

"I've received very positive responses from the clubs you played. Penny, I think you have a promising future if music is really what you want." Her words registered but I couldn't file them where they belonged. "We need to sit down and talk about your plans, as soon as you're ready."

I thanked her, but said I couldn't think about anything right then.

"That's another thing," she added. "You are focused and professional. I like that you take performing so seriously."

If she only knew. Beyond smoking a joint and finding Brian, I wasn't thinking of anything. My heart had stopped the minute I walked inside the building and realized I would see him in less than an hour, and then after that night I may never see him again.

I promised Madeline that I would call her soon, and struggled to gain the focus she believed I had. I couldn't pull up a song powerful enough to replace Brian in my head. Not a damned one. So, I changed directions. I opened my heart to all the pain it could hold, hoping that the pain would generate the performance of my life.

Whether it was my best performance or not, the audience responded longer than any other had, including the talent show at school. Each time they died down, Craig whistled to get them going again. I smiled and bowed, until my cheeks hurt and I was embarrassed to stand there any longer. They continued to clap after I left the stage.

The band followed and stood around me back stage. They took turns hugging me and telling me that they had enjoyed our ten weeks together, and wishing me luck. Brian stood back until the others had walked away.

"You tore the place down tonight," he said. The words meant less to me than the look in his eyes. "Raven, you do have extraordinary talent. I hope you use it well."

"I guess this is it," I choked out, wishing he would say it wasn't so. "I don't have much time so I'll just say what I have to say quickly. Thanks for everything. I'll never forget one second I've spent with you."

He hugged me, the same as the other guys had, without adding anything personal or intimate. "You know where to find me," he said.

"My heart is with you, wherever you go." He squeezed my arm and walked away.

And I will always love you sang in my head.

My sobs came five minutes into the drive home. Sharon held my hand and supplied fresh tissues periodically. Finally, she asked Craig to pull off at the next restroom so we could steal a roll of toilet paper because we were both out of tissue.

I downed the rum in a stall and she handed me a Valium when I came out. "These don't leave an odor behind," she said. "I started smoking cigarettes as a disguise, but it didn't fool my mother. Fortunately, Tinker isn't a pain in the ass like Craig, so I don't have to worry about it anymore."

"Thanks for understanding, Sharon." I sincerely meant that, and forgot why I hadn't wanted to accept her as a real friend before.

"No thanks necessary," she said. "Someday soon you can tell me what's really eating at you. I think I know, but the guys are waiting on us now."

Chapter 36

I survived the next few weeks by staying mentally paralyzed. I smoked outdoors during the day and washed the smell from my hair before Craig came in from work. At night I lived on Valium. With enough chemicals I could have sex with my husband once a week or so, hoping he didn't know I pretended he was someone else.

Jason demanded every minute of Craig's attention in the evenings, because I didn't give the child any of mine during the day. Whether because of Jason's increased demands on him, or preparing for the holidays, or plain old lack of interest, Craig didn't seem to notice that his wife was present in body only.

I developed a steady progression of illnesses, which fortunately weren't alarming enough to warrant a suggestion from Craig that I should see the doctor. Between Thanksgiving and Christmas I had a sore throat, menstrual cramps, and several headaches that I called migraines, although I wasn't sure what symptoms were required in order for a headache to qualify as a true migraine.

Craig offered sympathy, which mostly annoyed me, and called on others for assistance. Now that he had Jason potty trained, his mother agreed to watch him occasionally, and Irene helped out more than she ever had. Even Gary came by on a Saturday to help Craig and Jason decorate a Christmas tree.

Sharon became my new best friend, as long as our time together didn't include Jason. She didn't want kids of her own or to see kids that belonged to anyone else. She kept me well stocked with Valium and pot, often not charging for the pills since her insurance covered

277

prescriptions. She also introduced me to Cocaine, but I shied away from buying any. Not only was it out of my budget, it made me horny, and not for Craig.

The only good times I had during those weeks was when the band got together to rehearse for the New Year's Eve dance. We worked up a few new songs and brushed up on the old ones. It felt good to do something that I loved again.

"I was scared we had lost you," Boomer said after the first rehearsal ended. "We figured you'd be ready to run off to greener pastures after working all that time with Nashville pickers."

I stopped Mike, who was already halfway out the door. "I need to talk to you about that now that we're all together."

Craig reminded me that it was past Jason's bedtime and he was still at his parents' house. I said I wouldn't take long.

"Believe it or not, I missed you guys while I was away," I told them. "I liked working the bigger clubs, though. Would you be interested in getting out of here? I made some good connections and I think we can book some nice places."

Mike danced from one foot to the other, like he wanted to run out the door but couldn't find his way. Tommy wrinkled his brow and looked at his watch.

"Explain what you mean by getting out of here," Tinker asked.

"Out of the VFW for starters," I said. "They've been good to us but I think it's time to move on. I want to do something big with my singing, so eventually we'll have to leave town. It's not going to happen here, and I'm not getting any younger."

"You're only twenty-two-years old," Craig said, following his announcement with a nervous laugh. "That's hardly over the hill, Penny."

"We all have other jobs to consider," Tinker reminded me.

Craig drove the stake in my heart with, "And families."

"Why don't you give us a little time to think it over?" Mike asked. "Put together your ideas and how they fit in with the connections you made and we can meet after the holidays to talk about it."

For once, Craig allowed his disappointment in me to show. As soon as we were in the car, he told me that he wished I had talked my ideas over with him ahead of time. "I felt like an idiot when I learned about your plans at the same time as everybody else." His tone stopped just short of angry. I remembered Momma's anger over the talent show. But this was different; I hadn't planned to keep anything from Craig.

"The idea just popped into my head after Boomer said what he did about me taking off for greener pastures. I wasn't planning to say anything before then."

"Penny, I don't believe you. You've had something on your mind for weeks," he accused.

"I've had a lot on my mind," I said. "Not just one thing. Are you saying that you want me to stay with this group, at the VFW, forever?"

"Not forever. I just think you need to stay here with Jason while he's little. Your one-nighters were hard enough on this family. He needs his mother at home all the time."

I struggled to clear my head and put together a convincing response. "Do you think it would be easier for him if I waited until he starts to school? I don't. Right now he's flexible. And I can't wait until I'm old if I'm serious about making this a career."

He pulled into the drive at his parents' house and asked me not to mention anything about this in front of them or Jason. "We can talk about it later, after he's asleep."

I waited in the car while Craig went in so I wouldn't be tempted to mention the wrong things in front of the wrong people, and so I could swallow a Valium and a shot of tequila. Screw him, and his parents. I didn't need their approval, or their advice, or their sympathy.

By the time Craig carried Jason to his room and tucked him in with a stuffed animal, I was sound asleep in our bed, still in the clothes I had worn to rehearsal.

* * *

"Irene, I don't need Craig running my half of our life. I'm twenty-two-years old and perfectly able to think for myself." I ranted as I slapped Miracle Whip on bologna sandwiches, the best I had to offer when she dropped in for lunch. "And I sure don't appreciate him telling me who I can talk to, or when, or about what."

I slammed the plates on the table and sat down to watch Irene and Jason eat. She rolled her eyes over to Jason, silently warning me not to carry on in front of him. I huffed and went to the bathroom to calm my nerves while she carried on a two-year-old conversation with him.

I sat on the floor and waited until she tapped on the door. "You can come out now. Jason's on his bed with a book. Come out and kiss him so he can go to sleep."

I brushed past her, saying nothing until I had kissed Jason and closed his door. Then I confronted her. "Irene, you're doing it again, too. Stop bossing me around like I'm a child. I thought we got beyond this in Owensboro."

"Stop acting like a child so I can stop treating you like one," she said. "Sit down and listen for a minute."

Begrudgingly, I did as I was told.

"It's obvious to me, and probably to everyone else, that you are miserable. I'm on your side Penny, as long as you get your head together and go about this reasonably."

"What does that mean?" I relaxed a bit, waiting for her advice instead of fighting the lecture for a change.

"You need to make some decisions. I don't care what you decide, just be honest with yourself and admit what you want. Is it Brian?"

"It's Brian." Before she said anything else, I added more. "And it's music. I miss them both. And I'm discouraged with motherhood and this house and not having a car of my own. And I hate sneaking outside to smoke and in the bathroom to drink. Irene, I hate my life."

"Is that all?" She laughed and took a deep breath like she was going to speak.

"No. I forgot my parents, and Craig, and his parents. I hate them too."

She chewed her lip for a second and then took another breath and started before I could interrupt again. "You know what? I think I'm a little jealous."

"Jealous? My life is horrible and you're jealous?"

"I wish I had been brave enough to take such an honest look at my life when I was still young enough to change it. You are, Penny. You have plenty of time. But you have to be absolutely certain that you know what you want before you make changes."

"I'm not sure what I want. That's the problem. Craig doesn't deserve to be hurt. He has never hurt anyone in his life, especially not me. How can I even think about destroying his perfect little world?"

"Be serious. Do you really think Craig's world is perfect? How long do you think he can go on pretending he doesn't notice that you're a walking zombie, with little or no interest in him? Penny, he's nice, not insane."

"Tell me what to do, Irene." I reached across the table and grabbed her hand, hanging on for dear life. "I'm not strong enough to make these decisions on my own."

"You have to make them. Remember, you need to do what's best for you, and you're tired of people trying to run your life," she said. "Stop and think about your dad for a minute. He sacrificed his happiness for what he believed was best for you. But he never asked you what you wanted. Craig will do the same for Jason if you let him. Do you think your father did what was best for anyone concerned?"

"No." I didn't need a second to think about my answer. "I expected you to take up for Craig. I thought you'd tell me what a great guy he is and how you'd never forgive me if I hurt him."

"I love Craig. And you're right. I think he's one of the greatest guys I've ever met. I also know that he loves you very much." She pried my hand off of hers before I cut off circulation. "But sometimes love isn't enough. And great guys can't always give us everything we need or want."

She shook her hand back to life and I got up to refill our tea glasses while I tried to make sense of what she had said. How could love not be enough? All my life I had wanted nothing more, and when I got it, it wasn't enough. Why?

"You were a child when your parents forced you to marry Craig." She spat the words out, disgusted. "What did you know at the time?"

"I knew that I wanted out. Anything beat living with my parents, so they didn't have much trouble forcing me to marry him."

"Exactly," she agreed. "You knew what you didn't want, and you recognized a better opportunity. But you didn't know anything about love or marriage, and you hadn't dated anyone else to know if Craig was the man you really wanted to spend the rest of your life with. I wish I would have tried harder to get you away from them."

"What do you mean tried harder?"

She looked at her glass instead of at me. "I asked your dad to let you come live with me until you finished school, instead of marrying you off to Craig. I begged him, and even promised I wouldn't let you see Craig until after you graduated."

"What did he say?"

"He said your mother would never agree to that. He wouldn't even discuss it with her. That's when I threatened to throw them out of the house, hoping that would influence him. It didn't work. Maybe I should have involved the authorities—charged them with abuse or something."

I walked around the table to hug her. I had seen her cry a few tears during our bitch session in Owensboro, but that was nothing compared what she unleashed this time. "Thank you," I whispered. "You did all you could, and it means the world to me."

She wiped her eyes, looking embarrassed, and said she needed to get back to work. "You keep your head straight for a few days and think things through," she advised. "You'll make the right decision."

I promised I would, and I did everything in my power to keep that promise. Unfortunately, I wasn't as strong as either of us thought I was.

I stayed completely straight and sober for two days. Physically it wasn't so bad, but emotionally I crashed. I couldn't make a decision because dozens of thoughts begged for my attention all at the same time.

Did I love Brian, or had I only thought that because he offered an exciting diversion? Chances were good that I'd tire of him the same as I had with Craig. Could I leave Craig and Jason and not miss them? Would I be worse than my mother if I left my son? Did Brian want me?

None of that mattered as much as the music, and I had as many questions about that part of my life as I had about my relationships. Was I good enough to make it, or were the clubs as far as I would go? Were Brian and Madeline serious when they offered to help? Where would I stand without them if they weren't?

Maybe I could talk Craig into moving to Nashville where I could have my real life *and* my music. I'd only have to give up Brian, and he may not have wanted me anyway. Maybe I could have them both.

When Christmas rolled around, I still hadn't made any decisions.

Craig's dad let him have the week between Christmas and New Year off, even though he had used his allotted number of vacation days to stay home with Jason while I was on the road. Craig took it upon himself to tell Nana we would spend a few days in Crayfield.

We left the day after Christmas, packing Jason's Santa toys in the back seat of the car to amuse him while we drove. He and Craig sang Christmas songs and talked nonsense while I stared out the window and thought how ugly winter was. The trees looked as bare as I felt—them with no leaves and me with no chemicals.

Nana spent most of the time in bed while we were there. Wanda said she had only been getting up to use the bathroom and eat. Sometimes they carried meals to her on a tray because she didn't feel like getting up at all. After she forgot Jason's name, I was sorry we had gone there. I pretended to have another migraine so I could spend the day in bed at the barn house.

Gwen brought lunch to me and stayed to talk. "Is your headache better?" she asked when she found me sitting in the living room.

"It comes and goes," I lied. "I thought I would sit in here for a while and see how things went."

"You can't deal with Nana, can you?" She smiled sympathetically when I tried to act surprised at her question. "Don't feel ashamed. I'm sure it was a shock for you to see how much she had changed."

"Is she going to die?" I asked.

"It can't be long. She's already made it a year longer than her doctors gave her," she reminded me. "Penny Sue, I think she'll be glad when it's over but I don't know what will happen to him."

I closed my eyes and tried, unsuccessfully, to stop the moan that choked my heart and throat before it worked its way out.

"Sorry," she said quickly. "I guess I haven't done much to help your headache."

I said I needed to get back to bed so she would leave me alone. In addition to mourning the loss of Nana and feeling sorry for Pappy, she had given me something else to stress over. Why did anyone want to be in love? Misery was the best possible outcome. For his years of love and devotion, now Pappy got to end up alone, with a broken heart.

I didn't want to see any of them again. Not Nana, or Pappy, or Wanda, or Gwen, or Craig, or Jason. Not even Irene, and especially not Brian. I wished I could close my eyes and will myself to another planet.

Craig wouldn't let me leave without saying good-bye. "What's wrong with you, Penny? This might be the last time you get to see her. You have to go over there and say good-bye at least."

"I can't do it," I argued. "You don't understand. I can't look at her like this."

For once he stood firm. "You'll go if I have to carry you over there. I won't let you hurt her, or do something that you'll regret later."

The only thing I regretted later was allowing him to drag me to see Nana. She and I both cried, and she wouldn't let go of me when I leaned over the bed to hug her.

"I love you, Penny Sue. You take care of those boys and make a happy life. And tell your daddy I love him too," she said. "Will you do that for me?"

After Jason dozed off in the car, Craig tried to talk to me. "Aren't you glad now that you went in to see Nana?"

"No." I answered honestly. "She asked me to do things that I can't do, so now I have to live with that. I feel worse than I've ever felt in my life."

I wasn't sure I'd ever forgive him. Or Nana.

Chapter 37

Sharon warned me ahead of time that my band members weren't planning to go on the road with me. I wasn't surprised, or disappointed. "Tinker won't give up his job at Ford. I'd kill him if he even thought about it," she admitted. "He has ten years seniority and great benefits. I need that medical plan. Penny, you know that."

I told her it didn't matter to me. I offered them the chance to come if they wanted but wouldn't have hard feelings if they didn't want to leave their lives to chase my dreams. I would find a new band and everyone would be happy.

"What about Craig?" she asked. "Does he want to go? I guess it's easier for him, since he works for his family. He could probably come back to his same job if things didn't work out."

"He hasn't said for sure," I admitted. "He wants me to stay here until Jason is older, but he hasn't said what he'll do if I insist that I want to go. Sharon, it doesn't matter what he does. I'll do this alone if that's how it has to be. This is something I have to do."

I couldn't tell her that I hoped Craig wouldn't want to go. She might tell Tinker, and he might tell Craig. I didn't want him to hear it that way.

"And Jason? You'd really leave him?" She tried to sound disapproving, but I knew that was exactly what she would have done in my position.

"If I have to," I said, walking away from her to take my place on stage.

The regulars at the VFW gave me a warm welcome back, cheering when I walked across the stage and took the microphone, like I was some sort of star or something. They had become like an extended family to me. I would miss them when I was gone.

That night, I gave my VFW audience the best I had and took what I could get in return. I reached into their hearts with my voice to claim permanent residence there, and to thank them for their loyalty. Hopefully, they would forgive me for leaving, and still buy my records and concert tickets one day. When I got famous, I would come back to see them and sign autographs. Maybe even sing at the post.

During my breaks, I walked through the crowd to wish everyone a Happy New Year. I posed for pictures with the regulars and said I was pleased to meet strangers that I hoped I would never see again, at least not for a long time.

I sang with Nana in my heart that night. She hadn't made it to hear me sing with a band, and never would. As I scanned the dance floor, I realized that some of those people might not be around when my records came out either. Most of my fans were old. It was time to get out and meet younger audiences.

Thoughts of Nana led to thoughts of my dad, and Nana's request for me to tell him that she loved him. He didn't deserve her love by my way of thinking, but maybe he did deserve to know that she was dying just in case he wanted to make things right with her. If my feelings continued in that direction, I might go to see him before I left town. Maybe I'd take a picture of Jason since he probably didn't even know he had a grandson.

Because his poker buddies and their wives had agreed to join them, Ralph brought Irene to the New Year's Eve dance and gave her a chance to play proud mother. Irene wore a new dress, and her hair on top of her head. She looked prettier than I had ever seen her.

Craig walked away early one break to change a string and tune his guitar. I sat with Irene and wondered if I would ever feel as close to Jason as I did to her. I hoped she would stay in his life after I was gone and give him what she had given me.

The dance was a sellout, making it a success from the post's perspective as well as mine. I drank what I wanted all night and Craig stayed out of my business because it was New Year's Eve, a night when everyone was expected to drink. Everyone except perfect Craig, that is. After the countdown at midnight, he even handed me his glass of champagne.

I was glad Sharon and Irene were there to celebrate my last night, even though neither of them knew it might be my last performance before I left town. No one knew my plans. The decision making process had nearly destroyed me, but I had finally made my mind up after saying good-bye to Nana. I had to move on, away from the people I loved. I didn't want to turn into another Pappy, devoting my life to love that would eventually make me miserable.

Jason slept over with Craig's parents, meaning Craig would expect sex. For the first time in months, I was a willing participant. I wanted to leave Craig with a positive last memory of me, and hopefully one that would soften the disappointment when he discovered that I, and half of our savings, were gone.

I had studied used car ads in the newspaper, trusting that prices would be similar in Nashville. The money I earned on my *tour* would buy a decent car and feed me for a while. I took enough from the new house fund to pay for three month's rent, which I hoped would get me settled. Without me, Craig probably wouldn't want to leave Irene's rental anyway. And there was always the pretend house in the barn if he wanted to go there.

The rest of my inventory included a bag of pot, fifteen Valiums, one suitcase stuffed with clothes, and a tote bag of personal items. And a one-way Greyhound bus ticket to Nashville.

* * *

On New Year's morning, I begged off when Craig said it was going to go pick Jason up from his parents' house. "I have a headache, so it would be great if you stay and visit. I'll recover faster if you keep Jason over there."

"Hangover?" he asked, but in a teasing instead of accusing tone.

I closed my eyes and rubbed my temples. "Could be. Stay and eat black-eyed peas, or whatever she makes for this holiday? I'll be fine if you give me a couple of hours."

"Why don't you call me when you're ready for us to come home?" he asked on his way out the door. I nodded, feeling terrible that those be his last words.

As soon as he was out the door, I dressed and gathered my things. I considered calling Irene to drive me to the bus station but changed my mind almost as soon as the idea hit. A cab was safer because it would be too hard to say good-bye to Irene.

A last look around what had been my home for thirteen years gathered very few good memories. There wasn't a single neighbor I wanted to have a last look at or word with, or any mementos I wanted to stick in my bag to take with me.

I left two notes that I had written ahead of time, one on the bed for Craig and one for Irene on her workstation. I left my key with Craig's note, realizing that I was forfeiting my right to come back in without an invitation, even if I changed my mind later and wanted to come home.

I had the cab driver take me to Harvey's first, where I asked him to wait while I delivered an envelope to my parents. Daddy answered the door at the top of the wooden stairs that barely clung to the outside of the building. I wasn't sure he recognized me. He looked older than Pappy, very tired, and his eyes gave no sign that anything was going on inside his head.

"I'm leaving town and thought you should know a few things in case I don't come back," I said, handing him the envelope. I didn't wait to see him open the picture of Jason, or read my letter about Nana. He didn't invite me in, or try to stop me when I turned to walk back down the stairs.

The bus was crowded when I boarded so I walked down the aisle until I found a seat in the rear where I could sit alone. The last thing I wanted was conversation with a stranger. I needed to close my eyes and decide where I would go when I arrived in Nashville.

The idea didn't hit me until the bus pulled into the terminal at the other end of my trip. Claude would surely remember me, and keep an eye on me if I stayed a few nights at the Swingin' Door. I rubbed the rabbit's foot in my pocket before I collected my bags, and sat down to decide how I would get to the hotel. I had no idea how far it was from the bus station, or even which direction to go.

"Is someone picking you up?" I looked up to face the owner of the question and recognized the middle-aged man who had sat one row up on the other side of the bus aisle from me.

"Yes," I said. "He'll be here soon."

"This isn't the safest place for a young lady to sit alone," he raised one brow and I felt uncomfortable. "Do you want me to wait with you until your friend arrives?"

"No, thanks. I don't want to be any bother," I said, meaning that I didn't want to be bothered, and wondering if I should have said my husband instead of *he*.

"No bother," he said, taking a seat on the wooden bench beside me. "I'd rather sit here than worry or read about you in the papers later."

I spotted a row of payphones across the lobby. "I'll go call my ride to see if he has already left," I said. "I'll be right back."

Lugging everything I owned with me, I made my way through the crowded bus station to the phones. Only one had a directory still attached to the metal shelf, so I waited for it to be available.

"Is this Claude?" I recognized his voice but asked anyway, hoping by some miracle he would remember mine. He didn't. I had to describe myself and explain twice before he remembered me at all.

"We get lots of contest hopefuls," he said apologetically. "I can't keep track of all of you."

The lie about spending my first night with Craig at the Swingin' Door jogged his memory. "Ah, yes, with the pain-in-the-rear roommate. I remember now. Happy New Year. How are you?"

"I'm in Nashville, at the bus station," I said. "This trip was rather sudden so I didn't make a reservation. Do you have room for me?"

He did have a room, and a shuttle van, which he promised to send. "Stay put until you see the shuttle pull up at the door," he ordered. "It's a green van with yellow lettering on the door. He ought to be there in ten minutes."

I thanked him and went back to relieve the man who didn't want to worry about me. He preferred to wait until he saw me safely in the hands of my driver.

"I'm Jerry Fremlinger," he said. "We haven't introduced ourselves."

I relaxed and said my name was Penny Martox. A woman sat on the other side of me and the three of us talked until the van pulled up. I didn't hear much of what she said because I concentrated on planning my future. Jerry Fremlinger insisted on carrying my suitcase to the door.

"I want to register as Raven Coal," I told Claude when he pulled out the paperwork. "That's my stage name and I'm here on business. If anyone calls, they'll be looking for me under this name."

"Suit yourself," he said. "It don't matter to me what name you use so long as you pay your bill. Any preference on the room?"

I shook my head. Any room would do, as long as I had a bed, a shower, and a phone.

"Want a single? You came alone this time, didn't you?"

"Yes, I'm alone. A single is fine. If you have something close to the office, I'd like that," I added. "I've never stayed alone before." I hoped that would get me extra sympathy and protection.

He put me in the first room past the vending area behind the office. "You holler if you need anything, and keep the door locked and the curtains drawn," he warned. "There are lots of weirdos around here these days."

Before I reached the door he had another suggestion. "If you want anything from the canteen after dark, call down here so whoever's at the desk can look out for you."

I unpacked everything, filling the drawers and hangers, and junking the counter so I wouldn't feel homeless. It wasn't the nicest hotel room I had been in but, on the other hand, it wasn't as shabby as the home I had left either. And I had more space than my parents had allotted me for ten years.

I looked at the clock. Craig would have returned to the house by then and found my note. I left no destination but was sure he would guess Nashville, not that I thought he would try immediately to find me. He would hold up and pretend nothing was wrong in front of Jason, and maybe call Irene and Sharon. He would wait until Jason was in bed to grieve or search for me.

It was hard to take my mind off him since there was nothing else to do. I couldn't contact Madeline or look for a car or an apartment on New Year's Day. And there was nothing I wanted to see on television.

Despite Claude's warning, I opened the drapes to watch traffic and made a game of trying to guess who was in the cars and where they were going. Some of those cars could have carried famous performers to each other's homes, or back to their own homes after exciting performances or parties the night before. Even the traffic in Nashville was more promising than home.

Later, after closing the drapes again and checking the lock on the door for the third time, I closed myself in the bathroom with the ventilation fan on and smoked a joint while I soaked in the tub. I was relaxed enough to sleep when I came out, but first I looked through the phone book and made a list of used car dealers who had the same phone exchange as the hotel. In the morning I'd get a map and start looking.

My stomach woke me in the middle of the night. An over-ripened banana was all I had eaten the day before. I was too nervous before I left the house, and afraid to spend the money when the bus made a stop at the Kentucky/Tennessee line. The machines were right outside the door, so I didn't heed Claude's advice and call the office for assistance, I just ran out to buy a bag of pretzels. I wanted a Coke to go with them, but didn't waste the time or money.

I missed having Brian in the next room. Even on the few nights when he had been forced to sleep in his own hotel rooms instead of mine, I knew he was there if I needed him. As I fought for sleep that stayed just out of reach, I thought about calling him. His number was in my purse two feet away. I smoked another joint instead, and went back to sleep.

I slept through the complimentary continental breakfast in the meeting room. Claude saved two pecan Danishes in a napkin for me. When I went down to ask if he had a local map, he pulled them out from behind his counter and handed them to me.

"I get the feeling this trip isn't as happy as the last one," he said, handing the map to me. "Are you okay?"

I told him some truth and some fiction. "Things weren't working out so well with my husband, so I came to Nashville to see if I could make it on my own. Maybe things will be better between us if I make it big."

"How do you figure that?" he asked.

"If I make some money, and I can get a car, and we can move out of the back of the beauty shop where we live, I think we'll both feel better," I explained. "He won't have to work so many hours for his dad and he won't be so stressed. And I won't feel like such a burden."

He raised his eyebrows like he expected more, but that was all I wanted to tell him.

"And he's okay with you coming down here on your own? There weren't any jobs where you came from?" His tone removed the question. Claude either didn't believe me, or he didn't approve of the arrangement; that was obvious.

I dropped my eyes and played with the corner of the napkins my breakfast was wrapped in. "There's more to it than what I told you but I don't think I'm ready to talk about it. I'm trying to be positive and make the best of a bad situation." I managed to make my voice quiver on the words *bad situation*.

He crossed the office to get a local map from a metal rack in front of the window. "Here you go, but I can probably point you directly to just about anything you want in this town," he offered.

"First, I need a car," I told him. "Something cheap, so I'll have to look on used lots." I laughed, nervous and louder than I planned. "And I need a job and a place to live. I need everything."

"Irma, that's my wife, might ought to talk to you then," he suggested. "She's got an ear open all the time for things along those lines and she's forever fixing folks up together. Somebody in the neighborhood needs a plumber and she just happens to know a couple of plumbers from church. She's likely to know folks that have a car, a job, and a room available for you to rent."

I said that would be wonderful and he agreed to *hook us up over the phone*. She would be at a church function until later that evening, but he'd have her call my room later. I hated to waste what was left of the day, but said I would wait for her call.

"There's a cafeteria around the corner," he said. "The food is good and the prices even better. You ought to like it if you ain't looking for fancy. Try to get over there and back before dark. Between the panhandlers and tourists, you can't walk up the block without people hitting you up for something."

Claude was right about everything. Howard's Cafeteria was plain, and a bit rundown, but the food was delicious and I ate all I could hold for less than three dollars. A bum on the street asked for my spare change on the way back and a tourist offered me a good time if I would accompany him to a strip bar.

Irma called and said she was certain she could *hook me up* with everything I needed if I gave her an hour or two to make some calls.

I decided I should wait until I had a car and a place to live before I contacted Madeline. I made no plan to contact Brian, but hoped Madeline would let it slip to him somehow that I was in town.

If Craig hadn't called Irene the night before, she would have been in to work and found her note. Even if she didn't understand why I hadn't talked to her about my plan, I believed she would understand why I had to leave. I would call her as soon as I settled in and had some good news to tell her.

Each time Jason popped into my head, I told myself that he was better off without me. Irene had asked me to compare Craig to Daddy. I thought it made more sense to compare me to him. I was the unhappy one in our house, and the drugs and alcohol I used to fight my unhappiness were very unfair to Jason.

Maybe Craig would replace me, and find a new mother for Jason. I hoped it would be someone like Irene, not me, or either of our mothers.

Chapter 38

Irma was a no-nonsense woman who seemed overly excited to have inherited me as a project. Claude advised me to be ready at nine, and not a minute late, and she would take me to look for a car.

"Don't keep her waiting," he warned. "Nothing gets her going worse than a person who can't be on time. And, believe me, you don't want to see her when she gets going." He winked and added, "Learned a long time ago, she's easy to get along with as long as things go her way."

Still, when I opened my door at exactly nine o'clock, I wanted to ask her for identification. She looked closer to my age than to Claude's, and like she belonged on the cover of a magazine. Maybe Good Housekeeping or something, she looked too domestic for Glamour.

"Irma?" I double-checked before I let her in.

"Yes, are you Raven? Are you ready?"

She stayed at the door without coming inside so I grabbed my purse and turned out the light in a hurry. She started talking before I had a chance to be uncomfortable about not having anything to say.

"Claude tells me you're new in town and need pretty much everything. Well, you've met up with the right person. I know everyone in my neighborhood, and hundreds of people at church, and more at the hospital where I do volunteer work on Thursdays. And Claude and me both have truckloads of kin. Once we get the word out to everybody we know, and they ask around to all the people they know, we can usually come up with just about anything." I figured it was a good thing I didn't have anything to say because I wouldn't have had a chance.

She led me to her black Cadillac, unlocked my door, went around to get in hers, and checked her hair and teeth for lipstick in the mirror, talking the whole time and never looking at me. "My cousin bought a Chevrolet Nova for her daughter, Victoria. I need to tell you, Victoria is as spoiled rotten as they come, and she already had her eye on a Buick Regal, so she turned her little nose up at that perfectly good Nova. Christine, my cousin, parked that Nova out in the front of her house with a *for sale* sign in the window and bought the Regal for Victoria. I would have made her buy it for herself, but Victoria hasn't done anything on her own and she's twenty-six years old. I love her, but she's rotten as they come. So the Nova is available and I'm taking you to see it now. It's green and I reckon you'll have to like whatever color you can get at this point, huh?"

I waited a few seconds to be sure she was through and it was my turn to talk before I spoke. "Green is fine. Do you know how much she's asking for it?"

"She has twelve hundred posted on the sign but trust me you can talk her down to eight. I know she didn't give any more than that for it, and she doesn't need to make a profit off of you just because Victoria is so spoiled. Tell her that's all you have to spend. How much space are you hoping for?"

"In the car?" The question came so fast on the end of the car conversation that I didn't know she had moved on.

"Living space. Claude says you need a place to stay. My friend Dorothy, from the hospital, rents space in her basement. It ain't nothing special, but it's clean and private. Even has a private bathroom. There's one big room with a bed, a dresser, a couch, a dinette set and the bathroom, of course. She'll let you share her kitchen upstairs. She's not much of a cook from what I hear, but she's not home much no way. You'd have a parking space out by the alley. I'll run you by after we finish up with the car. She let the last girl stay for a hundred dollars a month, but she had cats. You don't have pets do you?"

"No, I don't have pets," I answered. "I've never had a pet in my life and don't plan on getting any now.

"The walls down there are concrete, but they're painted, and she put a nice rug on the floor. It looks decent enough. Kind of cozy really. I doubt you can hang anything on the walls though, because of them being concrete."

She looked over at me, but didn't stop talking long enough for me to respond.

"You need a job I guess, to pay for all this. Are you looking for something in music? Most everybody comes here with that in mind, but they end up doing something else because those jobs are hard to come by. Lot of the younger ones work over at Opryland when it's open, but then they have to find something else during the winter months. What kind of work did you do before you came here?"

I told her I had never worked, thinking my experience at Harvey's and the VFW didn't count as real jobs. "I learn fast, and I'll so just about anything."

"Do you type? Do you want to work in an office, or a store, or a restaurant? Sometimes those retail jobs turn out real good because you get the discounts."

"I'll try anything," I repeated.

"Don't let just anybody hear you say that or they'll try to stick you in a strip bar or scrubbing toilets somewhere. You need to brush up on what you want to say." She nodded, obviously approving her own advice. "Decide what you will and won't do and keep a confident answer on the tip of your tongue."

I watched to see if she ever stopped to breath. The words seemed to flow effortlessly from her mouth. In the short time I had been with her, she had already said more words than I had heard from either of my parents the last year I lived with them.

"Go ahead," she coached. "Practice on me."

It was my turn finally, and I had nothing to say. Before she thought I was rude, I said the first thing that came to my mind. "I could work in a restaurant, or a bar. I don't know how to type."

"You need to learn. I have an old standard typewriter at home that I'll dig out and let you practice on if you want. Most people use electric now, but the letters are in the same places so it'll still help you learn. If you plan on working for tips, you're going to need to be more outspoken."

I wondered if anyone was outspoken around her. It didn't seem possible unless they talked over the top of her words.

She turned off the main road, onto a narrow tree-lined one with few houses in sight. It was like going from the city to the country in the space of two car lengths.

"Christine lives back here," she explained. "About a mile out this road. Remember to tell her that you only have eight hundred dollars to put out on a car. There's a rusty spot over the right rear tire that you can point out if you need to talk her down."

Farms and trees divided the few houses on the road. We passed one car between the turn off and Christine's house, where the green Nova still sat with a for sale sign in the window.

"Did anybody even know the car was back here?" I asked. "It doesn't look like this road gets much traffic."

"See, you have a good head on your shoulders." Irma looked at me with a big smile. "Christine runs a small business on her own and didn't even have the smarts to figure that one out. Even after I told her that nobody was ever going to see this sign unless she drove the car around town, she didn't put any effort into it. It just sat right there killing her lawn."

Christine came out when she heard our car doors close. She looked as young as Irma, and even more attractive. I thought they must have good genes in their family. They both wore outfits that I would have saved for a special occasion, and had their faces completely made-up and not a hair out of place. They might have passed for twins if Irma hadn't frosted her hair.

I smiled to myself, remembering how Lori wearing our twin dresses at least once a week until we outgrew them.

Christine also talked as much as Irma, only her tone was softer. She still made her point, though, even when they both talked at the same time.

"It seems like a great little car, but we don't drive it much," she said, opening the door for me to sit in the driver's seat. "Shelton pulls it out on the highway occasionally to blow out the engine and keep it running, but that's about it. If you decide you want the car, you can take it with you today, as long as you brought the money."

She handed me the key and pointed out how quiet the engine was after I had started it up. I didn't know anything about engines, but was pleased that it had started on the first try. Sometimes I had to pump the gas pedal and crank the key a couple of times before Craig's car would start.

"I only have eight hundred dollars to spend," I said, looking disappointed. "I can tell it's a good car so if you still have it after I find a job and save up the other four hundred I'll come back."

Irma and Christine both started at once. "It has a rusty spot," Irma said.

"We might be able to work something out," came from Christine.

"Let's go inside and talk it over," Christine suggested. "I have a fresh pitcher of sweet tea and some of those cheese crackers you love, Irma."

We followed her through a side door, into a kitchen that was bigger than our living room/kitchen combination at Irene's place. White ceramic trimmed with tiny red flowers covered the floor, the walls, and the counters, and a red and white tablecloth covered a huge round table in front of the floor-to-ceiling bay window. I thought they might have to call the authorities to pry me out of that room again; it was more comforting than the red bedroom Nana had put together for me in the barn house.

Irma and I sat at the table while Christine poured tea and explained how she happened to own the Nova. I didn't tell her that Irma had already explained about her spoiled daughter, nor did I listen to whatever Irma said while Christine talked, because I was too busy trying to imagine how it would feel to live in a house like Christine's.

From where I sat at the table I could see into the living room. She had white furniture on a dark wooden floor, and porcelain dolls everywhere – on the couch, on the walls, on the mantle, in cabinets, and one in a wooden cradle on the floor. Each of them wore a different colored dress, most of them with matching hats.

"You can go in there and look at the dolls if you want," Christine said when she noticed me staring at them.

"I'm sorry. I didn't mean to be nosy," I said. "They caught my attention and I couldn't stop looking. I've never seen anything like it."

Irma pushed her chair back and grabbed my hand. "Come on, I'll take you for a tour. She has them all over the house. Everywhere. You ain't seen nothing like Christine's dolls."

Up close, I saw the fine details. The dolls had eyelashes, tears, little bitty teeth, and even freckles on some. There were baby dolls with pacifiers, adult dolls with jewelry, and everything in between, with every possible combination of eye and hair colors.

"Christine makes these dolls," Irma told me. "Remember when I said she ran her own business? This is what she does. She has a little shop out back, with a kiln and a sewing machine. She can make up a doll to look like anybody if you give her a picture and a couple of weeks."

I was speechless, but they didn't notice because they had gone on to talk over each other about something else while I examined the fingernails on a tiny baby doll that looked so real that I half expected him to open his eyes and cry.

"Raven needs a place to stay so I'm taking her over to see Dorothy's basement apartment. Dorothy expects us at noon, so we need to wrap up this car business," Irma said.

Christine narrowed her eyes and shook her head. "That Dorothy's a strange one, but she's easy enough to rent from because she's never at home. Always out trying to spread her weirdness around town or drive other people as crazy as she is."

When Christine backed up what Irma hinted at earlier, Irma decided Dorothy wasn't so bad. "Wait and judge her for yourself. Some people actually like her because she does a lot of good for others."

Christine settled on eight hundred dollars without putting up any fuss over it. "I'll be glad to get it off my lawn," she said. "You go ahead and take it now if you want and we can transfer the title tomorrow. I have to go downtown to deliver some dolls anyway, so I can meet you."

After we exchanged money and keys, and made arrangements to meet at the transfer office, Christine invited me to come visit any time. "You'll have to come back and meet my daughter, Victoria. She'll show you around town and introduce you to some friends your age."

Irma pulled me out the door, lecturing me on the importance of being on time. I followed her to Dorothy's house in my Nova, enjoying the quiet engine and the break from chattering women. At a stoplight, I ran my hand across the dashboard and soaked up the feel of my very own car. I hadn't expected ownership to be such an emotional experience.

Dorothy lived up to Christine's description. Strange didn't quite cover the peculiarity of this woman. She wore her hair, which looked like she had never cut it, twisted into a six-inch cone on the top of her head, and a generously cut dark skirt that nearly touched her ankles. White tennis shoes with no laces and a gray blouse finished the ensemble.

She fit well alongside Irma, speaking as few words as possible. "Come," she urged, in a voice so soft that I wasn't sure she had really spoken at all.

Irma filled in the blanks. "She'll take you downstairs to see the apartment. Follow her."

Dorothy unlatched the lock on the kitchen side of the basement door and walked down the stairs, sideways, stopping both feet on each step. After Christine's bright kitchen, the basement apartment seemed especially dreary, but it was clean and had everything I needed.

"Hundred too high?" she asked.

"No," I answered, figuring I should minimize my conversation to match hers.

Again, Irma intervened. "Raven hasn't found a job yet and she's living on a shoestring. If you could give her a break the first month it would be nice, maybe half off?"

"Sure," Dorothy whispered.

"And right now she's paying to stay at the motel, so the sooner you can take her in the better it will be for her."

"Anytime."

Irma prompted me by stretching her eyes.

"I have the money with me and could move in tomorrow if that's okay." I could pack my things into the trunk of my car and check out of the hotel before meeting Christine the next morning.

Dorothy nodded. I stepped back; afraid the twisted cone would spring loose and leave me buried in hair.

"Fine," Irma directed. "Then everything's settled. Give her the key now and she'll move in tomorrow. Raven, go ahead and pay her before you get the key. Tonight, Dorothy can write out a list of the rules she expects you to follow while you live here and give them to you tomorrow when you come back."

"I will," Dorothy said. "Park out back."

We followed her up the stairs and she pointed to a gravel parking space at the edge of the alley. She handed me a key and smiled. "Back door."

"Now all you need is a job," Irma said when we walked out the front door. "Don't let Dorothy upset you. It takes her a while to warm up to people. Once she's used to you, she'll talk more, although she never says a whole lot unless it's necessary. She told me once that she always has a prayer in her head and sometimes it's hard to talk around it."

"I understand that," I told her. "I do the same with songs. I keep a song in my head all the time, or at least in my heart. Thanks for all the help, Irma."

"Think nothing of it. I'm always glad to help anyone I can. It keeps me busy and out of trouble. Well, you have my phone number. Never think twice if you want to use it."

I thanked her again and started toward my car. She stopped me before I got in. "Raven, I'll keep my eyes open for a job, and I'll call you here if anything comes up. Good luck, and keep in touch."

I drove back to the hotel, making notes of the streets so I could find my way back to my new apartment the next day. Irma had managed to find such good deals for me that I splurged and had dinner at a Sizzler Steak House.

I had an urge to find a store and buy a red and white blanket or quilt to replace the faded blue cover on the bed in Dorothy's basement. Maybe I could recreate the cheerful atmosphere that Nana had put together for me, and that I had just seen at Christine's. In the end, I chased that urge away, deciding that I couldn't spend money on anything that wasn't necessary. Not until I after I had a job. I found a liquor store, where I bought a bottle of tequila to keep me company that night. That felt necessary.

When the phone in my hotel room rang, I expected to hear Irma or Christine on the other end of the line. A male voice took me by surprise.

"What's Penny doing tonight?" The question bothered me. Why would this guy use my name instead of asking 'what are you doing', like a normal person?

"Who are you," I asked, still trying to identify the voice.

"Don't tell me you've already forgotten me. That's not very good for the male ego."

Craig? Brian? Claude? Who would be offended if I didn't recognize his voice? I knew their voices and was sure it wasn't any of them. Tinker maybe? No, he'd never call, even if he knew where to find me. He'd have Sharon make the call.

"Tell me who you are or I'll hang up," I threatened. Nobody knew where I was. Maybe it was a prank call. No, he had used my name. I suspected that he had used my name purposely, to make me feel the fear that was creeping into my drunken body.

"I'll give you a hint," he said. "I'm someone who cares about you and thinks you are beautiful."

The clue was worthless and I still didn't recognize the voice so I hung up. The phone rang again and I let it go without answering.

Sometime after I had fallen back to sleep, the phone rang again. I wasn't sure if it was day or night, and answered without thinking.

"Don't hang up, Penny. I didn't mean to scare you earlier," the same mystery voice said. "I hoped you would recognize my voice and be happy to hear from me."

I cleared my head and focused on the clock.

"I wouldn't be happy to hear from anyone at three o'clock," I said, quickly reminding myself that there was one person I had welcomed several times at that hour, even later. Surely I'd recognize Brian's voice. I had replayed every word he had spoken to me a million times over. "I'll hang up again if you don't tell me who you are and what you want."

"It's Jerry Fremlinger, from the bus. I wanted to make sure you got settled in okay."

My heart pounded and I looked up to check the curtains and the locks. "I'm fine. How did you find me?"

He snorted. "The hotel shuttle was a good clue, Penny. I called there and they said you weren't registered, but I saw you in the parking lot yesterday. All I had to do was wait until you went into your room and get the number. The front desk put me straight through when I asked for you by number instead of name."

He sounded proud of his resourcefulness, so I tried to set him straight. "I don't appreciate you tracking me down this way, or calling. You're scaring me."

"I mean no harm, Penny." It bothered me that he kept using my name. "I liked you and thought maybe I could talk you into going to dinner with me. I'll take you anywhere you want to go. Hopefully, you'll choose something better than Sizzler."

"Please, don't call again," I said and hung up on him. After the call disconnected, I removed the receiver from the cradle so he couldn't get through if he tried again, and pushed a chair in front of the door.

Claude came to the door the next morning. I looked out the window before moving the chair to open the door.

"Your phone must be off the hook. Christine has been trying to get through," he said. "When you didn't come down for breakfast I thought I'd check on you."

I told him about my calls from Jerry Fremlinger and he promised he hadn't told him, or anyone else, that I was there.

"He's following me," I explained. "He told me where I ate dinner last night. This is scary."

Claude rubbed the back of his neck. "I don't want you leaving here alone or leading him to your new place," he said. "Let me think on this a spell. Come down to the office and eat your rolls while I think."

I sat behind the desk while he checked two guests in and made a few calls. Now that I had met Irma, my impression of Claude was completely different. His relaxed attitude and sparse interactions struck me as a break from Irma's overbearing personality more than the inactions of a feeble man as I had once thought.

"Christine will pick you up here," he said. "Leave your car where it's at, and your things in the room for now." He laughed. "If this guy wants to tangle with Christine and Irma, I pity him. Stick with them today."

I reminded him that I was supposed to check out and move into Dorothy's basement. "I can't afford another night here if I can avoid it."

"You're checked out already as far as money and registration is concerned. Run on with Christine now and let Irma handle the rest. She's on her way."

Christine took me to transfer the car, circling blocks and backtracking to make sure no one was following us. Before returning to the motel, I went with her to run her gift shop errands. As we walked out of the last shop I noticed a help wanted sign in the front window.

"Do you think they'd hire me?" I asked. "I don't have any sales experience but I'm sure I could learn fast."

"I don't see why they wouldn't hire you." She looked over her shoulder and up and up and down the concrete corridor, which made me feel safe and liked. "I can put in a good word for you. I know the manager."

We turned around and went back in. It was a part-time position, two days a week, which was better than nothing, and it paid enough to feed me.

In Christine's car I got to talk a little more than in Irma's. "In one day, I got my first car, my first apartment, and now the next day I got my first job, thanks to you and Irma. You can't imagine how excited I am," I said, forgetting about Jerry for a few minutes.

"And this is just a start, Raven," she said. "Hopefully, many good things will happen in your future."

Irma waited for us in Claude's office and started talking the second we walked through the door. "We've got it all settled. The housekeeper carted your things out like they were dirty laundry. It's in the trunk of Claude's car. We want you to go back into the room, wait for us to leave, and give us two hours. Then, cover up with the robe we left on your bed, put your hair in a towel like you just come out of the shower. Come out and go to the office. Claude will take you in the meeting room and slip you out the back door to his car. I'll go back to your room in the robe and towel."

I giggled. "This sounds like a movie scene."

"You'll have to leave your car here tonight so Jerry won't know you've checked out. Claude will take you on over to Dorothy's. I'm going to stay in your room and let my nephew, Alvin, in. Hopefully with Jerry watching. And if he calls back, Alvin will answer the phone, and we'll know that Jerry didn't see you escape to the new place."

Irma's plan worked. I moved into Dorothy's. Jerry called twice that night and got Alvin both times. Claude said Jerry was dumber than a box of rocks because his number was listed in the phone directory. Alvin's brother Charles, the cop, paid Jerry a visit and assured him that I was safe under their watch so he didn't need to worry over me anymore.

Chapter 39

I broke four of Dorothy's neatly printed house rules the first night for sure; five if the other four didn't meet her expectations for maintaining Christian behavior. I drank alcohol, used a drug illegally, skipped a night of toilet scrubbing, and left a light burning when I went to bed.

Creating a whole new life and out-smarting a stalker all in one day deserved a celebration. It wasn't my fault that my car was sitting in the parking lot at the Swingin' Door Motel and I was stranded in my new room to celebrate alone. And I sure hadn't asked my stomach to reject the Valium/tequila combination, or planned on passing out before I had cleaned up the mess or switched off the lamp.

I would have broken the light rule on purpose even if I hadn't passed out, because the basement was spooky. I wanted to be able to see if Jerry Fremlinger found me down there. Chills ran through my body every time I remembered the way he said my name. I never wanted anyone to call me Penny again.

June Winster, the manager of the gift shop, called me the next day and offered me three days to get settled before I started to work. My training would begin on Thursday, giving me plenty of time to unpack, and to call Madeline and maybe even meet with her if she was available and I got my car back in time.

I carried Madeline's phone number in the pocket of my jeans and waited until I heard Dorothy leave the house. She didn't have a regular job, but volunteered at church functions, hospitals, and nursing homes every day according to the schedule she left with my rules.

I preferred to make my calls when she wasn't there because she still made me uncomfortable. Why was it that the people who talked the most seldom paid much attention to what others said, and people who never said much seemed anxious to hear every word others said, especially when the words weren't meant for them?

Madeline's secretary said she wasn't in. "She's doing a contest today and tomorrow, so we probably won't see her back in the office until Thursday or Friday. Do you want me to leave a message on her desk for you?"

"Another contest?" I was surprised there would be another so soon after the one that I had won.

"She runs them one after the other," the secretary explained. "I didn't think she'd get a decent turn-out with this one being so soon after the holidays, but I was wrong. She has over fifty competing today. Did you want to enter?"

"No," I answered quickly. "There's no message. I'll call back at the end of the week."

How could I have been so naïve? Obviously the contest meant nothing. Someone else would win this week and I'd be forgotten. Brian was probably getting ready to spend the weekends with another lucky winner, forgetting he had ever met me.

I was crazy to move to Nashville before verifying my connections, and I deserved to spend the rest of my life in Dorothy's basement. Suddenly my appetite left and I changed my mind about the breakfast I had planned to make after I called Madeline. I went back to my room in search of an escape.

It was too early to drink and I wouldn't risk smoking in the house. A dirty bathrooms or wasted electricity was one thing; the smell of pot in a closed up basement was another. I put my coat on, took a joint from my purse, and stepped out the back door.

Dorothy's next-door neighbor called to me from her back porch. "You must be the new boarder. It's nice to meet you." She lifted the lid off her metal garbage can and placed a plastic bag inside.

I waved and said yes, I was the new boarder as she walked toward me wiping her hands on the dishtowel she wore on her shoulder.

"I'm Bertha Whitehouse," she said, offering her hand so I would have to meet her at the fence. "I've been over here twenty-eight years come next June."

"I'm Raven Coal. I've been here twenty-four hours come five o'clock. Happy to meet you." Only, I wasn't particularly happy to meet her. Not right then, anyway.

"You're sure a sight prettier than that last girl, and friendlier too." She adjusted her glasses and looked me over. "If you need anything, or just want some company, my door is always open," she offered. "Dorothy don't talk much so I'd imagine it can get pretty lonely over there at times."

I thanked her, unsure whether to call her Bertha or Mrs. Whitehouse. I decided on Ma'am, to be safe. "Same goes in return, Ma'am. I'm here if you need me."

I said good-bye. Figuring she'd watch me from her window, I decided I should walk farther down the alley to smoke. She'd most likely watch me from her window.

After a smoke and a walk around the block, things didn't seem as hopeless as they had earlier. I lived in a nice neighborhood for the first time in my life, even if my basement room was dreary. I had a new car, even if it wasn't with me. And I was still a good singer, even if Madeline and Brian weren't the contacts I hoped they'd be.

And I had Claude and Irma, and Christine and Bertha Whitehouse to make me smile. Irma could probably line me up with a record deal within twenty-four hours if I asked.

Feeling relaxed and more confident, I returned to the house only to discover that I had locked myself out. I went to Bertha's and sat in her kitchen eating oatmeal cookies while she told me about her late husband, their two sons, and her six grandchildren. Dorothy came home at five and let me in the house.

Claude and Irma brought my car to me after dark and said they thought I could safely leave the house without worrying about Jerry. It sounded good, only I had nowhere to go.

Dorothy came out of her shell and offered up a few phrases. She offered to share the spaghetti she made for supper and invited me to join her bible study group at the church that night. I accepted the food, which we ate in silence after a long prayer, but declined the study group. "I'll stay and clean up the kitchen while you're gone," I offered. She didn't respond, or say good-bye before she left.

I felt trapped standing at the sink washing dishes. The thought of another evening alone in the basement depressed me, so I decided I would enjoy the freedom of having my own car and some money, and go out.

Victoria already had plans by the time I worked up the nerve to call her, but she made me glad I had worked up the nerve to call. She told me about Danny's Den, a country music club that she thought I could safely go to alone.

"They may let you sing," she told me. "On weeknights they have amateur performers. If you get there early and signup for something on the band's list before they run out of slots, you get to sing. Try it out and see how you like it. I'll tag along the next time if you decide to go back."

I dressed in jeans and a denim work shirt, planning to draw as little attention to myself as possible since I still had an edgy feeling from my experience with Jerry. It took courage to go out alone, but staying home felt like an even worse idea.

Danny's Den didn't look any bigger or nicer than the VFW from the outside, but there was a line of people that stretched from the door all the way into the parking lot. I moved in close to the group ahead of me, hoping other people would think I was with them.

"Do you know how much the cover charge is?" I asked a girl who backed into me. Maybe when she realized I was alone and new, she would invite me to join them. She answered my question and jumped right back into conversation with her group, without giving me a second thought.

At the door, I handed over my three-dollar cover and asked if I had arrived in time to sing. The attendant handed me a song list. "Pick your songs, fill out the bottom of the form, and put this in the box on the left-hand side of the stage. If you're selected, they'll call your name." She continued to accept money from others and let them pass around me while she talked.

I thanked her and followed the crowd down a dark, narrow hall to the club area. Tables were already full and people stood in the aisles. It was my first time being in a club without protection and I was sorry I had been so hateful about people trying to look out for me in the past.

I found standing room at a side bar and settled in, ordering a beer after my second shot so I'd have something in front of me to hold my seat.

"How can you mix drinks like that and not get sick?" the guy next to me asked. "I end up with a killer headache if I switch around like that."

I smiled. "Please, don't give my head any ideas."

He asked a lot of questions. Did I come there often? Was I alone? Was I new in town? Planning to stay long? I answered honestly and without detail, except to say that I was meeting friends who hadn't shown up yet.

I put the song list aside and reconsidered the situation. Did I really want to sing with a band I didn't know, in front of strangers who probably had come to Nashville hoping to see stars? They'd be disappointed no matter how good I sounded.

When I looked at the list, the decision got easier. Some of my best songs were on it. I checked my first three choices, "Harper Valley PTA", "Crazy", and "Your Good Girl's Gonna Go Bad", wrote my name and the state I lived in – Tennessee - on the bottom, and asked my friend to save my place while I turned it in. He offered to take it to the box for me, and I let him which was just as well because I might have backed out otherwise.

We had moved into chairs at the end of a long table of tourists when I heard my name called for the next set. "If your name was announced and you are still present and want to sing, you should come to the right side of the stage during this break," someone instructed from the DJ booth. "If we don't hear from you during this break your name will be removed from the list and you will have to submit another sign-up sheet to get back in."

"Go on," my new friend urged. "I'll save your seat and watch your drink."

It wasn't too late to back out. What if no one responded? Most of the people who had been paying attention to the music seemed to reserve their applause for the person they had come with, and I had come alone. The people at the bar didn't clap for anyone.

My friend got up and playfully pulled me out of my seat, which drew attention from the others at our table. They joined him in encouraging me to get up, so I left the table to claim my turn.

"Raven Coal, you will go on second," the coordinator instructed. "You'll do your first choice song. What key do you need?"

I told her my key and stood behind the first singer to wait, rehearsing "Harper Valley PTA" in my mind until the band members took the stage from the other side. I looked out into the audience to smile at the people I had been sitting with, hoping they'd notice when I went on and remember to clap for me.

When I finally looked closely at the stage, it was half way through the first song. I wanted to determine which member was the band leader, so I could make good eye contact and reduce the possibility of a screw up if they played a different arrangement than I was used to singing.

I chose Brian, once my head stopped throbbing. Had he been there the whole time and I hadn't noticed? It didn't seem possible. How could I walk up there and stand that close to him without my heart jumping out of my chest?"

The first song ended and the DJ announced my name. It was too late to back out. Brian's head jerked back when he heard my name, and his eyes met mine as I walked onto the stage. Everything fell into place.

He smiled, as though truly happy to see me, and then counted the song off and played it exactly as I had done it for weeks on the road. Not only did my table of tourists remember to clap, other tables joined them. I said thank you and returned the microphone to the stand.

Brian motioned for me to come to him with a jerk of his head. "Where are you sitting?" he asked. "Can I come talk to you on my next break?"

I pointed out my table and returned to my seat on shaking legs. My new friend talked through the rest of the set, but I didn't hear anything he said. When the set ended, I excused myself and went to meet Brian, before he got to the table and I was forced to admit that I didn't remember my new friend's name.

"What are you doing here?" he asked. "I was shocked when I heard your name announced, and a little disappointed that you didn't call to tell me you were coming."

Why don't you hug me, like old friends normally do? Why aren't you somewhere with the latest contest winner? Why are my legs shaking? I had a million questions for him too, but didn't ask any of them.

"I didn't know I was coming here tonight," I answered. It wouldn't have mattered if I had because I didn't know he'd be there anyway. "It's nice to see you."

"It's great to see you," he returned. "I think about you often. Are you in town on business?"

Often? I thought about him all the time. Every minute of every day. "Indirectly," I answered. "I live here now, and hope to have some business eventually, so it's pre-business I guess. I'm just trying to get settled in right now."

Twenty minutes of small talk passed quickly. "Will you still be around after the next set? It's the last one. "I'd like to talk more. Are you alone?"

"I came alone," I answered. "Both, to Nashville, and here tonight. I'll wait if you'll walk me to my car. I don't want to walk out alone after the parking lot clears."

He looked surprised. "You? Being cautious? I'm glad to hear it. Wait for me by the stage and I'll walk you anywhere you want to go later."

I returned to listen to the last set with my new friend. "Someone you know, or was he offering you some advice?" he asked.

"I used to work with him. We did a road trip together a while back and he may be able to help me out while I'm here," I said, hating that I figured he would probably explain me the same way if anyone asked. "Someone I'm in love with," felt much better but I couldn't say those words to anyone.

My friend invited me to get something to eat after Danny's closed, and asked for my phone number when I said I couldn't go. I told him I didn't have a phone, and that I was married, both true.

He wished me luck and said he was a regular at Danny's and he hoped to see me again. "Here's my number," he said, handing me a business card. "If you decide you'd like to talk to me outside of here, give me a call."

Brian walked me out and sat inside my car so we could turn the heater on and talk in comfort. He wanted to hear about my move, where I was staying, and what my plans were. "I can't believe you didn't call me," he repeated. "Were you ever going to let me know you were here?"

"I didn't know what to do. Brian, I didn't know if you would want to hear from me. I had planned to call Madeline and let her know I was here, and figured if she thought you were interested she would let you know."

"Why? I left everything open to you, Raven. You were the one with the husband. I didn't try to influence your decision either way, but I thought I made it clear that I was available if you wanted or needed me, for anything."

I didn't know what to think. Maybe he had said that to me before, and I didn't want to hear it. Or maybe he was saying what was convenient now. And, there was the possibility that he said it when I was too messed up to remember.

"I'm confused about a lot of things," I said. "I tried to separate my personal life from the music, but it's all mixed up. I need something to either clear my head or muddle it further so I won't think at all. Do you have anything?"

"At home. It's not a good idea to carry it around, or to sit in public parking lots smoking," he advised. "Want to come home with me?"

Dorothy's rules stated that I couldn't bring anyone in to sleep over, but said nothing about me staying out all night. He hadn't asked me to spend the night – only to smoke a joint. Jumping to conclusions would only lead to heartache so I tried to stop.

"Should I follow you?" I asked, hoping it wasn't far so I would be able to find my way back.

"You can follow me, or ride with me and I'll bring you back to your car later."

Later tonight, or later in my life? Should I ask? Did it matter?

I drove to the back of the building where we moved into his car and left mine hidden from the main road. I was especially grateful that I hadn't driven when his house ended up being at least fifteen miles out, and in a secluded area much like the one where Christine lived.

Brian's house was smaller than Christine's, but still nicer than most I had been in. He showed me both bedrooms, three bathrooms, and the kitchen and living room, saving the best for last.

"Come down here," he said, opening the basement door. "I have a surprise for you."

A pool table filled most of the room at the bottom of the stairs. He opened a door and let me peek at a laundry room, and then rushed me across the room to another door. "Here's the part you'll like."

I wasn't appropriately excited because I had never seen a recording studio before. It looked like a soundboard to me. "Nice," I said, with little enthusiasm. "Is this where you practice?"

Brian explained the equipment in the room without laughing at me. "You can practice in here anytime you want," he offered. "You can also record your voice and see how you'll sound on records."

We went upstairs to the room where he kept his pot stored in a coffee can under the bed. He rolled the joint and told me to hold it while he ran to the other bedroom and brought back the pillows from that bed to prop behind us before he lit it.

"I didn't forget what you like. This is some good stuff, so it's best if you plan to stay here if you start on it," he warned. "I'll take you back in the morning."

I agreed to stay. He changed from work clothes into sweats. I took my shoes off and curled my legs on the bed. He smiled. "That's my girl. Make yourself at home. I've pictured you here many times."

I didn't make it back to Dorothy's for two days. Brian and I smoked, talked, made love, sang in the studio, and then went back to Danny's and started all over again. Strangely, I thought of Craig and Jason while I was with Brian. As my actions pushed them further from my heart, my head refused to let them go.

On the way to his house the second night, Brian mentioned Madeline, a topic that I had avoided. "I would have called Madeline to come hear you tonight, but she's tied up with another contest. She'll be happy to hear that you're in town, though. Or have you already called her?"

"I haven't talked to her," I said, not mentioning that I had called but didn't reach her.

"Good. My feelings would have been hurt if you had talked to her and not me."

"I told you I thought about telling her I was here so she'd tell you," I reminded him. "That way I'd never have known if you rejected me."

He pulled on his lips and frowned. "Why do you have so little faith in me?"

"It's a personal problem. I don't have faith in anyone really. Now, why don't you explain this contest business to me? I'm not sure I understand."

"Madeline owns a booking agency and her husband is a top executive for Algram recording label. Madeline sponsors these talent contests, hoping that the two of them will pick up new talent for their businesses. It's really not a bad idea, and a very cost-effective way to scout."

"And your roll?" I asked.

"Occasionally she hires me to oversee the musicians for the solo portion of the contest, or to judge. It's a two day job and not too bad. She decided to send you out on that trial road trip, to check both you and some of those clubs out. I didn't have anything else going on at the time so I went."

I fought off the song that kept interfering. *"You don't have to say you love me, just be close at hand."* This conversation may have been going my way, so I needed to hold on to it.

"Any more questions?" he asked.

Since I had missed half of the answers to my previous questions, I said no and let the song take over until we reached the house. *"You don't have to say forever, I will understand, believe me, believe meeee."* I may never know if he had done it before, or if he planned to do it again.

When we arrived at his house, I rushed inside, anxious to have physical pleasure drown out emotional chaos.

Chapter 40

Dorothy talked plenty when she got mad. My two-day disappearance cleared the prayers from her head as effectively as chemicals cleared songs from mine, and freed her tongue.

"Lord only knows what can happen to a young girl when she runs the streets in the middle of the night," might have been the first complete sentence I had heard her say. "I sat up here for hours praying for your safe return. I had visions of you lying dead in a crashed up car off the side of some dark road. And I imagined that you had been drugged or raped or had your throat slit by some pervert. Lord have mercy, Raven, the possibilities were endless and I thought of every one of them."

I bit my cheeks, thinking she must have learned her logic from Momma. If they were endless, how could she have thought of every one of them? She twisted her fingers until I thought they might break, and the pile of hair on top of her head wobbled. I felt too sorry for her to laugh.

"I'm very sorry I worried you, Dorothy. I didn't realize you would feel responsible for me when I moved in here. I should have called to tell you I wasn't coming home." The rules prohibited phone calls after ten, but I didn't mention that. Maybe the rule didn't include calls from me to her?

"This city is full of evil. The devil lurks around every corner, ready to dig his filthy claws into girls like you. Raven, you need to be especially careful, looking the way you do. Beauty is a curse because the devil likes the pretty ones best."

I questioned the accuracy of that statement but didn't want to make trouble with another adult. "I promise I will watch out for the devil, and the next time I'm not coming home, I will call and let you know."

She wrung her hands faster. "I don't want to hear any details about where you were or what you were doing for two full days and nights," she said, although I believed she secretly wanted to hear every detail. "I'm afraid my heart wouldn't survive even the thought of some things."

I honored her wishes and spared her an explanation.

"I'll continue to pray for you," she said. "Again, I strongly encourage you to join my bible study group. You can be saved, you know. God forgives those who ask."

I thanked her for the prayers and said I would think about the study group, only because I thought that might end the conversation.

"Did your car break down?" she asked, looking like she might be unable to live without those details she didn't want.

"I ran into an old friend," I said. "He has a big house with a recording studio in the basement. We worked on music until it was too late to drive home so he offered me his guest room for the night. I slept most of the day and then we worked again last night and lost track of time. I was safe."

She closed her eyes and waved her hands through the air. Her lips moved but no sound came from them. I wanted that to mean the prayers were retreating back inside her head, but it didn't.

"May the good Lord bless your soul and enlighten your mind." She changed to a tone that didn't sound like her regular whispering voice or the patronizing tone she had been using since I came home. I stared at her distorted face, because her eyes were closed and I could get away with it.

"Forgive her, oh heavenly father. She's young and misguided," she continued.

I cleared my throat because I didn't like her talking about me as though I wasn't there. "Dorothy, I've taken up enough of your time already, worrying you all night and then using up all your prayers today. I'm going to my room now so you can forget about me and relax."

I backed toward the stairs as I spoke, then darted down them when she took a breath. I could still hear her praying for my lost soul long after I was in what should have been my safe area. I replaced her voice with a song.

Dorothy went back to her regular quiet self the next morning, but I steered away from her as much as possible anyway. She asked once again if I wanted to go to the bible study and accepted my *no* without pushing the issue or praying over me. Still, without words, she let me know how disappointed she was in me. She reminded me of Momma in that way.

June Winster worked me every day the first week. It was her opinion that employees retained information better when they repeated the process often. Since early January was a slow period in the gift shop business, she wanted me there to wait on as many customers as possible.

Irma and Christine came into the store on my third day and invited me to lunch. June said to take as long as I needed since we hadn't had a customer all morning. We went to a nice restaurant in a hotel downtown - Irma's choice. I remembered Claude telling me about the cafeteria when I stayed at the motel, and understood why he had made the comment about it not being fancy. Irma probably preferred this place to any he would choose.

Irma stood across from me, loading cherry tomatoes on her salad plate, and asked how things were going with Dorothy. "Has she tried to drag you to church yet?"

I laughed. "Only to bible study group so far. I have a feeling she'll work up to more soon. I did get her to talk," I said, immediately sorry when she asked how. For all I knew, Irma would disapprove of my staying out for two nights as much as Dorothy had.

It was too late to back out, so I told her. "I ran into an old friend at the club and spent a couple of nights at his house. She thinks I've turned my soul over to the devil."

"Stand your ground with her, Raven. Just because you rent from her don't give her the right to run your life when you're outside her house," Irma advised. "She's a busy-body, with her nose in everybody's business."

Christine snorted. "She's worse than a busy-body. She's a nut case if you ask me. Dorothy is jealous of anybody that has fun so she convinces herself that they must be sinners."

Christine brought up the club again after we were seated. "Victoria was happy when you called her, and very sorry that it was on a night when she couldn't go. Did you sing at Danny's?"

"I did," I told her. "I'm glad she told me to go there. Maybe we can all go one night." I turned to Irma. "Do you think Claude would come hear me sing once? He helped me win that contest."

Irma and Christine came to hear my one song the next night. They brought Claude and Shelton, and Victoria and her date, and a dozen or so friends and relatives. Brian came to the table during his breaks and helped me remember the new names.

"That one sure puts a spark in your eye," Irma commented after he returned to the stage. "Is that where you disappeared to for those scandalous missing nights?"

I didn't need to answer; she went on talking.

"I'd say he's a heap better to look at than Dorothy, and much better with conversation, too. So, you knew him before you came to Nashville? You said you ran into an old friend," she reminded me when I looked surprised.

I nodded.

"Should I guess the rest? Raven, I'm not judging you and you won't get no preaching from me. Lord knows Dorothy has that covered for both of us. Just take a little advice from an older, more experienced friend," she warned. "Don't complicate your life if you can avoid it. Do things in the right order."

How could she know so much about me? She reminded me of Irene, and that was a heap more pleasant than Dorothy reminding me of Momma. By the time we left that night, I missed Irene so much I wanted to cry.

"Why don't you call her?" Brian suggested. "You can come to my house to make the call. You'll have privacy and you won't have to worry about running up Dorothy's phone bill."

I thanked him, but said no. "Ralph would be asleep already and he's not very nice about late calls, even from Irene when she's out of town. Besides, I need to get to bed. I have to work tomorrow."

The truth was, I didn't know if I was ready to make the call. Irene was connected to Craig and Jason. If I called her, I would hear about them.

"Think about it," he encouraged. "Eventually you'll have to face everyone you left behind, and make decisions about where you're headed. I won't rush you. Just remember that the offer stands when you're ready."

I pulled my car keys from my purse and held them so he'd know I was ready to leave. He stood up to walk me to the door.

"Another thing you can keep in mind," he added on the way. "My house is available to you any time you want to invite guests, for as long as they want to stay."

What would Irene think if I invited her to come stay at Brian's house? Could it be any worse than what she must already think of me for running off without saying good-bye? She might hate me for walking out on Jason, and hang up if I called her. I wasn't ready to find out.

I left Brian with a quick hug and went back to Dorothy's to break a few more rules. I drank so much that I overslept the next morning and was almost late for my last day of training. With no time to shower, I dressed quickly, brushed my teeth and hair, and ran up the stairs to leave. Dorothy waited at the top of the stairs with her hands on her hips.

"The light," she said, staring down the stairs into my space.

"I'm late," I argued, but she didn't accept my excuse. I ran down the stairs and turned out the light. She was still standing at the door when I returned.

"An idle mind is the devil's workshop," she preached. "If you'd spend your free time reading the bible instead of running around your life might turn around."

I didn't have time or inclination to explain that my mind was far from idle, and that I didn't want to turn my life around. I opened the door and said I had to go.

"You'll have to show some initiative, Raven, or I can't allow a sinner to stay in my house. I can't lift you up if you don't want to be lifted."

I nodded to acknowledge that I had heard her nonsense, and walked out before she could say any more. Since when was leaving the light on or being pretty a sin? Christine was right; Dorothy was a certifiable nut case. And I lived with her.

I needed to find a full time job and get out of there, into a real apartment without a prison warden watching over every move I made. I thought of nothing else the whole day while I stocked the shelves that June had left me to organize on my own.

"Congratulations," she said at the end of the day. "You learned quickly, and you are a very hard worker. I couldn't be more pleased with your training period."

Good. I thanked her. "I've enjoyed working here. If you can give me more hours, I'd like to work as much as possible."

"The most I can do right now is call you in if someone else needs a sick day. And we can use you to cover vacations," she offered. When I looked disappointed, she tried harder. "Things pick up at Christmas. And of course, if anyone quits, you'll be given first consideration for their full-time position."

I couldn't wait a year for Christmas, or wish for my co-workers to get sick or quit. I needed a second job. And I didn't want to ask Irma or Christine to help. They had done enough already.

My car headed for Brian's house before I realized what I was doing. "I need another job," I said as soon as he opened the door.

"You quit?" He sounded disappointed.

"No, I need two jobs. I have to get out of Dorothy's house."

"Danny might have something at the club," he suggested. "Can you handle working that late and still get up for your other job?"

"I'll do what I have to do. Will you ask him about it when you go in tonight?"

I stayed to have dinner with him and then went back to my prison when he left for work. He promised to check out the job situation and let me know something in the morning.

I soaked in the tub until my pills kicked in, turned out the lights like a responsible tenant, and went to bed early. Irene raced through my dreams when I finally got to sleep, only she was in my new life, in Irma's spot. She didn't look or act a thing like Irma. I woke, feeling sad that maybe that meant I had replaced one of them but soon realized the message was that my feelings for them were the same. They both made me feel safe.

When I fell back to sleep the dream picked up again. Irene ran toward me with a smile on her face. But the smile changed into scorn when she finally caught up to me. I read the questions in her eyes, even though she didn't ask them aloud. How could you? Don't you have a heart? Had I really believed that I could walk away and never look back? If nothing else, I owed Craig the courtesy of a divorce so he could move on and find the wife he deserved.

What was wrong with me? I was as crazy as Dorothy. I had planned to never go back, and at the same time, planned to sign autographs at the VFW. That was senseless, so I really had no plan at all. Nana would say, I ran off half-cocked.

Nana! I should call and check on her. She probably didn't care anymore, since she had already said good-bye, but Pappy would be hurt that I hadn't called. And Wanda and Gwen would know that I was a loser if I never called or visited again. Love was a burden.

Maybe they didn't know anything yet, and I could call without an explanation. Craig wouldn't have wanted to worry Pappy with our problems. I doubted he would tell anyone I was gone until I failed to show up at Jason's high school graduation.

I gave Brian time to wake up on Saturday morning before I drove out there and knocked on his door. He smiled when he saw me on the porch. "Another nice surprise," he said as he took my coat.

"You may change your mind soon," I warned as the tears found their way out. "I've been holding this back for a long time, and now I don't want to cry alone. Either hold me or roll a joint."

He held my hand and led me to the couch, where he held me while I cried. He must have wondered if I was going to cry forever because the thought sure crossed my mind, often. Neither of us talked until I broke the comfort of his arms to go after a tissue. As often as I needed them, I ought to have learned by then to keep them in my pocket.

"I'm an idiot," I said, blowing my nose without thinking how unattractive it might be to him. "I didn't plan anything out. Here I am, completely lost."

He scratched his head. I noticed for the first time that it looked like he might have less hair on top. "You aren't completely lost, Raven. I know exactly where you are, and can even tell you how to get back if you want."

"Get back to where?" I asked, aiming the question at myself more than at him. "I don't know where I'm going, Brian. I don't have a clue."

"Come back over here and sit down," he said, patting the couch beside him. He pulled me into his arms again and waited until I relaxed before he started to talk. "Again, Raven, I'm not in a position to advise you. I'm here to support you, whatever you want to do and wherever you want to go. Are you sorry you came here?"

I played the question again in my head, stalling until I pulled my myself together. "No, I'm just sorry I didn't think it out better before I came. I left without telling anybody. Ran away like a chicken."

"Nobody? Do you know why?" he asked. "Did you run off on the spur of the moment, or had you at least thought about it a little before you did it?"

"What is this?" I laughed. "A quiz?"

He squeezed me. "No, I'm just trying to ask questions that might lead you to answers. You don't have to tell me your answers, as long as you find them for yourself."

"I didn't tell anybody because I was afraid they would talk me out of it. I planned my escape, but didn't think about what would happen after I got here."

"Danny says you can serve at the bar, or work the DJ booth, or maybe some of each if it's a job you're worried about. He needs a DJ on Wednesday and a bartender on Saturday."

"That would help," I said, partially relieved. "Thanks for asking him."

I rested my head on his shoulder and worked up more tears. I had to go all the way back to childhood to identify the source of my sadness. I missed the special people in my life. My heart ached the same as it had when Momma and Daddy had snatched me away from Nana and moved me to the city. This time I had done it to myself.

"I'm a horrible person, Brian." I pulled my used tissue out of my pocket and wiped at my nose again. "I can't tell you what I'm thinking or you will hate me."

He kissed the top of my head. "I'll never hate you, Raven. You couldn't make me if you tried."

He didn't understand. I didn't have to try. I hurt people naturally. It was something I was born to do, just like singing. "How can you say that?" I asked. "You don't know everything about me. You don't know what I might do, or how much I can hurt people."

"But I know how I feel about you, and who I am," he answered. "I know that for a time my life was better because you were in it. No matter what you did before that time, or what you may do in the future, you can't take away what I already have."

"It's too bad everybody can't be like you," I said. His words sounded good, but obviously he didn't know how easily love could turn into pain, especially when I was involved.

"Everybody can't be, but many people are," he told me. "I'm sure there are other people in your life who love you unconditionally, and probably want to hear from you now."

He went to the kitchen for drinks. I closed my eyes and tried to digest everything he had said. I grasped the meaning but, hard as I tried, couldn't open my heart to pull it in. I was exhausted from crying, so he sat my water on the table and suggested that I nap while he ran errands.

I had nearly dozed off when he stopped beside me on his way out. "Here," he said, sitting the phone on the floor beside the couch. "The offer still stands if you decide to make some calls."

I couldn't sleep with the phone beside me. I turned my back to it and even put my head at the other end of the couch. After tossing until I was seasick, I knew it was my chance to prove to Brian how wrong he was about me. Other people weren't like he was, and he wouldn't be like that anymore once he found out that the people who knew me best could hate me.

I dialed the shop first and got no answer. Irene must have let the girls close up for something special, like when they all went to do hair and make-up for Lorraine Robertson's wedding.

Curiosity made me call her home number. I almost hung up when Ralph answered but decided he was the least likely person to criticize me. I said hello and asked for Irene.

"Penny? Is that you?" He sounded nervous, but not angry.

"Yes, Ralph. It's me. I called the shop and didn't get anybody. Is Irene there?"

"She gave the girls off because she's having a new floor put down over the weekend. She's gone to the funeral," he said. "Aren't you down there?"

"I'm out of state," I said. My hand shook out of control or I might have hung the phone up to avoid what he was going to say next. My head was empty—not a song in reach—and I wanted to scream.

"So you don't know? Penny, it's your grandmother," he said. "Man, I'm sorry I have to be the one to tell you. The funeral was this morning."

"It's not your fault, Ralph." I wanted to say more but couldn't pull any air into my tight chest to push it out with. Does Irene hate me seemed like a question that didn't need an answer at that point. Surely everyone hated me for not being there.

"Give me your number and I'll have her call you when she gets back. Hold on, let me get a pencil." He put the phone down and I heard him rummage through the drawer by the sink for a pencil. I pictured everything in Irene's kitchen, and wished with all my heart Daddy had listened when she tried to talk him into letting me live there instead of getting married.

Ralph was back on the phone talking to me, but I couldn't make out his words over the screaming in my head. If Daddy has listened to Irene, I wouldn't have married Craig, and I wouldn't be in Nashville missing Nana's funeral, and I wouldn't be a worse mother than Kitty Marilyn Treeton Martox.

"Penny, are you there? I have a pencil now, so you can give me the number."

Brian took the phone from me and gave the number to Ralph. I hadn't even heard him come in, but I did hear him explain that I didn't have a phone in my apartment so she could call there any time and he would make sure I got the message. He said I was fine. At least, I thought that was what he said. But his words sounded far away.

Later, I heard him call Dorothy to tell her that there had been a death in the family and I wouldn't be home for a couple of days. I kept my eyes closed until I drifted off to sleep again.

Chapter 41

I woke before daylight, stiff and disoriented. I wasn't in the damp, musty basement at Dorothy's house, and I sure didn't remember being in this bed when I went to sleep. Before total panic set in, my eyes adjusted to the darkness and I recognized Brian's room. Why wasn't he in the bed with me?

The furnace hummed somewhere in the basement under me; other than that I heard nothing. I checked his bathroom first--on the chance that he was there in the dark--and then tiptoed through the house until I found him sleeping on the couch. The pillows and quilt from the guest room ruled out the likelihood that he had accidentally fallen asleep in the living room.

I didn't blame him for wanting to avoid me but understanding didn't stop the hurt. He had wanted to believe that it was impossible for him to hate me. But, now that he knew I ran out and missed Nana's funeral, he obviously knew I was a heartless bitch, and there was plenty to hate about me.

Tears burned my swollen eyes again. Nana was gone. Nana, who had saved my life when my own mother wanted me dead, and who kept loving me all those years when she didn't get to see me. Nana had who shared sentences with Pappy because she knew how to love. Nana, who had died without her son or her granddaughter there to return her love. I didn't even wonder if he went back after he read my letter; I knew he didn't because I was just like him.

I went back to the bedroom and buried my face in the pillow so Brian wouldn't hear me cry again. My throat filled with salty phlegm and choked the breath right out of me. I hoped I was self-destructing so I wouldn't have to face the next day, but instinctively I gasped for air and kept on living.

Brian was a light sleeper; I had learned that in the hotels. He would wake if I tried to slip past him to get my purse and leave. I was trapped, and would have to face him again before I could get out of the house. The thought was unbearable.

I pulled the coffee can out from under the bed and took it into the bathroom where I could maybe close the door and turn on the light without waking him. Using two papers, I rolled a fat one and considered filling the tub. A long soak in warm water would help my tense muscles and relieve some of the stiffness, but I figured the water would wake Brian and I scratched the idea.

Would I ever be free to do what I wanted without fear of letting someone else down? I had escaped my parents and ended up with Craig. Then I left Craig and wound up with Dorothy. I had come here to avoid her, and relinquished control to Brian. Would it ever end? When I got my own apartment, could I retreat from the rest of the world and just be a person on my own?

I lit the joint, turned out the light, and sat on the floor. I smoked until I burned the tips of my fingers trying to hold on. As usual, Brian had the good stuff. The weight lifted from my body and I rested my head against the wall to enjoy the peace.

Brian found me on the floor and carried me back to his bed, where he ignored my protests. "Let me up," I demanded. "I need to go home. I only stayed this long so I wouldn't wake you."

"You can leave when you're straight enough to drive again," he said. "Stay in here and sleep this off. I promise I won't bother you."

You won't touch me, I thought, because I won. I made you hate me and I didn't even have to try. Simple job for me. He walked away and left me with those thoughts. And he kept his promise. He didn't bother me until late that evening.

"Sorry to wake you, but I thought you must be hungry. You haven't eaten all day." He stood beside the bed and talked, like he would be contaminated if he came close enough to touch me. "Do you feel like getting up, or would you like me to go out and bring something back?"

Without looking in his direction I asked him to bring something back. Anything, as long as I didn't have to make a decision. As soon as he was out of the house, I got my purse and coat and left.

At least Dorothy didn't have any love invested in me. I couldn't hurt her because she appreciated excuses to pray. I cried the whole way from Brian's house to the gravel lot in Dorothy's back yard, planning to forget Brian and Danny's Den. I'd stay at Dorothy's, work at the gift shop until someone else quit, and stay out of the Devil's path. My life was over.

My stomach burned with hunger but I didn't stop in the kitchen to eat after I saw Dorothy sitting at the table with her bible. She looked up from her reading long enough to offer sympathy for my loss, and prayers, of course. I said I was tired and headed for my room before she tried to make me pray with her.

Sleep was my only hope of escaping the pain I felt, so I took a couple of pills to make sure I would be out for a while. Soon, I would have to call Sharon, or find someone else with an endless supply of nerve pills. I was probably still on Craig's insurance and could get my own prescription. The shape I was in, any doctor would believe I needed them.

Sometime after heavy sleep moved in, I heard knocking on the back door. I couldn't move so I was relieved to hear Dorothy shuffle across the kitchen floor. "Go away," she shouted.

"I need to see Raven," Brian yelled back.

"She can't have visitors right now. Go away or I'll call the police."

"I don't want to come in or disturb you," he said. "Just bring her to the door so I can see that she's okay and then I'll leave. Please."

Dorothy's voice was clearly hysterical. "Leave us alone!"

He knocked again, this time on the window above my bed. Dorothy stomped across the kitchen. I heard her pull the receiver off the wall phone and shout, "I'll call the police. Don't think I won't. Last warning."

I pulled myself up. I couldn't let the police come and see me the way I was, and I couldn't let Brian get arrested because, in Dorothy's twisted mind, he was the devil for knocking.

"I'm coming," I called up the stairs.

She met me at the back door. "Don't open that door, Raven. I won't have that maniac in my house."

I looked at the clock on the stove. "Dorothy, it's eight thirty. You said no phone calls after ten and no visitors overnight. I'm not breaking any rules, so why are you doing this?"

"You need your rest."

I opened the door and told Brian to hold on before I responded to her. "You aren't my boss or my mother. You can't make decisions for me or control my life this way."

I stepped out the door to show him that I was okay. She followed.

"This is a private conversation," I told her. "Would you rather we have it in my room?"

She shook her head. "Neither of you are welcome in my house. I'm a decent, Christian woman. I can't have you here, Raven. You disregard my rules and carry on like a loose woman. I want you to take your things and leave now."

I sank to the ground, too discouraged to argue and too tired to carry my things out. Brian handed me his keys and told me to open the trunk and wait in the car for him.

"No, load the things in my own car," I said, without getting up.

"Come on, Raven. It's too cold to sit on the ground and you're in no shape to drive." He spoke patiently, as though he were talking to a child. "We'll come back for your car as soon as you feel better."

I was out of tears, finally, and fight. He was right; I couldn't drive. And now he was treating me the way everyone else had, because I had proven that I couldn't be responsible for my own life.

"Make up your minds," Dorothy demanded. "I'm tired of standing here in the cold."

Brian helped me up and answered for both of us. "I'm taking her with me now. We'll be back tomorrow to get her things. They'd better be here, untouched."

"That woman is insane," he muttered while he opened the door and helped me in the car. "You don't have to live this way."

"I can't afford to live any other way. Brian, you should have left me alone. I've lived this way most of my life. I'm used to it." I couldn't afford to go back to the motel, even if I accepted both of the jobs Danny had available.

"You'll stay with me until you get your life settled," he said.

"Is that an order?" I didn't have the energy to open my eyes or raise my voice.

He answered calmly. "It's an offer that I don't think you can afford to reject, at least not tonight. You'll stay on your own terms. I don't make rules like Dorothy."

"Thank you," I said. "Why are you doing this?"

"When I came home with your food—your favorite by the way--a Buddy Boy—and you were gone, I was worried. You were very upset, Raven. I had to make sure you were okay."

"I'm starving," I said, wanting to respond only to the safe part of his response. Did he think I would kill myself? "Did you save my Buddy Boy?"

"I called Claude to get Dorothy's address. It wasn't easy to track you down, either. I called the motel and he wasn't working. So I had to explain that it was an emergency involving a personal friend of Claude's and beg before the guy finally agreed to take my number and have Claude return my call. Then Claude wouldn't tell me anything until I explained how upset you were when you left here."

I opened my eyes and glared at him so he would know I didn't appreciate him sharing my business, hoping the glare worked when I couldn't keep both eyelids opened at the same time.

"Don't worry," he said. "I told him your grandmother passed, and you had been very close to her. "Still, he cleared it with Irma before he gave me the address. They care about you, Raven."

"You should have just let me sleep it off instead of upsetting Dorothy."

"And you should have let me know you were leaving. You can't keep running away from people, Raven. I will be happy to honor your wishes, but you'll have to tell me what they are before I can."

"I can run if I want," I said, unable to hold either eye open any longer.

He didn't argue. He didn't say anything else until we arrived at his house.

"I won't force you to do anything you don't want to do," he said before he turned the engine off. "You can run if you want, or you can grow up and stay here until you make a real plan this time." He turned the engine off and started in on me again. "If you really don't want to be here, I'll pay for you to stay at the motel. Or if it's me you want to avoid and not the house, I'll go stay somewhere else."

I opened the car door before shooting back at him. "Stop trying to be so nice. It gets on my nerves."

I stayed a step behind him until we were inside the house. He left me standing in the living room and went to the kitchen.

The couch looked inviting. I was exhausted and the pills weren't wearing off. Instead, though, I sat in a chair so he wouldn't be able to sit close to me if he came back into the room.

"Do you want your food cold, or reheated?" he called to me from the kitchen.

I didn't want to accept anything from him, but I was too hungry to resist. He knew that, just like he knew I was stranded at his house without my purse or my car. "Cold," I yelled back. He had purposely made the decision to leave my things behind and whisk me away from Dorothy's. It was the same thing all over again, just like when Momma and Daddy drove me out of Crayfield. Why did the same miserable pieces of my life keep replaying like a broken record?

He brought the cold sandwich and fries to me on a plate and sat on the couch to watch me eat. The first bite expanded in my mouth and refused to pass the lump in my throat. I chewed slowly, fighting tears and nausea. I finally left the room to deposit that bite, and the rest of my uneaten food, in the trashcan outside the kitchen door.

Rather than return to the living room and face him, I sat in a chair at the kitchen table and leaned forward to press my face on the cool wood. The swelling had spread from my eyes into my cheeks, and to make matters worse, then my throat was raw, too.

My face and head felt like they were on fire, yet the rest of my body shivered. I called back memories of Nana, thinking if I could just choke again, I might be able to fight the urge to breathe. It didn't work. The tears only made my face and head feel worse.

Brian went into the guest room, I figured, either to get the quilt and make his bed on the couch again, or to prepare that room for me so he could take his back. Was he keeping a promise to me, or did he not want me near him? And why the couch instead of the guest bed? Did he have to make sure I couldn't sneak out?

After turning the faucets on to fill the tub in the guest bathroom, he came after me. I offered no resistance when he pulled me from the chair and led me to the bathroom.

The walls were the same beige color they had been before, but the brown accessories had been replaced with yellow. Steam from the water in the bubble bath he had drawn filled the room with the aroma of Lilies of the Valley.

I pulled in a deep breath, allowing myself a moment of absolute peace before I turned and ran. How could he?

It was raining and I didn't have a car. I was stuck in that house, with a man who knew how horrible I was and was determined to torture me. I ran down the basement stairs, through the game room, and into the far corner of the studio, where I slid down the wall into a spiritless heap of misery on the floor. My stomach growled, my head burned, my heart ached, and I breathed – only because my stupid lungs wouldn't pay attention when I willed them to stop.

Brenda Lee's voice filled my head this time instead of my own. When had I started hearing me sing instead of her, and why was I switching back now? *Alone. . . just my lonely heart knows how. . . I want to be wanted. . . wanted. . . right now, not tomorrow but right now. . . I want to be wanted*

But I can't be, I argued with the song. I don't know how to be loved. I fight love away, every time it finds me. I can't get anything right.

How did he know? Nobody accidentally guesses Lilies of the Valley and bright yellow. Someone must have told him.

Brian gave me some time alone before he came to the basement. "I didn't mean to upset you. Irene thought the bubble bath would comfort you. I added the yellow on my own after she told me about your grandmother's bathroom. That stuff wasn't easy to find on a Sunday night."

He sat on the floor near where I lay but didn't touch me. "I don't know what I can do to help you through this. I've never lost anyone close to me."

Lucky Brian. I had enough experience for both of us. I had lost everyone close to me, at least once already. Now I had lost Nana for the second time, and forever. He couldn't possibly understand.

"There's nothing anyone can do to help me," I cried. "Brian, stop trying. It's useless. You don't deserve this, so let me out of here and you can get on with your life before I ruin it."

"Can I hold you?" he asked. "I want to at least share what you feel, but I'm afraid I'll make things worse if I touch you."

I moved over and put my head in his lap. He stroked my hair and back. I didn't say a word; afraid he would stop if I broke the spell. I knew it was wrong to encourage him, but it felt too good to stop. He didn't know love could be so cruel, and I was selfish.

"When did you talk to Irene?" I finally asked.

He continued to run his hand through my hair when he answered. "She called while you were at Dorothy's. That's another reason I came to find you. I hoped to bring you back and surprise you. She's going to call again at eleven."

"Does she hate me?" I couldn't have felt any worse, so I figured I'd get the question out of the way.

He shifted his legs under my head and I grabbed on tight so he wouldn't even think about getting up. "No, she doesn't hate you. She loves you, and she misses you, and she's worried about you. She wants you to be happy, Raven. Can't you believe that?"

I waited to see if he volunteered information about Craig or Jason. He didn't, so I sat up and leaned against him, not ready to give up the comfort of his touch completely.

"I can't decide if I want to sing, or make love," I told him. "I need to do something intense."

He laughed. "And I can't decide if that's a slap in the face or a come-on."

"You never touch me anymore," I said. "Not like that anyway."

"Only because I'm trying to let you be in control of your own life," he said. "I thought that was important to you?"

I told him I wanted to sing one song. He turned the equipment on for me. I sang "Til I Can Make It on My Own" and walked away from the microphone.

Brian wrapped his arms around me and whispered. "Raven, you can lean on me until you find the morning sun, and the hurting memories can't find you." He tried to take me upstairs, but I couldn't wait that long. I pulled him down, right there on the shag carpet.

"I'm too old for this," was his strongest argument. I proved him wrong for real that time.

Chapter 42

Irene didn't have much to say over the phone other than she missed me, everyone in Crayfield sent their love, and she wanted to come see me "I'll be officially retired after Thursday." The only time I had heard her sound that excited was the day Jason was born. "I'm turning my station over to a new girl that Linda found, and I'm going to take it easy and enjoy life.

"Good for you," I said. You deserve a break."

"Glad you think so. I thought maybe I'd leave Ralph here and drive down to celebrate with you this weekend, if you don't have other plans already."

I raised an eyebrow at Brian. "You want to visit this coming weekend?" He nodded and pointed to the guest room.

"That would be great. Maybe you could come on Thursday, in time to go to the club with us. I can only sing on weeknights."

She said she would let me know within the next few days whether she would come on Thursday or on Friday, and hung up without mentioning Craig or Jason. I was worse, because I didn't even ask about my own son.

We waited until Dorothy had come home from her volunteer job the next evening before we went to pick up my things. Brian respected Dorothy's insanity and waited outside while I carried my things up the stairs and out of the house by myself. I left the bed unmade and a toilet that hadn't been scoured in days, and considered us even. She refused to return my rent money. Brian wanted to argue for a pro-rate but I told him she had given me a break in the first place and I just wanted out of there.

When we got to his house he told me to go inside and he would carry everything in. "You can take the guest room, or share my room," he offered. "It's your choice, just tell me where to put your things."

"Can we drop everything in the kitchen while I think about it?" I asked. Irene would be there in a few days. Did I want to share the room with her, or let her think I was insensitive to her connection with Craig by moving in with Brian? Maybe I wanted to have my own room for a while, anyway, in a home where nobody wanted to control me. I wasn't sure.

"We can do whatever you want," he said. "Just remember you'll do all of the cooking as long as your stuff sits in the kitchen."

"Put it in the guest room if that's the deal," I decided. Cooking had been my way to please my father and my husband. Brian had never eaten a bite prepared by me and I wanted to prove I could hold on to him without feeding him.

He put my bags on the closet floor and I thought how sad it was that everything I owned fit in that small space. I learned to live small growing up in two rooms without a dresser or toy box of my own, and never broke the habit when I grew up. Maybe one day things would appeal to me. Hopefully, it wouldn't happen until I could afford to buy them.

"You were born for the road," Brian observed. "Not only are you talented, and fun in hotels, I've never seen a woman travel as lightly as you do, or accept change so easily. That's in your favor as far as the music business is concerned."

That was the first mention he made of my singing career since I had first come to Nashville. It excited me, and reminded me how much I missed singing.

"I'm cheap and easy," I teased. "Every man's dream."

I didn't waste time unpacking, since I wasn't sure where I wanted to stay. "Want to work on music tonight?" I asked. "I used to play around at song writing. Maybe we can come up with something good if we work together. Collaborate? Is that what they call it?"

We spent the evening in the studio, completely forgetting dinner. Brian recorded my voice so I could hear it played back. Once I admitted to myself that I sounded good, my next stupid thought was that I wished Momma could hear me. She would have to admit that I was good. Why did I care?

Brian took me to a neighborhood bar that served fried fish sandwiches until midnight. It was my first time in a bar that didn't feature live music, so I sprung for the five-for-a-quarter special on the jukebox. While we listened to my songs and waited on the bartender to call our name to pick up the food, Brian taught me to throw darts.

In the middle of dinner, he reached across the table, took my sandwich out of my hands and put it on my plate. "Come on," he said, "dance with me."

I pushed his hand away. "I'm eating. And you know I don't know how to dance."

"Then it's time to learn. How can you sing to dancers if you don't dance yourself?" He pulled me out of the booth and wrapped his arms around me.

"Nobody else is dancing," I protested.

"Then we'll start something new. Just relax. Hold me close and move with the music, it's very sensual so I think you'll enjoy it."

I felt like an idiot, but enjoyed the dance enough to thank him when the song ended. On the way back to the house, after another dance and two games of darts, I thanked him for the entire day.

"I don't think I've ever had so much fun," I said. "Unless it was that time we jumped on the beds in that hotel. Remember that?"

We both laughed, thinking about jumping from one bed to the next. "Don't get any ideas about mistreating my furniture that way," he warned. "We'll save that for the next hotel."

He planned to stay with me, at least through another hotel visit. I leaned across the car and kissed his cheek.

Irene arrived on Thursday, twenty minutes before we had to leave for Danny's. I showed her around the house while Brian carried her things to the guest room and left them with mine.

"See what I mean?" he asked. "She brought more than you, and she's only staying the weekend. Now, if you want to ride with me we need to leave soon."

Irene gave her hair a flip in the mirror and we left. From the backseat of the car, she spoke nervously. "I planned to get here earlier in the day but the girls at the shop surprised me with a cake and gifts for my retirement and I didn't get out as soon as I wanted. I hope you aren't embarrassed by the way I look."

Something had changed. Irene acted like we hardly knew each other. I told her she looked great to me, and then sang along with the radio to escape the silence that followed.

She seemed to warm up a bit when Brian introduced her to the band as my dearest friend, and found us two stools at the end of the side bar, where I had stood the first night I came to Danny's. She ordered a wine cooler. I had a shot, and explained the amateur singer routine.

"I accidentally lucked into Brian one night shortly after I came to town. Someone suggested I come to this club, and here he was. Talk about a surprise when I walked on stage," I explained. "I nearly peed my pants when I saw him there."

"So you didn't leave to be with him?" she asked. "I thought it was planned this way."

"No. He didn't know I was coming. Nobody did. I came to see if I could make it on my own."

"Craig tried to tell me that," she said. "I figured he just didn't know about Brian. He said you tried to get the whole band to come with you."

I nodded. "They didn't want to give up their jobs. I don't blame them."

"I'm sorry, Penny. Or is it officially Raven now? I said I would support your decision but I have to admit that I was disappointed when you took off the way you did."

"Everyone here calls me Raven. You can call me whatever you want," I told her. "I couldn't say good-bye, Irene. I wouldn't have had the courage to leave if one of you had cried or asked me to stay."

She hugged me. "I do understand. Are you happy?"

I ordered another shot and told her I couldn't talk about that right then. "I can't risk crying in here. When I get started these days, I can't stop. We can talk about it when we get back to the house."

I gave the song list to Irene and let her choose the ones she wanted me to sing. Her first choice was also Brian's favorite from the country list, "I Will Always Love You", and I hadn't done it yet at Danny's. I knew his real favorite was "Misty Blue" but it wasn't on the list because Danny only allowed country music in his club.

I wasn't called until the last set. During the break before, Brian pointed out two men sitting at a table in front of the DJ booth and told me that they were bigwigs in the business. "The guy with the beard is from Arista records. The one in the hat is a concert promoter who handles lots of big names. You might get a break tonight."

"Why'd you have to tell me that?" I asked. "Now I'll be nervous."

"Be you," he advised. "That's better than nervous."

We left Irene alone at the bar when the break ended. She was deep in conversation with Danny by the time we reached the stage.

"I think Irene is having a good time," Brian told me before we parted ways. "Are you glad she's here?"

I said I was happy she had come, but something seemed different and it made me a little sad. I thought she was enjoying herself, but I wasn't sure.

Pressure improved my performance. I sang directly to the men at the bigwig table, as though my life depended on impressing them. In some ways it did. Without a break, I wasn't sure I could ever support myself.

Brian winked when I glanced his way at the end of my song and reached for the mic stand to relinquish my position to the next amateur. I hated singing one song a night, especially when it felt as good as the one I had just finished. My body was full of energy, begging for stage release.

Danny had another shot waiting for me when I returned to the bar. Irene pushed the glass my way and looked up with tears in her eyes. "I had forgotten how good you are," she said. "I miss hearing you sing."

"You're going to get another chance," Danny told her. "The big guy wants to hear another song."

I tried to hide my excitement. It probably didn't mean anything more than he wanted to show that he had influence and could bend the rules wherever he went.

Danny proved my point. "Normally, I wouldn't let you cut line this way, but I like to have people like him come around. It's good for business. Word gets out they're in here scouting and everyone who wants a break comes in. You'd best trot back up there and get ready."

"He told me who they are," Irene said. "This is so exciting, P - Raven. Knock his socks off, girl."

The second song, "I Fall to Pieces", an old Patsy Cline favorite, felt even better than the first had. I received the kind of response I had missed since leaving the VFW, and knew I had to get out of Danny's with or without the big guys. I'd call Madeline again if nothing came of that night.

Danny's cleared out almost immediately after the last song on weeknights. There weren't many regulars, since much of the business came from people who were only in town a night or a week, hoping either to be discovered or to run into someone famous.

The guy in the hat, whose name turned out to be Eugene Browles, approached us at the bar and introduced himself. "You have a lot of talent, young lady, and a great look," he said, ignoring Irene and Brian. "Is anyone representing you?"

I didn't understand the question so I caught Brian's eye for support. He extended his hand to Eugene and introduced himself.

"I would like to talk to you about your plans," Eugene told me. "Maybe we can talk on the phone tomorrow." He handed me his card. "Call me if you'd be interested in opening some concerts."

I swallowed and tried to find the perfect level of confidence so I wouldn't sound like a star struck hopeful I truly was. "Thank you. Maybe we can talk tomorrow."

When we were in the car and safely out of hearing distance of anyone connected to the club, Brian and Irene let loose. "This could be something big," he said.

"I'm glad I chose this weekend to come," she squealed.

I was too nervous to say anything. I didn't want to get my hopes up until I knew what this was all about.

Brian went to bed soon after we reached the house. Irene and I sat against the headboard in the guest room and talked all night. I told her about Irma and how she rushed in to help me find a job and a place to live. I laughed until tears ran down my face telling her about Dorothy and my short stay in her basement apartment.

When it was her turn, she started with her decision to retire. "I didn't enjoy the work anymore and realized that I put more effort into my business than my marriage. I seldom saw Ralph, and when I did we didn't have much to talk about."

She caught me up on general gossip; Betty Grand got engaged to the man she had been dating for eight years and Mrs. Quick sold the grocery on the next block. She ended with the part I dreaded.

"Craig is holding up well. He was hurt when you left, but not surprised. I don't think he was angry, either. Penny, I do believe he understands."

I exhaled the tension that I had harbored for weeks. "Irene, I don't want to hurt him. Craig has been wonderful to me. I just couldn't do it anymore."

"I know, baby." She held my hand. "I don't think badly of you. For Jason's sake, I wish things could have been different, but I don't expect you to sacrifice your happiness for anyone. Not even that baby. I blame your parents for the whole mess. You shouldn't have been a wife and mother at that age. They forced you."

She hesitated for a minute. "Jason is fine, by the way. Craig's mom watches him while Craig works. I go over and visit, or take him out with me a couple times a week. You can't pretend he doesn't exist, Penny, or that you don't love him."

I blinked away tears, not ready for the mood change.

"It's okay," she said. "I may be the only one who truly understands how you can walk away from that boy. Penny, I watched your life. Any time a negative thought creeps up about you leaving, I think about how you would have been happier if your mother would have just left you and Jerold to pursue her own music interests. I'm on your side."

Her attempt to console me only reminded me that I was exactly like my mother. I appreciated her support anyway.

"Does Jason hate me?" She would know, because she knew my son better than I did.

She shook her head. "He misses you, but he doesn't get stuck on it. He asks about you but then in a few minutes he runs off to play. He'll be fine."

"Will you give him extra hugs for me?" I asked.

Irene changed the subject. "Your friend Sharon got herself in a mess of trouble. She was pulled over for driving on the wrong side of the road. They found all sorts of drugs in the car, some right on the front seat in plain sight. She spent a night in jail before Tinker could get her bail."

Poor Sharon didn't have enough sense to be careful, or to realize how lucky she was that Tinker kept his nose out of her business. She could have kept everything she wanted right in the house, and used it in front of him, and he wouldn't have said a word. Why would she risk getting caught like that?

Brian was a lot like Tinker. I hadn't thought of that before. He didn't care if I drank and smoked. I was sure he knew about the pills too, although he had never mentioned them. I wouldn't make Sharon's mistake. I would appreciate him and keep my problems at home.

Home? Had I mentally settled in? And why had I thought problems, pleural? I didn't have a problem, now that I was with someone who didn't care what I did.

"Are you getting sleepy on me?" Irene asked. "You got quiet all of the sudden."

"Sorry. I guess I am tired," I said, embarrassed to admit that my mind had drifted away from her.

"You need rest so you can be at your best when you call that Eugene guy tomorrow anyway," she reminded me. "Let's go to sleep and we can talk more later. I'll be here two more days and we'll stay in touch after I leave."

Before I turned out the light she said it wouldn't bother her if I went to sleep in Brian's room. I kissed her cheek and said I loved her before I left.

* * *

Eugene Browles made an offer after I lied and said I had my own band. He wanted me to be the warm-up act for the warm-up band for Christofer Moore, a newcomer with an unpredicted number one song and, therefore, no plans for a concert tour.

"Nobody expected him to do this well," Eugene admitted. "Now we're scrambling around trying to throw together a concert tour. So far, we've booked seven cities."

My heart raced but I tried to catch every word so I wouldn't make the same mistake and be lost like I had been after the contest. Warm-up to a warm-up was a great deal to me. I'd be on the road, in front of large audiences, with not too much expected of me. It was a dream come true.

"There's not much money," Eugene warned. "But it's good exposure for all of you."

"Yes," I said. I would have done it free, so *not much money* was a bonus for me. "I want to do it, so tell me what I need to do."

We scheduled a meeting on Monday morning. He told me to bring my bandleader, a song list, and a picture if I had one.

I hung up the phone and screamed. "I can't believe it! I'm going on a concert tour with Christofer Moore!"

Irene grabbed me in a bear hug and we jumped all over the kitchen until Brian laughed and warned us to watch out for the furniture.

"Oh my God," I suddenly remembered. "Brian, I told him I have a band. You have to help me. I need a band before Monday."

He rubbed his head and looked at Irene. "She doesn't ask much, does she?"

I knew he'd come through. He came out of the bedroom later and stopped mid-sentence when he saw Irene sitting at the table while I mixed up the ingredients for a meatloaf.

"She cooks?" He asked Irene like I couldn't hear. "I had no idea."

I smacked his balding head with my wooden spoon and we all laughed.

"I came out here with good news, but the shock made me forget what it was," he teased.

"I can toss this mixture out the back door if that will help you remember," I said, moving toward the door.

"Hold on, it's coming back to me. Keith and Phil are in. Link has other commitments, but I think I know another guitar player we can work in with no problem. I got his wife and told her to have him call me when he comes in."

"Is this man wonderful, or what?" I asked Irene. "In one hour he can cover any lie I tell."

She smiled and agreed that he was wonderful. "You have to let me know as soon as you get a schedule. Now that I'm retired, I'll be able to come see you. Surely you'll have at least one show close enough for me to drive there."

The three of us celebrated for the rest of the weekend. Brian went out and came back with roses and two bottles of wine, one for her retirement celebration and one for my big break. "You have to share the roses," he said.

The next night we went out to dinner, and then stopped at the liquor store again. They got a bottle of wine. I got Jose Cuervo.

Irene smoked with us on Saturday night. "If my friends could see me now," she joked. "They'd swear I'm going through a second childhood. Forty-five years old and smoking pot for the first time."

"At least you had the decency to act like an adult somewhere between childhoods," I told her. "Unlike my mother."

My excitement faded once Kitty entered my head. I had spent most of my life pushing her out of my mind and wishing I never had to see or speak to her again, then in one weekend she popped up several times. What if I called her? Would she be proud to hear that I had been asked to warm-up the warm-up, or would she laugh at me again?

Before I went to bed I put Bruce Springsteen—Irene's favorite—on the stereo and turned it up so she could hear him in the guest room. That way she wouldn't hear the celebration I planned to have with Brian in our room, or his dishonest, worn-out protests about being too old to keep up with me.

Chapter 43

Keith and the endless supplies that he carried in his duffle bag helped me survive the trip. The first time I asked for something other than pot, he laughed and told me that he had something much better than Valium. He was right. Three Valiums weren't half as debilitating as one Dilaudid, and debilitated was only the beginning of what I wanted to accomplish. One Dilaudid with a couple shots of tequila was close to heaven – Eugene could bitch, the new guitar player could play in the wrong key, and Brian could rub the skin right off the top of his head and I didn't care.

The concert bookings were so haphazardly scheduled and spread across the country that we didn't have time to return to Tennessee between them. We traveled in an old school bus and stayed in cheap hotels, some far worse than the Swingin' Door, and nowhere near a decent restaurant.

Since none of us had driven our cars, we were at the mercy of group travel, or stranded. Brian and I were assigned to the same room, so I seldom had a minute alone. Everything was as uncomfortable as I could imagine possible.

Being warm-up to the warm-up meant that I was on stage before the spotlights came on, and while most ticket holders were still at home finishing up dinner or sitting in traffic somewhere. The few people in their seats didn't know or care who I was, nor did they understand that the sound crew purposely distorted my sound and volume so they could learn the room before Chris came on stage. They just thought I couldn't sing, talked through it, and were grateful when I left the stage.

"It's all part of paying your dues." I wanted to smack Brian every time he said that, and it must have been at least twice a day, the whole trip. It got to the point where he'd open his mouth and I'd say the words, and I wondered if frustrated was really what Nana and Pappy had felt when they finished each other's sentences.

He had no idea how much of my life before I met him had been wasted in dues. I had rehearsed in my head for fourteen years, sacrificing every thought and emotion to the cause. I had choked on Stinky Morton's tongue, and suffered through months of watching my mother strut around Harvey's Tavern bragging that she had taught me to sing when the truth was she had discouraged me in every way possible. Dues owed me a fucking refund.

And I had given up a husband who loved me, and a son who needed me, and Nana's funeral.

Without Keith, I might have killed Brian before the trip ended, or at least our relationship. As it turned out, I slept almost every second that I wasn't working, and Brian hung out in other hotel rooms the last few weeks, playing cards and watching television with the guys. A few nights he didn't come back to our room at all, and I didn't care.

Despite all of that, Eugene thought things had gone well and said he would keep me in mind if anything else came up. I didn't know whether to laugh because I had gotten away with something, or cry because this might be the best I could expect. I decided this was the perfect business for me; everyone involved was at least as confused as I was.

Brian seemed relieved when we finally pulled back into Nashville at the end of the trip. Even though he had never complained, I knew he must have been tired of me so I found myself hoping he wouldn't be ready to throw me out when we got home. I had given up my job at the gift shop before we left and hadn't saved one cent of the money I made while we were gone. What Keith didn't get, the bars and liquor stores finished off. I was too tired to start over with nothing again.

On our second morning back, I woke at ten o'clock to an empty place in the bed beside me. I was surprised, because we had both gotten into the habit of sleeping past noon while we were gone, and I knew he had to have been exhausted. The night before, he drove the last five hours of the trip home, helped unload equipment at Eugene's warehouse, and then carried our things into the house when we got home.

He wasn't anywhere inside so I went to the front door to see if his car was gone. He probably needed to catch up on his publishing company business after being away for so long, although I had never figured out what he did there.

Both cars were in the drive. I checked the laundry room and the studio, and found no sign that he had been anywhere. I couldn't imagine that he would have left with someone else without waking me or leaving a note, but that was the only explanation I could think of.

As I crawled back into bed, I heard a thumping sound come from the back yard. After a second thud I got back up and pulled the curtain back to look out.

Brian stood in the middle of the yard, throwing clods of dirt at an old doghouse sitting in the far corner of the property. I watched him throw two more balls and bend down to gather more.

Was he warming up for a spring softball league? Clearing the lawn before it was time to mow? Curiosity got the best of me so I dressed and walked out to ask what he was doing.

"Clearing my head," was his explanation. And it didn't sound encouraging.

"I didn't know you had a dog," I said, rather than ask what troubled his head enough to send him to the back yard to throw dirt.

"There are a lot of things you don't know about me," he said, blasting the roof of the doghouse with a baseball sized mud ball. "Rascal, my nine-year-old Boston Terrier, died a few weeks before I met you. He broke out of the yard while I was in the shower and ran under the mail truck. He bled to death before I got him to the vet's office."

"I'm sorry." I started to explain that I had never had a pet of my own but could imagine how sad it would be to lose one, but he didn't look at me so I didn't think he'd be interested.

"Do you know my full name," he asked, reaching for more dirt.

"Of course I do. Brian S. Clater. What's going on with you?"

"What does the S stand for? I'll give you a dozen pills of your choice if you can answer that question." He stopped hurling and turned to look at me.

I tossed the blame back at him. "You never told me."

"And you never asked. Where was I born? Do I have brothers or sisters? Are my parents alive?"

"I know your parents are alive because you told me you had never lost anyone close to you. I figure you would have told me these things if you wanted me to know them. Some people get upset when others pry into their business," I explained. "So I don't do it."

"Raven, you've been in my bed, and in my heart. You've been part of my personal life, and you thought asking my middle name would be prying?"

That explained what he wanted to clear out of his head. Me. Did he want me out of his bed too?

"I think you are afraid to know anything about me because you think I'll want to know about you in return. And you don't really want me to know about you," he accused.

I wanted him to shut up and go back to throwing dirt. I didn't like the conversation.

"You aren't going to respond?"

"You're wrong about the reason," I said. "It's too cold to stand out here and talk about this. I need a jacket."

He leaned over to pick up more dirt and let me walk away without trying to stop me. Did he want me to get a jacket and come back? Why had I gone out there and interrupted his private time in the first place?

I looked through his hall closet for a lightweight jacket while I tried to decide if I should go back out or not. I found a hooded sweatshirt and hung it on the doorknob while I used the bathroom. If he came inside while I was in there, he could assume that I had planned to return to finish the conversation.

I stayed there until I heard him come inside and close the back door. He left his shoes at the door and sat down in the kitchen. I carried the sweatshirt with me to the table and sat across from him.

"Do you plan to stay inside?" I asked. "Are you finished throwing dirt?"

"Yes. I feel a little better. Maybe you should try it sometime," he suggested. "Get rid of some of your stress without chemicals."

I folded my hands on the table between us before I spoke. "Do you want me to leave?"

He pulled his face and sighed. "Is that your solution to everything? Run away? Do you want to leave?"

I couldn't look at him. Why wouldn't he just spit the truth out? I was a disappointment, a burden, and he wanted me out of his life.

I kept my voice and eyes low. "I don't have anywhere to go."

"If that's the only reason you are still here, Raven, I'll give you somewhere to go. You aren't stuck with me and I never want you to feel like you are."

There. He had done it and we both survived. "Where?" I asked.

"Damn it, Raven, wherever you want to go. I'll send you back home if that's what you want. If you want to run further away, I'll help you do that, too. If you want to stay in Nashville but not with me, we can work that out. I'll do whatever you want, but you have to tell what that is because I sure as hell can't read your mind."

I swallowed repeatedly, hoping to force back the words that caught in my throat before they choked me. I couldn't tell him, or anyone else, how afraid I was to truly be on my own. I had failed at the Swingin' Door when I let the crazy man from the bus track me down. I blew it again by breaking Dorothy's rules and getting kicked out of her house. And this road trip had been a disaster. I couldn't make it on my own.

Fear mounted. Maybe he would change his mind if I apologized for my behavior on the road. Maybe he would let me stay until I found a job.

"You've done enough for me already," I finally managed to say, without choking or crying. "I appreciate that. If you will let me stay just until I get on my feet financially, I promise to stay out of your way and I'll earn my way. I'll cook and clean and do your laundry, and I'll pay rent as soon as I find work."

I raised my eyes to meet his, and to see how much damage he was doing to his face and head. I was prepared to beg if I had to. "Maybe Danny will still give me a job," I said, remembering how Nana had asked if I was working to help Craig. Had I taken advantage of Brian the way she thought I had of Craig? "I know I haven't done my share and I promise to try harder."

He dropped his hand on the table, causing my heart to jump. "I don't want your money or your labor. Raven, you still don't get it."

I raised my voice. "You said you can't read my mind," I reminded him. "Well, I can't read yours either. What do you want me to do?"

"For starters, you could wish me a happy birthday," he answered.

"Brian, I didn't know. I'm so sorry. Happy Birthday!" My voice sounded choppy and unnatural to me, so I could imagine how it sounded to him. I kept trying, hoping to find a tone that changed the miserable look on his face. "I'll make a cake, and fix you a special dinner. What do you want?"

No matter what happened after that day, I could at least make the rest of his birthday pleasant.

"Thank you." He tried to smile. "I don't care about a cake or a dinner. The point is you didn't know it was my birthday because you've never cared enough to learn even the most basic things about me."

"That's not fair," I protested, rising from the table to wipe up the mud trail that I had tracked from the back door to the hall closet. "You can't say I don't care about you just because I didn't ask a lot of personal questions. Everybody is different. I hate questions. You obviously like them. Maybe I thought I was being nice by treating you the way I want to be treated."

My voice rose more. I shouted and scrubbed the floor harder with each word. "Maybe I care about you but I just don't know how to show it."

I tossed the muddy rag down the basement stairs, washed my hands in the sink, and opened the cabinet doors to look for cake ingredients. "I'll have to go to the store before I can make anything," I complained, rearranging everything on the shelves and not finding what I wanted. "How old is this stuff? When was the last time you ate oatmeal?"

When he didn't answer, I slammed the cabinet door and walked over to move his hand and rub his scalp for him. "Are you going to tell me how old you are, or should I guess by looking at your head?"

He pulled my hand away and held it. "Thanks for asking, Raven. I'm not as old as you probably guessed by looking at my head. I'm thirty-seven, and the S stands for Shane. The rest of the men in my family have full heads of hair, and that's why you'll never meet my three younger brothers."

"Are you serious? You have three brothers and you won't let me meet them? I never pictured you as the jealous type."

He laughed. "Until we make a trip to Colorado you won't meet them because they would rather go to Siberia than Tennessee. My parents, on the other hand, may drop in any time so keep your legs shaved and the kitchen clean."

"You'd better be lying," I warned.

"Exaggerating," he said. "They usually give me at least a week's notice before they come. But they'll call sometime today."

"Can I stay?" I worked up the courage to ask since he obviously wasn't throwing me out if he mentioned going to Colorado.

He pulled me into his lap. "You are welcome to stay as long as you want to be here. I thought I could do this with no conditions, but I can't Raven. I have to ask a few things of you."

"That's fair," I admitted.

"I want you to promise me that you will throw dirt, or scrub footprints off the floor, or go to the studio and scream when you need to clear your head. Stop carrying your sadness, or whatever it is, inside until you need to shut down with chemicals to avoid it. Let it out for God's sake, before it destroys you."

Some of it wanted out right then. I walked away from him to lean against the counter and leave space between us so he wouldn't feel the fear as it slipped out.

"I can't," I confessed. "There's enough ugliness inside me to fill the world if I let it out. I could throw your whole yard around and not put a dent in my sadness. Brian, you don't understand."

"I want to understand," he said gently. "Help me."

I turned to get a glass of water so he wouldn't see the damned tears that were as much a part of me as blinking. He didn't need to spend his birthday listening to me cry again. While the faucet still ran, I splashed my face with cold water and then dried it and my tears on the hand towel. He came up behind me and wrapped his arms around my waist.

I leaned into him and exhaled. "How can you help me if I don't even know how to help myself? I don't know how to do what you've asked, but I promise I'll try."

"You can help both of us at the same time," he said "Let it out a little at a time. Tell me one thing that hurts. Then if you feel better you can tell me another, and another, until it's all out."

I nodded. "I'll try. But not now. It's your birthday. Let's go to the grocery and plan your dinner."

I had made promises that I wanted to keep, but I knew I would need help. Cuervo was better than pills for this job.

Chapter 44

Periodically, I got loaded and told Brian the details of another pathetic event or stage in my life. When I told him, on the night of his birthday, that my first memory was of my mother giving me her car key so I could drive off the cliff, I thought I banked enough sympathy to cover the next year of screw-ups and pills.

I hated taking advantage of him that way but didn't know how else to survive. Besides, he seemed to need to take care of me as desperately as I needed him to do it, so things worked out well for both of us. Sometimes I balked at his doting and pretended I still wanted independence and privacy. And he tried to convince me that he wanted me to be strong, but it was all a game for both of us.

He half-heartedly asked me to give up booze and drugs at times, but still came home with what I wanted more often than not. It was easier than listening to me complain, or explaining to Eugene and Madeline why I pouted through rehearsals and meetings. I upheld my commitments on stage, but was a bitch otherwise.

Brian carried me, sometimes literally, all over Nashville for interviews, auditions, and performances. He stood silently beside me in studios while I eked out demo tapes and back-up vocals, and finally a song that we had written but never sold to a major label.

"You'll make it, it's just a matter of time," he promised, month after month. "Ninety percent of this business is being in the right place at the right time."

"Being straight when that time comes around might help too," Madeline pointed out once, but Brian silenced her with his eyes.

Poor Brian. Madeline was right but he took forever to admit it. I was so far out of control that I couldn't have held onto a deal if it had been branded to my palm. He didn't want to see that any more than he wanted to admit that he had given up his own career to push mine.

Putting his career aside was a big mistake, because I hated both of us as a result. I hated him for humoring me when I didn't deserve it and I hated him when he stood up to me. It started to feel like Craig all over again. I hated me when I told him the truth, and I hated me when I lied. Neither of us could do anything to make either of us happy, so he would have been better off to leave me alone and work on his own life.

Irene visited often the first couple of years, but hadn't come back since I said I didn't want to see pictures of Jason with Santa Claus. I tried to say that I didn't mean it after she got so upset—that I was drunk and had something else on my mind—but she wouldn't listen.

I called her later to explain that the pictures broke my heart and made me want to drink more. She didn't have children or a drinking problem, so she couldn't understand. She said she would stick with my child and I could stick with my drinking and hung up.

Good news came shortly after that so I let it go. After spending a night or two in hundreds of small town dives, I finally got my first booking in a decent club in a big city.

"Chicago," Brian said enthusiastically. "And we'll have an extra day so I can take you to see some of the city while we're there. We can turn this into a small vacation."

I fought through a haze and remembered that Chicago held some significance in my life other than being the home of big lakes, museums. My eyes wouldn't open, but I managed a smile and slurred a few words about having friends in Chicago.

Brian never let anything go. He was obsessed with every word I uttered, determined to find a hidden meaning somewhere that would unlock my sanity and return me to him a normal person. He hounded me for days until I finally told him about the Sawyers.

"Your parents need to be shot for what they put you through," he said. "How could they keep you from your best friend that way?"

"She wasn't much of a friend after all," I said, instead of telling him that she had been my only friend. "She just stopped answering my letters when I needed her the most. I think she was jealous because I had a boyfriend before she did. I'm not interested in seeing her after all these years of silence. I wouldn't have anything to say to her."

He didn't mention it again for a few days, but when he picked it up again he said I had cried when I talked about Lori.

"I was drunk. It didn't mean anything," I said. When would he finally admit that pure craziness came from my mouth when I was drinking? Sometimes, even when I wasn't drinking, I didn't mean half of what I said, and I couldn't keep things straight in my head. Somewhere he had read that truth comes out of a drunken mouth, and chose to believe that instead of me.

"I'm the drunk, Brian. Take it from me. I'm the expert on this subject. It's pure bullshit. I'll say anything when I'm drinking, either to get my way or because I can't remember the truth. Stop listening to me."

He went to the library, or to Madeline's office, or maybe to the damned FBI, and searched until he found a list of Sawyers who lived in the Chicago area. Then he spent days, and God knows how much money, calling them until he found Lori's mother.

"They're coming to hear you, Raven. Lori and her husband, and her parents, and one of her sisters. I don't remember which one." He announced the plan as though I should cheer and thank him. The fit I threw didn't change his mind.

"Why can't you stay out of my business? I'm not going now," I threatened. "Call Madeline and cancel because I'll never step foot in Chicago now."

He shook his head and walked away. I had a right to think for myself, and he ignored it. I threw an empty bottle that clipped him on the shoulder and he kept on walking. I considered myself the winner of that round.

When I heard Madeline's voice in the living room the next morning I thought Brian had honored my request and called her over to cancel the Chicago booking. My head hurt too much to decide if I wanted to stick with that decision or not. It was one of the best jobs she had booked for me, and I was drunk when I told him to cancel. He should have known to ask me again before he followed through.

Before I decided what to do about Madeline and Chicago, I heard other voices. Eugene and Keith were there, and someone else whose voice I couldn't identify. I wasn't in the mood to face a crowd, so I decided to stay in bed and deal with Madeline later.

Brian had other plans. He came to get me.

"I'm not ready to get up," I shouted. "You should know better than to invite people here this early."

"Raven, you don't have a choice in this. We want to talk to you." He walked over to the bed to help me up but I turned away from him.

"Too bad," I said, pulling the covers over my head. "I'm not getting up now."

He picked me up and carried me to the living room, where my unwelcomed audience waited. Just about everyone I knew in Nashville was there – the musicians who had traveled with me, Madeline and Eugene, Claude and Irma, Christine and Victoria, Danny, and one of his waitresses. It looked like a Tupperware party, with everyone squeezed next to each other on the couch and in chairs brought from the kitchen.

"You can all leave now," I said as Brian stood me on the floor and held me up until I caught my balance. "I'm not sure why he invited you here this early, but he was crazy whatever the reason. I'm not ready to get up."

Eugene moved from the chair he had been sitting in and Brian tried to help me into it. I smacked his hands away.

"I'm going back to bed. Maybe you misunderstood me the first time. I'm not ready to get up."

Brian's face twitched. He looked to Irma for assistance. Like a traitor, she jumped up and stood beside him, and went into one of her endless spiels.

"Raven, honey, we hate to wake you before you're ready, but we've all come together here because we are worried about you. You're a beautiful, talented girl, and we love you. We want what's best for you."

"Then let me sleep," I begged.

She ignored me. "Nobody here, especially Brian, wants to make you mad or hurt your feelings. And we certainly don't want you to feel like we think bad things about you. We just believe it's time for you to take a long, hard look at where the drugs and alcohol might take you if you aren't careful."

I looked around the room at all of my friends who remained silent while she attacked me. How had he convinced them to do this to me? They were traitors, especially Keith. What was he doing there?

"I don't know what Brian told you, but things aren't all that bad. Shoot, I still have brief moments of sobriety and a lucid thought once in a while. I can spell my own name. Both of them. Did you all know my name is really Penny Sue?"

Irma reached toward me but pulled her arm back when I stared her down. I was ready to smack her away the same as I had Brian.

I turned my attention away from Irma before her sad dyes drew an apology out of me. "Keith, you're a hypocrite," I said. "How can you sit here and act like I have some big problem that you don't have? How can you show your face in this group?"

He didn't waver the way Brian and Irma had. He held my eyes with his. He didn't try to soften his tone to appease me. "Raven, did you hear me deny that I have a problem? This is about your problems today, not mine. We don't have time to run through mine," he admitted.

"See, you're a hypocrite and a traitor," I repeated.

"Not really. I admitted that I have a problem. The difference between you and me is that you have this room full of people who love you enough to want to help with yours. If this was happening in my living room, you might be the only one sitting there. But, I hope you would care enough to show up. And you have a lot of talent at stake. Shooting me down won't fix anything for you. This isn't a contest to see who's worse."

I stared at him without a response.

"Why not sit still and listen for a few minutes?" he asked.

I knew I didn't have a choice. Brian and Irma blocked my path to the bedroom, and everyone else filled the space between me and the front door. I flopped into the chair that Eugene had donated and sat straight, with my teeth clenched and my arms folded.

"Say what you came here to say and get it over with. Just remember, I'll never feel the same about any of you when this is over." I poured most of my anger into the look I gave Brian.

Irma took charge again while Brian licked his wounds. "All we ask is that you listen, Raven. We'll work out hurt feelings later. Today is about talking openly about how much we love you and worry about you."

I interrupted what sounded like a carefully planned speech since she stayed on topic. "Can you get to the point, Irma, I can't take it if you plan to talk all day."

"Okay. We think your drinking and drugging are out of control. We're worried and we want to help you," she said.

I stared at the floor and waited, but she stopped short of her usual lecture.

"If that's all, I'll go back to bed now," I said, rising from my chair. "I've heard what you came here to say."

"Sit down, Raven," Eugene ordered. "You aren't getting off this easy."

"And you aren't the boss of my private life," I shot back. "Eugene, I do what I'm contracted to do for you. If you have a complaint about my work, fine. Otherwise, don't say another word."

He called my bluff. "As a matter of fact, your work is exactly what I plan to address. You look like hell, and you have become a bitch to get along with. Your voice won't carry you if you don't pull the rest of your life together. We're all pulling for you to do that, but the choice is entirely yours."

Brian worked up the nerve to come near me again. He stood behind my chair and rested his hands on my shoulders. I hated him but let him stay there because it felt good to feel like one person might be on my side.

I waited to see what they were going to do, but no one seemed to have planned the next stage. They stared at me, all except Claude, who hadn't looked me in the eye once since I came into the room. I thought he might cry if he sat there much longer.

"Other than looking like hell and being a bitch with a drinking problem, do you have any other complaints? Maybe I can't cook and I don't call my friends as often as I should? I'll help you a little. I seldom make my bed and I'm a terrible mother. The worst mother ever. Victoria, what did you come her to complain about? Did I forget to use my napkin at dinner the other night?"

Tears filled her eyes and I almost wished I could take it back. She probably wouldn't have come unless pressured by Irma and Christine.

"Raven, I love you just the way you are," she said between sobs. "I only came to try and convince you to save your career and your relationship with Brian. He loves you so much."

I laughed. "Brian loves me? He does a great job of hiding that fact. If calling in a crowd of people to humiliate me is love, I'm not interested."

Keith came forward and knelt on one knee in front of me. I half expected a ring and a marriage proposal to finish off the insanity that had already happened, but the proposal was for something different.

"Raven, I sort of feel responsible for what happened to you. You made the choices, but I paraded them in front of you." He covered his mouth and coughed. "I apologize. If you want to work at cleaning up, I'll go to some meetings with you or something. Maybe we can get clean together."

Damn him. I couldn't be mean after that. He hadn't forced me to do anything, and here he was taking the blame.

"Keith, I drank and drugged before I met you. You aren't responsible for anything I've done, and it's not your job to clean me up. But thanks for the offer."

"If you aren't ready now, the offer will still stand anytime you change your mind," he promised, getting off his knee to hug me.

"I think we've done all we can do here," he said to the others. "Raven knows we care. The rest is up to her, in her own time."

Claude spoke his first word of the meeting when he agreed. Our guests filed out, each stopping to hug me before leaving. I kept my arms folded and my eyes down, making no effort to return their affection or acknowledge their words.

Most of them offered to be there if I needed them for anything. Victoria echoed Keith's offer to accompany me to meetings or treatment, although she didn't have a drinking problem that I knew of. Claude told me to stop by the motel for a visit soon.

While Brian showed them out and closed the door, I went back to bed and pulled the covers over my head. Maybe I'd wake later and discover that this had been a nightmare. Even better, I might completely forget it before I woke.

I lay in bed until early evening, with my eyes closed and my thoughts racing. What had Brian told my friends to convince them that I needed help? And why would he have done that?

Maybe my plan had backfired. I had convinced him that I really didn't know what I was doing when I drank. It was my fault. I drank too much and took too many pills, but only because I enjoyed it, not because I had to. There was a difference, and I could explain that to him.

I had made a fool of Brian. Obviously he had cried to others about my not remembering things, and they believed that I was on the way to skid row and needed meetings and treatment centers and constant help from them. That should be easy to fix. I might even spare him the embarrassment of looking like a fool by letting him think that he had helped me.

"I'm not going to pretend that whole show-down wasn't the most ridiculous thing you could have done," I told him. "But I believe you thought it was necessary because of all the sob stories I've told you. See why I don't like to talk about my personal life? I get it all mixed up."

"My intention was not to embarrass you." He approached me slowly to see if I was going to throw things or smack him away. "Are you very mad at me?"

"No. But if you ever do anything like that again, I won't forgive you," I warned. "Brian, things aren't nearly as bad as you made them out to be. I drink and drug because I like it. I'm not an alcoholic or addict, and I don't need meetings. I could stop any time I wanted, I've just never wanted."

"Are you sure?" he asked. "There's no shame in needing help."

"I'm sure. If it will make you happy, I won't touch a thing for a while to show you."

I made the offer, sure he would want to smoke a joint or open a bottle of wine before I would. He'd be sorry he ever brought this up.

He carefully avoided conflict the next few days. I let him bribe me into honoring my commitment to do the Chicago show, never letting on that I had planned to do it all along.

"Since you're forcing me to see the Sawyers," I accused, "I want something new to wear. They haven't seen me since I was an awkward twelve-year-old in the early stages of puberty. I want to look my best."

Anxiety over seeing Lori again consumed my thoughts for a few days. Would she look and act the same? Had I disappointed her by not becoming famous? What would she think of me for leaving Craig and Jason? Surely, all of the Sawyers would hate me for leaving my son.

I didn't need anything; I wasn't having DTs or breaking out in sweats. But I wanted something to calm my nerves. Meeting old friends and planning a big show were stressful situations that would play on the nerves of any normal person. Wanting something to offset that stress didn't mean I had a problem.

Brian had thrown out the coffee can long before, and only brought pot into the house one joint at a time, on special occasions. Same with alcohol, a bottle of wine here and there, or shots when we were out, but nothing on hand at home.

I had approximately ten pills hidden in a sock in the back of my drawer, set aside for emergencies. I thought of them every day, and even checked to make sure they were still there at times. A week had passed since Brian's big intervention and I hadn't taken one yet.

Chapter 45

Brian left me alone in the hotel room while he went to help with some last minute changes to the stage set-up. As soon as he was gone, I pulled the treasured sock from my cosmetic bag and secured a Valium in my bra. One pill wouldn't do much harm as far as my promise was concerned, but it would do wonders for my nerves if the meeting with the Sawyers turned out to be as difficult as I predicted. I didn't plan to use it unless absolutely necessary to save my sanity.

"We should have thought to meet them for dinner," Brian said, as we waited in the hotel dining room for our server to return with our orders. "We could have spent this time getting to know them before the show."

Brian couldn't get it through his head that I didn't want to see them at all, or maybe he just refused to believe I meant it. Probably, because he held onto every friend and relative in his life, he didn't understand how I could just as easily turn loose of the people who wanted to leave mine.

Over the years he had suggested that I go back and resolve things with Craig. "If you never intend to return to him, divorce the man," he said. "You both need a clean start and you'll feel better if you finish the things you left hanging."

He also tried to convince me that I needed to go to Crayfield for a visit, reminding me how badly I felt about not going back to see Nana before she died. "Don't repeat the same mistakes over and over, Raven. Your grandfather might not be around long. Often, the spouse dies of a broken heart soon after losing someone they've loved and lived with for so many years."

And he stayed in touch with Irene, even though I stopped speaking with her. I recognized her number on his phone bill once and questioned him about it. "She still loves you and wants to know how you are," he explained. "I'm sure she would rather hear it from you, but I'll keep calling if you want."

So, his obsession with the Sawyers shouldn't have surprised me. I braced myself to make it through the reunion and hoped he wouldn't encourage or accept any get-togethers other than seeing them at the club as already arranged.

I sipped my water before I responded. "Yes, it's too bad that you didn't think to invite them to dinner." I said it only because it was too late for him to call them. "I'm not sure I want to do my originals," I said, to change the subject. "I'm afraid this isn't the place for surprises."

"We can change them if you want. Let me know soon so I can tell the guys before we go on stage."

I wrote my alternate choices, "Downtown" and "Don't Cry Out Loud" on the inside of a match book and gave it to him so he could run it up to Keith's room before we finished dinner. I knew Lori liked "Downtown" from the pool, and I threw in the other just because I didn't have to stick to country.

I watched for the elevator doors to close, then went to the bar for my first shot in weeks. I shook my head and walked away when the bartender offered to pour a refill.

Brian came back to the table as I finished off the last of my salad. He watched and laughed at me. "You do that on purpose, don't you?"

"Do what?" I asked.

"I finally get it. You save your salad and eat those raw onions at the end of the meal so they'll stay on your breath."

I batted my eyes innocently. "What makes you think I'd do that?"

"To irritate Keith. You know how he hates onions," he accused. "I watch him back away when you run over to share his microphone. Raven, you're so mean to that poor guy. Just be careful not to forget your breath when you talk to other people."

I knew he meant the Sawyers. How could he be so obsessed about people he had never met?

The room setup was between that of a club and a concert. There was no dance floor, but the seating was similar to that in a club, with small drink tables surrounded by comfortable seats. There were four tiers of tables, and standing bars around the perimeter of the room.

The stage lights were on and the house lights low when I came out, so it was impossible for me to see beyond the front tables. I wasn't sure I would have recognized the Sawyers anyway.

The shot of tequila, the excitement of my first classy room in a big city, the relief of getting past Brian's sensitive nose with my drink, and a touch of spring fever all combined to fuel one of the most energized performances I had delivered in years. I brought the audience to their feet twice, and they screamed for more after I had left the stage.

The club owner caught me as I walked backstage. "Will you do a couple more?" he asked. "We'll add another three hundred to your check for fifteen more minutes."

The guys left the decision to me, and I accepted. The stage lights went back on and the applause started again. We waited for the audience to order another round of drinks, and then I charged back onto the stage feeling bigger than life.

At the end of the encore, applause carried me all the way to my dressing room where, for the first few minutes, I forgot everything, the way I had in the early days of performing.

Brian raced through the door without warning. "I brought someone to see you," he announced cheerfully.

I turned to see him pushing Lori Sawyer toward me. She looked exactly as she had on the first day in second grade. She had the same short, blonde hair, and a new layer of the baby fat she had later lost for the bikini.

"You haven't changed a bit," she said. "Oh Penny, you're so good! Mom cried through your whole performance because she's so proud of you, but I thought we might have to carry her out of here when you sang "Don't Cry Out Loud". I always knew you would end up beautiful and successful." She stopped and just stood there staring at me.

"You didn't change either," I said. "You look the same and you still talk as fast as ever."

Brian beamed like a proud matchmaker. His persistence had paid off. The reunion was successful because we were flattering one another.

"Are you coming out soon?" Lori asked. "Everyone is anxious to see you. Especially Georgia. I think she was as excited as I was. This is all she's talked about since the first time Brian called."

Lori's excitement was contagious. I had forgotten her ability to energize and carry me. It all came back—her encouragement and faith and love—in a flood of emotions. I missed her thirteen years' worth in a second, and bounced back with an equal amount of happiness from my side, too. I was going to see my real family.

"I'm ready." I turned to gather my things off the dressing table but he took my bag from me and said to go on.

"I'll take care of everything back here and join you when I can."

The Sawyers jumped to their feet as Lori and I approached the tables they had pushed together to form their party. Mrs. Sawyer ran to meet me halfway down the aisle, and hugged me so tight I was afraid she had crushed the pill in my bra. She passed me off to Mr. Sawyer, and Georgia pulled me away from him for her turn.

Lori interrupted Georgia's stream of compliments and pulled a tall, thin man forward to meet me. "This is my husband, Todd. He's terribly shy, but you can hug him anyway."

"Shy my ass," Georgia scoffed. "Lori just never shuts up long enough to let the poor man get a word in."

A bartender brought a bottle of champagne and glasses for everyone. Mr. Sawyer poured as we all settled into seats, me between Lori and her mother. Lori shut up and allowed Todd to make a toast. "Here's to a long over-due reunion, and hoping for a break soon for one of the best singers I've ever heard."

We made a dramatic production of clinking glasses and mushy talk, and then emptied our drinks. Mr. Sawyer refilled the glasses as quickly as we drank, and the bartender brought another bottle.

"I'm getting ready to announce last call and turn the house lights up," the bartender told me. "But that's only to clear out the other customers. Your party is welcome to stay. We'll open the bar to you again after they're gone."

Brian came out while the lights were up and Mr. Sawyer immediately placed a drink in his hand.

"Drink up," he said, holding the bottle close to Brian's glass. "You have two to go before you catch up to the rest of us. We're drinking to old friends and to Penny's success."

"I'm all for both of those," he said. He killed two drinks and held his glass out for the refill. Todd pulled another chair to the table, putting Brian across from me, between him and Mr. Sawyer. Brian winked when he caught my eye.

I lost count, both of the bottles the bartender delivered to our table, and of the refills I had from each. Brian, on the other hand, appeared to be keeping track of every drop I had. I imagined he was waiting for me to lose control and embarrass him.

"Penny?" Lori waved her hand in front of my face and teased. "Earth to Penny. Please come in."

"I'm sorry," I said when I realized I had drifted away from the conversation and everyone was looking at me. "Nobody has called me Penny for years. I almost forget it's my name sometimes."

"I don't blame you for that," Georgia said. "If I were you I would want to forget that part of my life, too."

"Georgia!" Mrs. Sawyer intervened. "Forgive her dear. She doesn't tolerate her drinks very well. Georgia, that was a very insensitive thing to say."

"But well deserved from what I've heard," Brian said. "Every time Raven tells me anything about her childhood, I wonder what kind of monsters she had for parents. I can't imagine some of the things they've done. Raven is still troubled by her childhood."

Tears of shame and anger stung my eyes. How could he humiliate me in front of them? The Sawyers sat in an unprecedented silence, waiting for an explanation. I delivered my version, so he couldn't give his.

"Poor, troubled Raven has a problem with drinking and drugs," I admitted. "She'll use anything she can put her hands on in order to block out the horrible childhood memories. But don't worry. Saint Brian over here is always willing to rescue her from herself before she causes too much damage to anyone else."

Lori put her arm around me. "It's okay, hon, we love you no matter what. Do you have any contact with your parents? Are they still together? I always thought it was interesting that they hated each other so much but stayed together all those years."

"I haven't talked to them in years," I told her. "As far as I know, they're still together. I don't think it is interesting, Lori, I think it's appropriate. They deserve each other."

I excused myself to the restroom, where I dug the Valium out of my clothes and swallowed it without a drink. Why did Brian have to ruin the mood? Everything was going so well, and I was enjoying myself for a change. And they believed I was happy and doing well. He blew it.

I sat on the counter and waited for the pill to meet the alcohol and relieve the pain. Lori came to find me.

"I'm sorry for Georgia's big mouth," she said. "Are you okay? Mom was right. Georgia can't hold her tongue when she drinks."

"I'm not upset with Georgia. Believe me, I do understand both the point she tried to make, and the loose tongue."

Why hadn't the pill worked? I wanted to talk without feeling, but the pain was still there.

"I've done enough drinking for all of us, and when I've had too much there's no telling what might pop out of my mouth. So I can't be upset by what Georgia said. Brian's another story though." The disappointment rolled out with my words.

She wiped a tear off my cheek. "Cheer up. I don't think he meant to upset you. Come on, let's go back out and have fun again."

I followed her back to the table, concentrating on walking without a stagger. Brian was deeply involved in a discussion with Mr. Sawyer about how he had rescued me from the depths of hell and tried to give me a decent life.

"You make me sound like your charity project," I accused. "I never knew I was such a burden to you." Finally the pill kicked in. The eyelids drooped and my words detached from my emotions.

"Raven, that's not what I meant," he said.

Georgia defended Brian. "While you were gone, he told me how much he loves you. He didn't say a word about thinking you were a burden, Penny."

I ignored Brian and Georgia and tried to salvage my reunion with Lori. "Do you work? Have children? Tell me about your life. I'm tired of hearing about mine."

She and Todd hoped to have three children one day, but not until he finished school. "He went two years and then quit to work full-time so we could get married. If we ever save enough, he'll go back. I work in the billing office at the phone company. It's a pretty good job, but not as exciting as yours."

"Did you ever get a piano?"

She shook her head. "But it looks like you found a good replacement." She nodded at Brian.

"Fortunately, I don't have a fan club yet, so I'm still holding that position for you," I said, halfway serious.

My eyes grew heavier and my head weighed too much for my neck. I wanted to ask more, about her house and the other sisters, and was she happy, but I ran out of energy. My head snapped back just as my chin threatened to land on my chest, only to have it slowly return to the original position anyway.

"Maybe we should clear out so Penny can get to bed," Mrs. Sawyer suggested. "We've kept her out too late already. She's bound to be exhausted after working so hard tonight."

My friends scrambled to finish their drinks and gather purses and cigarettes from the table. Brian told them he was happy to have met them. I wanted to beg them not to leave, but I couldn't move my lips.

"We'll be here for another day." I repeated the thought in my head several times but couldn't speak or open my eyes to communicate without words. I didn't have the energy to push my tears out, so they collected inside and choked me.

Lori leaned down to hug me. I hoped she sensed my emotions, the way she had on the day we met because, again, I had nothing to give.

The Sawyers left the club. Brian carried me out and put me in the car after they were gone. He didn't say anything to me until the next morning. "I'm going to get breakfast. Do you want me to bring something back for you?"

I said no thanks without opening my eyes. I wasn't sure I ever wanted to face him again. It was his fault I had made a fool of myself in front of the Sawyers. Why had he mentioned my problems in front of them? Did he think they would continue his intervention plans?

While he was gone to eat, I showered, hoping to wash away the pain and shame of the night before. I couldn't forgive Brian or me. Together, we had ruined my pathetic life.

When the hot water ran out, I sat in the tub and let cold water pound my face until I had no tears left to cry. The phone rang in the other room but I didn't care. The guys had left early that morning, and I didn't want to talk to Brian. No one else knew where to find me.

Much later, I turned the water off and crawled over the side of the tub to lay curled and shivering on the bath mat. I lost track of time; it seemed like Brian had been gone long enough to have eaten breakfast and lunch.

I figured he wasn't coming back. I didn't care except for the fact that I didn't have money to get home without him. Eugene would make arrangements if I called him, but I wasn't ready to let anyone know that I had failed again. We had the room for another day so I would sleep and deal with the problems later.

My bag was beside the door where Brian had dropped it when we came in the night before. I found the sock. One pill would make me drowsy. Two or three would put me where I had been at the club, heavy and unable to speak. But I would still think and that wasn't good. Four would knock me out but I'd wake sometime in the middle of the night, starving and alone. That was even worse.

I swallowed eight pills, one at a time, while I watched the red light on the phone blink. Maybe he had called to say good-bye. He always tried to do the nice thing.

Chapter 46

A rising sense of doom interrupted my sleep. I couldn't connect my brain to the rest of my body so the only thing I knew for sure was that I had screwed up again. The stiffness in my back made me suspect that I had been asleep for a very long time.

As I fought my way to consciousness, I heard voices but couldn't identify the speakers or understand their words. Not another intervention. The voices mixed together to create deceptive sounds – a faraway din at times, and a loud hum of near-by voices at others. Maybe some people were close and others far away and I juggled my focus between the two. Maybe I couldn't focus at all. I couldn't tell.

If Brian had organized another humiliating group intervention, I really wouldn't forgive him. I warned him the last time. He couldn't be stupid enough to do this again.

Maybe that hum was my brain shorting out instead of nosy do-gooders waiting to confront me about my problems. I couldn't deal with either so I gave up the struggle and fell back into the fog.

"I'm sure I saw her eyelids flutter, like she was trying to wake up." The words registered that time, but I still didn't recognize the voice. It was a loud female but not Irma. That was as close as I could get.

Who would stand beside my bed to watch me sleep? I needed to know.

The struggle remained internal at first. I tried to clear the fog from my head and focus. I didn't want someone I couldn't recognize to stand over me and stare, so I taxed my brain for a memory of that voice. I still found nothing in my voice bank. I would have to wake up and look at her.

It was as though someone had glued my eyes shut, and the lids ripped a layer of skin off my eyeballs when I tried to force them to open. The pain briefly paralyzed my thoughts again and took my breath away.

When I regained a bit of clarity, I willed my hand to rub my stinging eyes, but my arms didn't respond to the command my brain made. They were heavier than my eyelids and as resistant to movement.

Terror overrode pain for a minute while I conducted a quick inventory. My lips were sealed as tightly as my eyes. My head was on fire. My throat was raw and mute, and tasted like blood. My arms had turned to lead, and my legs were missing. I was paralyzed. How had this happened?

Useless adrenaline pumped through my paralyzed body and exploded in my head. That pain released my voice. I let out a scream that intensified my pain to new, excruciating levels.

The mystery woman grabbed my hand and held it while she spoke. "You're okay, Penny Sue. Try not to move until a nurse gets here."

Why was she there, and why was there a nurse? That probably meant I was in a hospital, so why hadn't they fixed me?

I started putting things together. Brian had finally managed to stick me in a treatment center without my permission. Damn him. They couldn't hold me against my will. Where was my will? My legs instinctively tried to run; they weren't missing after all, only leaden like my arms and eyelids.

The heaviness spread from my limbs to the rest of my body. If I didn't force myself to get up, I would sink through the bed I was in and crash through the floor. I would die.

The struggle was pointless. Fatigued, my heavy body disappeared into darkness. Where were the white lights that were supposed to carry me to the other side? This was worse than death. I was stuck somewhere between life and death, unable to make it to either side.

My heart pounded furiously, refusing to be sucked into the hole. I tore loose to fight with both arms and legs. The woman who had been watching screamed for someone else to come help her hold me down.

She was either there to kill me, or she wanted to push me into the dark hole that was worse than death, and I had to escape. I screamed louder and fought harder.

"Penny Sue, stop it," she ordered.

Why did she call me that name? I had said repeatedly that I never wanted to hear that name again, but nobody cared what I wanted. Just like nobody cared that some crazy lady was holding me down in a bed somewhere trying to kill me. Where was Brian?

I kept screaming until the other voices separated from the hum and spoke individually.

"I'm here, Raven." It was Brian, the traitor. Had he come to save me, or to help the woman kill me?

I felt him walk toward the bed and decided he probably wanted to help the woman; otherwise he would have thrown her out. I screamed and fought until someone in the room and asked Brian and the woman to leave.

"I'm giving you a shot to help you relax, Mrs. Osburn," she said. Mrs. Osburn sounded stranger to me than Penny Sue had. Where was I, and why didn't she know who I was?"

I wanted to refuse the shot but didn't have the energy left to fight her.

* * *

"Your mother has been here for three days. She never left your side until you woke up and we had to sedate you," the nurse explained when I woke again later. "Would you like to see her now?"

Who did she think was my mother? The screaming had left my throat too raw to ask, so I tried to communicate fear with my eyes and shook my head. Penny Sue. It was my mother. I should have known. Of all the people who called me Penny Sue, she was the only one who would want to hurt me. She had come to kill me and get me permanently out of her life this time. Nurses weren't supposed to allow things like that to happen.

This time when I cried the tears felt good. They soothed my dry, scratchy eyes.

"How about Brian?" the nurse asked. "He's here too, sitting with your mother and Irene in the waiting room. They're all very worried about you."

I mouthed Irene's name. She was the only one I thought I could face; yet when she finally walked into the room I couldn't look her in the eye.

"You scared us, Penny." Her voice cracked. "We thought we lost you a couple of times. Thank God you're finally awake."

My tears continued to flow freely. I was relieved that she wasn't trying to hurt me. I was confused, but at least I wasn't going to die.

When I finally looked at her, she looked as bad as I felt. Her eyes were swollen and red, and her hair unfixed for the first time since I had met her. I tried to smile, but my lips cracked.

"Don't try to talk if you don't feel like it," she said. "I don't want to upset or tire you. Let me know when you're ready to sleep, or just ready to be left alone."

I reached for her and she sat on the side of the bed to hold my hand.

"Your hair is a sight," she said, followed with an attempted laugh.

"Yours too," I whispered. "Water."

She jumped up and fumbled through my sheets until she found a call button for the nurse. "I'll order anything you want. Can you think of anything besides water?"

Irene talked while she spoon-fed me ice chips. "Brian found you unconscious in your hotel room and called an ambulance. You had overdosed on some pills. Do you remember that?"

I nodded. I remembered taking the pills, but nothing after that.

"That was three days ago. You've drifted in and out, but never completely woke up until now."

"My mother." The words felt strange.

"Brian called me. The hospital admitted you and started treatment because it was an emergency, but they asked Brian to contact your next of kin for authorization. Legally, that's Craig. He gave verbal authorization for treatment but couldn't get away to come here."

"Chicago?"

"Yes, you're still in Chicago. Penny, because I wasn't sure you'd be okay, I called Kitty. Please don't be upset with me for that. She was hysterical when she heard and insisted that she wanted to come here, with or without me, so I brought her. Can you imagine that? The two of us in a car for six hours?"

The news surprised me and my head swam again trying to make sense of it. Why would she want to be there? To watch me die?

"Brian is a walking zombie. He hasn't eaten or slept since he found you. He paces the halls and drives the staff crazy, asking about you and insisting that you be kept comfortable."

A nurse came into the room to check my temperature and blood pressure. "It's good to see you awake," she said cheerfully. "We need to get you out of that bed as soon as possible, so you need to start moving around and get ready. Do you think you can eat something? Soup?"

I nodded; hoping that meant the tubes could come out. "And a Sprite," I squeaked out.

She said she would order the soup and be right back with the Sprite. She handed me the call button and told me to let them know if I thought of anything else.

"Do you want to see Kitty and Brian?" Irene asked. "Lori Sawyer and her mother were here earlier. They keep in touch by phone when they aren't here. It was interesting when your mother and Mrs. Sawyer ran into each other. Kitty was edgy at first, but Mrs. Sawyer was nice. They've learned to tolerate each other."

It felt like a dream, or like watching my life on television instead of experiencing it firsthand. Irene explained things and I had delayed reactions. Sometime after the nurse had come and gone again, the news of my overdose settled in. Did they think I had intended to kill myself?

"It was an accident," I told Irene. "The pills. I just wanted to sleep, not die."

"I'm glad to hear that," she said, smoothing the hair around my face. "You can't imagine how sad I felt, thinking that you had intentionally tried to take your life. And how guilty."

"I can't see Brian right now. Tell him I'm sorry. If I let him in, I have to let Momma in too, and I need time before I can look at her.

She said Brian would understand. "How about Lori? Do you want to call her?

"I want to sleep." After three solid days in bed, I still felt like I needed more sleep before I could face life. I was exhausted, physically and emotionally, and every part of my being ached.

Irene kissed my forehead and said she would let me rest. "Try to stay awake until you eat something," she encouraged. "We need to get you strong enough to go home."

Home? Did I have a home? For three years, I had lived in Brian's home, always with the understanding that my position was temporary. One day I would make it big, or get a job, and move out on my own so he could get on with his life. Before that I had lived in Irene's house with Craig, at first as a gift because we were too poor to live, and then after that as a renter, resentful because I wanted a home of my own. And before that I lived in Irene's house with my parents, fearful of being evicted from the home that wasn't large enough to accommodate me in the first place.

And before that I had lived in the barn house that my parents refused to pay my grandparents for. Even after they gave it to me, it didn't count because, no matter how much love-filled hand-me-down furniture and bright paint and covers they put in it, it was still a barn. Not only did I not have a home, I had never felt at home for as long as I could remember.

Nothing in life had ever felt permanent. And that might have been a good thing in some ways.

The nurse brought my soup and found me crying. "Is there anything I can do? Under the circumstances we prefer not to use drugs, but if you truly need something I can call the doctor."

"I'm confused and sad, and in pain. Isn't it normal to cry when I feel this way? Crying almost feels good."

"Yes. It is normal," she assured me. "As long as you don't feel hopeless. Let me know when crying stops feeling good, and we'll get someone in here to talk to you."

"I'm scared, too," I said. "I'm not sure what you mean by hopeless."

"Desperate may be a better word," she said. "If you don't see any light at the end of the tunnel, let me know."

I dismissed her with a nod, because I couldn't find words for my questions. What if I couldn't even see the tunnel? Is that why I couldn't find the light when I hung in limbo between life and death? Could people be tunnels? If my mother and Brian were tunnels, did I need to talk to them before I'd find the light?

I sipped my broth and considered the questions and their possible answers. The broth soothed my throat and settled my stomach, and the tears stopped while I ate. When I finished, I pushed the portable table away from the bed and found the paper that Irene had left with Lori's phone number written on it. I might call her after my nap. I couldn't believe how resistant I had been to seeing her again, and now she seemed like the least complicated relationship I had, again.

Before the day ended, I remembered that the only way to get any sleep in the hospital was to be unconscious. An aide had interrupted my sleep to take my food tray and drop off a dinner menu. Shortly after she left, a volunteer stopped by to offer magazines and candy, neither of which appealed to me as much as sleep. I dozed off again and a social worker came in.

"Now that you are awake, we need to discuss your plans for disposition," she advised. "You'll be ready to leave acute care in another day or so, but will require continuing treatment. Has anyone explained your options?"

"Am I sick?" I hadn't thought to ask the nurse about my medical condition, assuming that I was okay since I was awake and not paralyzed.

"You are doing well, physically. Your doctor will be in to discuss those details with you later. We need to address the emotional and chemical addiction issues," she said.

My heart raced. What right did this stranger have to assume that she knew anything about me? What had Brian told them?

"I don't have an addiction issue and I didn't try to kill myself," I insisted. "This was an accident."

"It's difficult to accidentally consume the amount of chemicals you had in your body when you were brought here," she pointed out. "I'll leave my card with you. Think things over and I'll check back in the morning, or you can call me if you decide you're ready to talk before then."

I threw the card on the floor. I'd never be ready to talk to Paula Krowski, or anyone else, about treatment centers or disposition. Brian could give up his campaign to have me committed because I would never consent.

I didn't feel like sleeping anymore, and I didn't want to see Brian, Irene, or my mother. If I had known where to find my clothes, I would have walked out. They couldn't hold me against my will. Maybe Lori would help me escape.

Todd answered the phone. "It's great to hear your voice. Lori has been worried sick over you. Why don't you call her at work? She'll probably want to stop by to see you on her way home."

I hung up, relieved that he didn't sound disgusted with me. Maybe Brian hadn't reached everyone with his stories about my addiction problems. Anxiously, I dialed Lori's office number.

"I need clothes, and someone to get me out of here," I said. "My crazy mother is here, and Brian wants to send me to a treatment center. Lori, I didn't try to kill myself and I don't have half the problems Brian thinks I have. This is out of hand."

She promised she'd come help me as soon as she finished the report she was working on. "Keep your spirits up," she encouraged. "We'll get you out of there and away from them soon, I promise."

Chapter 47

"We have no medical reason to hold her in an acute care facility. Physically she is ready for discharge." The doctor addressed my visitors instead of me. I wanted to hurl the vase of roses Brian had brought at the doctor's head. I was an adult, capable of understanding his assessment, intelligent enough to make my own decisions, and deserving of his undivided attention. He was *my* doctor, in *my* hospital room, discussing *my* life.

"Have you declared me totally incompetent? Is that my final diagnosis?" I let him hear the anger in my voice.

"No, Penny, I haven't declared you anything other than medically ready for discharge," he answered calmly.

"Then why are you talking to them about me as though I'm not here? That's insulting to my independence. I'm the patient so anything you have to say about my condition or my discharge should be said to me, don't you think?"

Dr. Spratt smiled, showing a side I hadn't seen in him before. "Yes, as a matter of fact I do agree. And I apologize for insulting your independence. That wasn't my intention but I can see how you would have taken it that way."

I thanked him, and exhaled the rest of my anger.

"We can ask your visitors to leave the room and sit in the waiting room while we finish this visit if you prefer," the doctor offered.

Brian made a last appeal before I responded to the doctor. "Raven, please reconsider. None of us want to hurt you. We love you and want what's best for you. At least consider therapy if you've completely ruled out the treatment center."

We? He went from 'they deserve to be shot' to including my mother in his assessment of what was best for me? We had been through the same discussion several times already and I hadn't wavered in my refusal. He should just give it up.

"I have considered every option that was presented to me Brian, and my decision won't change no matter how many times you bring it up. I'm not interested in continuing with any treatment after I leave here. Please stop asking."

My mother defended me. "She knows how she feels. If she says she doesn't have a problem and she doesn't need treatment, I think you should get off her back about it. You know Brian, just because somebody likes to have a few drinks, or accidentally takes an extra pill or two, doesn't mean they're crazy."

How perfect. My mother finally ended up defending me, only because it was the only way she could protect herself. If I had a problem, she knew that meant she had a worse one. She also knew that when the counselors and doctors delved into my history they would realize that I came by my drinking habit through watching my parents sneak bottles out of vegetable bins, tool boxes, couch and glider cushions, and bar kitchens, to drink up what they should have spent giving me a decent home.

All I could do at the time was thank her publicly and hate her internally. I could legitimately blame her for all my problems, both genetically and through the way she had raised me. I was certain that even the sanest person alive would drink if she was their mother, and the counselors would understand.

My visitors remained in the room, silently staring. I told the doctor I wanted them to leave.

Irene opened the door and Momma ran out immediately. Brian hung back for a minute to rub his head and plead with his eyes. I looked away and he left.

"Something tells me they were surprised by your direct approach," the doctor guessed. "Was that out of character for you?"

"Do you think I'm crazy? Even if you know I'll disagree with your opinion, I want the truth," I told him. "Just promise you won't tell them if it's bad news."

He dodged the question. "Crazy isn't a term I use. I think you are depressed, and you suffer a great deal of anxiety, neither to dangerous extremes, and both easily treatable conditions. I also think you have a substance abuse problem, although I'm not totally convinced that you are an alcoholic or an addict. And whatever I think, I won't discuss it with them."

"I'm not," I replied. "Either one."

"There's a fine line between where you are now and where you could end up," he explained. "Balancing on that line will become more difficult the longer you stay there. I think you use alcohol and drugs to mask other problems that you aren't willing to confront. You may not be physically addicted, but I think your emotional dependency poses a serious threat to your health, both mental and physical."

"So in plain English, can you tell me what you think I should do?" I refused to look at him, lest he mistake that as surrender.

"I think you would benefit from al-anon meetings, followed by some private counseling once you've overcome your fear that talking to others means you are crazy."

"Al-anon? Everyone else seems to think I need AA."

"I believe your sadness is rooted in problems that existed long before you took your first drink or pill. Al-anon may return you to the source of that pain, and your biggest reason for drinking. But I won't discourage you from attending AA also, if you will. Perhaps a combination of the two would be most beneficial."

"I didn't say I would do either," I reminded him.

"No, you didn't. I'm just giving you my opinion. You are welcome do with it what you want."

"Do I need an appointment, or do I have to become a member or anything?" I asked. "Just in case I change my mind, how do I do it?"

"No appointments or memberships," he said. "In fact, you don't even have to tell them your name unless you choose to do so. We have information about both programs and local meeting times. Will you stay in Chicago when you leave the hospital, or return to Tennessee?"

I hadn't decided until that moment. Suddenly it seemed that there was no question about what I should do. "I'll be staying in Chicago, with friends," I told him. "I would appreciate having that information about local meetings."

He congratulated me on what he called a wise decision, and said he would have a nurse bring me a list of meetings and counselors in the area.

Brian didn't protest my decision to stay in Chicago the way I expected. By then he probably knew he couldn't change my mind. He left my clothes and cosmetics bag beside my hospital bed and promised to mail my other things to Lori's house when he returned to Tennessee.

"Make a list of the things you think you will need," he said, leaving no doubt that he believed I would eventually return to his house after a temporary visit in Chicago. "And remember, any time you want to come home, I'll either drive up here to get you, or send a plane ticket, depending on my schedule."

I took the easy way out for the moment. Rather than deal with the truth in person, I thanked him and started on the list he requested. Later, after he had adjusted to living without me again, I would tell him by phone or letter that I wasn't coming back. He could send what was left to wherever I ended up.

Momma hugged me good-bye, only because Irene hugged me first and she knew everyone would see that Irene loved me more if she didn't try to catch up. She didn't say she was happy that we had reacquainted, or encourage me to keep in touch when I got out of the hospital. And the only thing she offered me was an awkward sounding wish for recovery, not a home.

Lori used her lunch break to pick me up from the hospital and drive me to her house. "I would have taken the afternoon off, but we have our monthly staff meeting later today," she apologized. "And Todd was booked solid. I hate to leave you alone on your first day."

I said I didn't mind. "I don't expect you to entertain me, Lori. Just letting me stay for a while is plenty."

The house was smaller than Brian's and in a quiet neighborhood. It had never been a barn, it had a shower, and it offered a fresh start with people who weren't judging me, so it was perfect to me. Lori had decorated it in bright, cheerful colors that matched her personality.

I was envious that she had what I wanted, but at the same time happy for her. Why hadn't I ever thought to decorate a house to match my personality? Would it have been red or blue if I had? Red was what I wanted to be; blue was what I was.

"This will be the baby's room eventually, but it's yours for now," she said, showing me into a small room with a twin bed and dresser. "I'm sorry we didn't have time to fix it up some before you came. I hope you won't be too cramped."

I laughed. "Lori, have you forgotten that I grew up in the back of Irene's beauty salon with no bed or dresser? And do you realize that this is my first time to have a room—a bed even—to myself in my life, except for the couple of days I lived in a crazy woman's basement? This is great. A tug of guilt pulled at my heart. Brian had offered me a room of my own and I had made the choice to sleep in his bed instead.

"I never saw your home, remember? In all those years you never let me in."

"You wouldn't have cared, would you? You would have liked me just the same if you had seen that place, and how crazy my parents were. I'm sorry, Lori."

"I have to run," she said, looking at her watch. "Make yourself at home. There's lots to eat and drink in the kitchen, and the television is in the basement. Look around if you need anything."

I said I'd be fine, and walked her to the door. "Are you sure Todd doesn't mind if I stay? I don't want to cause trouble between you."

"This was his idea to begin with," she said, opening the door. "I wanted to make the offer but he actually brought it up first. Don't worry about us. And be warned, Todd speaks his mind, sometimes to the point of being rude. He'll let both of us know the second he thinks there may be a problem."

I unpacked the few things that I had brought with me to Chicago, thinking this may have been the bleakest move yet, as far as material possessions were concerned. In every other way it felt like my best move.

I sat on my bed to look over the papers that I had been given when I left the hospital. The name stamp—Penny Martox Osburn— was as unfamiliar to me as the house I sat in. I had wished away Penny Sue Martox, and run away from Penny Osburn. Who was I?

The difference with Raven Coal was that she had never existed in the first place, so she could easily evaporate and never be missed. Would I miss her if that happened? Although far from perfect, my time with Brian had been the happiest part of my life so far, but the fact that I saw it as time with Brian proved that I had failed in my quest for independence.

The telephone rang in Lori's kitchen and I didn't know if I should answer it or not. The odds that it would be for me were almost impossible. I let it ring.

After ten rings there was a brief pause and then it started again. I thought of Jerry Fremlinger and shook off a chill. When the caller obviously wasn't going to give up, I answered.

"Were you sleeping or something?" Georgia asked. "I thought you'd be tired of sleeping after your hospital stay. How are you?"

"I'm okay," I told her, wondering if I believed it myself. "I wasn't asleep. I just felt funny about answering someone else's phone."

"I purposely called while they're at work," Georgia said. "I've been given strict orders from Lori and Mom to stay away from you. They think I'm a bad influence."

"You? I can't imagine," I said, feeling a bit disappointed that Lori and Mrs. Sawyer had already taken over Brian's role as my protector.

"I'm the black sheep in this family," she said. "I've already lost two husbands to my drinking problems, if you listen to them tell it, anyway. There were actually other problems but they didn't see those. Enough about me, though. I called to see if you need anything, and to give you my number."

"I guess I need everything, but I don't expect you to get it for me," I said with a laugh. "I have a costume and two pairs of jeans. And a toothbrush and make-up. I was just going through my bag to see if everything was there before you called."

"I'm a size seven, so you can probably wear my clothes if you want to borrow a few things," she offered. "Also, I'm not working right now so I'm available if you need me to drive you anywhere. I'm officially still married, but ditched, so I still have a home and another month or two on my unemployment benefits so I won't be kicked out any time soon. And I'm bored shitless during the day, so call me anytime."

I found a paper in the trashcan by the phone and a pen on the table and wrote Georgia's number down for later. Surely, Lori and Mrs. Sawyer wouldn't expect me not to communicate with Georgia forever.

Georgia's offers relieved some of my anxiety. Dr. Spratt had accurately diagnosed me. Depression and anxiety fit well. I needed many things, and clothes and transportation were the first steps toward the rest. I couldn't look for a job in a costume or jeans.

Lori hadn't set anything out for dinner so I abandoned the thought that I should have something ready when they came in. I had never lived in a home where both adults worked during the day, and no one was there to have dinner on the table at the end of the day. I had a lot to learn about their lifestyle.

Todd arrived before Lori, and welcomed me to his home. There was a brief period of tension when I tried to decide if I should stay in my room or join him in the living room, where he had settled with the newspaper. I didn't want to appear rude, nor did I want to invade his privacy.

If I offered to make dinner, would he think I was rude for not waiting until they led the way so I could follow their regular routine? If I didn't offer he might think I was lazy. Maybe I should have gone back to Brian's where I knew the routine.

Fortunately, Lori wasn't long behind Todd. She cleared up the discomfort as she passed the door to my room. "Don't feel like you have to stay in your room," she said. "Make yourself at home."

I said I'd be out soon, and used my paperwork as an excuse for sitting there. "The hospital gave me a whole stack of literature so I've been reading most of the afternoon to get it out of the way."

Todd suggested pizza for dinner. We called Lori's parents and met them at a small restaurant near their house.

From the looks of the neighborhood, the Sawyers had made the right decision when they moved to Chicago. The worst house in this area was better than the best house in our old neighborhood. I forgave Mr. Sawyer for moving his family away from me and felt another surge of relief.

"We're very pleased that you've decided to spend some time with Lori," her mother said. "She has never forgotten you, or forgiven her father for moving us here away from you. Maybe you girls can catch up on all of those missed years now."

Mrs. Sawyer confirmed my belief that Jason deserved more than I had to give. I had spent hours – days even – listening to him jabber and staring into his eyes, and never figured out what he thought about anything. In less than ten minutes with me, she read my mind like it was a billboard that she couldn't get around. A wave of guilt stopped my heart. Good mothers understood children, their own and everyone else's. I wasn't a good mother and probably never would be, no matter how hard I tried.

"When you feel up to it, I want to have everyone over for a dinner," Mrs. Sawyer said while she distributed pizza slices on our plates. "Rachel and Sue are anxious to see you also. Sue lives in Wisconsin with a husband and two hyperactive boys, but she'll drive down if we give her a few days' notice. Rachel hasn't married yet, but she stays so busy that we seldom see her."

"Translation," Todd said. "Rachel lives with her boyfriend. Mom and Dad don't approve so she stays away to avoid the lectures."

"We don't lecture," Mr. Sawyer said.

"Maybe not," Lori said, "but you still manage to let her know you don't approve. And Pete knows you don't like him, so he's always uncomfortable around the family."

"I've never said that I don't like him, and neither has your father," Mrs. Sawyer said. "We haven't done one thing to make him think we don't welcome him."

"Sometimes it's what you don't say that means the most," Lori pointed out. "For example you haven't mentioned Penny's hospitalization. You act like she just dropped by my house for a vacation. When you avoid the obvious it makes people nervous, and they know you don't approve."

During the silence that followed, I worked at dislodging impacted cheese from the bottom of the shaker. Lori's statement expressed my exact feelings, but I didn't want to agree and hurt her mother's feelings.

I hoped Todd would jump in and break the tension, but he chewed his pizza and took another bite. My heart fluttered until my hands shook in response. Deep breaths didn't help and I couldn't remember the next step from the 'overcoming anxiety' pamphlet I had read earlier.

Mr. Sawyer spoke first. "Penny, I'm sorry they've upset you. Look at how uncomfortable she is, her hands are shaking."

Another piece of my world shattered. Mr. and Mrs. Sawyer apologized for others just like Irene and Brian and Craig had done for me. Did no one respect others? Were my expectations too great?

Todd put his arm around me. "Go ahead and say what's on your mind, Penny. We're all family here. Let it out and you'll feel better."

Let it out? He had no idea how big *it* was, or how long I'd keep them there if I said what was on my mind. I caught Lori's eye, hoping she would talk instead. Or maybe Mrs. Sawyer would just read my mind and save me the trouble of speaking.

"It's okay, Penny. You can say what you want, or say nothing at all if that's what you want," Lori said. "We're an outspoken bunch, except for Mom, so we're used to hearing things that we may not always want to hear. And we deal with it. You just do what makes you comfortable."

I smiled while I swallowed and tried to find out if the lump in my throat was pizza that hadn't gone down, or anxiety coming up.

"Lori's right," I finally said. "Avoiding the topic does make me think you are ashamed of me, and when I add that to my own embarrassment I kind of wish I wasn't here." Being outspoken wasn't easy. I was glad the words were out, but my body tied in knots waiting for their reactions.

"We aren't ashamed of you," Mrs. Sawyer assured me. "Honey, we love you. I simply avoided that issue because I wasn't sure you would want to discuss it. When you sang that song, 'Don't Cry Out Loud', I thought it came from your heart. You've never been one to share many of your thoughts so I didn't want to push you. Maybe singing is how you do it."

"I didn't try to commit suicide. It was an accident," I told them. "I wanted to sleep through the next day, and I misjudged the number of pills it would take because I forgot how much I drank the night before. I don't want to die."

"And we aren't going to let you die," Lori said, the same as Brian had said once before. "You stay here and we'll do everything we can to get you happy." Her eyes watered up. Another thing we had in common. "We shouldn't have moved here without you. We should have kidnapped you and brought you with us."

"It's not your fault I turned out like I did," I told them. "If anything, this family gave me the only hope I ever had. And Lori, you made me believe in myself. You made me a singer, and that is the best thing I've had in my life."

Todd winked at me. "Doesn't it feel good to say what's on your mind?" he asked. "Sometimes the good things come out along with the bad."

"Brian probably should have warned you not to get me started," I said. "It's not for the weak."

Chapter 48

Todd and Lori spent most of the weekend listening to me say what was on my mind. I told them about my life after the Sawyers had moved away, and how my mother hadn't allowed me to talk to Irene for a while because of her involvement, so I felt completely alone. And I explained how Craig had come along just in time to fill the emptiness so I naturally came to depend on him to be everything in my life.

I told them how my father had forced me to marry Craig, and my mother had let it happen rather than admit that she was sleeping with Harvey, even though she hated Daddy. And I told them how I was confused because, although I thought I loved Craig, I resented him at the same time because they had forced him to be with me.

"We were too young in the first place, and neither of us had ever dated anyone else to know what love was all about," I decided, identifying my problem as the words came out of my mouth.

In the middle of my sob stories, I threw in a few good things. I told them how nice it had been to go back to Crayfield and discover that I had a family that had tried to find me. "They loved me and welcomed me back, and Nana and Pappy gave me a barn house. Momma never let on that Nana sent cards and letters. All those years, she let me believe that they had given up loving me."

Through happy tears I described how Irene had finally ignored Mama and moved into my life and tried to be a mother and a friend to me. And for Lori's benefit, I described the excitement of singing in the first talent show, and then walked them through the stages of my singing career, if it could be called that.

"Wait until you see my costumes," I told her. "I have a couple that look like they jumped off the pages of your notebooks. Do you remember how many costumes you drew for me with those colored pencils? I thought for sure you would end up a famous designer."

I explained why I had run off and how I ended up with Brian and how I had been flailing aimlessly the whole time without catching hold of anything solid.

"I have put two good men through hell," I admitted, as much to myself as to them. "I thought Craig deserved more than me. And poor Brian. I ran to him every time I was afraid, and then pushed him away when he tried to comfort me. I loved him one minute and resented him the next, the same as with Craig. Truthfully, there was nothing either of them could ever have done to please me because I was miserable with myself."

"I haven't met Craig, but I can tell you that Brian adores you," Lori said. "You should have seen how worried he was before you woke up at the hospital. I honestly thought he might die of a broken heart if it went on much longer."

"You were there? Lori, I didn't know. Thanks, and I'm sorry I put you through that."

Todd raised his hand. "Penny, you don't have to apologize and say thanks every other breath. People do things for you because they love you, and because they want to do them. I can assure you that Lori sat at that hospital as much for her own sake as yours. It made her feel good to be your friend."

I needed time to work through that idea. It didn't feel right but I trusted Todd to know what he was talking about, and to be honest. When I remained silent, Lori assured me that Todd was right. "I couldn't have stayed away for anything. I needed to be with you to prove to myself that I was a true friend."

"You stopped answering my letters, Lori. I thought you didn't like me anymore. I was hurt and angry."

"I couldn't write any more after you married Craig. Nothing seemed real. You didn't sound like yourself and I didn't know what to say to the new person," she explained.

"You knew, didn't you? You knew I shouldn't have married him."

"And that you were drinking or using drugs, or both. You sent a crazy letter one time, Penny. It was so messy that I couldn't make out some of the words. And what I *could* read didn't make any sense. I wanted to write back and tell you that you weren't your mother, so you should stop acting like her."

"Why didn't you?" I asked.

"Because by then I had already been through too much with Georgia and her problems. She stayed furious after the move, and started drinking and drugging as soon as we got here. There wasn't anything any of us could do or say to get through to her. I assumed you would react the same as she did, and that would have crushed my feelings and broke my heart."

"You were right. It wouldn't have done any good to try," I said, thinking she might have been the one person who could have gotten through, but what good would it have done to tell her that when it was too late to change the past.

"I used anything I could find to occupy or numb my brain so I didn't have to think or feel. The songs worked for a long time. I just kept a song going in my head so I didn't hear anything going on around me, or my own thoughts. Eventually I needed drinks to block out life so I could sing, and drugs to sleep off the guilt caused by my drinking. And then I used sex to keep from wanting a drink."

Sex must have been more than Todd could handle. He yawned and said he couldn't hold his eyes open another minute. He kissed Lori good night. "Keep talking, Penny," he said to me. "You already look five years younger since you started tonight."

After he left the room Lori laughed. "I guess you finally found a subject Todd couldn't handle."

"Lori, I never put it all together like this before. One emotional dependency led to another. I've never had a real relationship because I didn't know what I was doing, but thank God I had Craig and Brian. Otherwise I would have drank or drugged myself to death, or maybe even gone from one man to the next looking for what I needed in the least likely places I'd ever find it. How scary."

She said she thought I was going to be okay, and that I'd find a true relationship the next time I tried, because I would understand things better. I agreed.

"Is Georgia okay?" I asked after Todd had left the room. "She called me, the first day I was here, and mentioned her drinking problems."

Lori looked around the room as though searching for words in the air. "Poor Georgia. Her life has been a series of catastrophes, most of which she could have avoided by making better choices. Sometimes I think she brings trouble into her life purposely, because she loves misery."

"Nobody wants to be miserable, Lori. She told me that you guys don't want her to come around me. I felt sad for her. I promise I won't offer her anything to drink if I see her."

"You have that backwards, Penny. We aren't afraid of what you might do. She'll drain you. She'll cry on your shoulder and beg for sympathy. But then, if you offer to help, she'll only get angry and turn on you. She gets vicious. I don't have any objections if you want to see her. My only concern is that she will take the energy that you need to help yourself."

"She sounds just like me," I said. "She offered to let me borrow her clothes, and to drive me if I want to go anywhere. Maybe I could ask her to drive me to some of those meetings. We may be able to help each other."

Lori wrinkled her brow and thought about my suggestion before she responded. "That may be a great idea, Penny."

"I'm not positive that I want to go yet, but I'm thinking about it."

"I'll warn you. We've tried for years to talk Georgia into going to AA, or getting some kind of help. Her first husband had great insurance that would have covered an inpatient treatment program, but she refused to even consider going. She just might do it with you, if she thinks she can help you."

I wondered how it would work if we went to meetings together, thinking we were helping each other. The al-anon idea was growing on me, because that meant my parents had the drinking problem, not me. Maybe Georgia could go to al-anon because she believed I had the problem. And then maybe Lori could go because Georgia and I both had a problem. This way nobody had to admit that they were responsible for the original problem.

"We may be onto something," I said, and explained my plan. "The doctor recommended al-anon to me, and it's not nearly as threatening as AA. I think I can do this."

Lori's eyes started to fade. I suggested we go to bed and continue the conversation the next day. As I lay in bed that night, I thought of all the times Brian had begged me to talk to him, and how the best I had ever been able to do was relate sequences of events from my past. Never my feelings. If I had known how good it could feel, I might have told him everything I had told them. Maybe more.

I didn't want to think about Brian, even to decide if I loved him or if I had only used him for drugs and sex. I was on my own, almost, and refused to backtrack and attach my emotions to anyone. Until I fell asleep, I planned my next few days. I would call Georgia and ask her to take me to an al-anon meeting. And I would finish telling Lori about my life. I would also look for a job. Even if Brian sent money with my clothes, as I expected he would, it wouldn't last forever. And I couldn't keep using him if I ever wanted to be independent.

Chapter 49

I accepted a cashier position in a small grocery store three miles from Lori's house. I lucked out because they had several students who wanted weekends and evenings, so I got Monday through Friday daytime hours. I rode the bus to work and home three days, and the other two days I took the bus in and Georgia picked me up in front of the store when I got off. We had time to eat dinner before our al-anon meeting.

I called Dr. Spratt to thank him for suggesting the meetings and reported, truthfully, that they had helped me to return to my roots as he had predicted they might. I told him I was also addressing my strange dependencies on sex and music. However, I credited Lori and Todd for as much of my newfound serenity as I did al-anon. Together, they had listened and talked me through some of the most painful memories that I needed to pull out and confront.

As I expected, Brian sent money with my clothes. He boxed up the things I had listed, and added my check for the Chicago gig and a personal check for five hundred dollars. He also included a letter, in which he said he missed me but wouldn't call until I let him know that I was ready to talk to him. He would wait as long as I needed, and either drive to Chicago to pick me up or send a plane ticket when I was ready to come back.

I turned loose of the shield that I had been holding between us and allowed myself to miss him. But it was still too soon to call so I sent a letter instead. I told him that I had been attending meetings and dissecting my past, and that I planned to stay as long as it took to feel comfortable being me. I sent my love to Claude and Irma, and promised to keep him up to date on my progress, if he really wanted to hear it.

As I wrote my letter to Brian, I realized that writing was a safe way to communicate difficult messages. Without exposing emotions that I wasn't ready to share, or being interrupted by reactions that I didn't want to see, I could express my feelings.

I thought about the days I had spent curled up in Irene's glider writing my good-bye letters to the Sawyer family. As a child, my goal had been to say what my parents had prevented me from saying to my friends in person. It became clear to me that night that those letters had turned into so much more. I had searched my heart and expressed feelings that I would never have found the words for if I had said good-bye in person.

"I still have my letter," Lori said when I asked if she remembered. "I must have read it a hundred times, and dropped tears on the paper until it blistered into bubbles and wouldn't lie flat any more. I still have it in my jewelry box, and I'll bet Mom still has hers too."

I started a new letter writing project and spent most of my free time sitting in my room collecting thoughts. I wrote to the people I had left behind, and to those who had left me behind, even Nana, who would never see my letter. It was important for me to finally tell her how sorry I was that I hadn't gone back, so I could forgive myself.

The letters to Craig and Irene were the hardest because my feelings were so mixed, and my understanding of the relationships unclear. I didn't know if Craig had stayed in my life out of choice as much as obligation. He had married me when he was young, and he felt sorry for me. I could never be sure he would have wanted to marry me under normal circumstances, and was pretty sure he would have stayed forever out of duty.

On the other hand, I didn't understand my feelings for Craig either. I loved him because he was the only person in my life for a long time. I loved him because I needed him and he didn't run. And then I loved him because I believed only a monster could not love him, and I didn't want to believe that I was a monster.

I gave him Jason, someone he could love forever and who would love him back just as much. Hopefully, Jason had replaced me in Craig's life, and satisfied his need to take care of someone.

I wrote to Pappy and Wanda and Gwen and tried to explain that love was so foreign to me that I hadn't understood how to accept theirs or give mine, but promised I was learning how to love so I could return to Crayfield and do it right the next time. I told them what had happened since I last saw them, and that I was finally taking charge of my life and it would include them when I had it pieced firmly together - if they still wanted me, which I was sure they did.

Proving how illogical my expectations could be, the letters to the people who had left me behind were easier to write than those to the people I had left. My feelings for my parents had been close to the surface for as long as I could remember. As soon as my pen touched the paper they rushed forth, begging to be released. Surprisingly, I discovered that I didn't hate either of my parents. They were too pathetic to hate.

Although Nana had dropped a few hints over the years, no one had ever explained the details of my parents' lives to me. I figured many things out on my own as I experienced similar situations and emotions in my life, and recognized that they had been in the same place at one time and never got out. They lived in that black hole forever.

Momma wanted to be a singer but ended up a mother instead, secluded in a barn house with a broken screen door, constantly under the scrutiny of a resentful mother-in-law. Daddy was supposed to go to college but stayed home to support his wife and daughter, and he accepted his fate like a martyr, making her feel like the villain.

Neither of my parents had the strength to demand their life back. Instead of living, they existed, like robots that no one cared to program. And they weren't smart enough to share their misery, so each carried a full burden.

They didn't know how to love me; consequently I didn't know how to love my son. It wasn't my fault that they didn't love me, nor was it my fault that I hadn't known how to be a mother to Jason. I could only forgive all of us, and hope Jason would be able to do the same in time.

Irene's letter was the longest. She had chosen to come into my life, the same as Craig and Brian, but her reasons for staying were more self-less and less deserved in some ways. She truly had offered herself to me as a mother. No matter what I did or how often I disappointed her, she never gave up on me. I believed that she got as much out of the relationship as I did, however, because she wanted so much to be my mother.

I needed more al-anon and private therapy before I could write to Jason. In my mind he was still a two-year-old boy, and I still didn't understand how to talk to a child. Whatever Craig had told him about me would have to do until I created a real me for him to know. I was sure Craig had presented me more positively than I deserved, and I wouldn't go back until I could live up to that image.

I wrote to Lori and Todd and Georgia, only to get my thoughts straight. I didn't send their letters because I had learned to talk to them about my feelings.

My excuse about not wanting to inconvenience Lori, or borrow her car, hadn't fooled Georgia. "You realize I see through your little scheme, don't you?" she asked over dinner before our third meeting.

"What scheme?" I acted innocent.

"Getting me to these meetings. I know Lori would gladly have loaned you her car, or driven you. This was something you guys cooked up to get me there."

"I really didn't want to go alone," I promised. "I didn't want to go at all originally, but when the doctor suggested al-anon instead of AA it seemed like a good idea. Both of my parents had drinking problems. I'm learning to understand them a little and that helps me understand myself."

"My parents don't drink," she said. "So what do you think my problem is?"

"You were unhappy about the move? That's what Lori said."

"We were all unhappy about the move. Lori cried for the first year, Sue walked around in a daze, and Rachel cut school twice a week and failed seventh grade. Why didn't I wet the bed or cuss out a teacher instead of turning to pot and beer? It's weird how one person can be so different. Think I was adopted?"

"You look exactly like your dad," I reminded her.

"Why am I so different? It doesn't make sense."

I realized she was serious when she waited for my answer. "Georgia, I don't know. I'm as new to this whole recovery thing as you are. I still don't know why I did it. I blame my parents, but I'm not sure that's honest. I hated them for drinking, so why would I do it?"

We ate in silence for a while, each of us deep in thought about our own reasons for drinking.

"I wonder if we'll ever know why we did it," she finally said.

"Notice you said did instead of do?" I pointed out. "Does that mean we've really quit? Have you ever quit before?"

"A hundred times. I made it three months once. I think my husband cursed every single day of that time because I was downright miserable to live with."

"Do you think we should try an AA meeting?" I asked. "I will if you will."

She shrugged. "I guess it wouldn't hurt anything. We don't have to go back if we hate it."

"We can do it tonight if you want. AA is in the basement so all we have to do is go down the stairs instead of up."

"Do we have to say our name, and admit the dreaded disease? They always do on TV."

I didn't want to let those words cross my lips either. Dr. Spratt had said that I might not be physically addicted. For Georgia's sake, I could do it if necessary.

"I guess we'll find out." I let that sink in while I dug through my purse for tip money. "We'll survive."

We sat in the back row at an over-crowded speaker meeting. "This guy must be really good," I whispered. "Can you believe there are this many people here?"

She shook her head as the chairperson called the meeting to order. They went through the same preliminaries that we had learned at al-anon meetings, and it felt painless at first.

Then the dreaded introductions started. They went around the room, each person stating their name and admitting their failure.

"At least you have an alias," she whispered. "Maybe I'll make one up real fast."

I wouldn't have thought of that on my own, but since she put the idea in my head, I tossed it around until the row ahead of me started calling out their introductions.

None of my names felt right. I hated Penny Sue. Penny belonged to Craig. And I needed to protect Raven. I am an alcoholic became the simpler half of the statement.

When my turn came, I used Penny Sue, because she was the most troubled of my three identities. And that was the name that my parents had used for me.

"Hello, my name is Penny Sue, and I'm an alcoholic." It didn't hurt like I thought it would.

After a few minutes passed I felt free. I still couldn't say for sure that I was an alcoholic. They called it a disease, but there was no lab test to prove it or medication to treat it. They had studied my blood at the hospital, and told me how many pills and drinks were in my body at the time, but they couldn't tell me if my body needed them, or would crave them again later.

Nor was I able to prove that I wasn't an addict. I knew I could go weeks without using and suffer no physical repercussions. But I couldn't measure the emotional disturbance that I felt, or know that it wouldn't grow to proportions that would seem unbearable in the future.

"I'm glad I did that," I told Georgia when we were back in the car. "What do you think?"

"I'm not sure. I know I don't get much out of listening to some old drunk tell his life story. Shoot, enough of that would make me want a drink to block him out."

"How did you feel about saying your name and admitting that you're an alcoholic?" I asked. "I was surprised at how good it felt to me, even though I'm not sure it's true."

"Honest? I hated that part. I felt manipulated. So many people have already called me that, and tried to force me to admit it when I didn't want to, that I felt like I was caving in to them. Penny, I'm extremely rebellious."

I tried to put myself in her place. Even when I knew that Craig hated my drinking, he hadn't nagged me or tried to force me to admit that I was an alcoholic. On the contrary, he had tried to pretend he didn't notice. And Brian's intervention plot had been a one-time attempt to wake me up. He hadn't harassed me except when I was in the hospital and he was worried. Georgia's experience was much different.

"Georgia, this is your business. AA is anonymous, so you don't have to tell anyone who wasn't in that room about it. I won't share your business with anyone," I promised.

After that night, Georgia and I continued our two night a week routine. We went to an al-anon meeting one night and an AA meeting the other. I never asked if she believed she was an alcoholic, or if she had quit drinking. It didn't matter to me. We were both learning to take control of our own lives and to solve problems in our own ways.

Lori didn't ask about the meetings, or personal questions about her sister. I still talked to her about my life and my feelings. One night when Todd was out, she brought up the subject of my future.

"Have you thought about what you plan to do?" she asked.

"Not really," I admitted. "I've been taking it one day at a time." Then it hit me. How could I have been so rude? They probably wanted their home and their privacy back. I had been living with them for three months, long past what most people would consider a visit.

"Lori, I'll look for an apartment. I've imposed on you guys long enough."

"I'm not trying to push you out," she said. "We don't care if you want to stay. The reason I asked is because I've wondered about your music. Do you miss singing?"

The real love of my life. Of course I missed it, and it was the one missing piece that I hadn't had the heart to confront.

"I do," I admitted, trying to hide the sadness from her. I wasn't sure I could talk about it.

"You're welcome to sing here. I'm sure you need to practice or something, and I just thought maybe you were embarrassed or afraid you'd bother us. We would actually enjoy it."

I thanked her but didn't commit to anything.

"Todd said you can have that space next to the laundry room if you want to have somewhere private. He'll clean his junk out of there for you."

I didn't want to tell her the truth. I wasn't sure I could sing anymore, and didn't have the courage to try and learn the truth. I sang because I was miserable, and singing was the only way I knew to release that energy. Now that I almost understood my parents, and I had forgiven myself and everyone else who had hurt me, I wasn't sure I had the negative emotions I needed to sing well.

I didn't realize the tears had started until Lori put her arm around my shoulders and handed me a tissue.

"Thanks, Lori," I said, wiping the tears away. "I'm afraid to try."

"Do you think you'll need to drink if you want to sing? If so, I can prove you're wrong. I heard you sing a million times before you started drinking and you were great back then."

I laughed. "Lori, you're the best friend anyone could ever hope to have. Do you know that?"

"I try to be," she said. "I want to do what I can to give you back that part of your life. I know how important it was to you, and how good you are."

"It's not the drinking or drugs I need," I tried to explain. "What I had before was raw pain. That pain motivated me. It was the reason I sang. I don't have that anymore."

"Wow, Penny, that is heavy stuff. I never thought of that." Tears filled her eyes and she reached for another tissue. "This is so unfair."

I tried to console her. Not only was I a crybaby, I was making everyone around me cry too. It wasn't the end. I had plenty of time to work through my problems. Maybe I was wrong. I just wasn't ready to find out.

"Nobody should have to be miserable in order to do what they love most. That just defies everything I want to believe in, Penny."

We cleaned the kitchen, saying little as she loaded the dishwasher and I covered the leftovers and put them in the refrigerator.

"Penny, do you think Georgia needed to be miserable for some reason? Could that be why she wanted to drink?"

It was my turn to console her. "We don't have to know her reasons, Lori. We just have to love her while she discovers them for herself."

I called Brian that night and told him about my fear of not being able to sing without some misery for motivation. He was relieved to hear from me, and said exactly what I needed to hear about my singing.

"If you decide you never want to sing another note, I'll be sorry for the people who will be deprived of your talent, but I'll love you just the same," he promised. "You aren't a singer to me, Raven. You are the beautiful woman I love, who just so happens to sing, the same as you make meatloaf and wear jeans to the grocery store. If you stop *doing* any of those things you'll continue to *be* the same woman and I'll continue to love you the same. All I want you to do is be."

I said I was ready to see him, and he agreed to visit the next weekend.

Chapter 50

Lori and Todd offered us the sofa bed in the basement if Brian wanted to stay in their home while he was in Chicago, so we would have privacy, and wouldn't have to share my twin bed. Brian opted for a hotel, but said he still wanted to spend time getting to know them better. He planned to stay for a week.

"I'll have to work," I warned. "I haven't been there long enough to accumulate vacation time yet."

"Raven, do you really want to keep this job? I'll send you the money you need while you're here," he said.

His question frightened me. Maybe I shouldn't have called him so soon. My independence was new to me and I wanted to defend it.

"I need my job," I replied firmly. "It isn't just about the money, Brian. I need to know that I can hold a job, and that I can support myself. I've thought about moving into an apartment even, to prove what I'm capable of on my own."

He inhaled deeply and held the breath while he pulled on his chin. I missed his nervous habits.

"Okay," he said. "I'll find something to do while you work, that's no problem. We'll have the evenings and nights to catch up."

"I have meetings on Tuesday and Thursday evening, but I'm free by ten on those nights." I felt guilty about the limited amount of time I had for him, after he came all that way to visit. "I'm sure Lori and Todd will entertain you while I'm out."

He smiled with one side of his mouth and little eye involvement. Something stirred in me, but it wasn't sexual. I breathed slowly, waiting for his response.

"Raven, do you want me here? I realize I sort of pushed this visit on you very suddenly. I just got so anxious when you called."

"I do want you here," I said. "I've missed you more than I knew. But I have to finish what I've started here, and that means I can't take any breaks from my responsibilities. I hope you understand."

He said he did. "We'll play this by ear. You call the plays and I'll follow," he suggested. "I'm happy to spend any time I can with you, and I don't want to compromise your independence or your progress."

Tears again. It almost seemed like I cried more now that I was happy than I had during my miserable years, and I wasn't sure I understood why.

"Did I say something wrong?" he asked.

"I don't know what's wrong with me. No you didn't say anything wrong. I appreciate your patience and generosity. I don't understand. I cried all the time when I was sad, and now I cry all the time when I'm happy."

"Whew." He laughed. "Glad it isn't me."

"You know what? For once in my life I'm not thinking that I don't deserve it. I'm just thinking I'm glad I have you. Do I have you, Brian? Are you here to stay?"

"With you? Yes, if you want me. If you mean in Chicago, we'll have to talk about that."

"You mean you would consider it?" I asked.

"Raven, I would consider anything that's important to you. I'll be honest, I don't think I would like Chicago, but if it were the only way I could be with you, I would strongly consider it."

Everything got confused again. This man expressed a desire to be with me under any circumstances. Instead of feeling stifled or stalked, I felt free. I wasn't afraid to let him love me, or to admit that I loved him. I was happier than I had ever been in my life, yet I cried too hard to speak.

He held me and laughed at me this time, because he knew I wasn't sad.

"Brian, I love you. I really do love you and this time I love myself enough to know what that means. And I want you to love me. I'm not afraid anymore."

"That would have been a beautiful speech without the big sniff in the middle," he teased.

"Want me to take it back?"

"No way. I'll treasure it, sniff and all. I love you Raven. Someday I hope you'll be free so I can marry you."

He reminded me that I still had a lot of work to do, but that didn't scare me or diminish the excitement I felt. Hope and serenity were new emotions to me. Once I had opened the door to welcome them, I became anxious to conquer the remaining work and find more.

"Todd and Lori won't let me pay board. I help with groceries and utilities. I should have enough for a divorce soon," I told him.

He opened his mouth to respond but I interrupted. "I have to do this on my own. And I'll have to go back before I can do it. That's only fair."

He agreed, and said he was proud of me. I told him I was tired of talking about me and thought we had other things to catch up on.

Todd used a couple days of comp time to entertain Brian while I worked. Brian told me they played basketball at a gym one day and went sightseeing the other. He lied. When we went back to their house for dinner on Friday night, they surprised me with a mini studio that they had spent those two days putting together for me in the basement. It was only a microphone, a stereo system, and a couple of small speakers, but it was everything I needed and more than I expected.

"I told them they should ask you first," Lori said nervously. "They wouldn't listen."

"You're under no obligation to use it," Brian said. "I thought I'd put it there in case you want it, but you don't ever have to use it if you don't want. Todd said Lori can play with it if you don't."

"I appreciate what you've done. Both of you," I said. "And you Lori, for considering my feelings. All of you are just too much."

They stared at me, waiting for me to let them know if I planned to use it. The doorbell saved me from having to announce my decision.

"You said you wanted me to get to know Brian, so I took a chance and dropped by," Georgia said. "I hope nobody minds." She looked at Lori with pleading eyes.

"I'm glad you came," I said. "They've just surprised me with a music studio downstairs, in case I decide to sing again. I'm glad you're here to share the excitement."

"I'm glad you came," Brian told her. "I want to meet all of Raven's family."

"We've been through some big things together," she said. "I think Penny will always hold a special place in my life because of that."

Lori asked Georgia if she had eaten, and said there were some ribs left if she was hungry. Georgia declined, but asked for a drink. "Water or juice," she clarified when Lori looked scared.

"I apologize, Georgia," Lori said quickly. "I reacted out of instinct, and that was cruel."

Georgia flashed me a little grin before she responded. "I don't want to bring the mood down here, so I'll keep this short. You don't have to second-guess every word you say around me anymore. I'm aware of my problems, and the bad attitude I've had for the last few years. Can we just start over now?"

Lori said that sounded great to her, and went to get Georgia's water. Todd told Georgia to find a seat and make herself comfortable. Brian looked confused because he knew nothing about Georgia's history. I had protected her anonymity, as promised, telling him that I attended meetings and that Georgia and I had become friends as totally separate issues.

While Todd initiated small talk to ease the tension, I thought about the microphone in the basement. Before the night was over, I would either have to go down and try it out, or explain that I wasn't ready.

My fear had diminished because I knew I wouldn't crumble if I couldn't sing. What remained for me was the possibility that I may be able to sing, if not now, someday.

Brian took my hand and squeezed it gently. "Are you okay?"

I nodded and tuned back into the conversation around me. Lori and Georgia were exchanging stories about their jobs, a safe topic. I knew both of them well enough to know that they enjoyed being able to talk, even if the conversation wasn't about much. I felt like a sister, allied to each of them individually, and still part of the bigger group.

"Do you remember that summer when your dad claimed me as a daughter so I'd be included in your pool membership?" I asked, after the work conversation fizzled out. "I feel like part of the family again. It's nice to see you two acting like sisters."

Georgia laughed and told the guys about Lori's bikini. "I felt so sorry for poor Mom. You should have seen her face when she realized that Lori had been hiding breasts all winter."

"What do you mean, you felt sorry for poor Mom? I was the one who never had clothes that fit," Lori said. "I didn't know I had breasts either."

"And I didn't realize I didn't have any until I saw Lori's," I laughed until I cried. "Talk about disappointment."

"You still don't have any," Georgia said. "Now, that's what I call disappointing."

Brian defended me. "I'm not disappointed."

I waved my hand to make them stop. I was laughed too hard to fully appreciate his vote of confidence. When I recovered, I remembered another time when I had enjoyed myself that much.

"I have a great idea," I said. "Do you guys want to come back to the hotel with us and jump on the bed?"

Brian let out a howl. "I can't believe you said that. I was thinking about that very thing. That was the last time I saw you laugh this much."

"What in the world are you two talking about?" Lori asked.

I told her how I had looked forward to my first night alone in a hotel room. "I planned to do all sorts of naughty things, like leave toothpaste in the sink, and not flush the toilet or put my clothes away, and I wanted to jump on the bed. Brian came to my room to visit, and I thought for a minute that I might have to act like an adult and miss the fun."

"She found out I was crazier than she was," he reported. "The old bald guy deceived her. If she expected mature and refined, she was disappointed."

"I wasn't disappointed," I said. "Anyway, if you haven't jumped on the bed as adults, you don't know what you're missing."

Todd raised his eyebrows questioningly at Lori. "What do you think?

"I think we're going to the hotel if you want to do this," she answered. "You aren't breaking my bed. Georgia? You in?"

"All I need is to get arrested for a wild party in a hotel room to ruin my reputation," she said. "Nobody would ever believe I was sober."

Lori laughed. "And since when do you care what anybody thinks?"

We drove to the hotel--Georgia included--and took turns jumping on the beds. During my last turn, a song automatically came out. "*I'm the happiest girl in the whole USA.*"

I only sang the chorus but they applauded like I had done a concert. I jumped down and hugged Brian.

"Are you ready to go back and try out your studio?" he asked.

"I don't want to keep Lori and Todd up, or bore you all. It won't sound good without music."

"But you have music," he said. "I brought tapes. You haven't checked your studio out closely enough. I got a couple of guys together and recorded tracks for some of your songs. They're in your tape deck."

"And we don't have anything to do tomorrow, so you can keep us up all night if you want," Todd said.

"Georgia, why don't you plan on spending the night," Lori suggested. "We'll have a slumber party, all of us."

"What would Mom and Dad say? A mixed slumber party," Georgia teased.

We went back to the house. Lori gave Georgia a gown and a blanket and pillow, and warned her that she'd be sent home the minute she jumped on any furniture.

Brian moved my microphone out of the storage room where I could be with them while they lounged in the TV room. I sang all of the songs on the tapes.

It felt rough at first, because my voice was out of shape. Soon I didn't worry about how I sounded, or how my throat felt. I focused on the emotional high and sang until I was hoarse and my audience was sleepy.

Georgia was completely out in a recliner. Lori's head rested on Todd's shoulder and they both had their eyes closed, although I thought they were still awake. As ragged as my voice was, I still sang "Take Me to Your World" before I turned everything off and sent them to their beds.

Georgia slept in the twin bed and Brian and I took the sofa bed.

"You've still got it," Brian said, after we had opened the sofa bed and settled in. "You sounded great. And I'd like to take you to my world, any time you're ready to come back."

"Not great," I corrected. "Don't ever lie to me about my music, Brian. It felt good, that's the important part. Thanks for putting this together for me. And keep your world ready. It won't be long."

I was sad when it was time for Brian to leave the next day. I made Todd drive him to the airport because I didn't want to say good-bye in public.

"I'm on the right track," I told him before he left the house. I need a little more time to pull everything together, but I know I can do it."

"I know you can too," he assured me. "Do what you need, and come back home when you're ready."

I wanted to say I was ready and leave with him then, but I controlled the urge. A few more weeks of meetings and the rest of the divorce money stopped me. Home. At least I knew I had a home to go to.

Lori held my hand while we watched Brian and Todd back out the drive. "He's great," she said.

"I know," I answered. "I don't know if it's a case of absence makes the heart grow fonder, or clearing my head of the garbage that made me finally see just how great he is."

She decided for me. "Probably both. I wish Georgia could find someone like him."

I asked for extra hours at work, determined to get the divorce money as quickly as possible. And I called Irene to ask her to find an attorney for me.

"I'm glad you are finally ready to do this," she said. "You'll feel much better, and Craig won't be stuck in a stage of uncertainty. He has a serious woman in his life. She loves Jason, and I think Craig will marry her after you go through with this."

I was relieved. This made things easier for me. The divorce should be simple, if we both wanted it. There would be no custody fight, and I didn't want anything from him.

On Thursday, Georgia didn't come to pick me up. I waited for thirty minutes in front of the store before I went back inside to call. She didn't answer her phone so I went back out and waited another twenty minutes, hoping she had been held up in traffic.

Finally, I called Lori to see if she had heard from her. She offered to come pick me up.

"Do you want me to drive you to your meeting?" she asked. "I can drop you off and come back later, or stay with you. Either way is fine with me."

"I think we should check on Georgia," I said. "She hasn't ever been late or missed a meeting since we started going."

Lori was unusually quiet as she drove to Georgia's apartment. When she saw Georgia's car in the parking lot she smacked the steering wheel with the butt of her hand.

"This isn't a good sign," she said. "Why don't you wait here and let me go alone?"

I insisted on going with her, and stood beside her while she pounded on the door.

"Maybe someone else picked her up." I shrugged. "I don't think she's here."

We had turned to walk back to the car when she finally opened her door. She didn't have to say a word; we could tell by looking at her that she had been drinking.

"Georgia! How could you?" Lori started but I stopped her.

"Don't Lori. We can't do that."

She walked away crying and left Georgia staggering in the doorway.

"Did you get a sponsor?" I asked. "Can I call someone for you?"

She shook her head. I wished her luck and told her to call me when she was ready to talk.

Chapter 51

I wasn't sure it was possible, but I thought Lori might have been more disappointed than I was. She cried all the way home from Georgia's apartment, repeating different versions of the same impossible question.

"How could she? How could she do this, Penny? What was she thinking?"

"Lori, we can't take this personally. Georgia has hurt herself, not us," I reminded her. "Believe me, she will hate herself when she realizes what she's done. We don't need to criticize her because she'll do enough of that on her own. I feel so sorry for her."

"She was doing so well. She seemed happy. Did she seem happy to you? What do you think happened?"

I had no idea, and tried to push it from my mind. I didn't want to consider the likelihood that nothing had to have happened to trigger her relapse. It happened to people every day, for no reason that they could identify. That meant the same thing could happen to me and I didn't want to think about it."

I was dangerously vulnerable. Brian was gone and Georgia was drinking.

Lori went to her room as soon as we got home, probably to cry or to call her mother. I went to the basement to sing and didn't come back up until bedtime. I said good night to Lori and Todd and headed straight to my room.

When sleep eluded me, I tried to find a song that would relax me. That didn't work anymore. Now I wanted to perfect the songs by deciding how to sing them with my ragged voice and lack of drive. They created more stress.

I turned the light on and tried to write. My thoughts refused to collect rationally, so songs and letters were both out of the question. After ten crumpled pages of unsuccessful attempts, I gave up.

To avoid waking Lori and Todd, I went to the bathroom in the basement and filled the tub. With no bubbles, nothing to drink, and no pills, the water alone did little to console me. I laid my head back on the edge of the tub and covered my eyes with a washcloth. I cursed Georgia for slapping me with reality.

At two o'clock, after tossing until I had sheet burns, I broke down and did the one thing that I thought I'd never do. I called my sponsor. There went my final hold on denial. If I needed a sponsor, I had to admit that I was an addict.

"Any time, I told you that," Virginia L. said after I apologized for calling so late.

"I'm scared," I told her. "I've tried everything I could think of to calm my nerves and nothing worked."

"And now you want a drink?" she guessed.

I hesitated. No, I didn't think I wanted a drink. I just wanted to feel better. "Actually, I don't think I do," I answered. "This is weird. Now that I've thought about it, I don't want a drink. I think I want to sing."

And I wanted Brian there with me. I wanted to feel safe. I wanted Georgia not to be drunk. I wanted a ham sandwich from Rene's Deli in Nashville, but I didn't want a drink.

"That's good," Virginia said doubtfully. I knew she didn't believe me. "The important thing is to keep working your program. At times like this you have to take one minute at a time, or even one second. Focus on the progress you've made and fight to hold on to it."

I promised I would follow her advice, and thanked her for her time, feeling much better. I wasn't sure how I would have done if I had had a drink or pill available to me at the time. Would I have taken them with me to the bathroom? If I reacted this negatively to Georgia's relapse, how would I react to one of my own? I didn't want to know.

"Keep working your program." Virginia's simple advice played again in my head. Skipping the meeting because Georgia hadn't shown up to go with me had been my big mistake. My recovery belonged to me, alone. I couldn't allow myself to become dependent on Georgia, or anyone else.

On Saturday morning I consulted the directory of meetings that I had picked up from the literature table at the first al-anon meeting I had attended. I located the weekend meetings in the area and asked Lori if I could use her car.

"You're welcome to use it," she said, "but I think I'd like to come with you, if you don't mind."

She had shown no interest when I invited her before. "I don't mind but why the change of heart?" I asked, hoping she wasn't afraid that I would skip again if she didn't tag along to watch over me.

"Because I don't know how to help Georgia," she admitted. "All these years, I've tried to tell her what I thought she should do, when I should have been asking her what I could do. The least I can do now is learn from people who know about the disease. Penny, I want to help her."

I hugged her. She looked defeated and as scared as I had felt the night before.

"Lori I'm glad you want to go and learn what you can. Just don't expect to learn how to help Georgia, or me. You can only learn how to help you," I warned.

"I thought al-anon was for the family of alcoholics to learn about their disease. Penny, I never believed it was a disease. I thought it was a choice. A mistake to be more honest."

"That's part of it," I explained. "You learn about the disease, and maybe how to deal more effectively with the alcoholic but you can't learn to understand or fix them. We don't understand ourselves, and no one else can fix us."

I noticed that I had spoken in first person and wondered if she had caught it also or realized the significance.

"What you will get are the tools you need to help yourself. We are really hard on you guys," I said with a smile. "We make you crazy with worry, and anger, and frustration. We don't mean to, we are just sharing the only things we have left. You'll learn how to cope, and not blame yourself."

She dropped her eyes and fumbled with the strap on her purse. I reran my words, wondering what I had said to destroy my best friend's confidence. I had known her since second grade and couldn't guess what brought her down and made her speechless.

"I do blame myself. Penny, life was easy for me. I didn't have to make tough decisions and my temperament allowed me to accept anything that came along. I cried after the move, but didn't think my life wasn't worth living. I expected Georgia to be the same so I didn't sympathize when she had problems. I wasn't a very nice sister when she needed me."

"It's not over yet," I reminded her. "You're still going to be her sister for a long time. Don't be so hard on yourself."

"What if it is too late?" She sounded terrified. "You saw her, Penny. She looked so old and sick. What if she never comes back?"

I didn't have an answer for her. I couldn't speak for Georgia, nor could I give Lori false hope. The only thing I knew for sure at that point was that I never wanted anyone to feel that much sorrow over anything I did. I thought about the people at my intervention, and decided I would write each of them a letter apologizing for the pain I had put them through, and thanking them for caring enough to want to help me.

I told Lori I wanted to go to an al-anon meeting that day and an AA meeting the next, and suggested she try both with me. She needed to hear from alcoholics who had been to the edge and back so she would understand that there was nothing anyone else could have done to stop them.

Lori told Todd where we were going and that she wouldn't be long. He said he might go with us the next time.

She asked questions in the car. Would she have to explain why she was there? Did they charge admission? Once we were there, she relaxed and soaked in as much information as she could. She collected pamphlets and exchanged phone numbers with the speaker after the meeting.

"I can't believe the love I felt in that room," she said as she unlocked the car door for me. "It's such a relief to meet so many others who know exactly how I feel. Thanks for bringing me here."

I told her we both owed Dr. Spratt for that, and agreed with her that the love in the group was what seemed to make the program work. Love was the answer to every question. Why had I been such a lonely child? Because my parents didn't know how to love me. How had the Sawyers made my life bearable? Because they did know how to love. Why had I clung to Craig? Because I wanted someone to love me. Why hadn't it worked? Because I didn't know how to return his love.

And I had run out on my son because I didn't know how to love. Or maybe I did. Maybe I knew I would hurt him if I stayed, like my parents had hurt me by not leaving me with Nana. I would have appreciated my parents more if they had been honest about not wanting to raise me, or if they had divorced. There may have been a time, when I was very young, when Daddy would have been a good parent alone. Maybe I loved Jason enough to know that Craig alone was better for him than Craig with me.

Was I rationalizing? Trying to excuse myself for running out on my son? I would find the answers, and I would write my letter to Jason, explaining my version of love and how afraid I once was of it.

"Love is such a complicated part of life," I said. "Do you ever think about how different people show and think of love?"

"I'm starting to," she answered. "I used to think it was simple, but I've changed my mind."

"Years ago, I tried to talk to my grandmother about love." I laughed, remembering her reaction. "She thought I meant sex, and got all nervous and didn't know what to say. And she loved better than anyone; she just didn't know how to explain it. So I asked Irene. She gave me great advice, only I didn't understand it at the time. She said I couldn't love anyone else until I learned to love myself. She was so right. I saw a sign the other day that said, *People need love the most when they deserve it the least*. That fits with Irene's lesson."

Lori turned into an empty church parking lot and parked her car. Before I could ask what she was doing, she leaned her head on the steering wheel and sobbed. Occasionally I had felt the same way after leaving a meeting where someone had told their story of abuse and broken promises.

"You can't let these stories depress you," I warned. "Hold on to the love and the hope of the meeting."

"It's not the story that got to me," she said. "It's what you said about going to your grandmother and Irene. Penny, your life has been so unfair. I hate to think what you've lived through, searching for love so much that you had to ask people to explain it to you. And you are one of the most loveable people I have ever met."

She pounded the steering wheel and cried harder. "I don't understand life sometimes. Things aren't fair."

I took her lead and let my own tears pour, but for another reason.

"Lori, I love you. You just validated all of the self-pity that I thought I wasn't entitled to." We sniffed together. "And the good news is that because you did that, I don't have to feel sorry for me anymore. I love me now, and I've discovered in the last week that I'm capable of loving other people too. I love you. I love Brian. And I know I love my son."

She caught her breath. "Oh Penny, I've wanted to ask you about him so many times. You never mentioned him, so I wouldn't bring it up first. I thought maybe Craig took him away from you and I'd open a painful wound."

I told her the truth, how I had run off and left him because I wanted to, and none of it was Craig's fault. I also told her that I believed with all my heart that he was better off with Craig than with me.

"I don't know what will happen now," I admitted. "I want Jason to know the whole truth about me one day, when he's old enough to understand. In the meantime, it will be up to Craig whether or not I see him. Irene says he is happy. I don't want to disrupt that, so if Craig thinks it's better for him not to see me until later, I won't.

"You aren't going to be here much longer, are you?" she asked. "I can tell you are getting better every day and I know you'll go back."

"I want to go back to Brian," I admitted. "I wish I could move him here, close to you, but he belongs in Nashville. I almost have enough saved for a divorce. I won't go back until I have at least hired an attorney and filed."

She wiped her face with the back of her hand and laughed. "I guess we can go home. There's no reason to sit in this parking lot all night."

I laughed with her. "I don't know, that felt pretty good, Lori."

"Maybe we should go out somewhere and cry more often?"

"Shut your mouth!" I said. "I've given up booze, drugs, sex almost, and crying is next on the list."

Todd looked at us like we were crazy when we walked through the door, laughing with our swollen eyes and streaked make-up. "Dare I ask, or is it a girl thing?"

"Don't ask," I warned. "You might get us started again."

I called Georgia the next morning and told her that Lori and I would pick her up if she wanted to join us for the AA meeting. She was embarrassed, but didn't let that stop her from going. I was proud of her. The following week, Mr. and Mrs. Sawyer and Todd joined the three of us for an al-anon meeting. Lori was so pleased with them that she volunteered to do a reading at that meeting. Then, Georgia was proud of her. Everything concerned with love seemed to work in a circle as long as everyone stayed connected, and the same emotions passed around the group.

Irene called me with the name of an attorney she had already talked to about divorcing Ralph. "I've decided that I don't want to be married if I still have to spend most of my time alone," she told me. "I'm not too old to make a new life."

I mailed the letters to my friends in Nashville, and told them I'd be home soon, to appreciate them in person. Until then, I hoped they could feel my love long-distance. I told Keith and Victoria I was ready to take them up on their offers to attend meetings with me if they still wanted. Brian already had a list of meetings ready for all of us.

I finished out the month at the grocery store, and then spent a week with Irene while I filed for the divorce and had dinner with Craig and his girlfriend. They said they would work me back into Jason's life, slowly so he wouldn't be confused.

And then I headed home to Nashville.

Message from Author

Penny Sue Martox aka Raven Coal represents a combination of:

- ❖ my daughter, who was musically gifted from birth and has spent many years trying to understand her parents and grandparents
- ❖ her father, a brilliant musician and loving man whose substance abuse problems caused relationship problems and an early death
- ❖ me, who has lived with a song in my head for as long as I can remember

I hope you will purchase and/or visit YouTube and listen to the songs that were used in this story. They are collected in one place at this link: https://www.youtube.com/playlist?list=PLskh4Ljg-4YALgd0zR3Ak70Dk3SU_-UIt

If you enjoyed Song in My Heart, please rate and review, and recommend it to friends and families.

I welcome feedback at SandyKnauerMorgan@gmail.com

Sample of Rena's Silver Lining on next page.

Rena's Silver Lining

Sandy Knauer Morgan

The snooze button renders a limited number of reprieves before it finally says screw you, it's my turn to go back to sleep. It was a screw me morning; the clock and I snoozed peaceably together for an extra couple of hours. When my eyes finally opened without an intruding alarm, light poured between the blind slats.

I threw back the red satin comforter, a gift delivered to my door two days after my mother's first visit to my new apartment, because the *disgraceful excuse for a bedcovering* (her words) I was using could be viewed as a poor reflection on her. Unfortunately, she neglected to replace the sheets, too, so on this day, the gorgeous red comforter still lived atop a yellow flannel fitted sheet and the orange and green striped top sheet that was the only thing I had to show for my last relationship.

In my rush to get to the shower, as though a couple of seconds would matter when I was already fire-me-please late for work, I failed to notice that the top sheet had wrapped itself around my leg tight enough to require surgical removal. The silver lining was that it hung on for dear life and minimized the carpet burns on my knees when I landed on the floor and skidded across the room. But it did little to protect the heels of my hands.

While standing under the shower, cursing the sting of carpet-burned hands, I pondered a couple of mind-shattering questions: Should I start sleeping on the floor to avoid injury and is it better to be screwed by an inanimate object than to not be screwed at all?

I sliced a sizeable chunk of skin off my bruised but not terribly burned knee with the dull razor I used to scrape the fuzz off my legs, and talked myself out of calling in sick before the third question came to mind. Was my alarm clock more useful than the men I had dated? It was there every day and had willingly screwed me three out of five days a week for the last year. Much as it hurt to admit it, this might have meant Mother was justified in criticizing the men I had dated. But, that didn't mean she still needed to nag me about finding (her word) a keeper every time she saw me.

Without doubt, the clock won, hands down. Or hands up as the case would have been if the clock hadn't been digital. It was nine fifty-five, an hour and fifty-five minutes after I should have opened my customer service window at Greenville Water Company's main business office – the last place I ever expected to work. I overslept on the day delinquent customers were scheduled for shut-off and that was inexcusable. Because I failed to wake on time to collect last minute overdue payments, some unfortunate souls might have to go to work without coffee or a shower.

Remembering my experience at Russell Jenky's deli the week before, I hoped it wasn't anyone who worked with the public. My first thought that day was that the new kid must have kicked a slice of dropped meat under the counter to rot again. He was surely another Jenky relative. Otherwise there was no sensible reason I could imagine to keep him and his sloppy work ethic around.

Clarice disagreed about the potential cause of the stink. She believed it had to be one of those exotic cheeses Russell brought in so he could add a gourmet column on the blackboard menu and raise prices. "Whatever it is," she said, "it's rank and has no business in a place where people are fixing to eat."

The smell ended up coming from Russell's wife, Gladys, who worked the register alone during that extremely busy lunch hour, wearing a multi-colored synthetic sweater. When she reached across the counter to deliver the change from my ten, I felt my stomach try to claw its way out through my throat. I held my breath and thanked her, and didn't inhale again until Clarice had finished paying for her meal and we walked away.

"It makes sense if you really think about it," I told Clarice, when my gagging subsided and we settled into the booth farthest away from the cashier. "Shouldn't a sweater make you sweat?"

With much less discussion than we normally devoted to our world-changing hypotheses, we decided warmer would be a more appropriate title for that article of clothing, at least for those of us who don't wear them for the purpose of sweating.

I would have to remember to ask Clarice to help me decide if clocks are inanimate. I finished my shower, band-aided a square of toilet paper over my knee to catch the blood, towel-dried my hair, and dressed in gray slacks, a lavender warmer, and my navy slip-on shoes. At least that's what I thought. Clarice informed me later that I was wearing one navy shoe but its odd mate was black.

"Rena," she whined, "you need to get to bed earlier so you can clock in before lunch and wear clothes that match. Maybe you could even put on some of that make-up you cleaned your bank account out to buy. No offense, but you won't ever get moved up looking like this."

By that time I enjoyed Clarice's whine as much as I cherished the advice she was becoming less and less reluctant to offer. But the first time I heard her speak, I thought fate had cursed her with the worst luck possible.

Ann Lyons hauled me into the customer service department on my first day and caught Clarice by surprise as she leaning over to put her purse in a file cabinet drawer. Without giving Clarice a minute to orient herself after rising, Ann asked her to show me around Greenville Water Company. Clarice smiled, sniffed, and said she was glad to meet me. I envied her composure, thinking it must have been positively humiliating to meet the new employee when her head was full of snot.

Ann left us alone and I discretely whispered that it wouldn't offend me if Clarice wanted to blow her nose. I'd wait.

"Girlfriend, I don't need a tissue. This is my regular voice," she explained. "I reckon I needed some offensive trait to counteract this beauty and stave off the heap of men bound to collect at my feet otherwise." She tried to laugh but it came out sounding more like a snort, probably, I thought, another symptom of the condition that caused her to talk like her head was full.

I laughed and said I was sorry, immediately afraid I had made my second big blunder. Surely, she was kidding. Clarice was anything but a stud magnet. In fact, she reminded me of Belinda Peakins, a girl I knew in college. Often, the less attractive girls (who would have been my crowd, had I joined one) would drag Belinda along when they went to clubs or parties, so they could ease their disappointment later by realizing someone got less attention from the guys than they did. Belinda, on the other end, laughed about ignoring the jerks that kept hitting on them because she knew she could do better.

After knowing Clarice for less than five minutes, I hoped no one had treated her the way my friends had treated Belinda. I wasn't sure how I felt about her laughing off what she probably perceived as me treating her the same.

I posted a quick reminder in my sub-conscience to look stave up in the dictionary, and concentrated the rest of my energy on Clarice's face. I hoped her expression would tell me whether or not she understood that I was laughing with her, and not at her.

Clarice drew the corners of her mouth back a tad bit further, exposing one more oversized, protruding tooth on each side. I wanted to count, because I was sure she must have twice the number of teeth the rest of us grow, but I was already bordering on rude so I focused on her eyes. I thought I saw a glint but couldn't be sure it represented warmth. It might have been a reflection off the rhinestone studs in the black plastic frames of her glasses.

"Let's just throw this out on the table straight away," she said. She tried another smile that was so wide she had to slurp to keep saliva from dripping out the corners of her mouth. She stretched her lips over her teeth and swallowed.

"Girlfriend, I own mirrors and I've been hearing my voice my whole life. You don't need to pretend you're blind or that I'm anything other than what I am. I don't. I like me just fine the way I am." She paused to slurp again before she said she hoped I would too.

I said thanks because I couldn't think of anything better to say.

"One more thing," she added. "I try to avoid the paparazzi, so if you're somebody famous we'll have to restrict our meetings to private places."

I wasn't sure I wanted her to call me girlfriend, but was pretty sure I liked Clarice just the way she was otherwise.

My life changed that day. Clarice McDaniels exorcised the normal, boring, twenty-four-year-old, semi-depressed, and slightly neurotic, Rena Boiles right in the middle of trying to convince the world that I was smarter, more beautiful, saner, and more successful than I truly was, or than my mother pretended I was when we weren't alone. Clarice McDaniels shamed the all-American-version of the liberated-woman right out of me, and truly liberated me from the box that controlled my life. Instantly.

Before meeting Clarice, I had never considered the important things in life, like the hidden meaning in my alarm clock, or the inappropriate titling of clothing. And nobody called me girlfriend.

Clarice turned the lights on and introduced me to a world I had never seen before. Seeing the world through Clarice's glow is about as good as it gets.

www.ingramcontent.com/pod-product-compliance
Lightning Source LLC
Chambersburg PA
CBHW051542250626
47157CB00001B/157